SORT
OF
SUPER

SORT
OF
SUPER

by Eric Gapstur

COLOR BY
DEARBHLA KELLY

ALADDIN

NEW YORK LONDON TORONTO SYDNEY NEW DELHI

ALADDIN

An imprint of Simon & Schuster Children's Publishing Division

1230 Avenue of the Americas, New York, New York 10020

First Aladdin paperback edition March 2022

Copyright © 2022 by Eric Gapstur

Also available in an Aladdin hardcover edition.

All rights reserved, including the right of reproduction in whole or in part in any form.

Aladdin and related logo are registered trademarks of Simon & Schuster, inc.

For information about special discounts for bulk purchases, please contact Simon & Schuster special sales at 1-866-506-1949 or business@simonandschuster.com.

The Simon & Schuster Speakers Bureau can bring authors to your live event. For more information or to book an event contact the Simon & Schuster Speakers Bureau at 1-866-248-3049 or visit our website at www.simonspeakers.com.

Color by Dearbhla Kelly

Book designed by Laura Lyn DiSiena and Eric Gapstur

The illustrations for this book were rendered in ink and colored digitally.

The text of this book was set in Gapstur and Gapstur Shouting.

Manufactured in China 1221 SCP

2 4 6 8 10 9 7 5 3 1

Library of Congress Control Number 2021940159

ISBN 978-1-5344-8029-2 (hc)

ISBN 978-1-5344-8028-5 (pbk)

ISBN 978-1-5344-8030-8 (ebook)

TO MICHELLE,
LIAM, AND HENRY

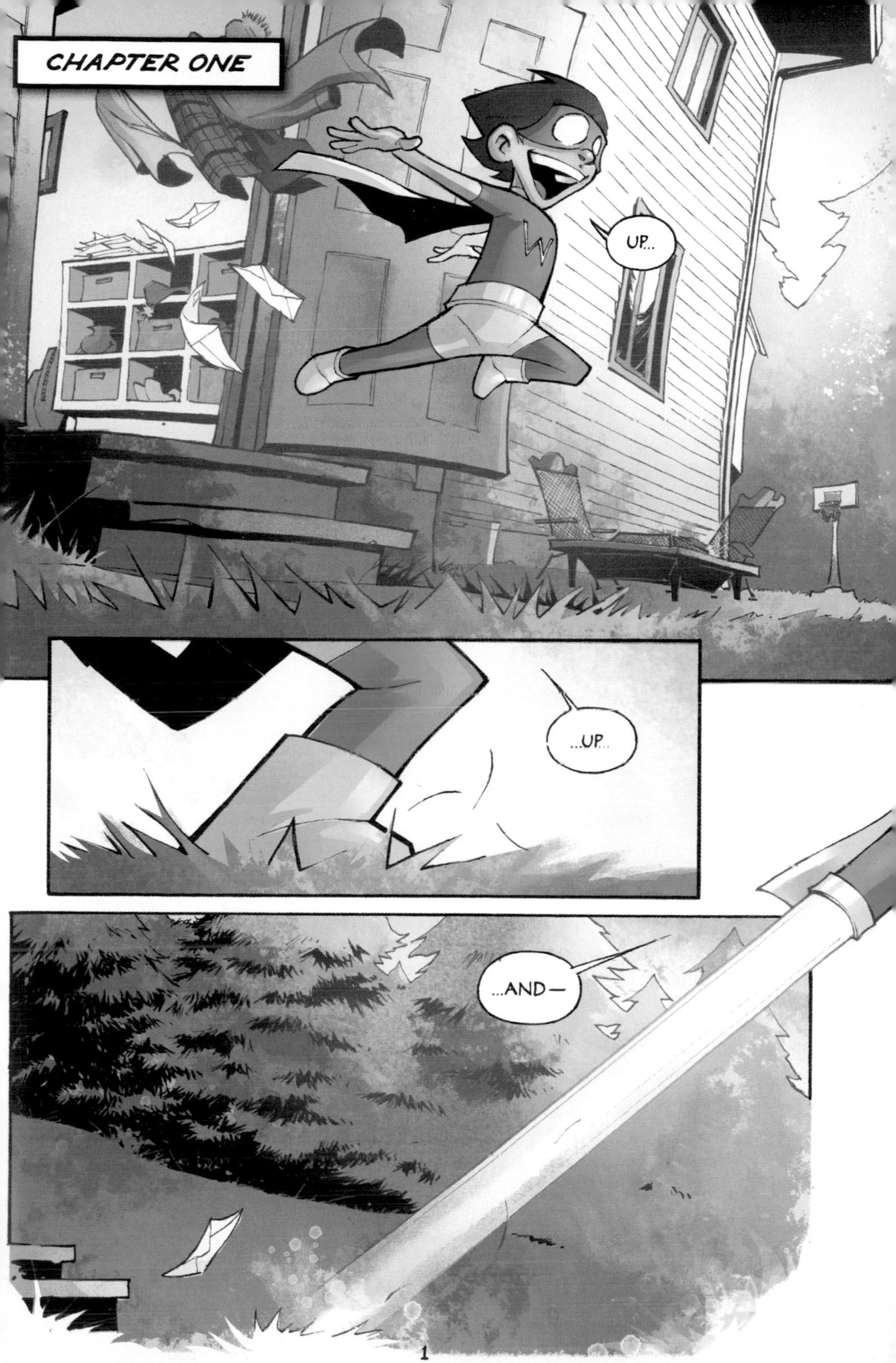
CHAPTER ONE
UP...
...UP...
...AND—

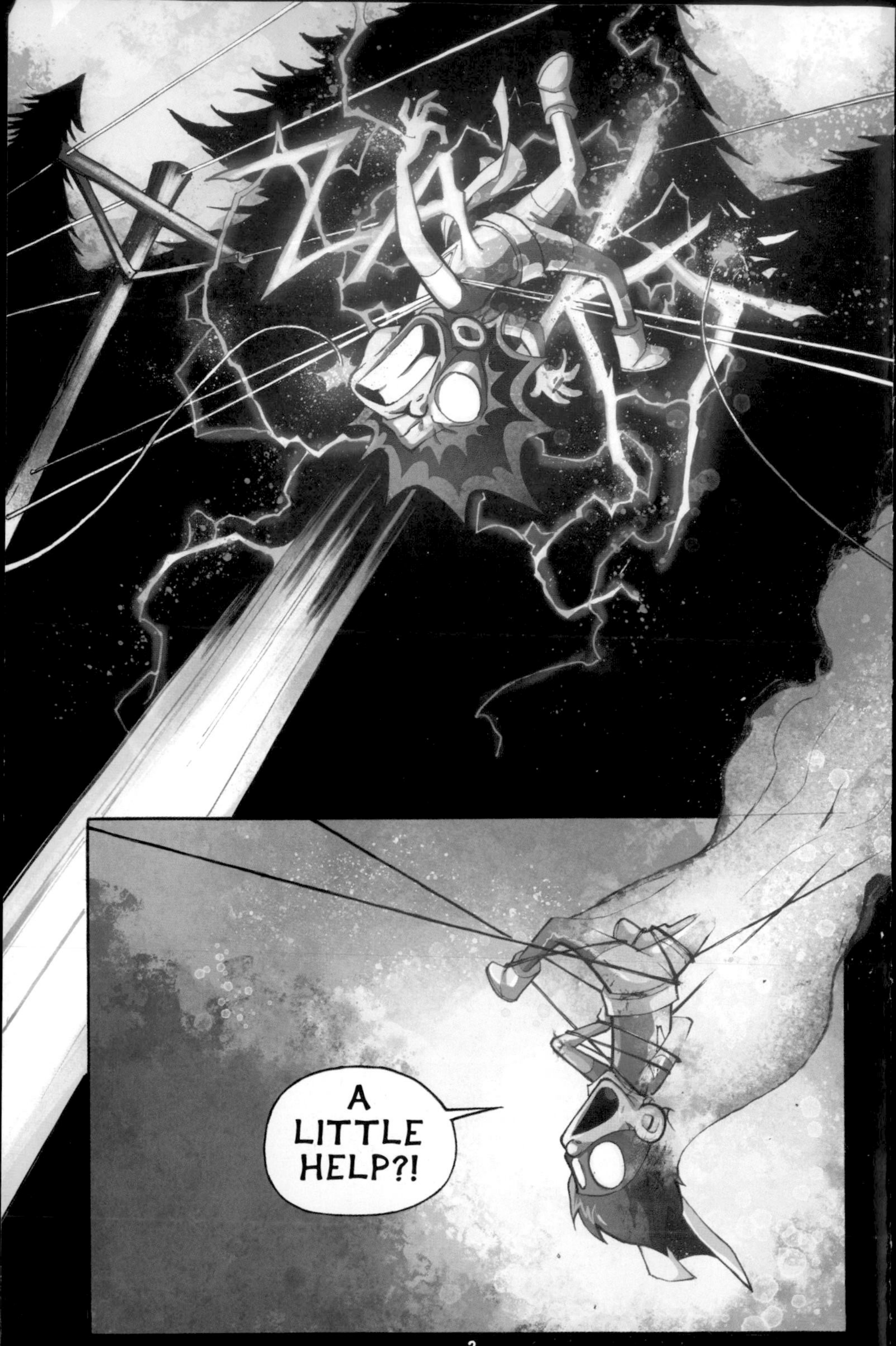
A LITTLE HELP?!

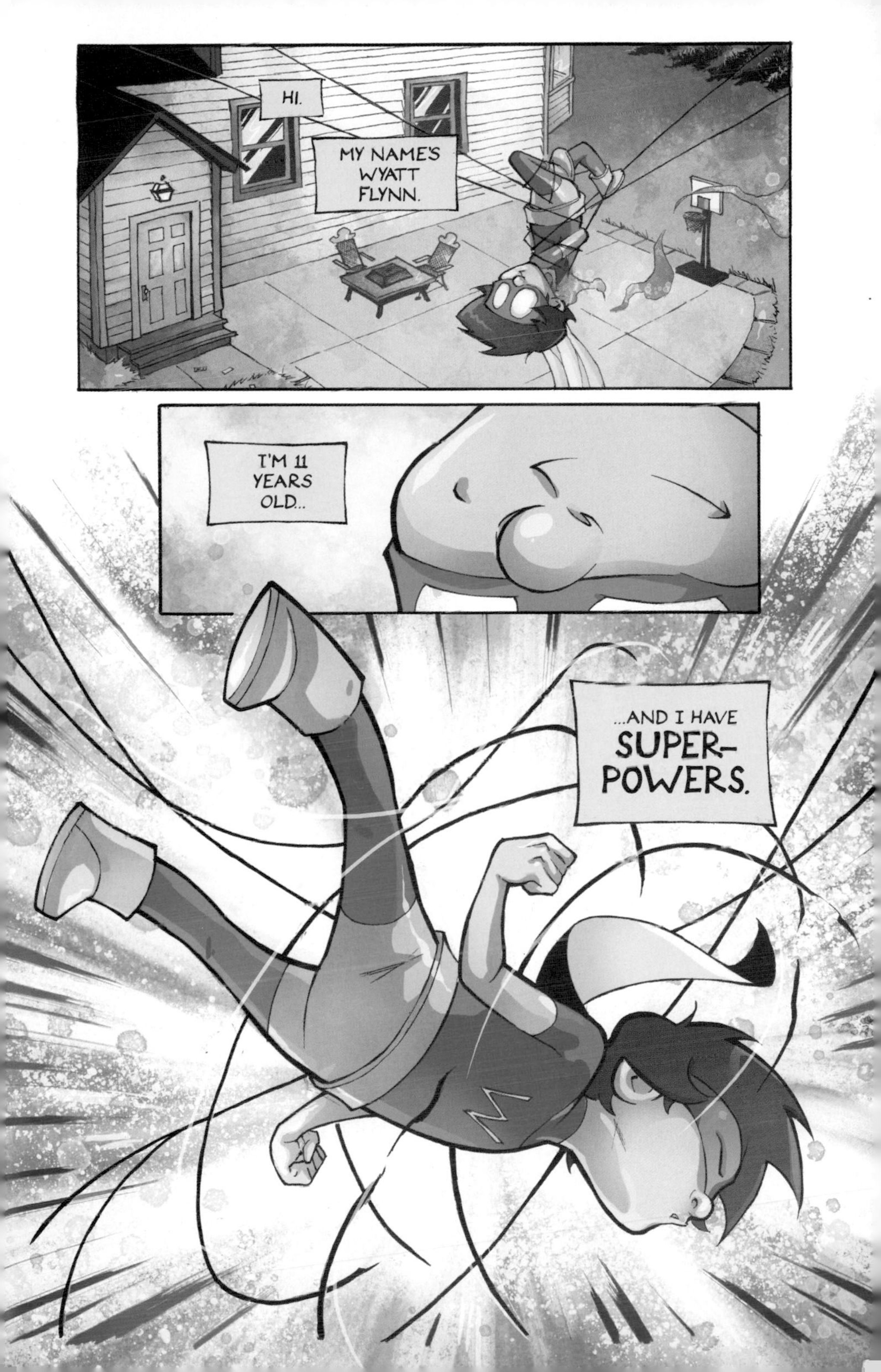
HI.
MY NAME'S WYATT FLYNN.
I'M 11 YEARS OLD...
...AND I HAVE SUPER-POWERS.

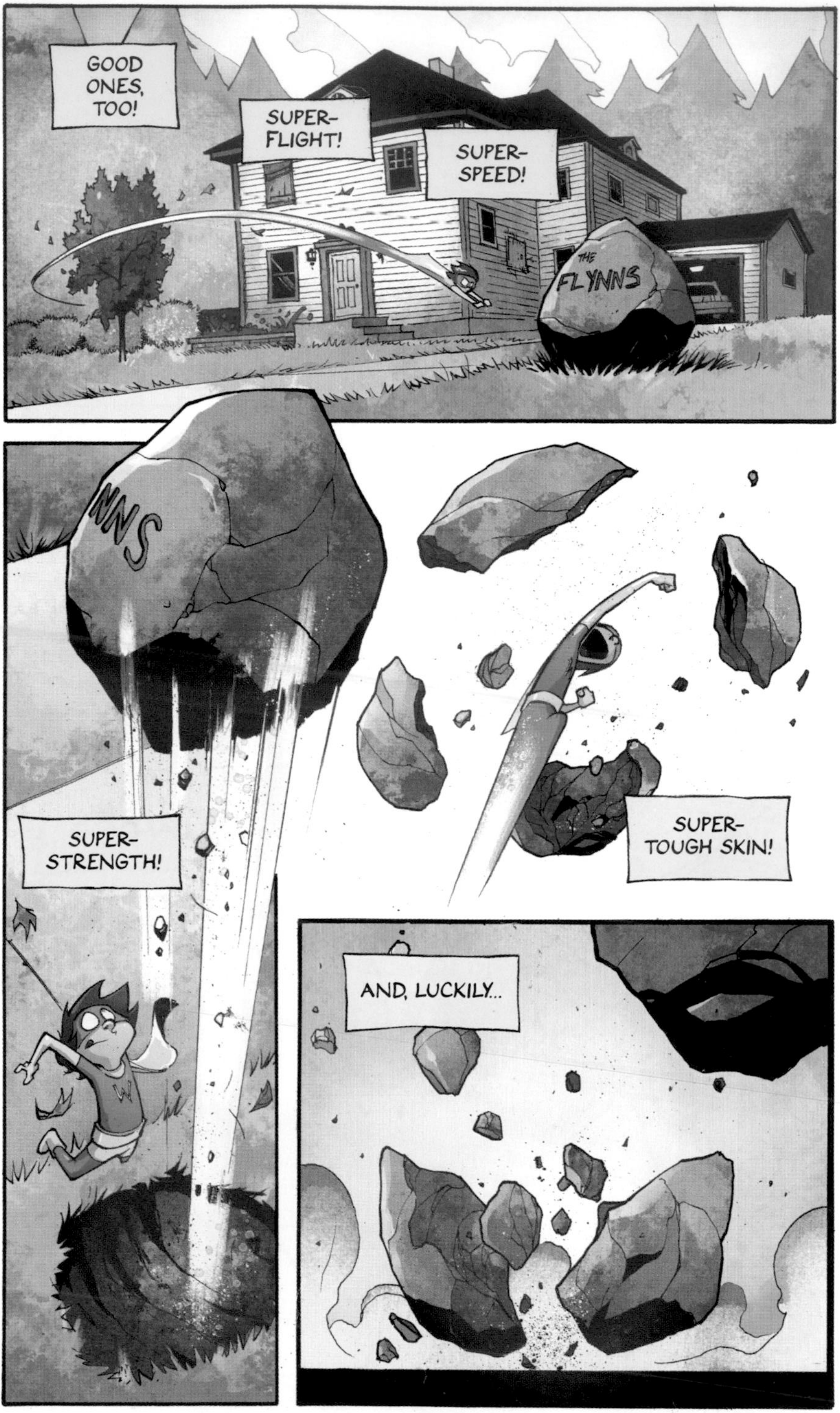
GOOD ONES, TOO!
SUPER-FLIGHT!
SUPER-SPEED!
THE FLYNNS
SUPER-STRENGTH!
SUPER-TOUGH SKIN!
AND, LUCKILY...

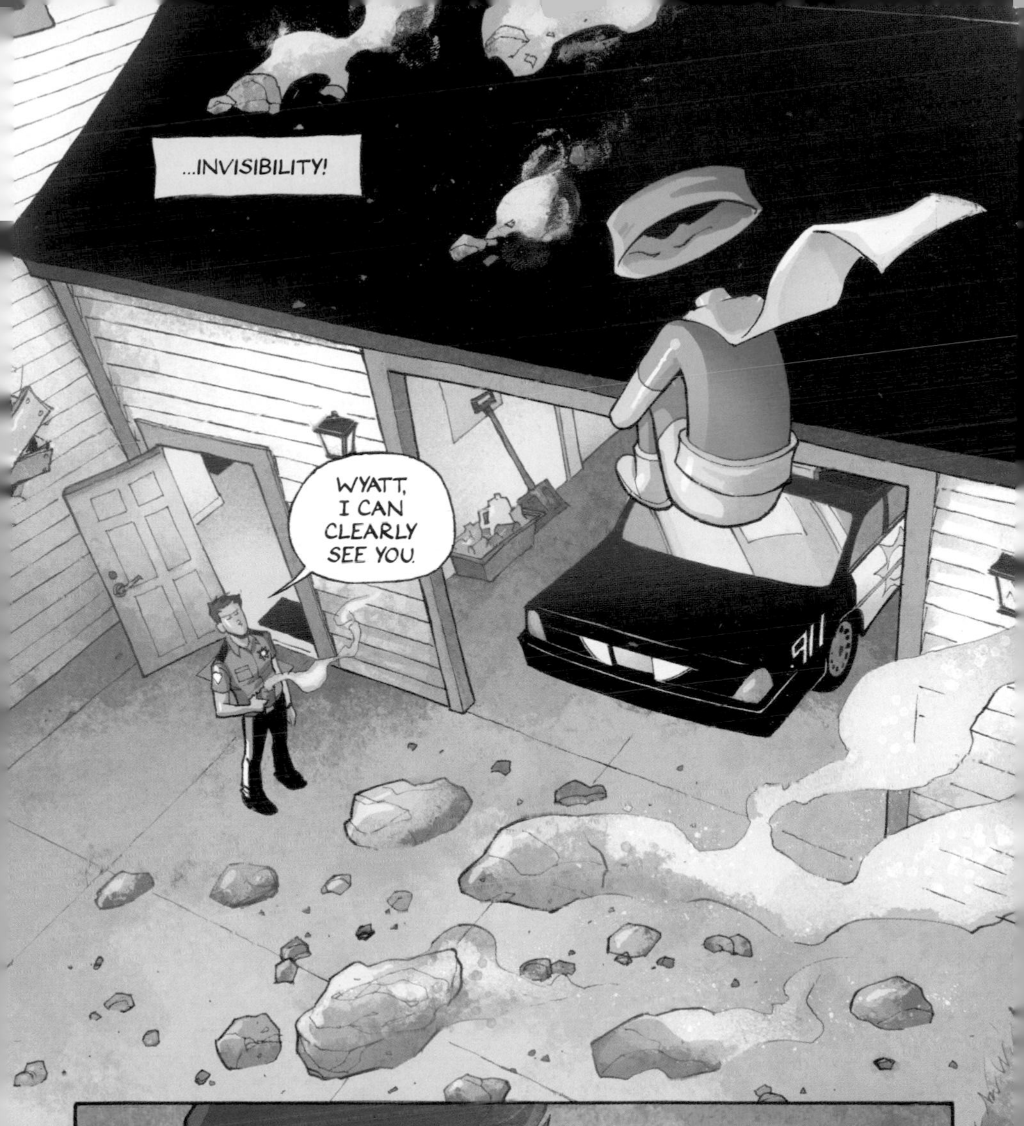
...INVISIBILITY!
WYATT, I CAN CLEARLY SEE YOU.

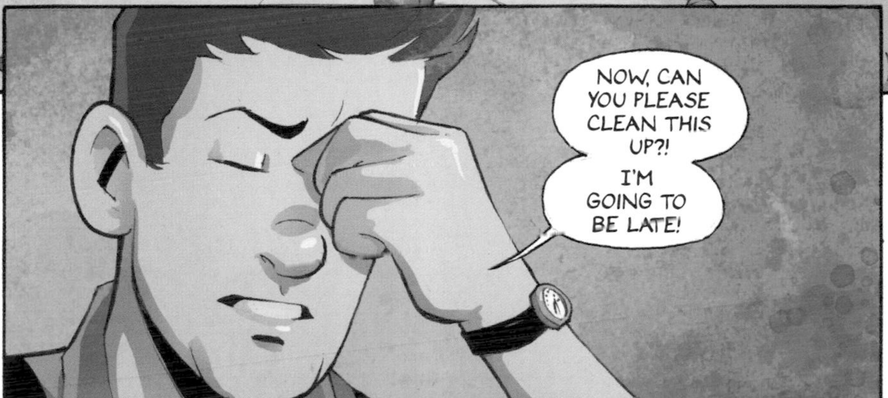
NOW, CAN YOU PLEASE CLEAN THIS UP?!
I'M GOING TO BE LATE!

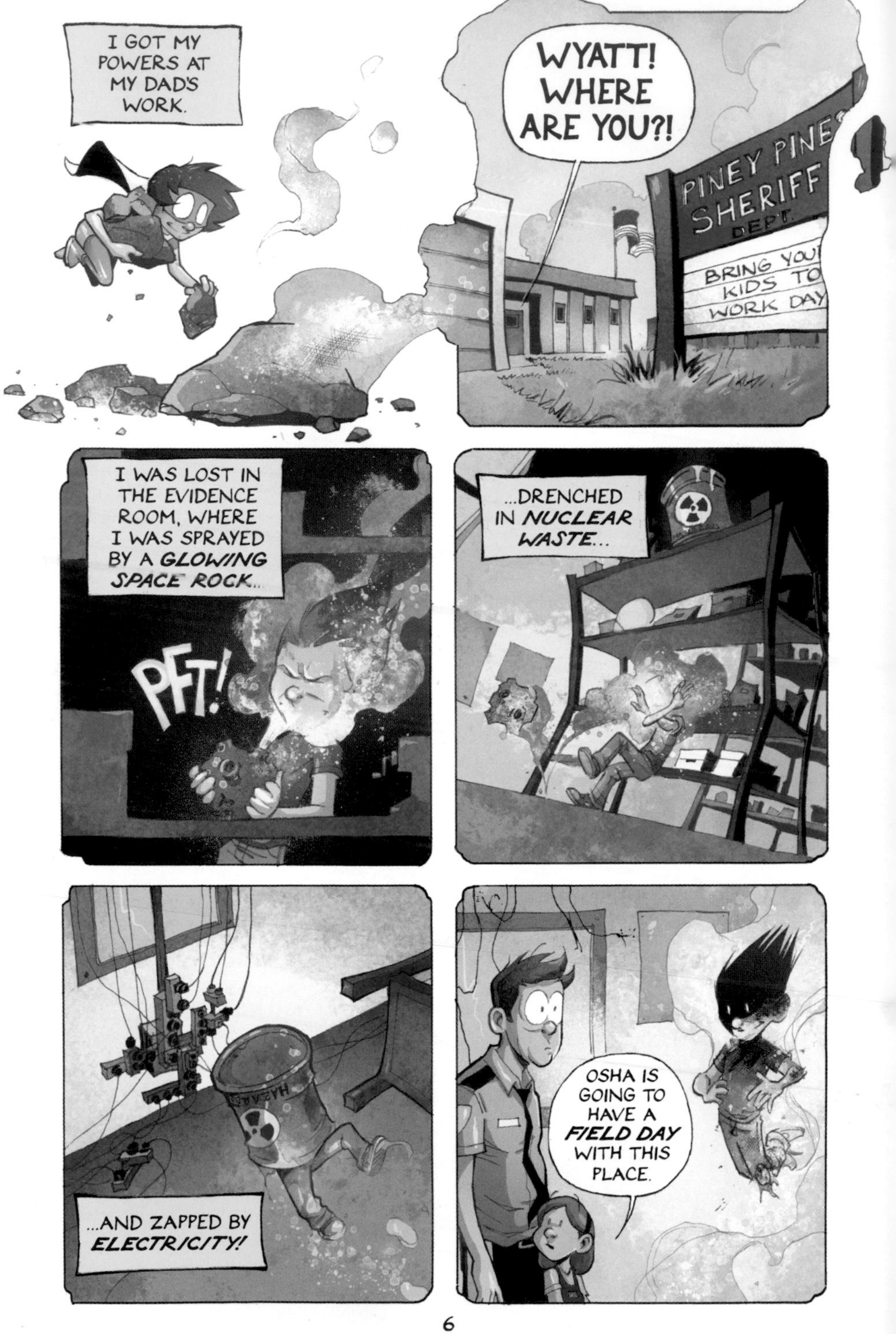
I GOT MY POWERS AT MY DAD'S WORK.
WYATT! WHERE ARE YOU?!
PINEY PINES SHERIFF DEPT.
BRING YOUR KIDS TO WORK DAY
I WAS LOST IN THE EVIDENCE ROOM, WHERE I WAS SPRAYED BY A GLOWING SPACE ROCK...
PFT!
...DRENCHED IN NUCLEAR WASTE...
...AND ZAPPED BY ELECTRICITY!
HAZARD
OSHA IS GOING TO HAVE A FIELD DAY WITH THIS PLACE.

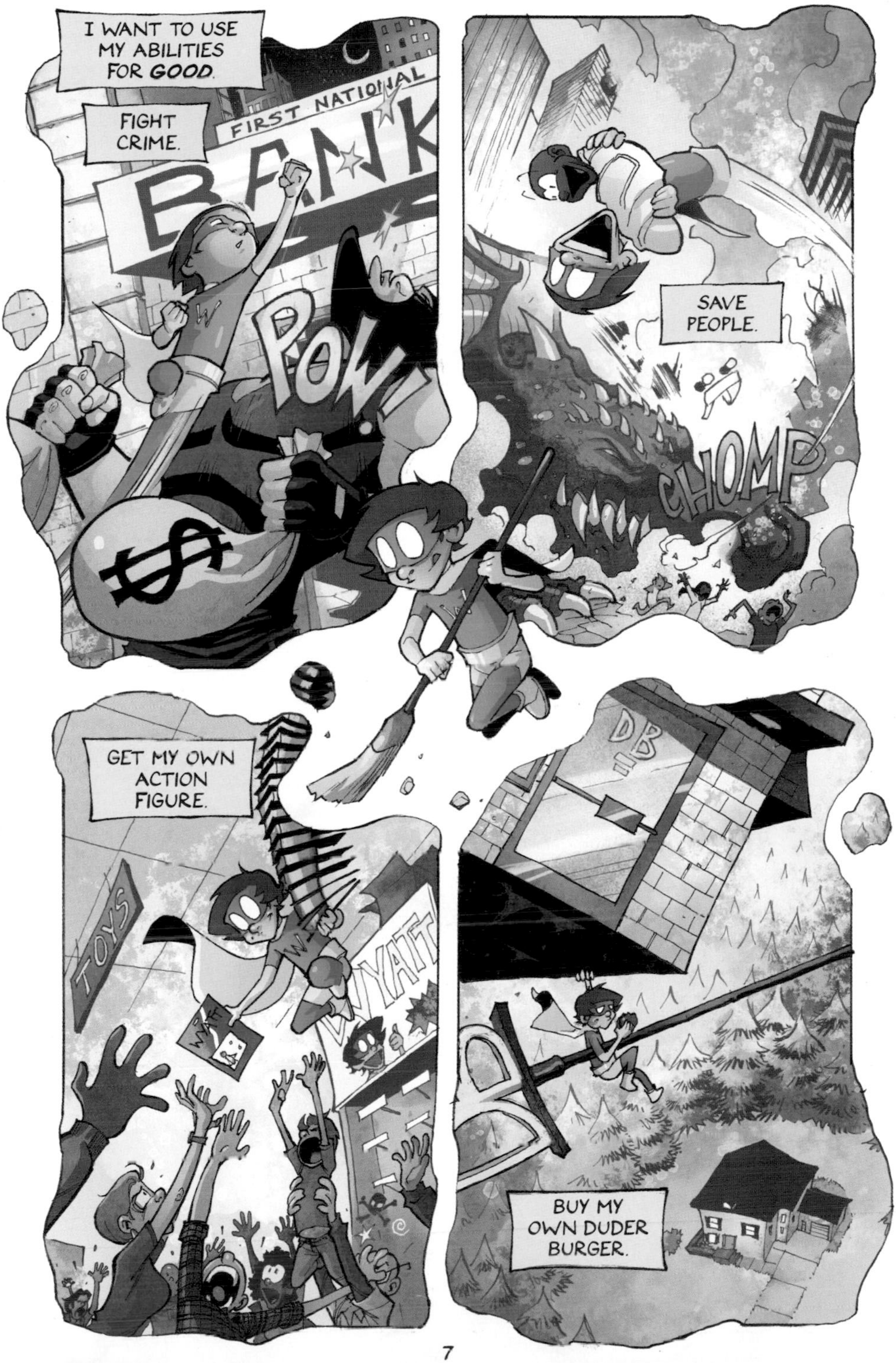
I WANT TO USE MY ABILITIES FOR GOOD.
FIGHT CRIME.
FIRST NATIONAL
BANK
POW!
SAVE PEOPLE.
CHOMP
GET MY OWN ACTION FIGURE.
TOYS
WYATT
DB
BUY MY OWN DUDER BURGER.

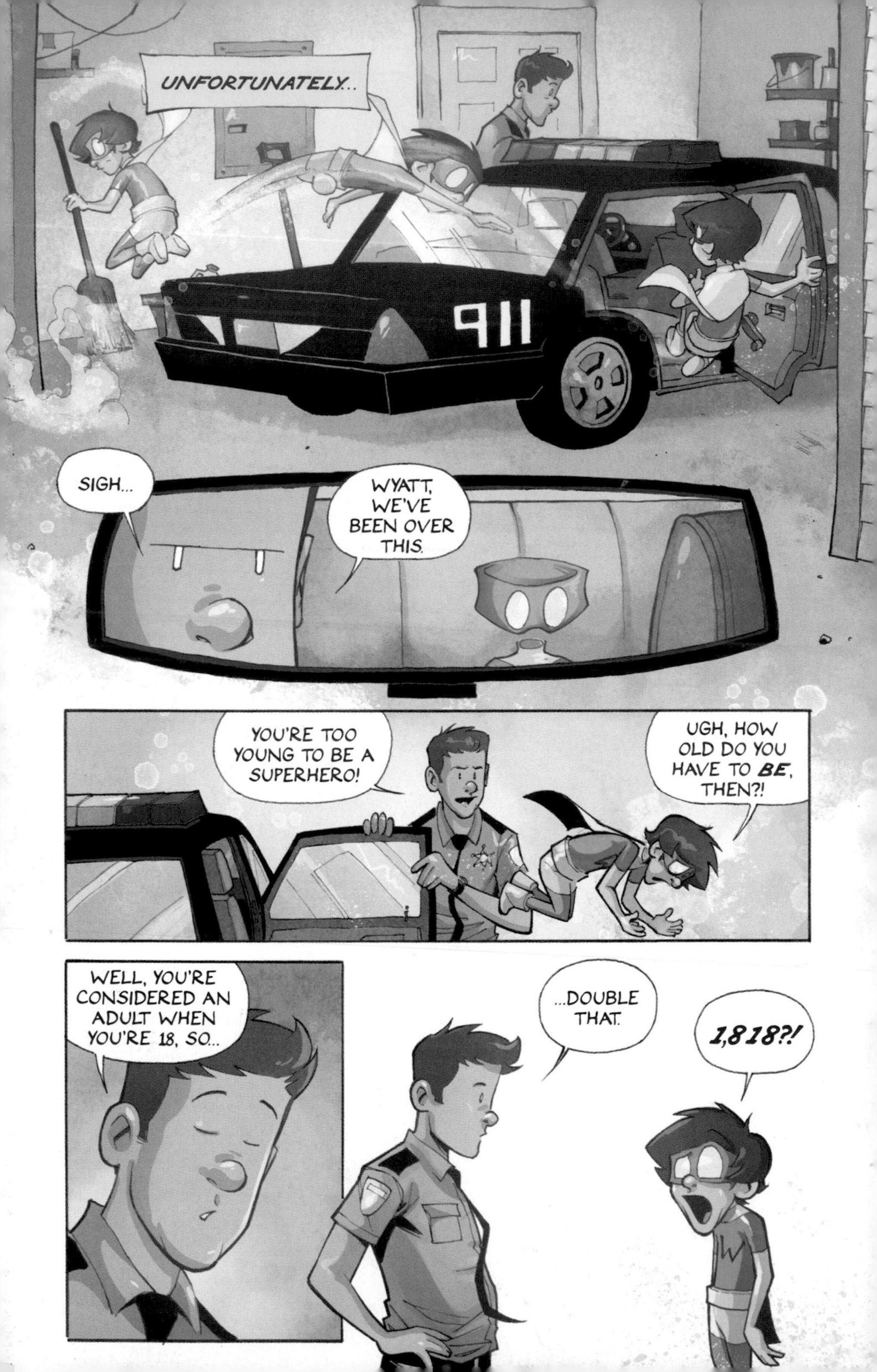
UNFORTUNATELY...
911
SIGH...
WYATT, WE'VE BEEN OVER THIS.
YOU'RE TOO YOUNG TO BE A SUPERHERO!
UGH, HOW OLD DO YOU HAVE TO *BE*, THEN?!
WELL, YOU'RE CONSIDERED AN ADULT WHEN YOU'RE 18, SO...
...DOUBLE THAT.
1,818?!

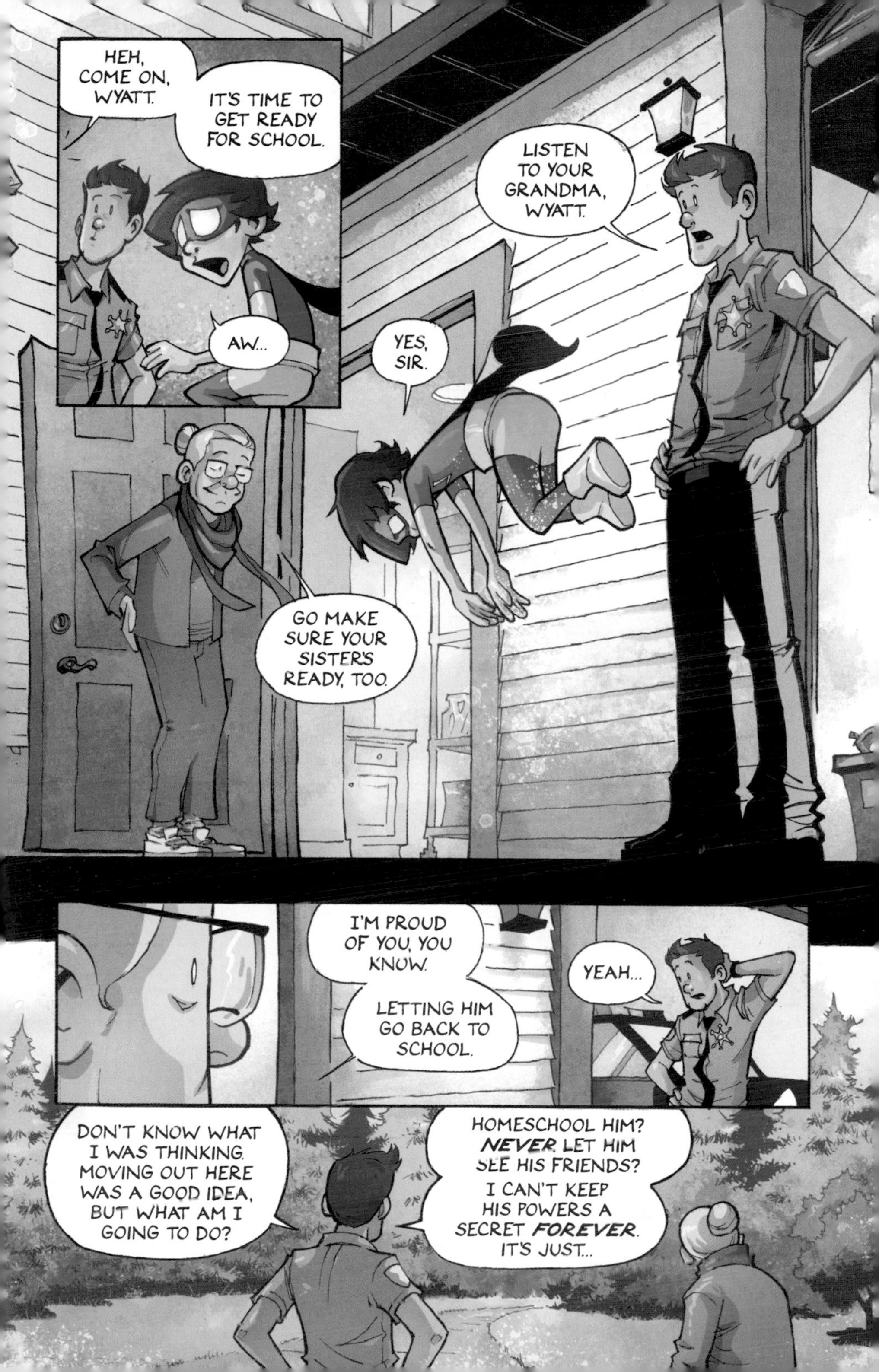
HEH, COME ON, WYATT.
IT'S TIME TO GET READY FOR SCHOOL.
AW...
LISTEN TO YOUR GRANDMA, WYATT.
YES, SIR.
GO MAKE SURE YOUR SISTER'S READY, TOO.
I'M PROUD OF YOU, YOU KNOW.
LETTING HIM GO BACK TO SCHOOL.
YEAH...
DON'T KNOW WHAT I WAS THINKING. MOVING OUT HERE WAS A GOOD IDEA, BUT WHAT AM I GOING TO DO?
HOMESCHOOL HIM? ***NEVER*** LET HIM SEE HIS FRIENDS?
I CAN'T KEEP HIS POWERS A SECRET ***FOREVER***. IT'S JUST...

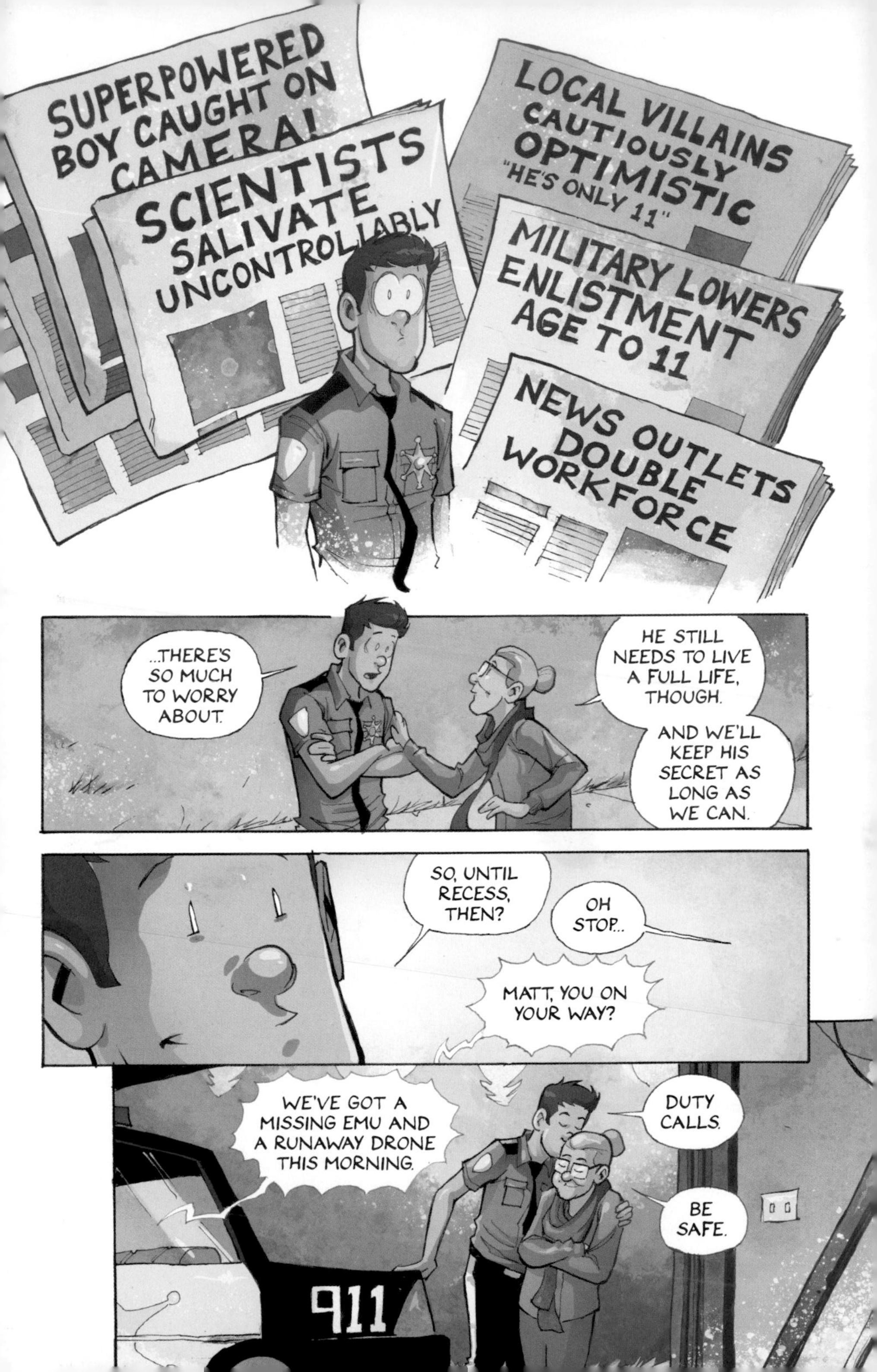
SUPERPOWERED BOY CAUGHT ON CAMERA!
SCIENTISTS SALIVATE UNCONTROLLABLY
LOCAL VILLAINS CAUTIOUSLY OPTIMISTIC "HE'S ONLY 11"
MILITARY LOWERS ENLISTMENT AGE TO 11
NEWS OUTLETS DOUBLE WORKFORCE
...THERE'S SO MUCH TO WORRY ABOUT.
HE STILL NEEDS TO LIVE A FULL LIFE, THOUGH.
AND WE'LL KEEP HIS SECRET AS LONG AS WE CAN.
SO, UNTIL RECESS, THEN?
OH STOP...
MATT, YOU ON YOUR WAY?
WE'VE GOT A MISSING EMU AND A RUNAWAY DRONE THIS MORNING.
DUTY CALLS.
BE SAFE.
911

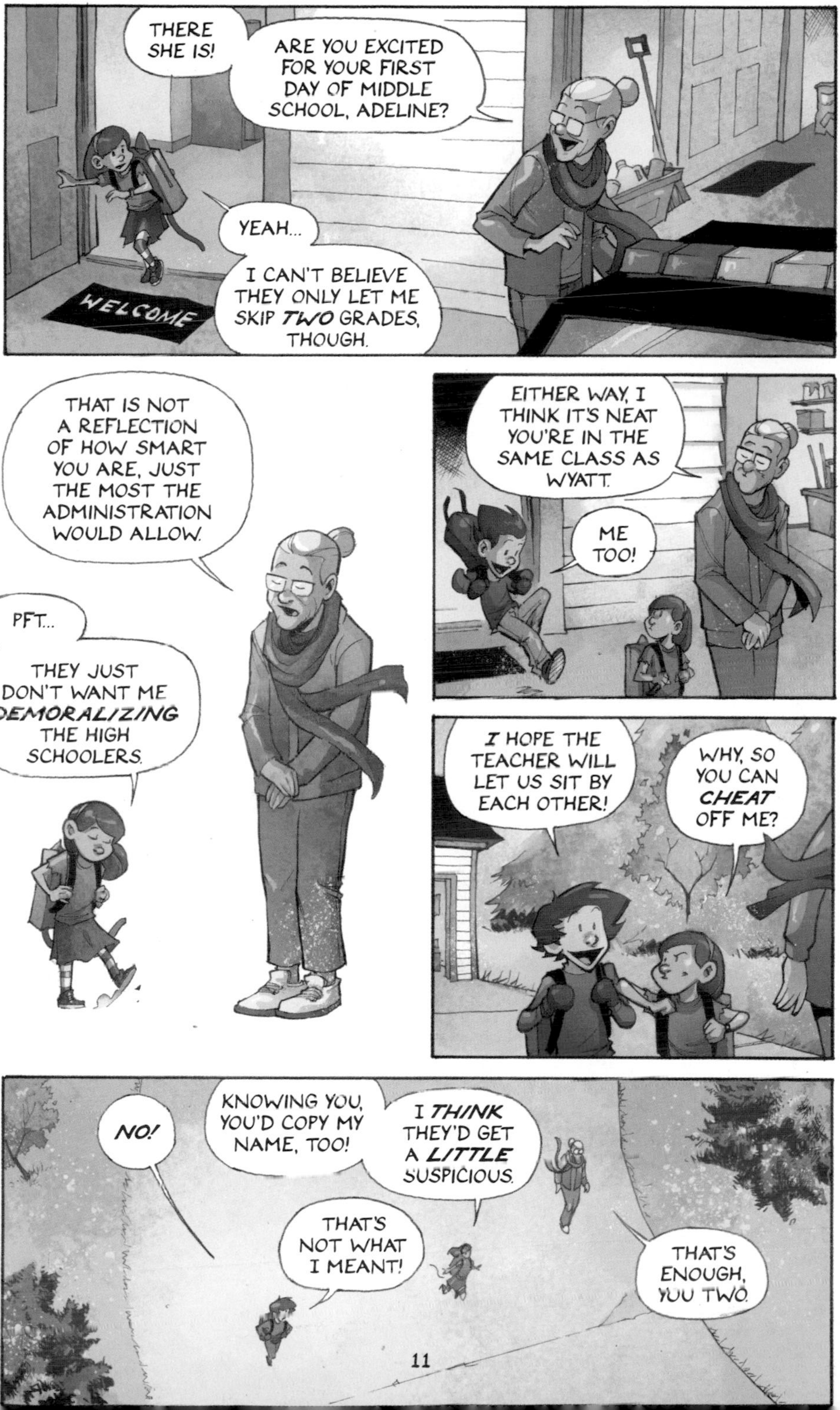
THERE SHE IS!
ARE YOU EXCITED FOR YOUR FIRST DAY OF MIDDLE SCHOOL, ADELINE?
WELCOME
YEAH...
I CAN'T BELIEVE THEY ONLY LET ME SKIP *TWO* GRADES, THOUGH.
THAT IS NOT A REFLECTION OF HOW SMART YOU ARE, JUST THE MOST THE ADMINISTRATION WOULD ALLOW.
PFT...
THEY JUST DON'T WANT ME *DEMORALIZING* THE HIGH SCHOOLERS.
EITHER WAY, I THINK IT'S NEAT YOU'RE IN THE SAME CLASS AS WYATT.
ME TOO!
I HOPE THE TEACHER WILL LET US SIT BY EACH OTHER!
WHY, SO YOU CAN *CHEAT* OFF ME?
NO!
KNOWING YOU, YOU'D COPY MY NAME, TOO!
I *THINK* THEY'D GET A *LITTLE* SUSPICIOUS.
THAT'S NOT WHAT I MEANT!
THAT'S ENOUGH, YOU TWO.

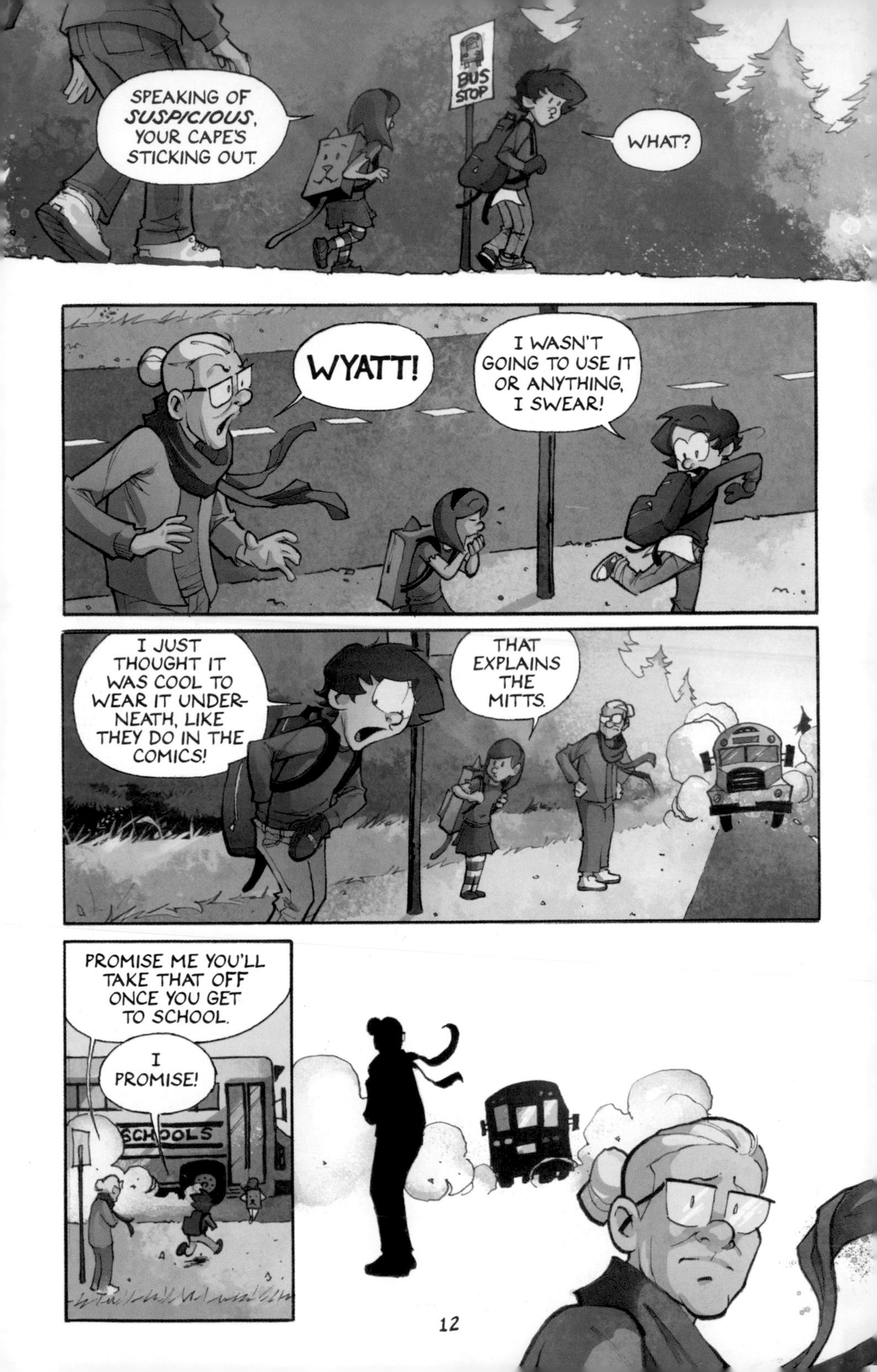
SPEAKING OF SUSPICIOUS, YOUR CAPE'S STICKING OUT.
BUS STOP
WHAT?
WYATT!
I WASN'T GOING TO USE IT OR ANYTHING, I SWEAR!
I JUST THOUGHT IT WAS COOL TO WEAR IT UNDER-NEATH, LIKE THEY DO IN THE COMICS!
THAT EXPLAINS THE MITTS.
PROMISE ME YOU'LL TAKE THAT OFF ONCE YOU GET TO SCHOOL.
I PROMISE!
SCHOOLS

CHAPTER TWO

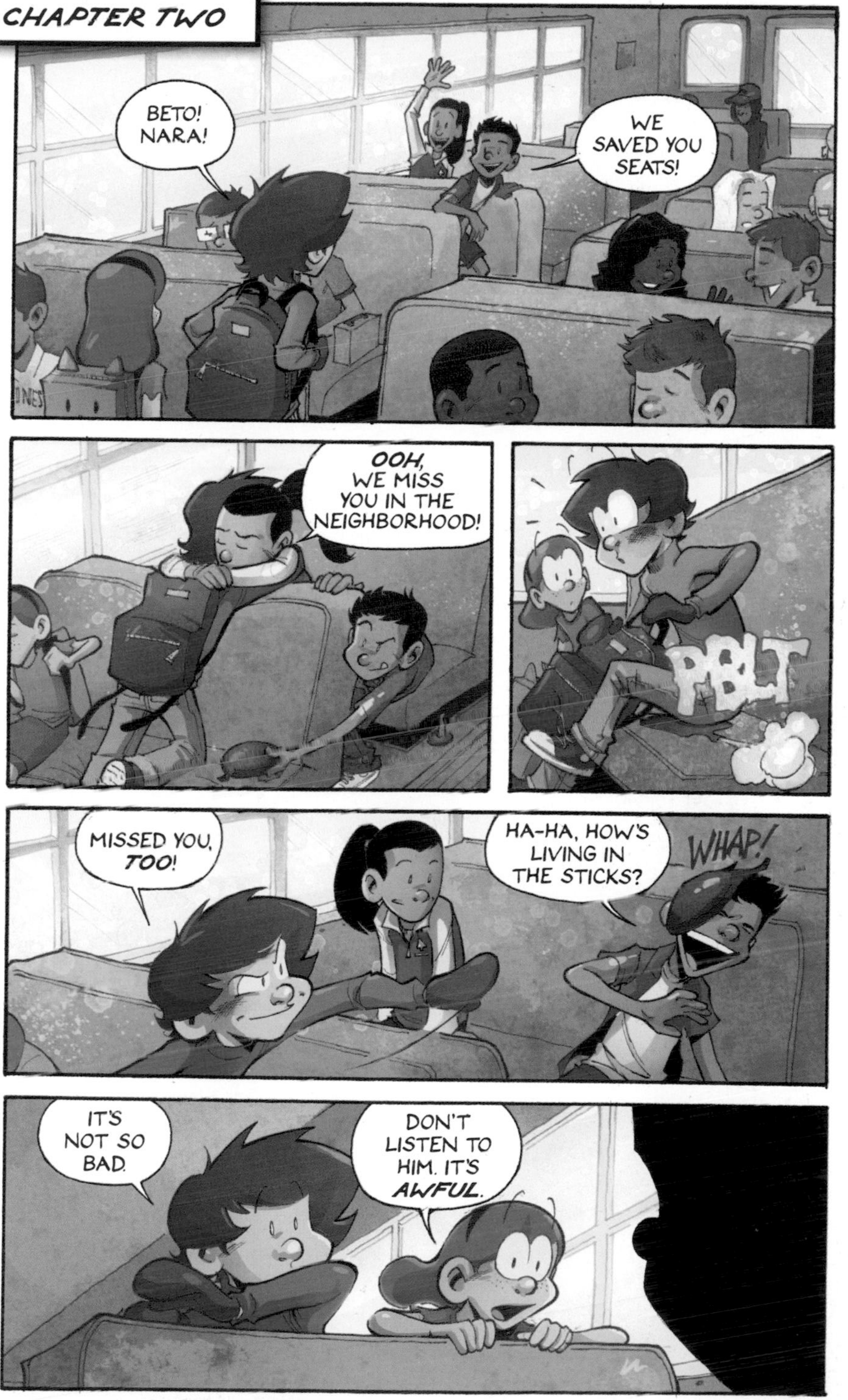
BETO! NARA!
WE SAVED YOU SEATS!
OOH, WE MISS YOU IN THE NEIGHBORHOOD!
PBLT
MISSED YOU, TOO!
HA-HA, HOW'S LIVING IN THE STICKS?
WHAP!
IT'S NOT SO BAD.
DON'T LISTEN TO HIM. IT'S AWFUL.

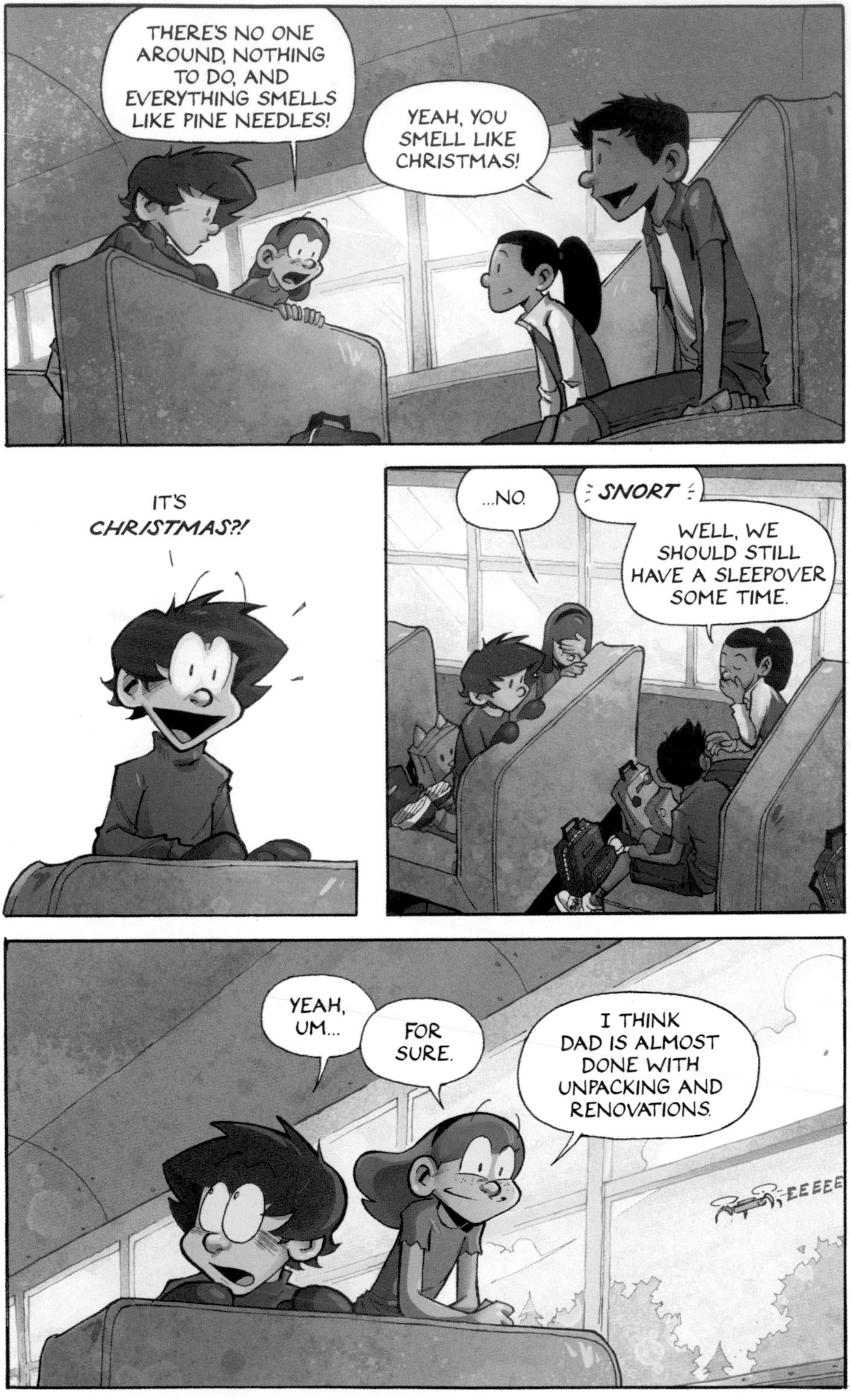
THERE'S NO ONE AROUND, NOTHING TO DO, AND EVERYTHING SMELLS LIKE PINE NEEDLES!
YEAH, YOU SMELL LIKE CHRISTMAS!
IT'S CHRISTMAS?!
...NO.
SNORT
WELL, WE SHOULD STILL HAVE A SLEEPOVER SOME TIME.
YEAH, UM...
FOR SURE.
I THINK DAD IS ALMOST DONE WITH UNPACKING AND RENOVATIONS.
EEEEE

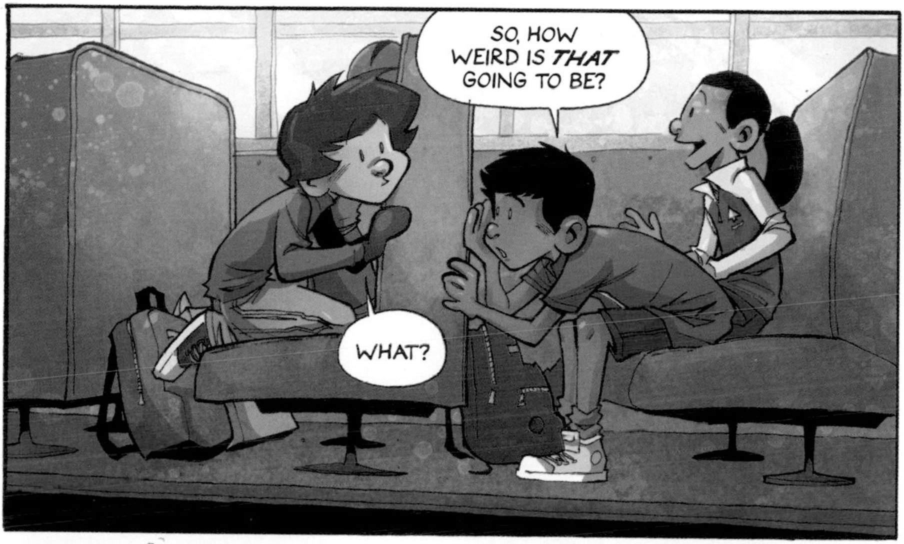
SO, HOW WEIRD IS *THAT* GOING TO BE?
WHAT?

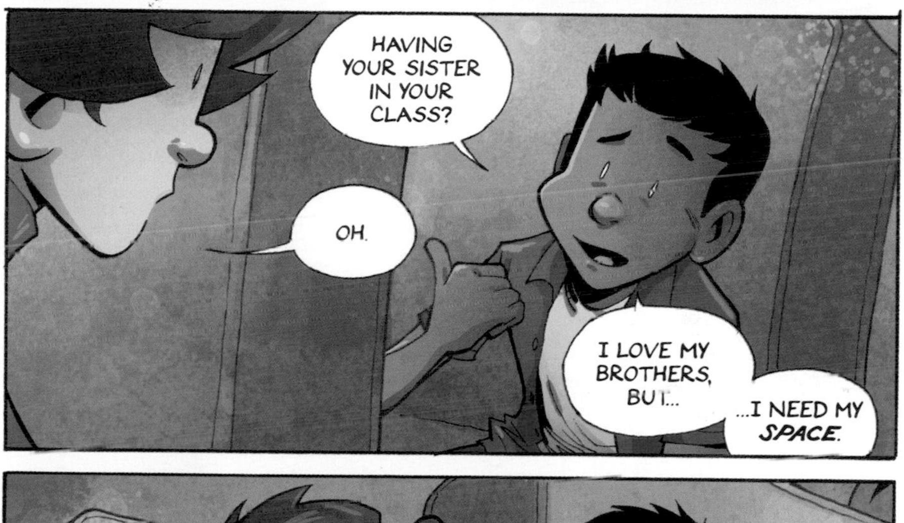
HAVING YOUR SISTER IN YOUR CLASS?
OH.
I LOVE MY BROTHERS, BUT...
...I NEED MY *SPACE*.

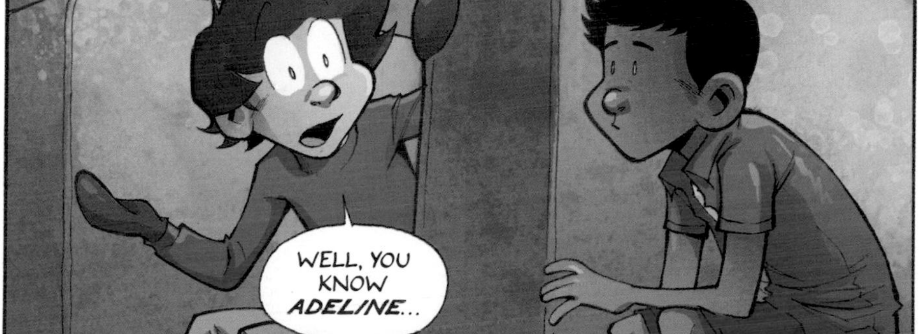
WELL, YOU KNOW *ADELINE*...

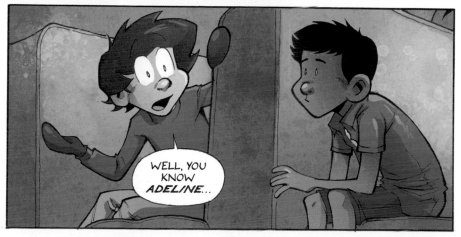

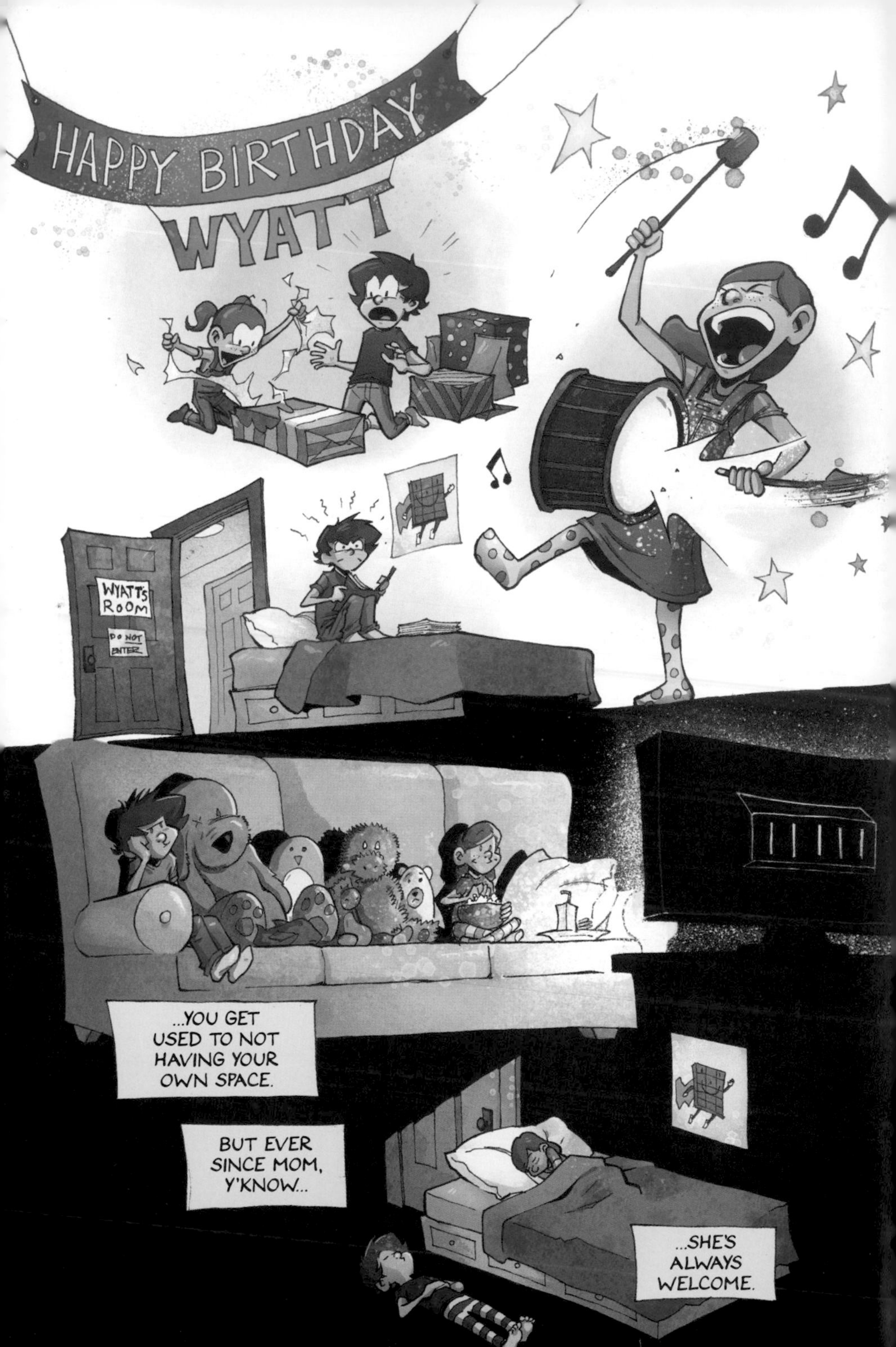
HAPPY BIRTHDAY
WYATT
WYATT'S ROOM
DO NOT ENTER
...YOU GET USED TO NOT HAVING YOUR OWN SPACE.
BUT EVER SINCE MOM, Y'KNOW...
...SHE'S ALWAYS WELCOME.

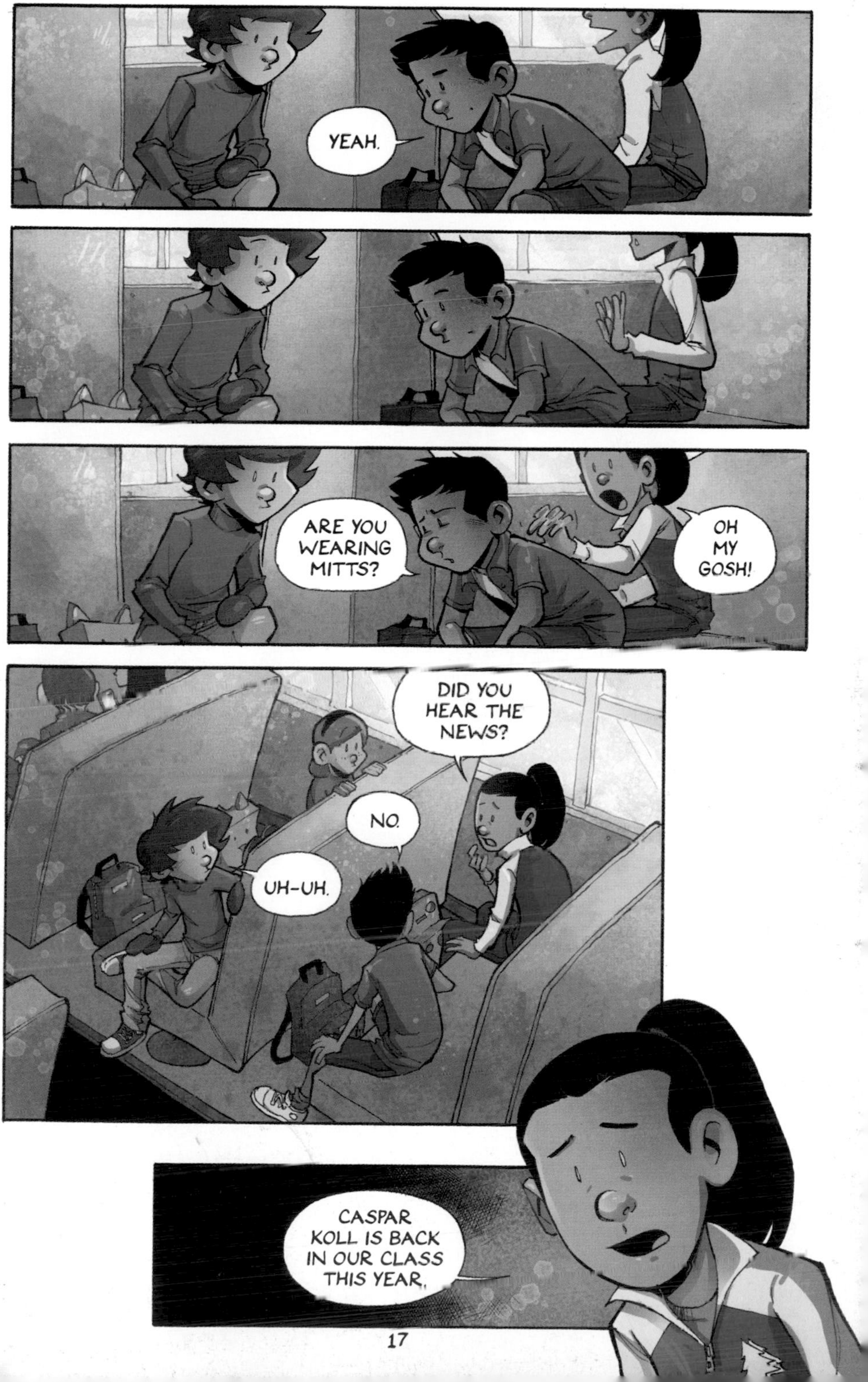
YEAH.
ARE YOU WEARING MITTS?
OH MY GOSH!
DID YOU HEAR THE NEWS?
NO.
UH-UH.
CASPAR KOLL IS BACK IN OUR CLASS THIS YEAR.

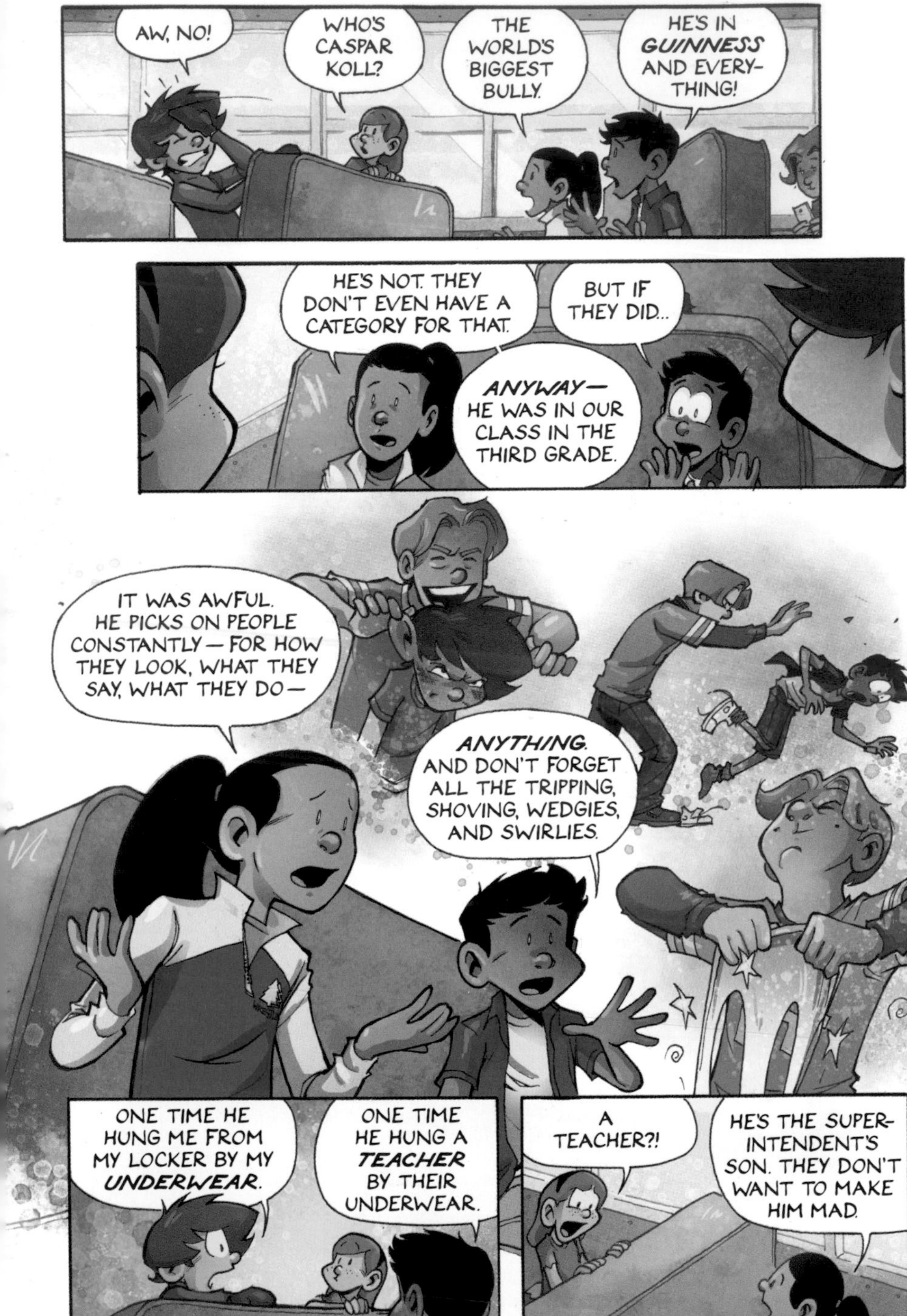
AW, NO!
WHO'S CASPAR KOLL?
THE WORLD'S BIGGEST BULLY.
HE'S IN *GUINNESS* AND EVERY-THING!
HE'S NOT. THEY DON'T EVEN HAVE A CATEGORY FOR THAT.
BUT IF THEY DID...
ANYWAY— HE WAS IN OUR CLASS IN THE THIRD GRADE.
IT WAS AWFUL. HE PICKS ON PEOPLE CONSTANTLY — FOR HOW THEY LOOK, WHAT THEY SAY, WHAT THEY DO—
ANYTHING. AND DON'T FORGET ALL THE TRIPPING, SHOVING, WEDGIES, AND SWIRLIES.
ONE TIME HE HUNG ME FROM MY LOCKER BY MY *UNDERWEAR*.
ONE TIME HE HUNG A *TEACHER* BY THEIR UNDERWEAR.
A TEACHER?!
HE'S THE SUPER-INTENDENT'S SON. THEY DON'T WANT TO MAKE HIM MAD.

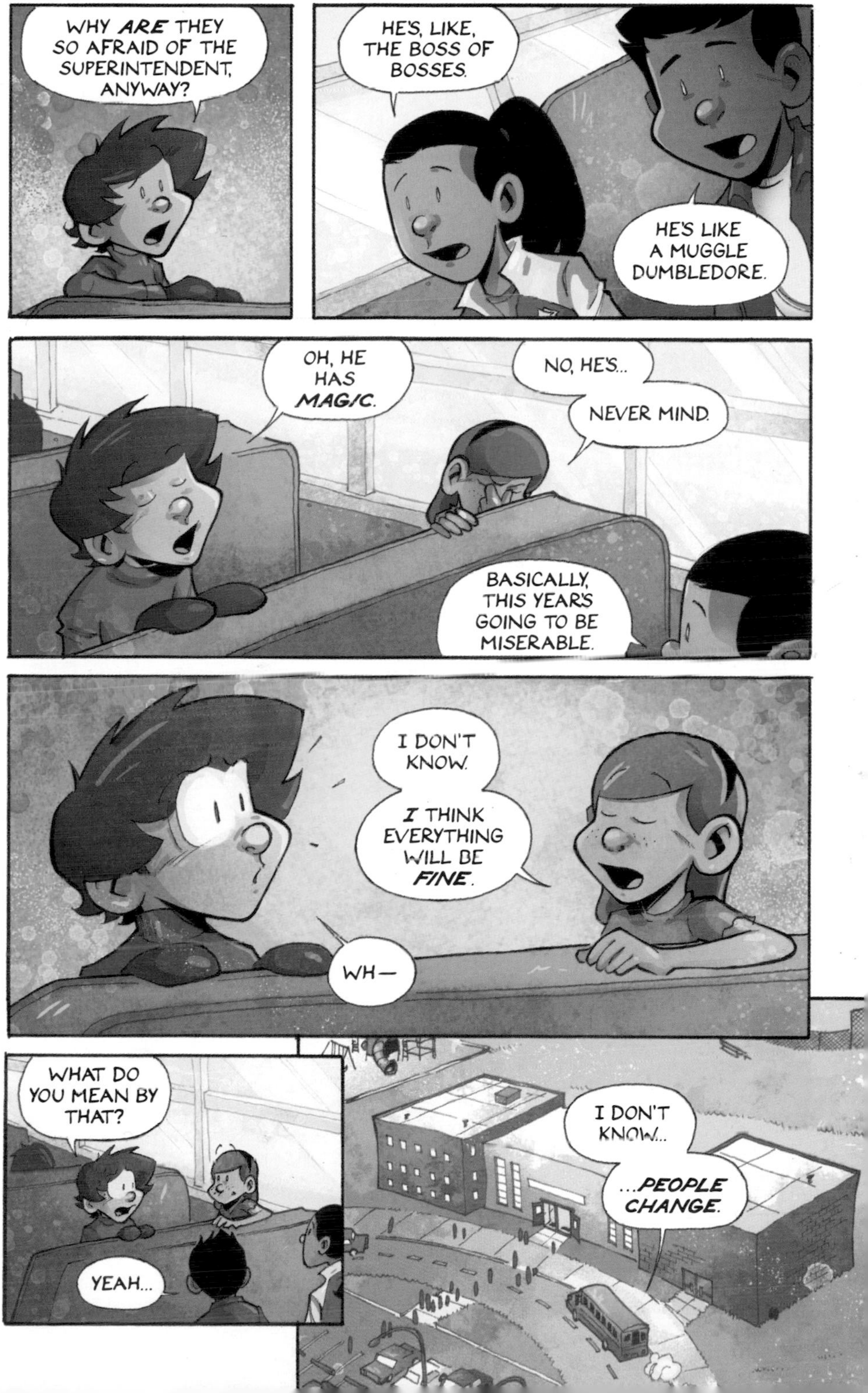
WHY *ARE* THEY SO AFRAID OF THE SUPERINTENDENT, ANYWAY?
HE'S, LIKE, THE BOSS OF BOSSES.
HE'S LIKE A MUGGLE DUMBLEDORE.
OH, HE HAS *MAGIC*.
NO, HE'S...
NEVER MIND.
BASICALLY, THIS YEAR'S GOING TO BE MISERABLE.
I DON'T KNOW.
I THINK EVERYTHING WILL BE *FINE*.
WH—
WHAT DO YOU MEAN BY THAT?
YEAH...
I DON'T KNOW...
...*PEOPLE CHANGE*.

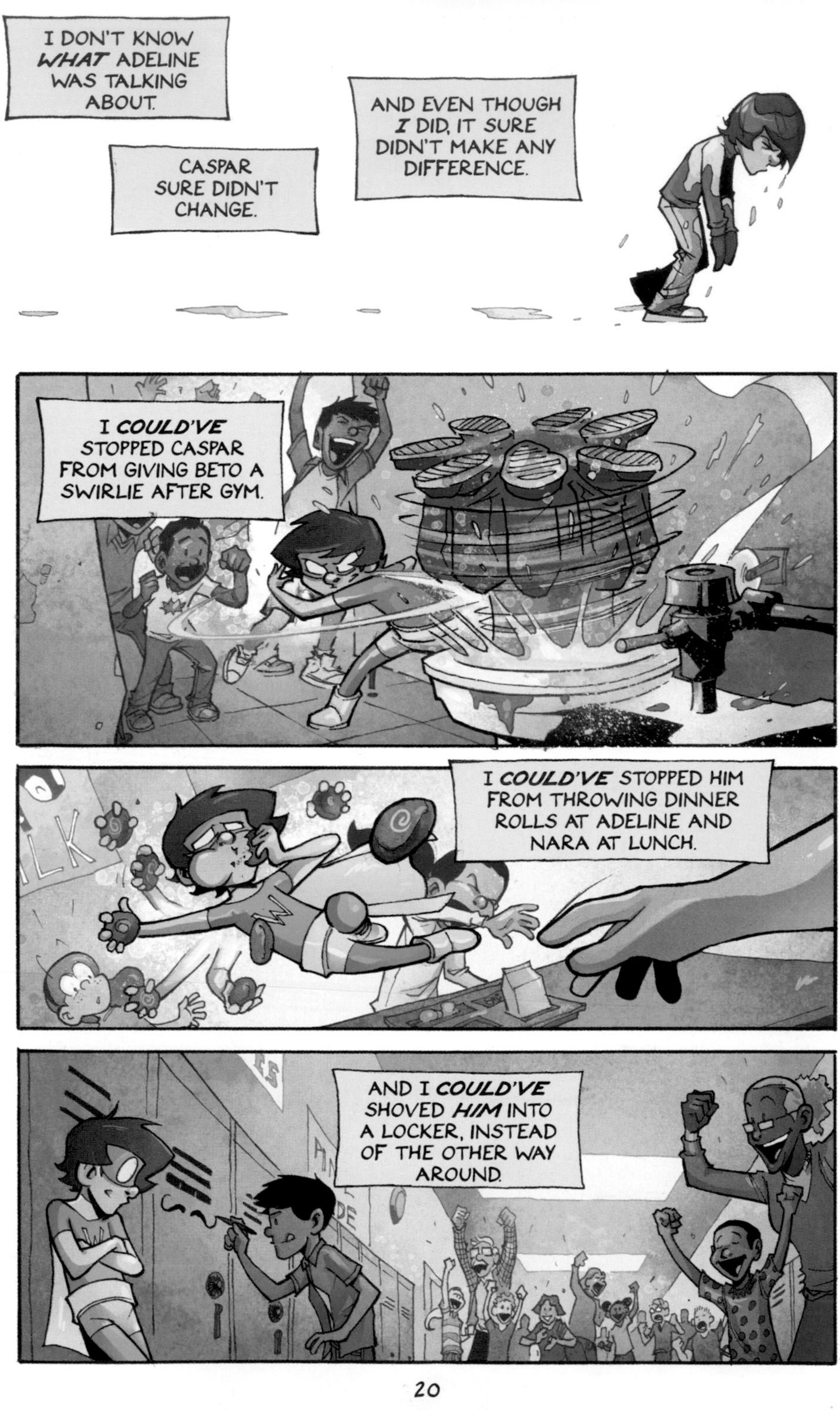
I DON'T KNOW *WHAT* ADELINE WAS TALKING ABOUT.
CASPAR SURE DIDN'T CHANGE.
AND EVEN THOUGH *I* DID, IT SURE DIDN'T MAKE ANY DIFFERENCE.
I *COULD'VE* STOPPED CASPAR FROM GIVING BETO A SWIRLIE AFTER GYM.
I *COULD'VE* STOPPED HIM FROM THROWING DINNER ROLLS AT ADELINE AND NARA AT LUNCH.
AND I *COULD'VE* SHOVED *HIM* INTO A LOCKER, INSTEAD OF THE OTHER WAY AROUND.

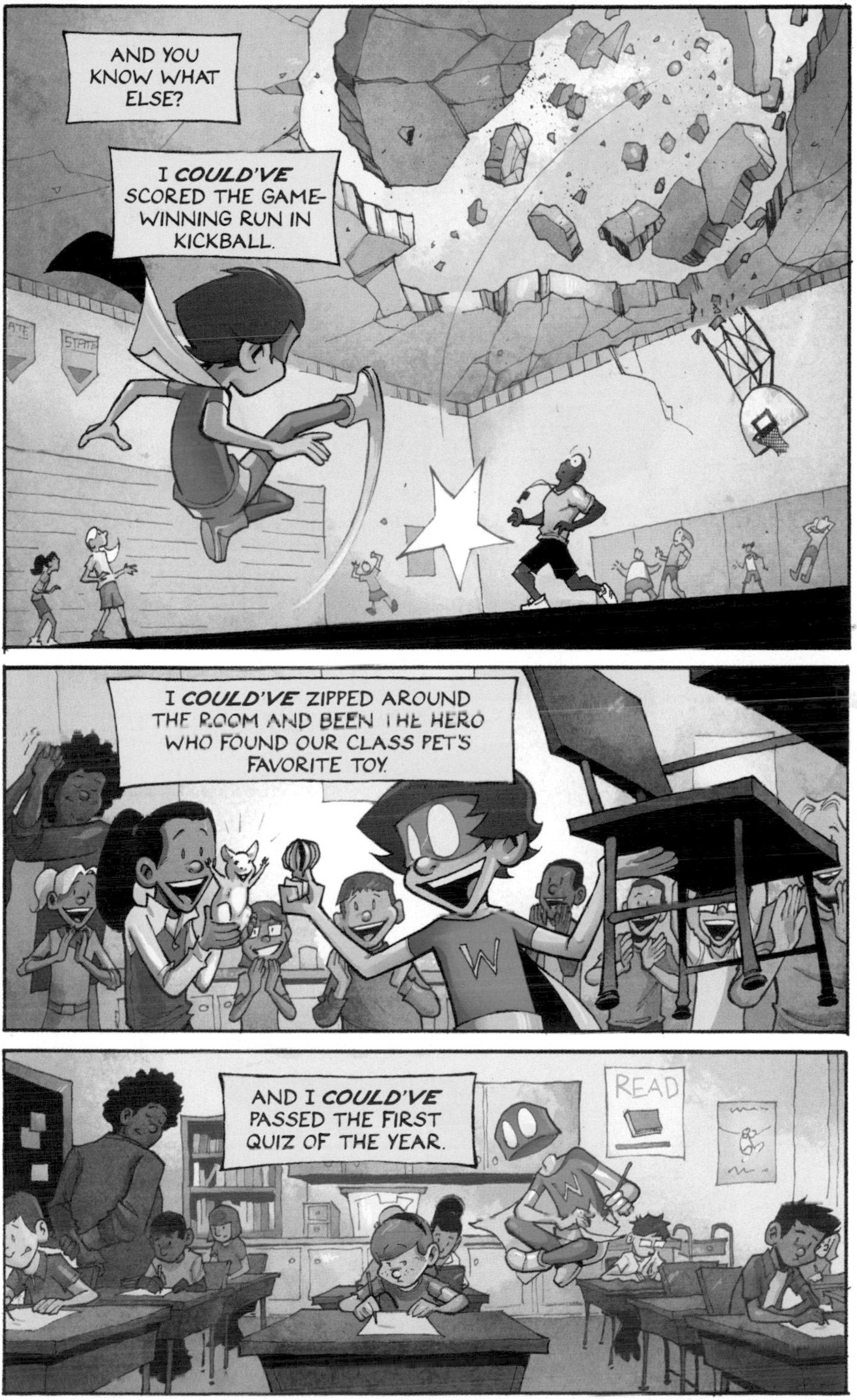
AND YOU KNOW WHAT ELSE?
I *COULD'VE* SCORED THE GAME-WINNING RUN IN KICKBALL.
I *COULD'VE* ZIPPED AROUND THE ROOM AND BEEN THE HERO WHO FOUND OUR CLASS PET'S FAVORITE TOY.
AND I *COULD'VE* PASSED THE FIRST QUIZ OF THE YEAR.
READ

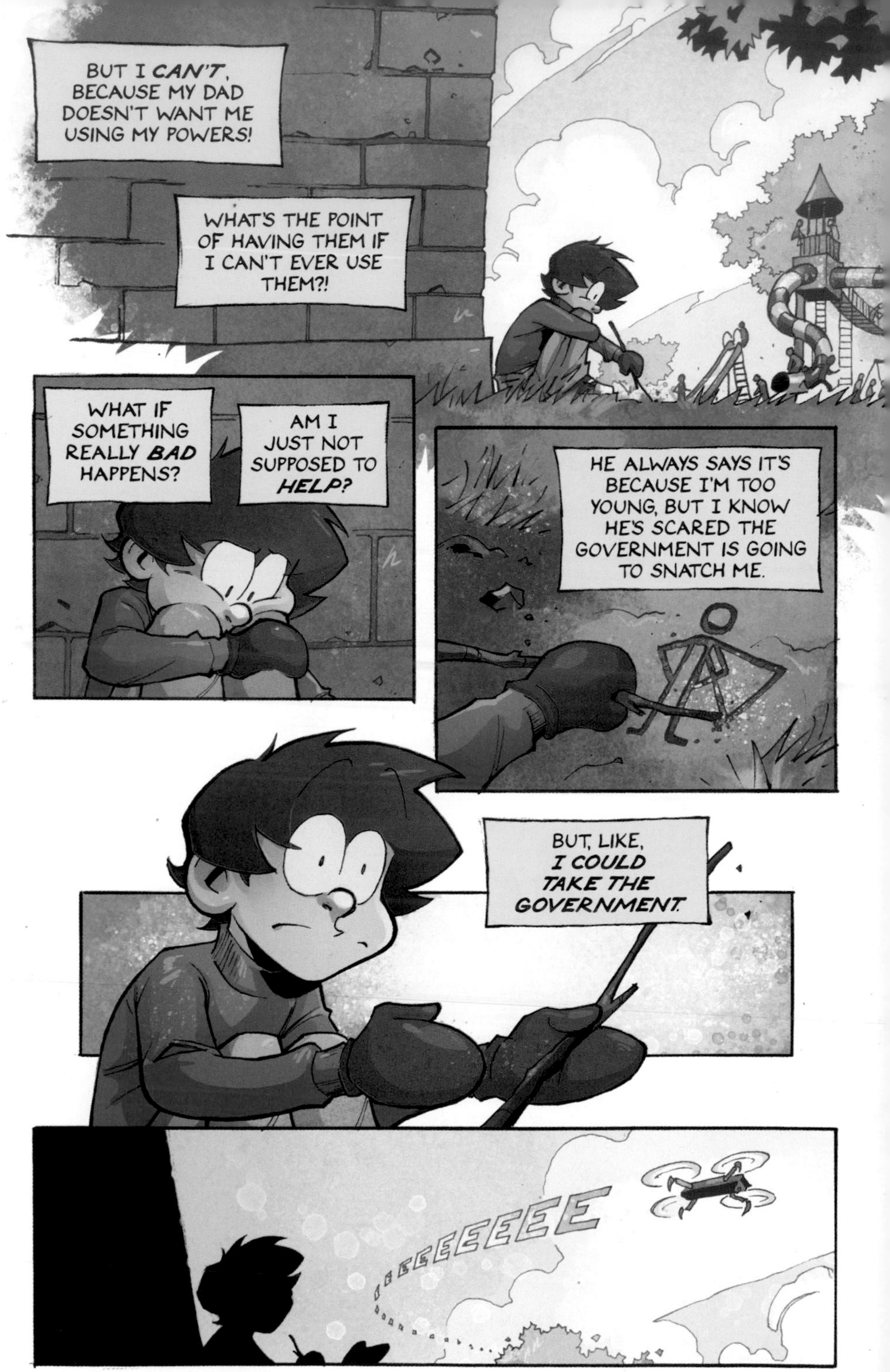
BUT I CAN'T, BECAUSE MY DAD DOESN'T WANT ME USING MY POWERS!
WHAT'S THE POINT OF HAVING THEM IF I CAN'T EVER USE THEM?!
WHAT IF SOMETHING REALLY BAD HAPPENS?
AM I JUST NOT SUPPOSED TO HELP?
HE ALWAYS SAYS IT'S BECAUSE I'M TOO YOUNG, BUT I KNOW HE'S SCARED THE GOVERNMENT IS GOING TO SNATCH ME.
BUT, LIKE, I COULD TAKE THE GOVERNMENT.
EEEEEEEEE

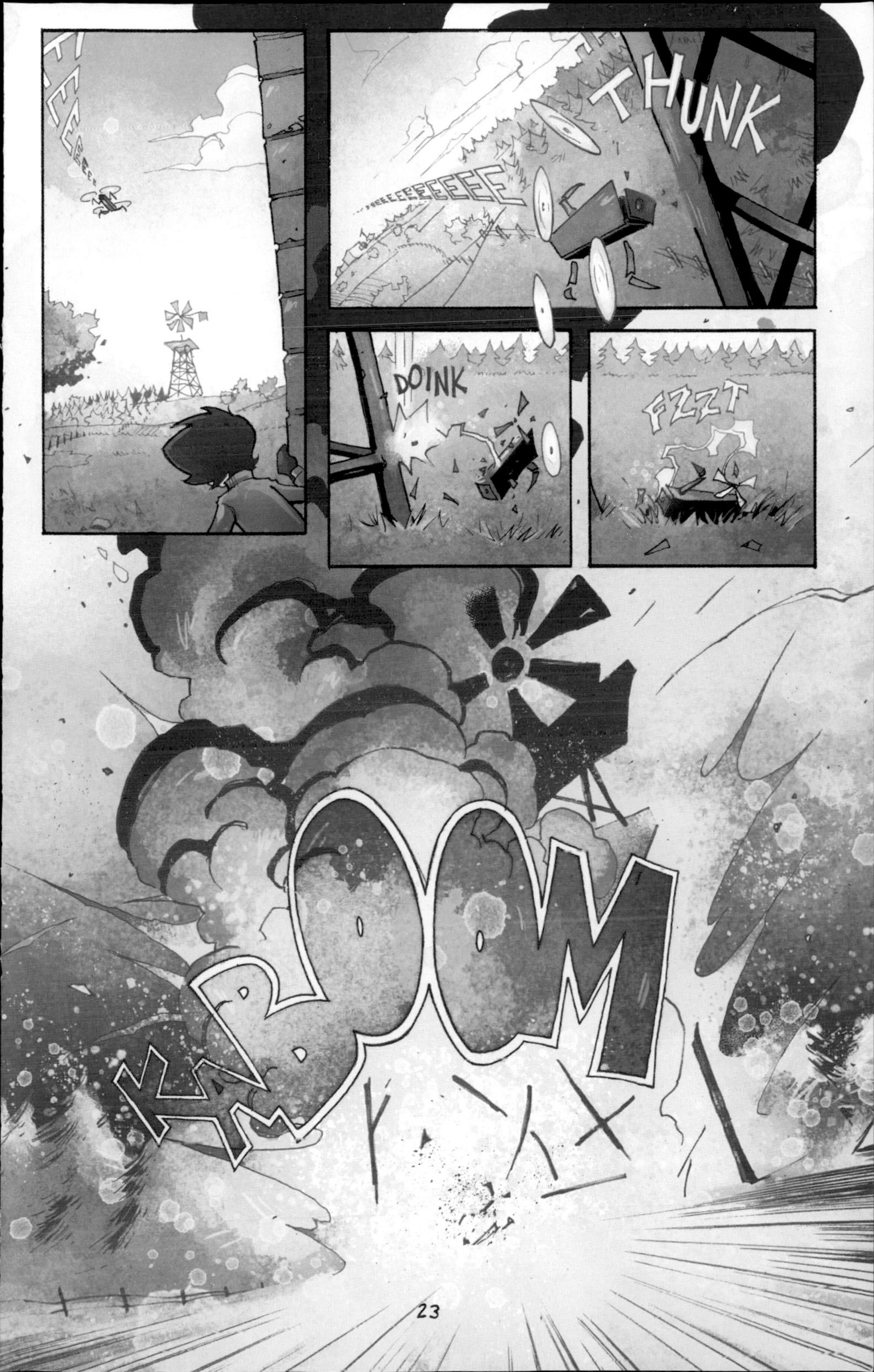
EEEeeee
...eeeeEEEEEEEEE
THUNK
DOINK
FZZT
KABOOM

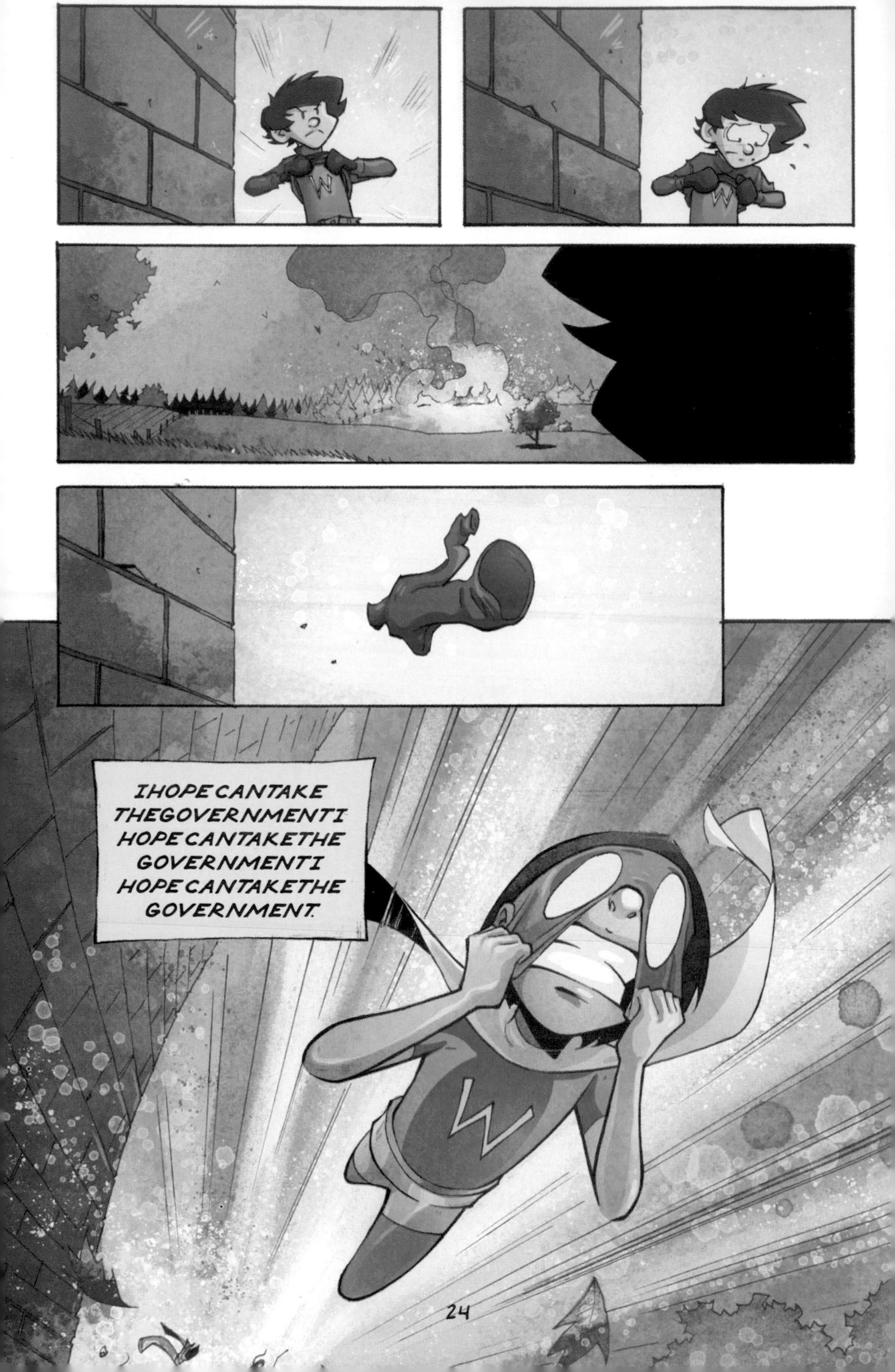
IHOPECANTAKE
THEGOVERNMENTI
HOPECANTAKETHE
GOVERNMENTI
HOPECANTAKETHE
GOVERNMENT.

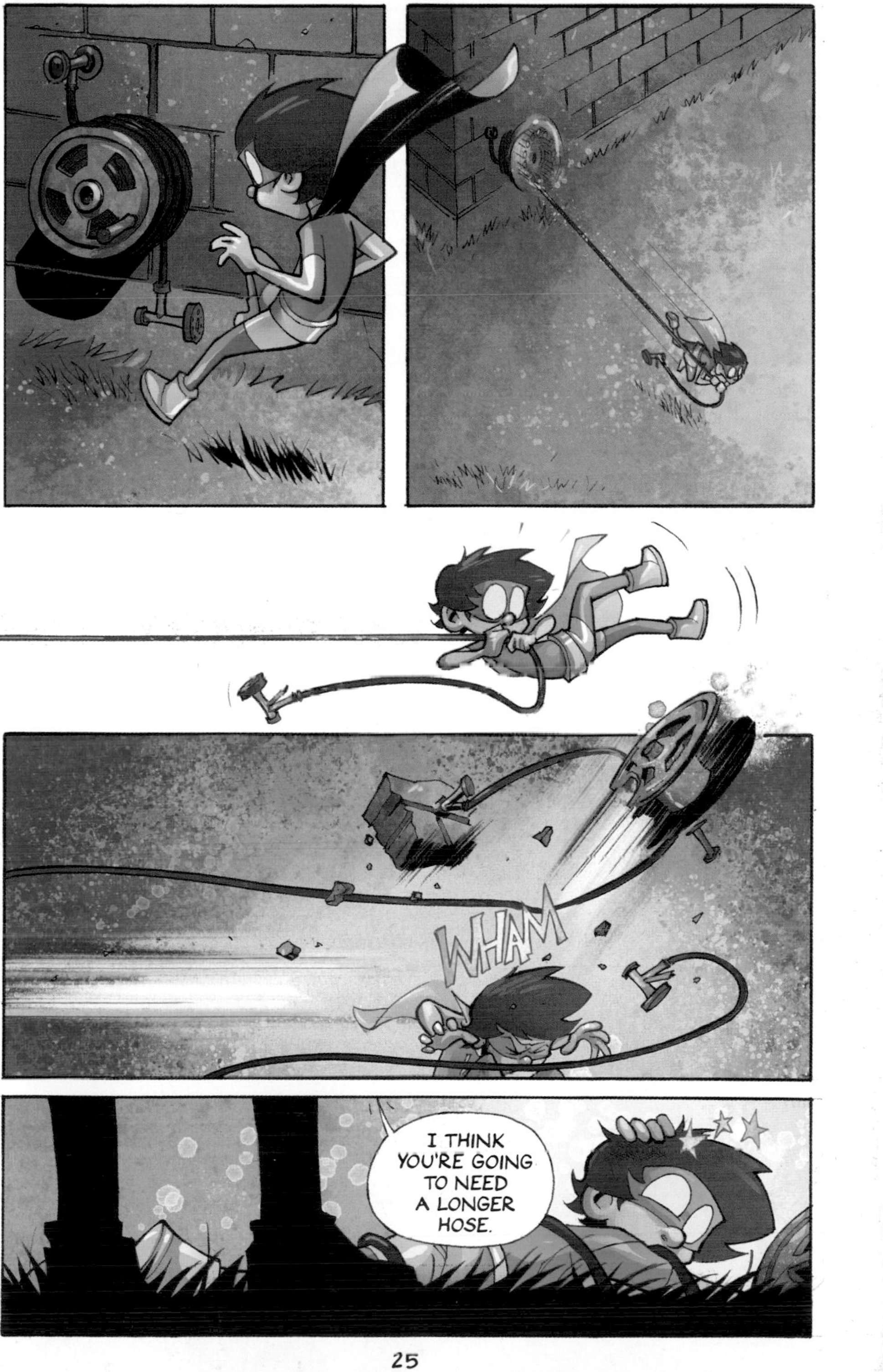
WHAM
I THINK YOU'RE GOING TO NEED A LONGER HOSE.

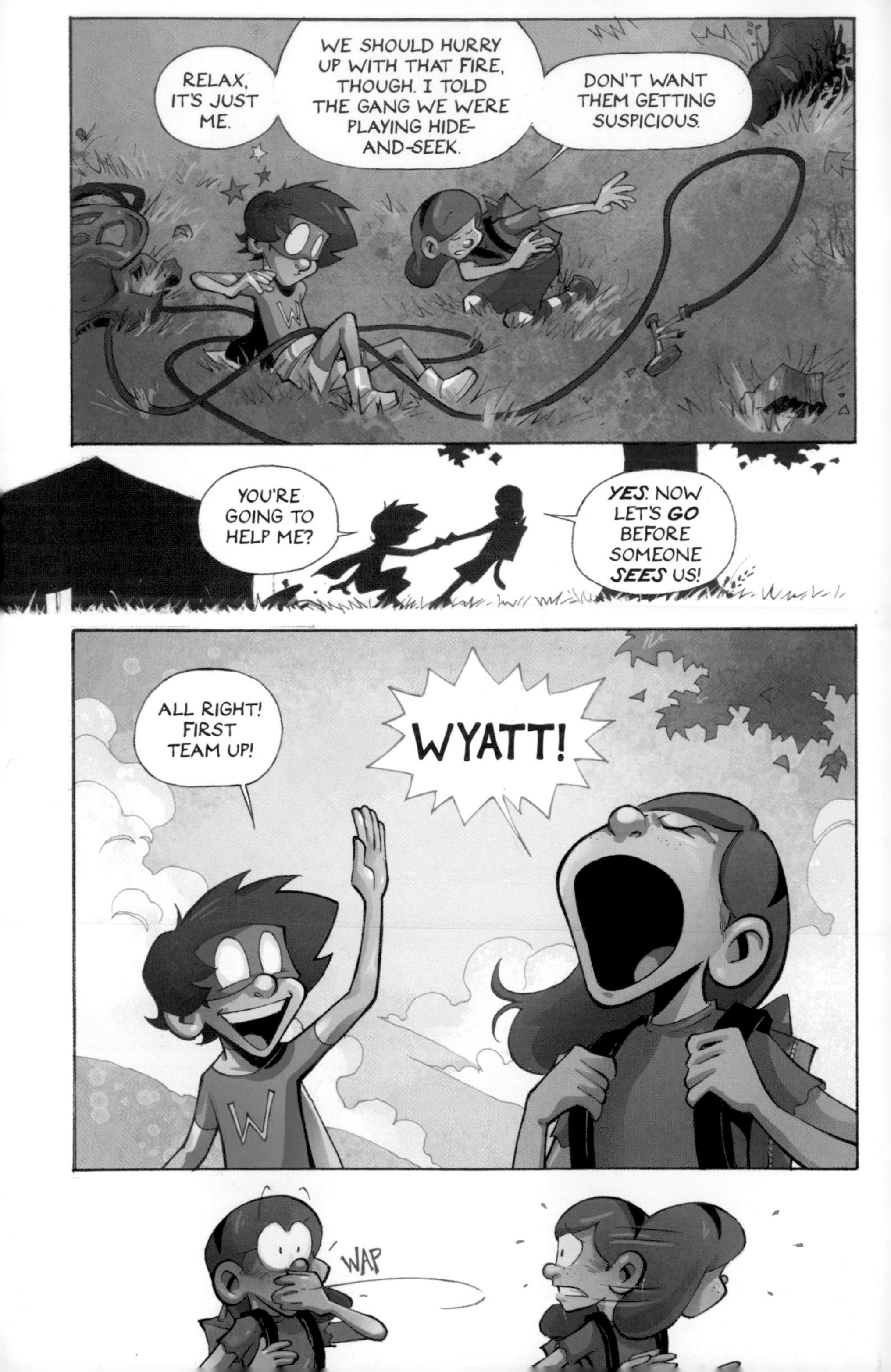
RELAX, IT'S JUST ME.
WE SHOULD HURRY UP WITH THAT FIRE, THOUGH. I TOLD THE GANG WE WERE PLAYING HIDE-AND-SEEK.
DON'T WANT THEM GETTING SUSPICIOUS.
YOU'RE GOING TO HELP ME?
YES. NOW LET'S GO BEFORE SOMEONE SEES US!
ALL RIGHT! FIRST TEAM UP!
WYATT!
WAP

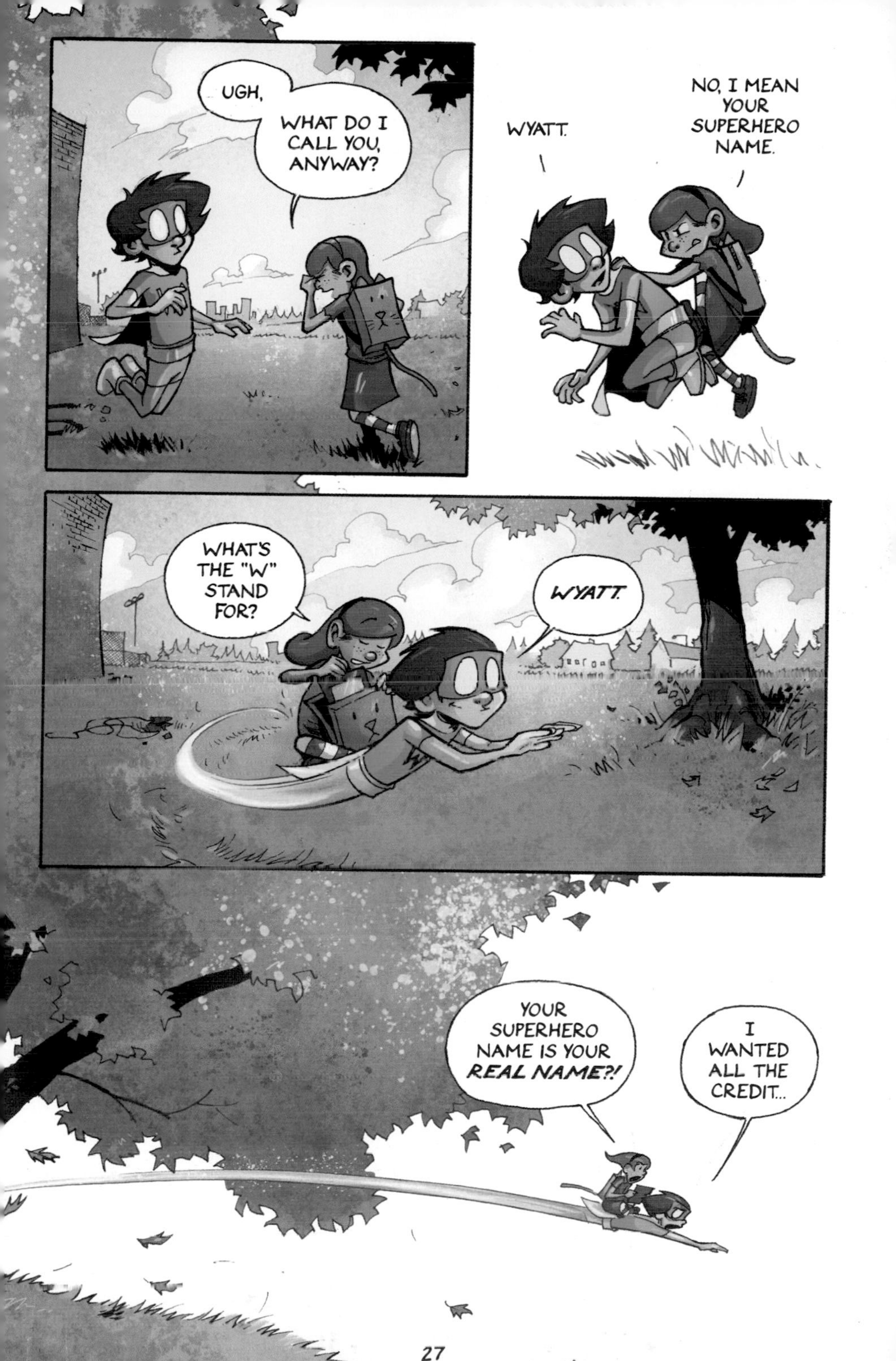
UGH,
WHAT DO I CALL YOU, ANYWAY?
WYATT.
NO, I MEAN YOUR SUPERHERO NAME.
WHAT'S THE "W" STAND FOR?
WYATT.
YOUR SUPERHERO NAME IS YOUR REAL NAME?!
I WANTED ALL THE CREDIT...

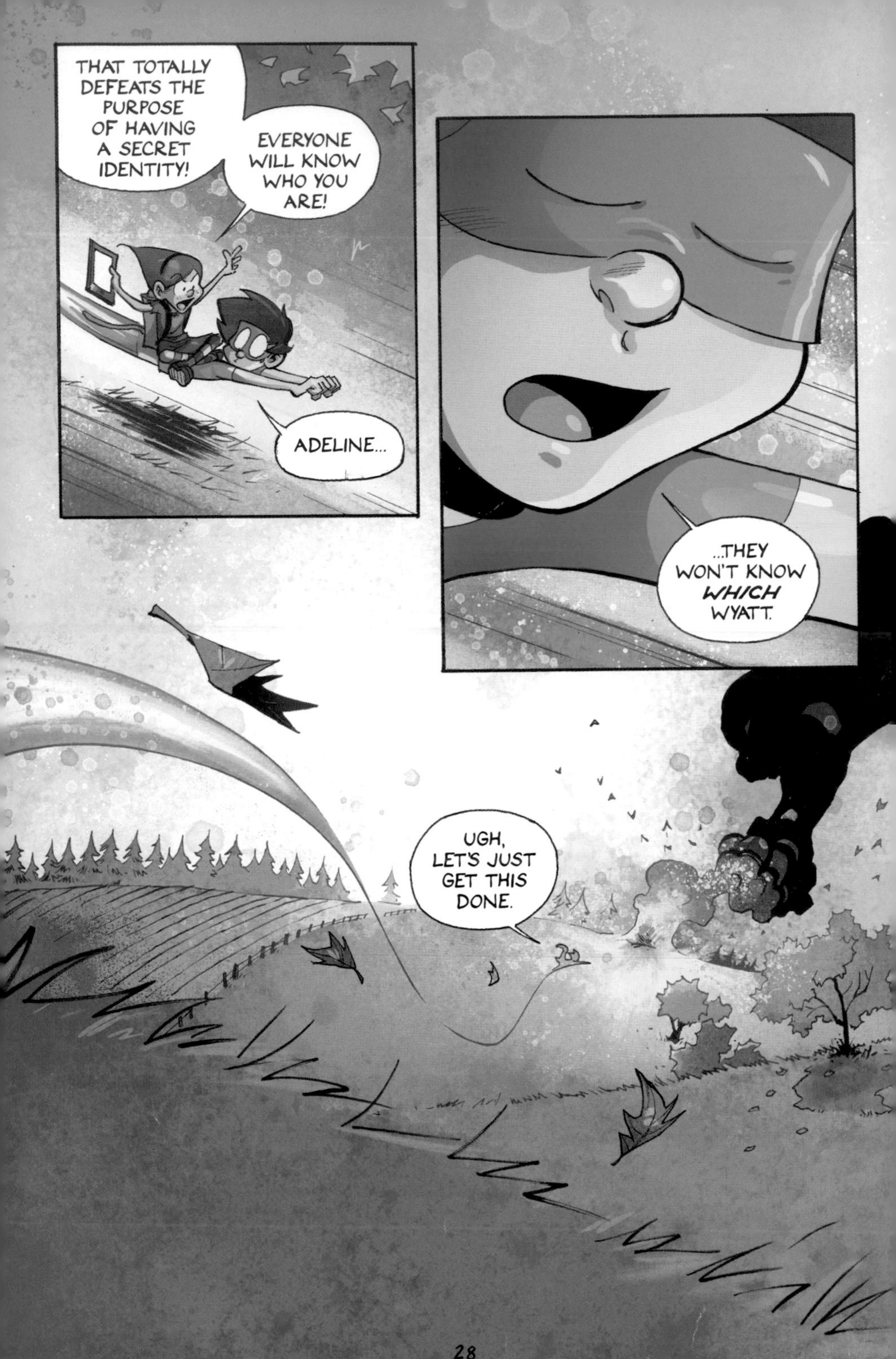
THAT TOTALLY DEFEATS THE PURPOSE OF HAVING A SECRET IDENTITY!
EVERYONE WILL KNOW WHO YOU ARE!
ADELINE...
...THEY WON'T KNOW *WHICH* WYATT.
UGH, LET'S JUST GET THIS DONE.

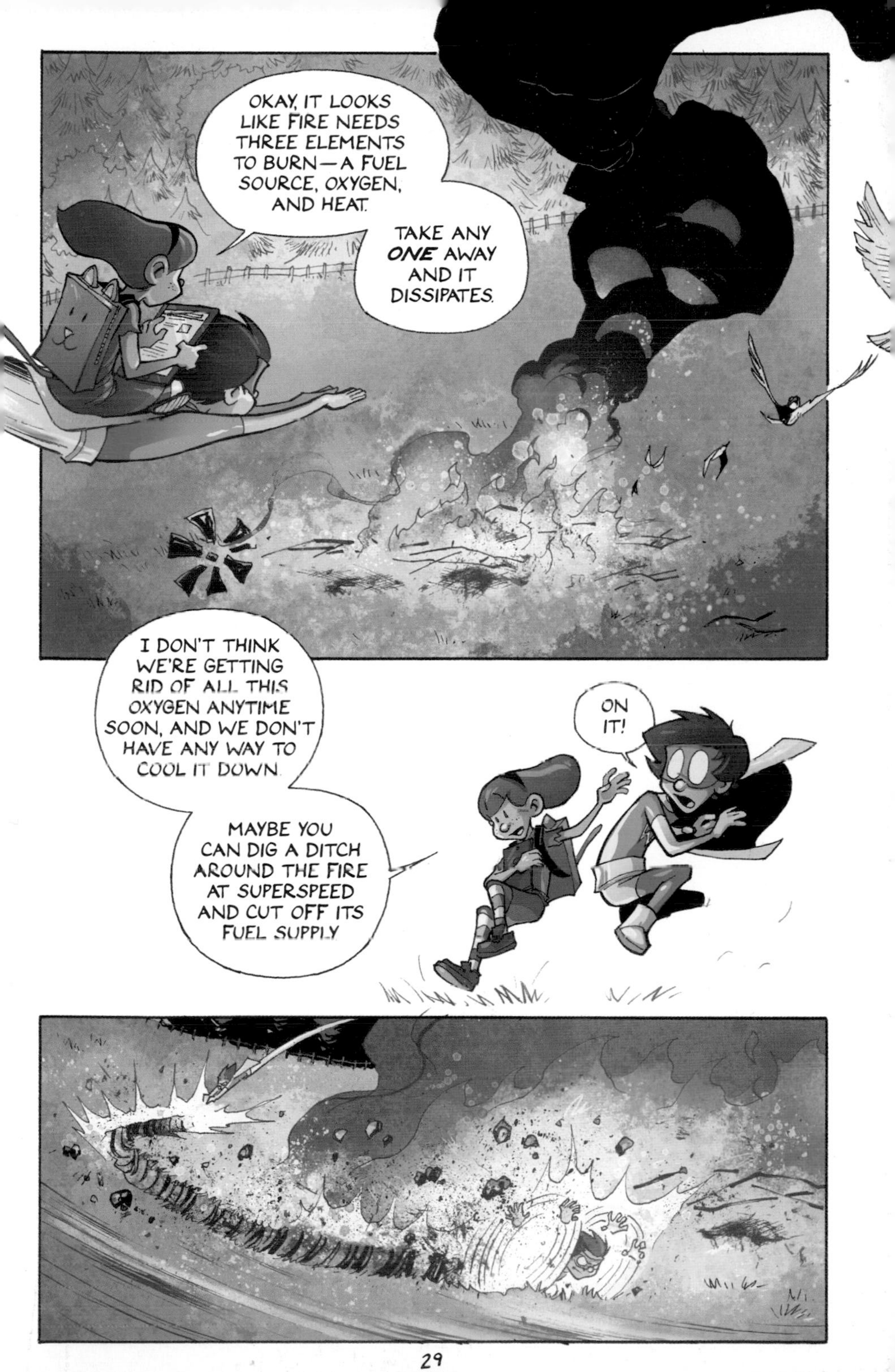
OKAY, IT LOOKS LIKE FIRE NEEDS THREE ELEMENTS TO BURN—A FUEL SOURCE, OXYGEN, AND HEAT.
TAKE ANY *ONE* AWAY AND IT DISSIPATES.
I DON'T THINK WE'RE GETTING RID OF ALL THIS OXYGEN ANYTIME SOON, AND WE DON'T HAVE ANY WAY TO COOL IT DOWN.
MAYBE YOU CAN DIG A DITCH AROUND THE FIRE AT SUPERSPEED AND CUT OFF ITS FUEL SUPPLY.
ON IT!

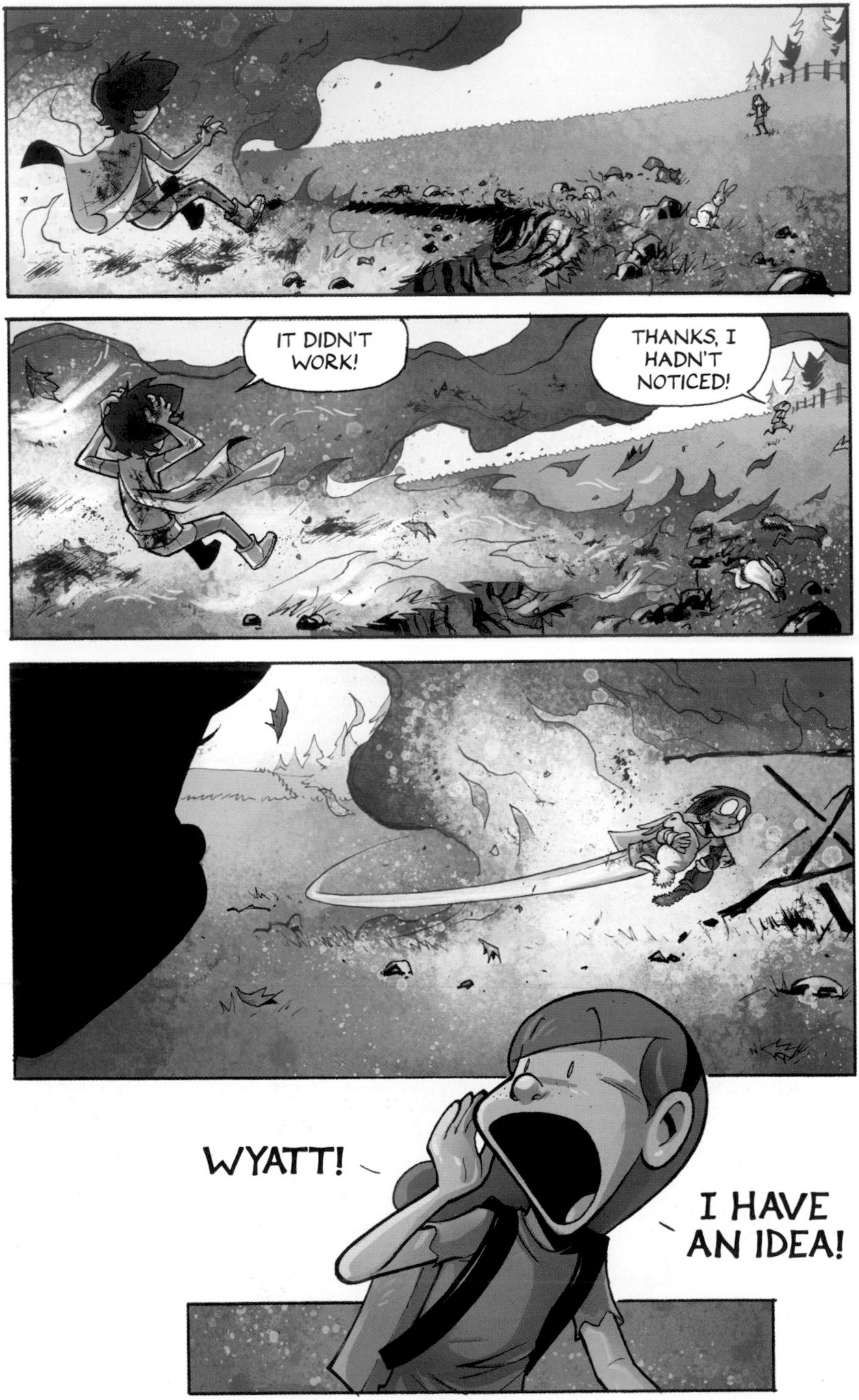
IT DIDN'T WORK!
THANKS, I HADN'T NOTICED!
WYATT!
I HAVE AN IDEA!

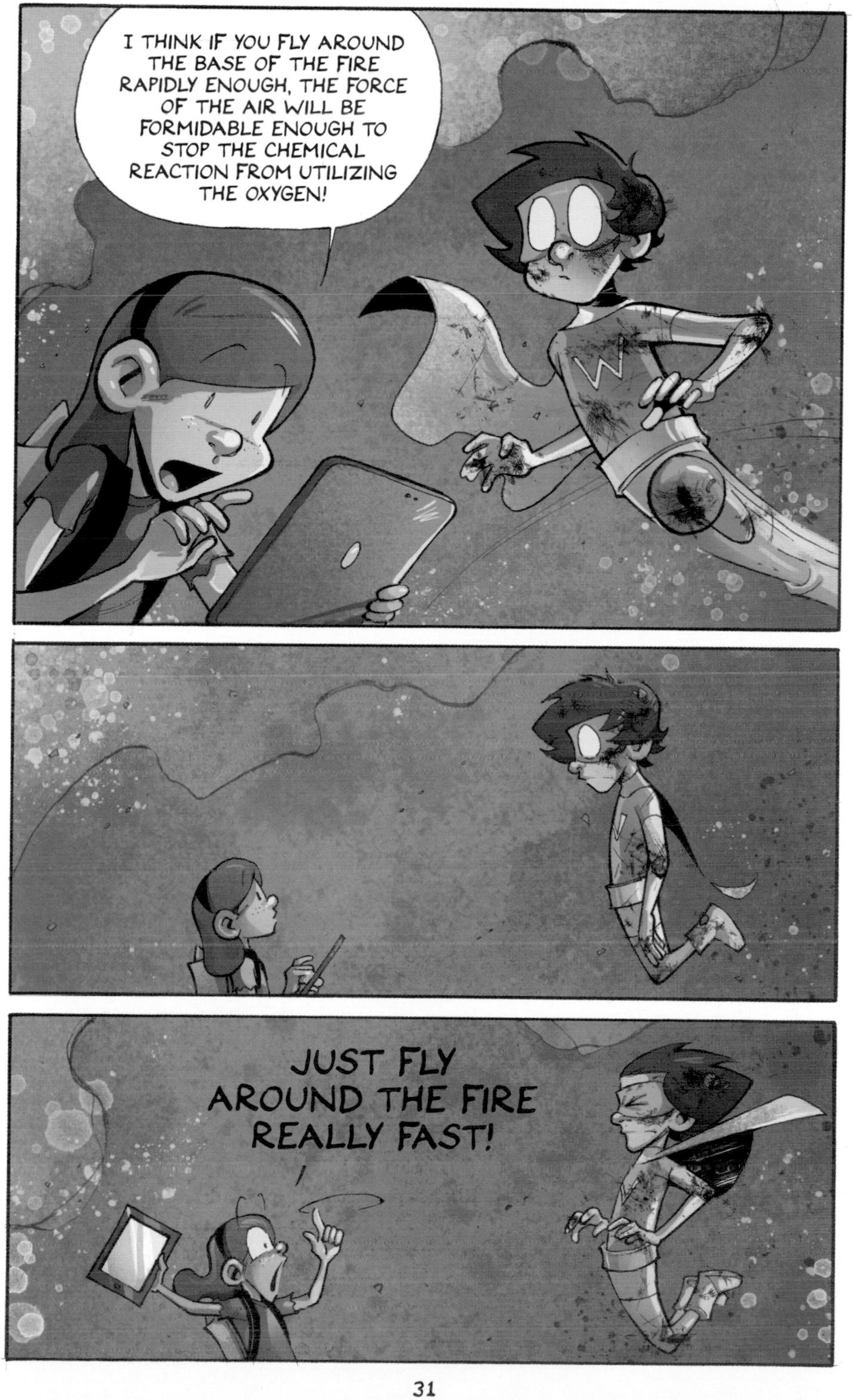
I THINK IF YOU FLY AROUND THE BASE OF THE FIRE RAPIDLY ENOUGH, THE FORCE OF THE AIR WILL BE FORMIDABLE ENOUGH TO STOP THE CHEMICAL REACTION FROM UTILIZING THE OXYGEN!
JUST FLY AROUND THE FIRE REALLY FAST!

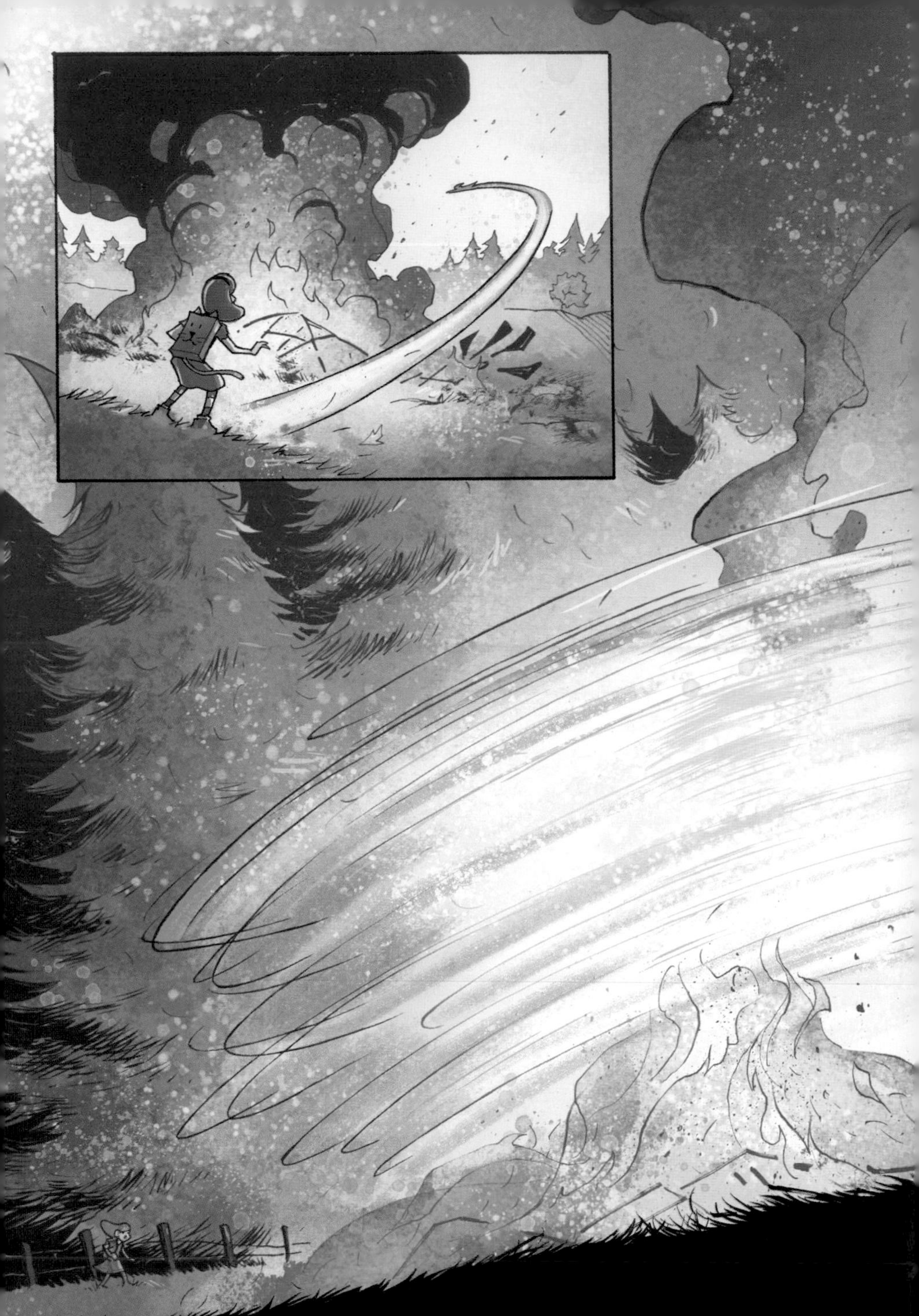

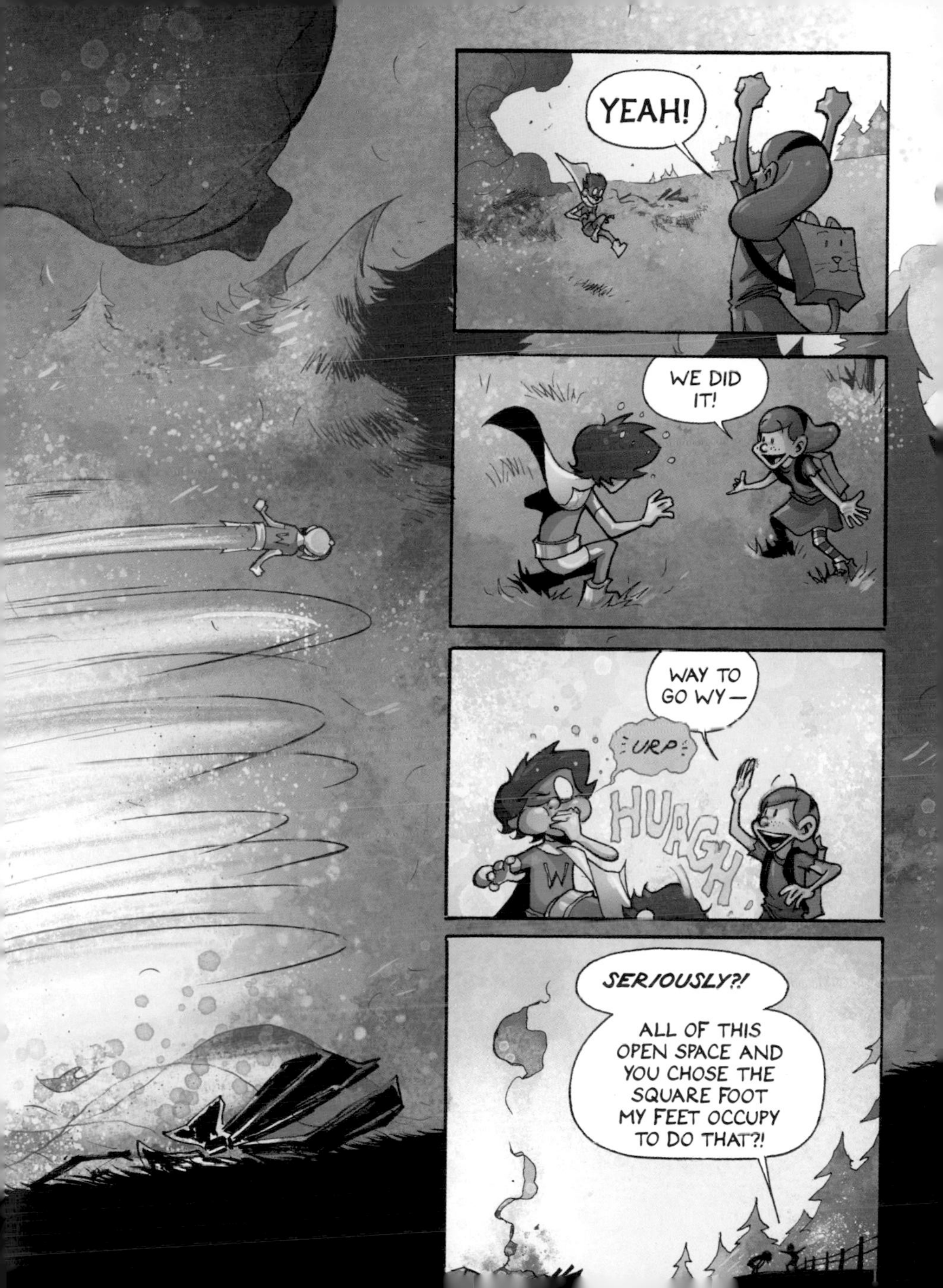
YEAH!
WE DID IT!
WAY TO GO WY—
URP
HUAGH
SERIOUSLY?!
ALL OF THIS OPEN SPACE AND YOU CHOSE THE SQUARE FOOT MY FEET OCCUPY TO DO THAT?!

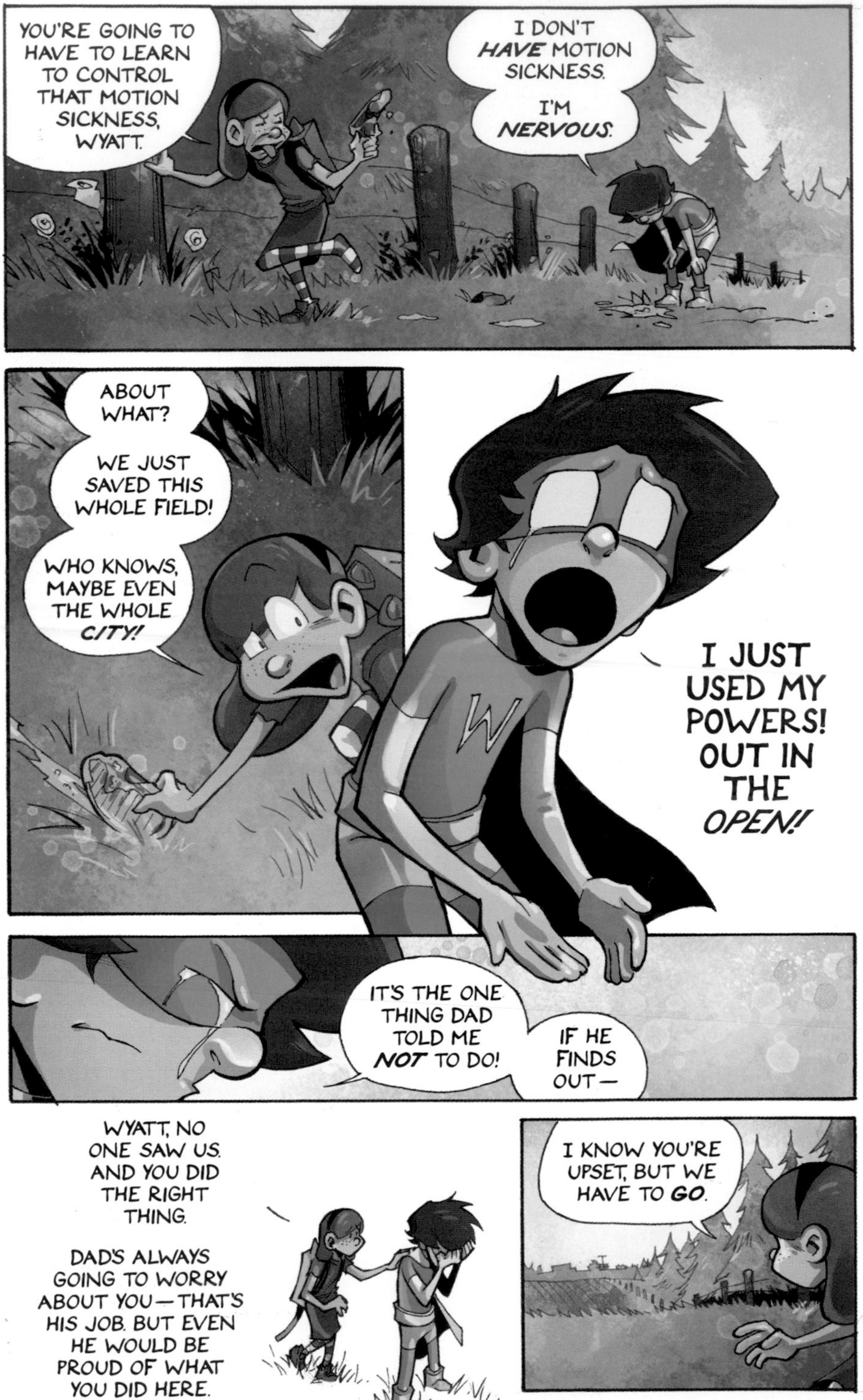
YOU'RE GOING TO HAVE TO LEARN TO CONTROL THAT MOTION SICKNESS, WYATT.
I DON'T *HAVE* MOTION SICKNESS.
I'M *NERVOUS*.
ABOUT WHAT?
WE JUST SAVED THIS WHOLE FIELD!
WHO KNOWS, MAYBE EVEN THE WHOLE *CITY!*
I JUST USED MY POWERS! OUT IN THE *OPEN!!*
IT'S THE ONE THING DAD TOLD ME *NOT* TO DO!
IF HE FINDS OUT—
WYATT, NO ONE SAW US. AND YOU DID THE RIGHT THING.
DAD'S ALWAYS GOING TO WORRY ABOUT YOU—THAT'S HIS JOB. BUT EVEN HE WOULD BE PROUD OF WHAT YOU DID HERE.
I KNOW YOU'RE UPSET, BUT WE HAVE TO *GO*.

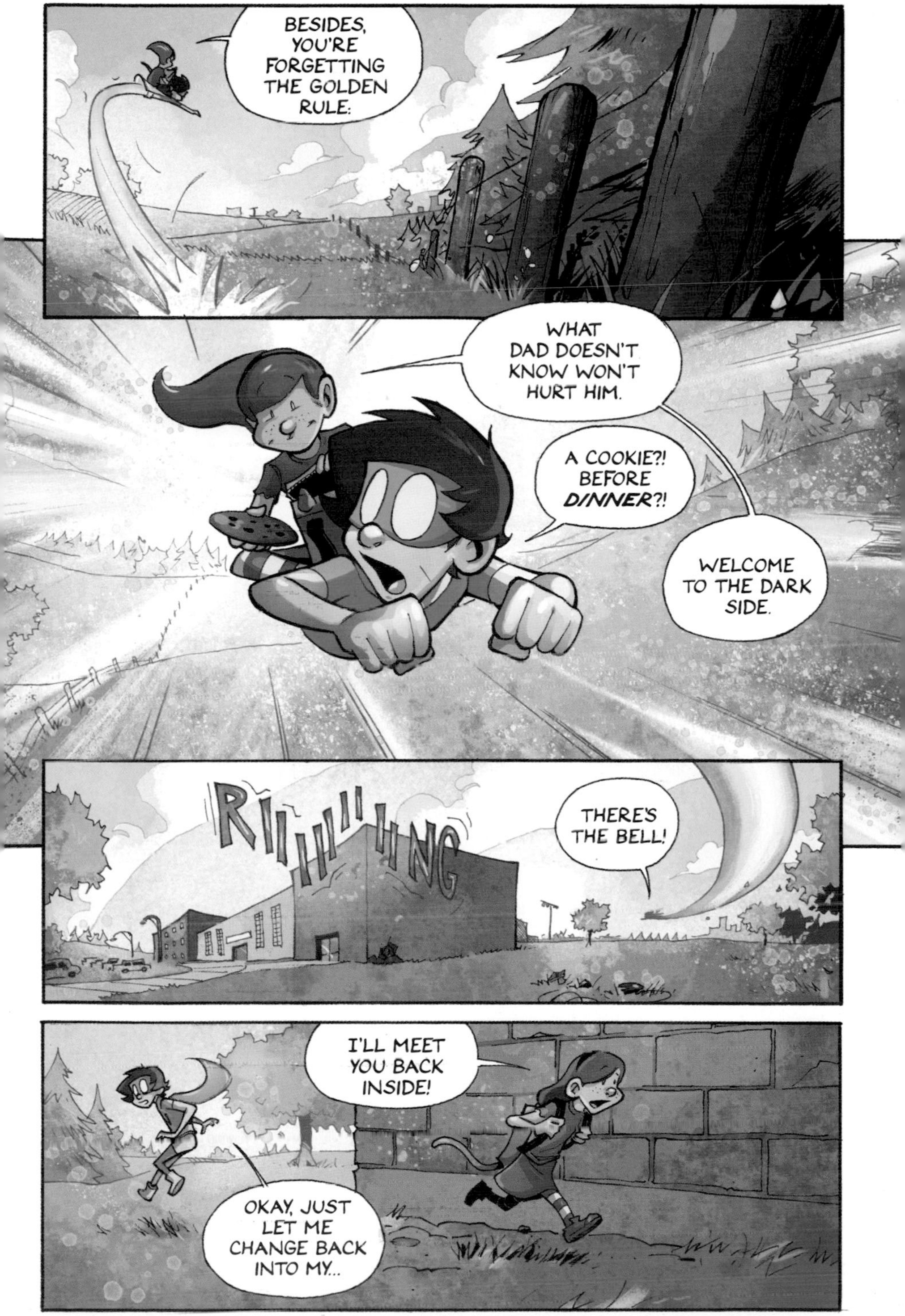

BESIDES, YOU'RE FORGETTING THE GOLDEN RULE:
WHAT DAD DOESN'T KNOW WON'T HURT HIM.
A COOKIE?! BEFORE *DINNER*?!
WELCOME TO THE DARK SIDE.
RIIIIIIIING
THERE'S THE BELL!
I'LL MEET YOU BACK INSIDE!
OKAY, JUST LET ME CHANGE BACK INTO MY...

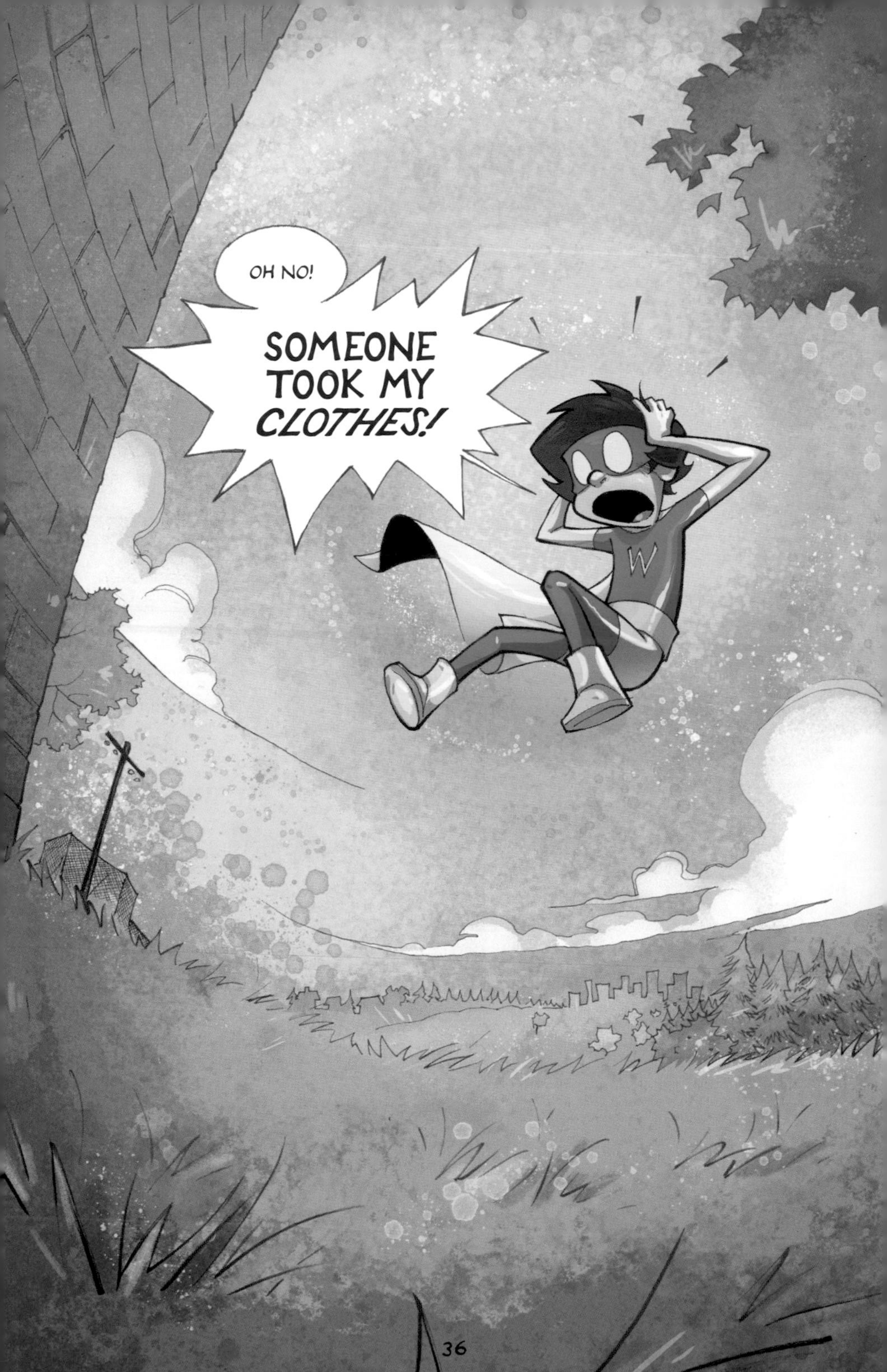
OH NO!
SOMEONE TOOK MY CLOTHES!

CHAPTER THREE

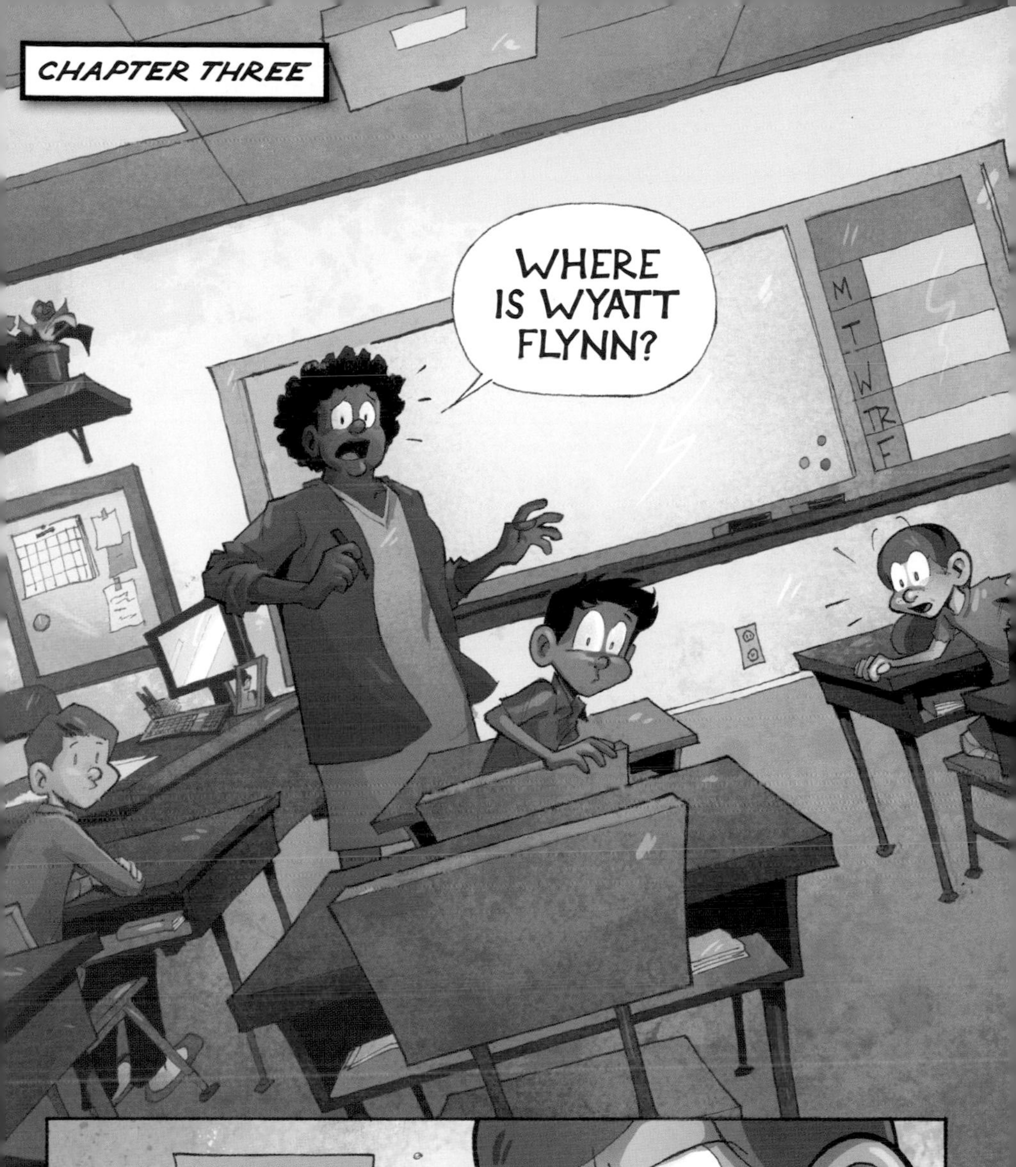
WHERE IS WYATT FLYNN?
M
T
W
TR
F

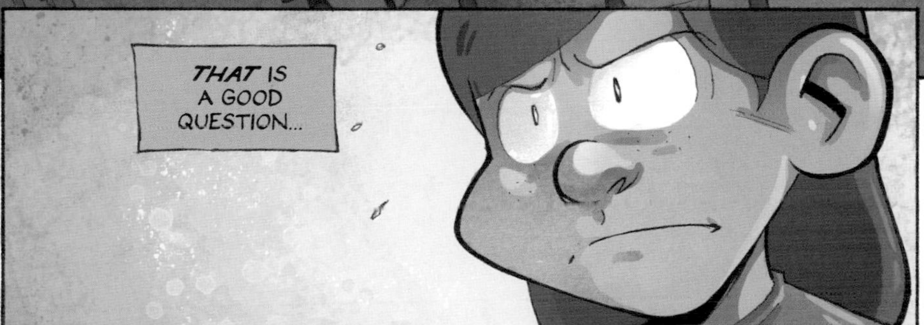
THAT IS A GOOD QUESTION...

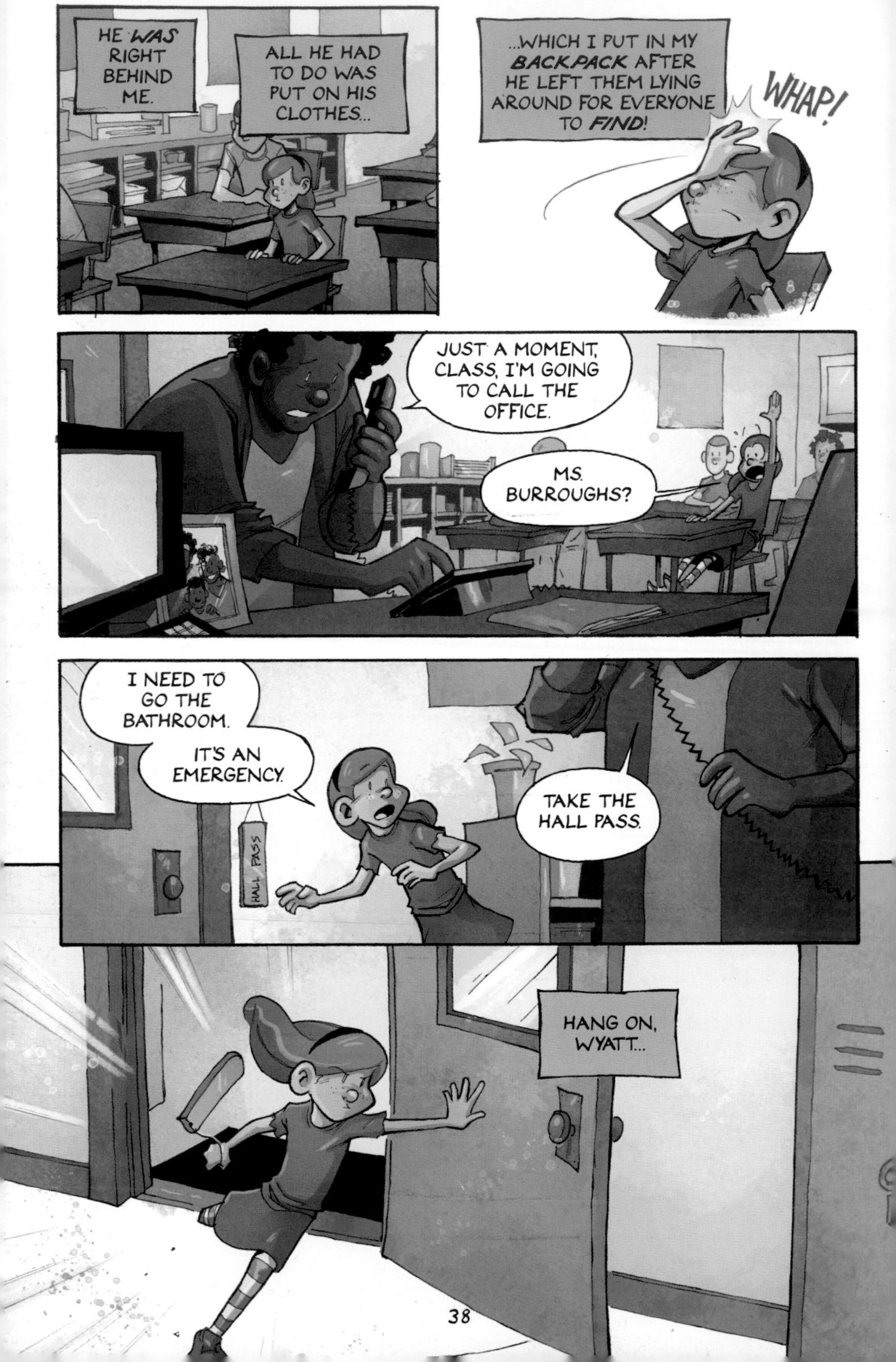
HE *WAS* RIGHT BEHIND ME.
ALL HE HAD TO DO WAS PUT ON HIS CLOTHES...
...WHICH I PUT IN MY *BACKPACK* AFTER HE LEFT THEM LYING AROUND FOR EVERYONE TO *FIND*!
WHAP!
JUST A MOMENT, CLASS, I'M GOING TO CALL THE OFFICE.
MS. BURROUGHS?
I NEED TO GO THE BATHROOM.
IT'S AN EMERGENCY.
TAKE THE HALL PASS.
HALL PASS
HANG ON, WYATT...

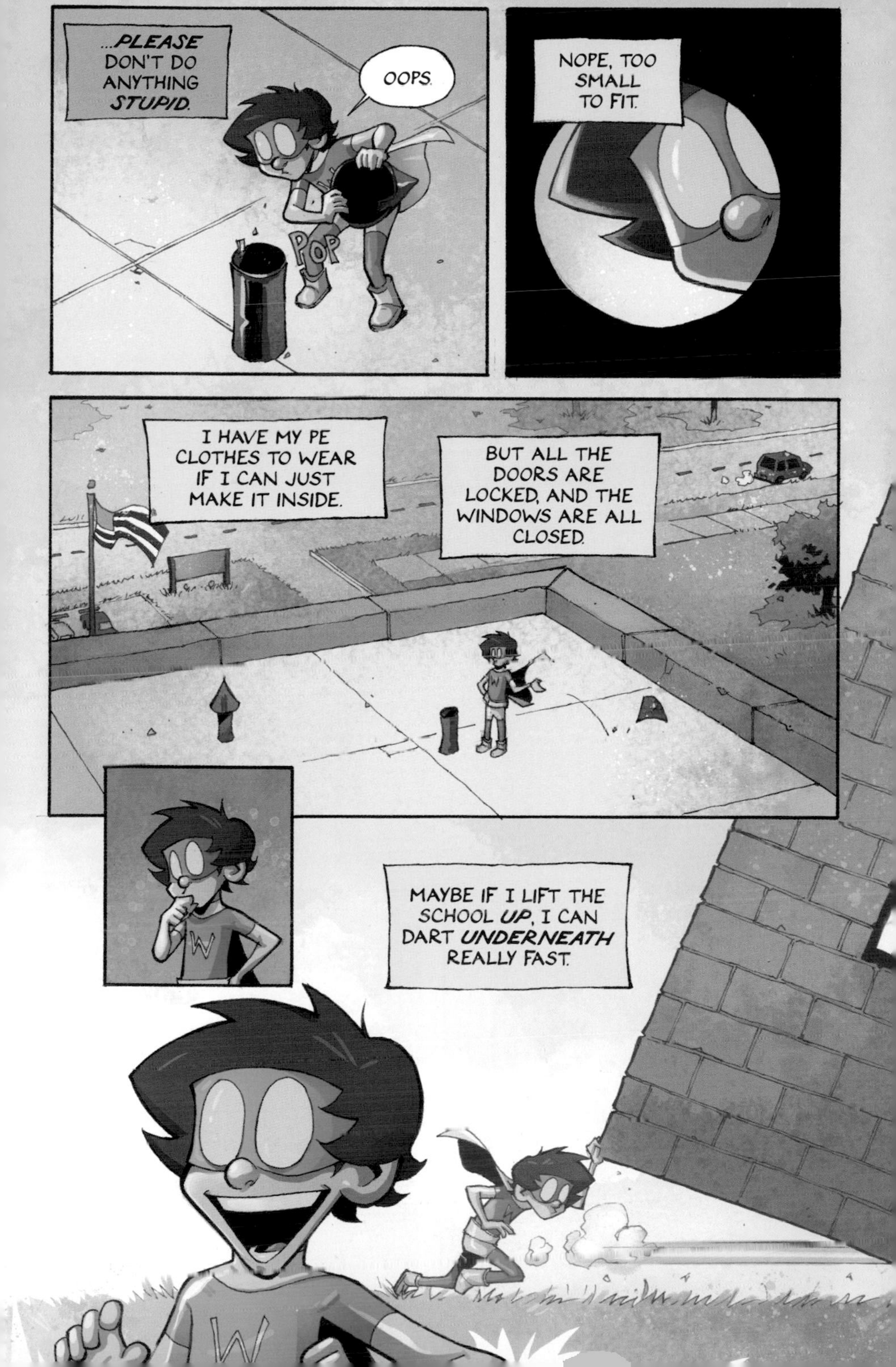
...PLEASE DON'T DO ANYTHING STUPID.
OOPS.
POP
NOPE, TOO SMALL TO FIT.
I HAVE MY PE CLOTHES TO WEAR IF I CAN JUST MAKE IT INSIDE.
BUT ALL THE DOORS ARE LOCKED, AND THE WINDOWS ARE ALL CLOSED.
MAYBE IF I LIFT THE SCHOOL UP, I CAN DART UNDERNEATH REALLY FAST.

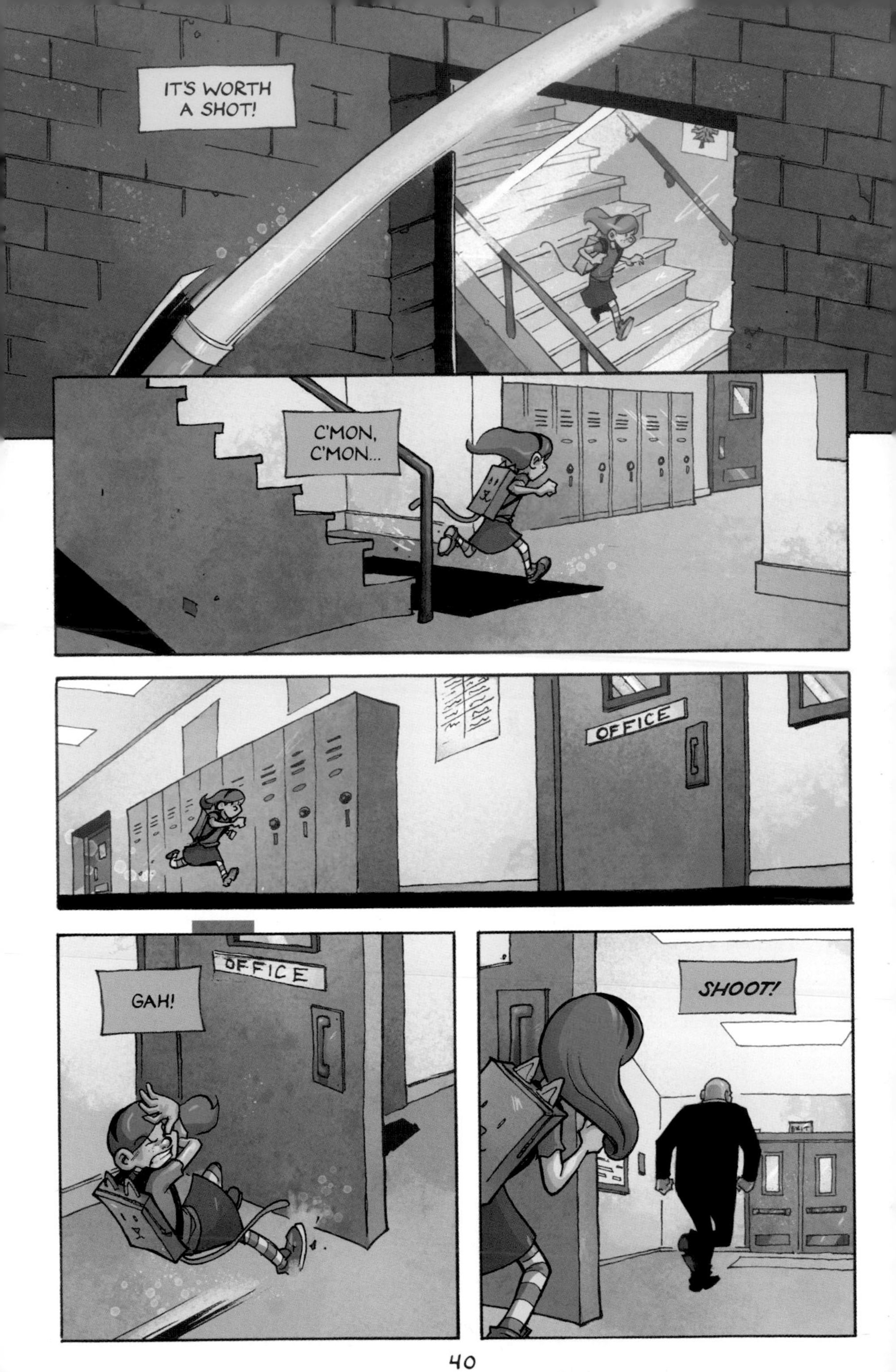
IT'S WORTH A SHOT!
C'MON, C'MON...
OFFICE
OFFICE
GAH!
SHOOT!

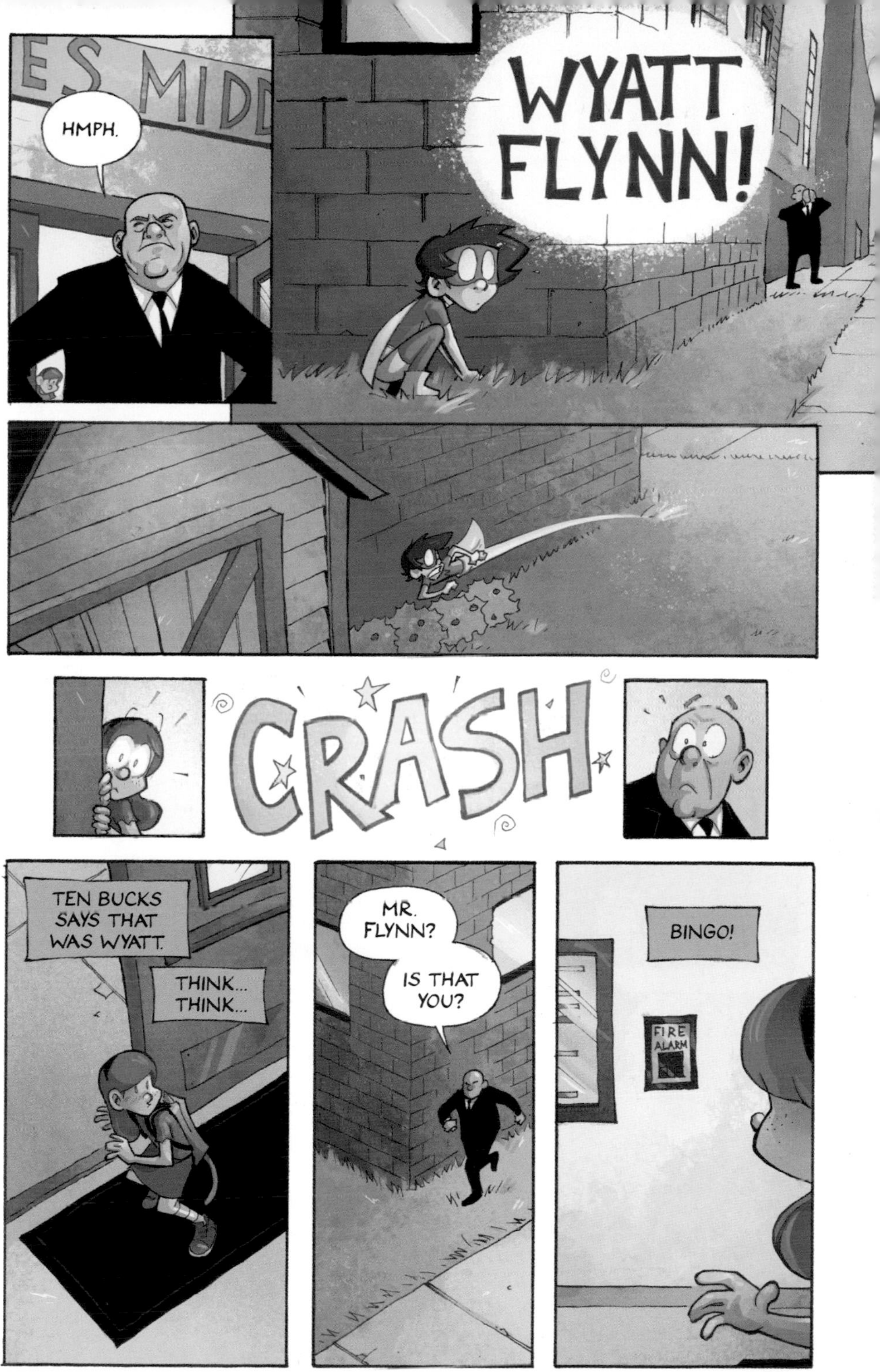
ES MIDD
HMPH.
WYATT FLYNN!
CRASH
TEN BUCKS SAYS THAT WAS WYATT.
THINK... THINK...
MR. FLYNN?
IS THAT YOU?
BINGO!
FIRE ALARM

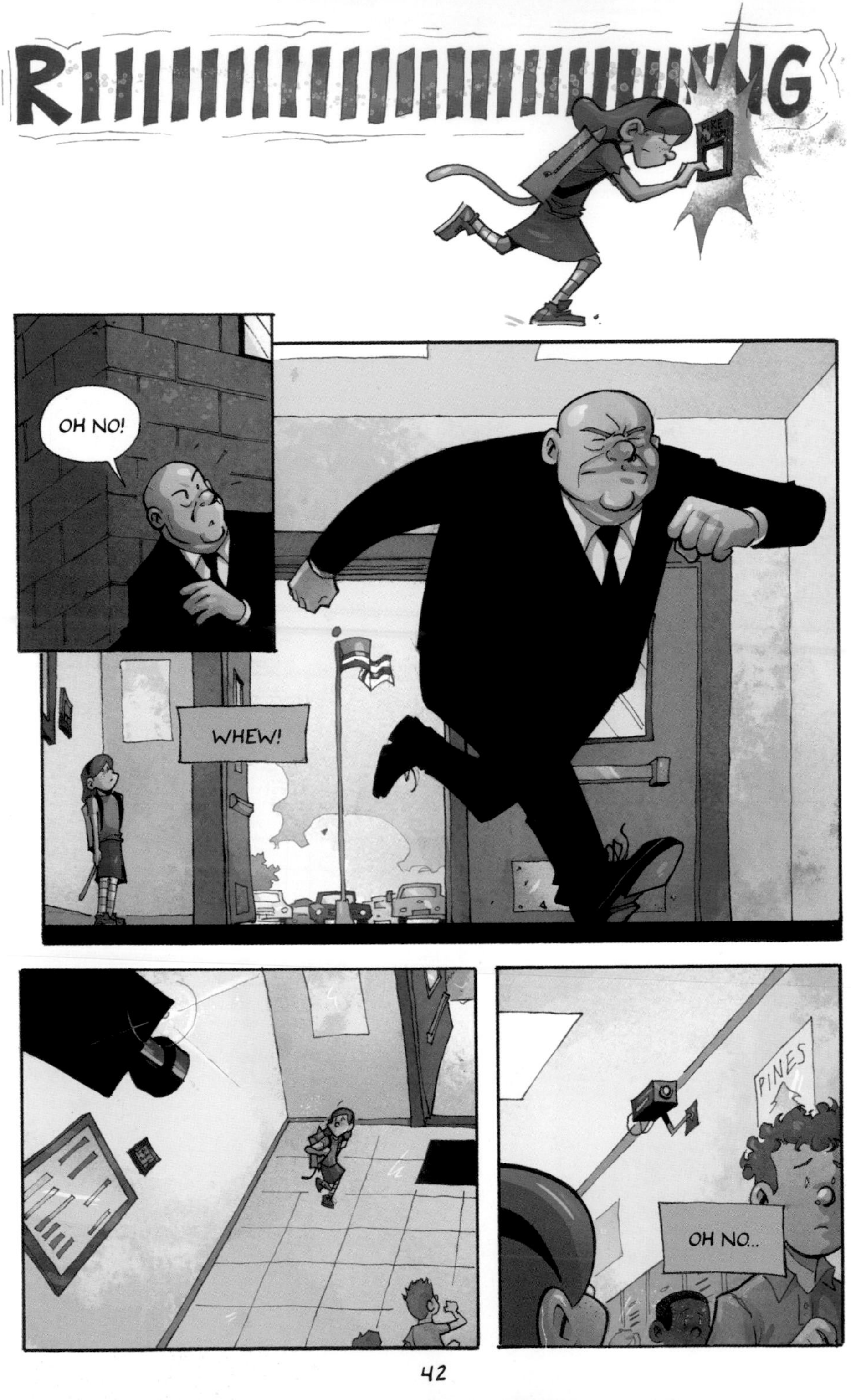
RIIIIIIIIIIIIIIIIIIIIIIIIIIIING
FIRE ALARM
OH NO!
WHEW!
PINES
OH NO...

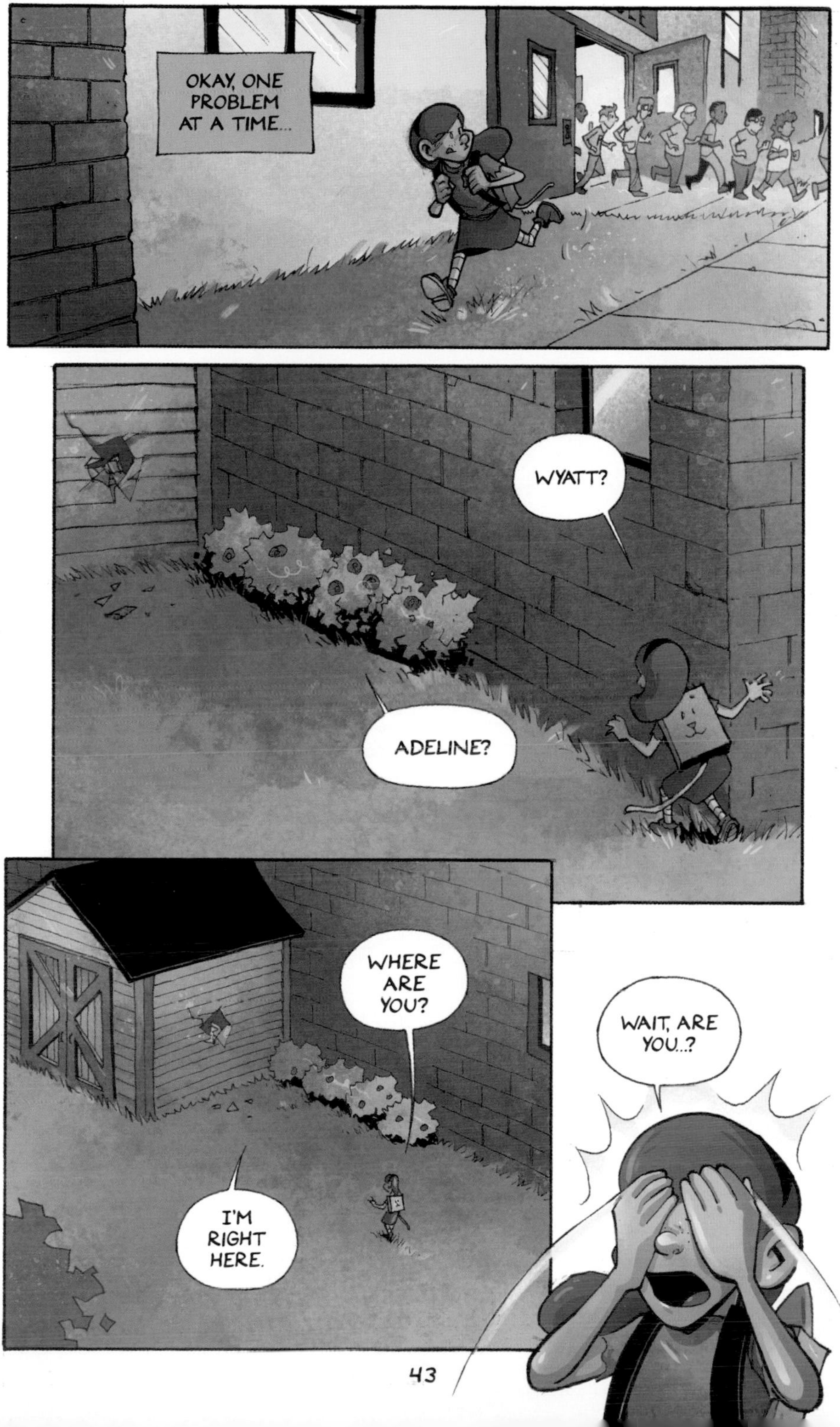
OKAY, ONE PROBLEM AT A TIME...
WYATT?
ADELINE?
WHERE ARE YOU?
I'M RIGHT HERE.
WAIT, ARE YOU...?

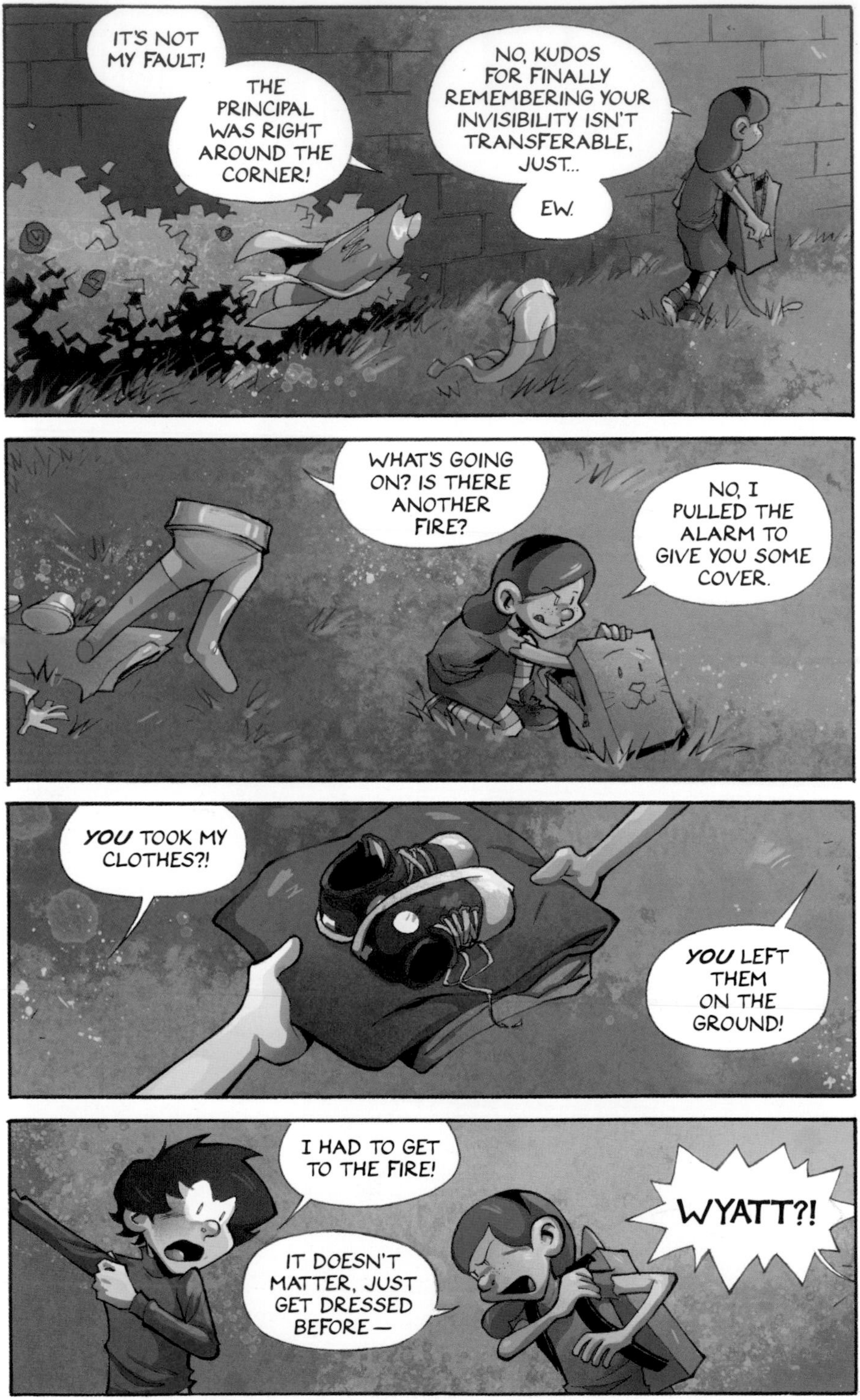

IT'S NOT MY FAULT!
THE PRINCIPAL WAS RIGHT AROUND THE CORNER!
NO, KUDOS FOR FINALLY REMEMBERING YOUR INVISIBILITY ISN'T TRANSFERABLE, JUST...
EW.
WHAT'S GOING ON? IS THERE ANOTHER FIRE?
NO, I PULLED THE ALARM TO GIVE YOU SOME COVER.
YOU TOOK MY CLOTHES?!
YOU LEFT THEM ON THE GROUND!
I HAD TO GET TO THE FIRE!
IT DOESN'T MATTER, JUST GET DRESSED BEFORE—
WYATT?!

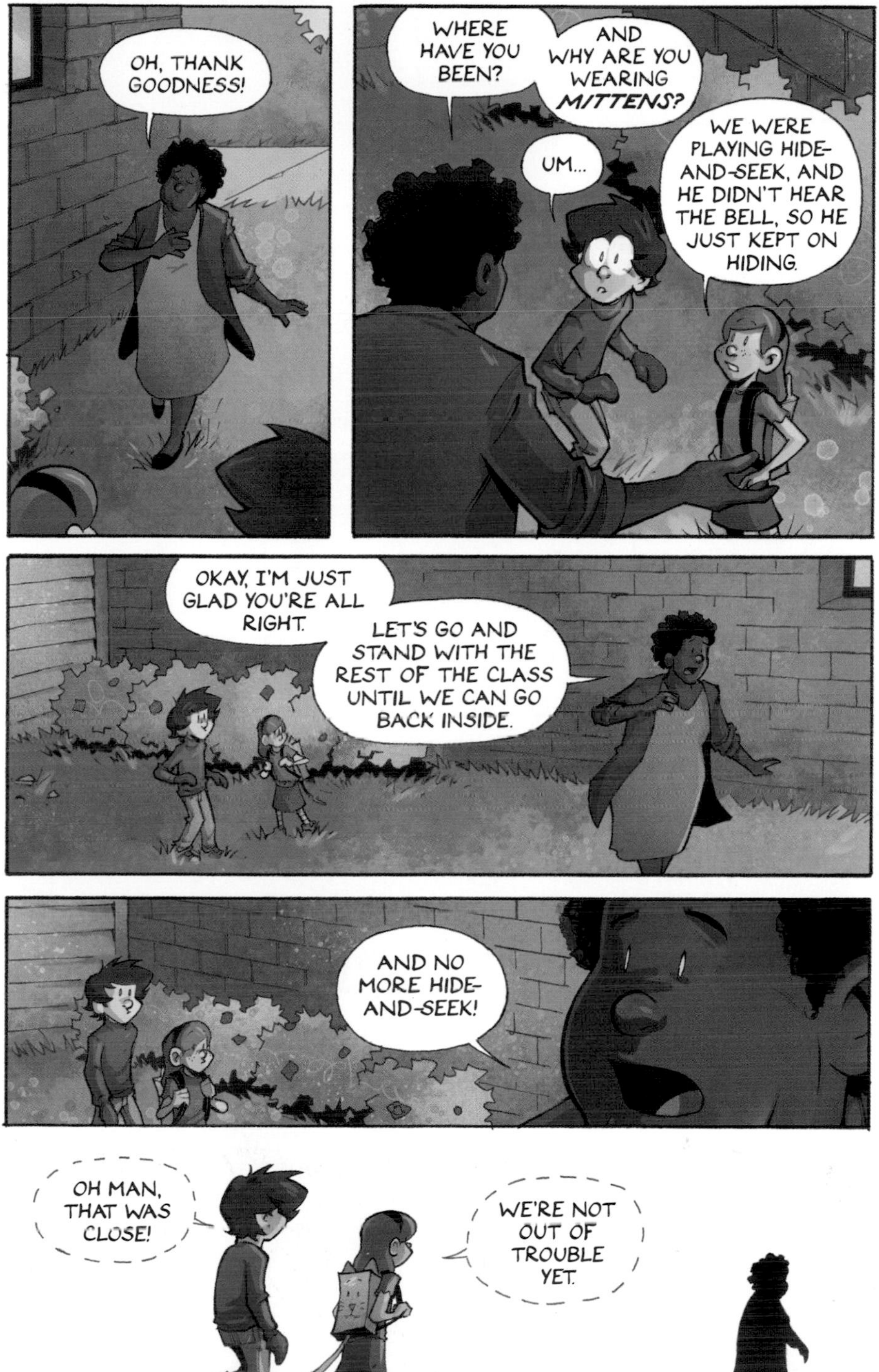
OH, THANK GOODNESS!
WHERE HAVE YOU BEEN?
AND WHY ARE YOU WEARING *MITTENS?*
UM...
WE WERE PLAYING HIDE-AND-SEEK, AND HE DIDN'T HEAR THE BELL, SO HE JUST KEPT ON HIDING.
OKAY, I'M JUST GLAD YOU'RE ALL RIGHT.
LET'S GO AND STAND WITH THE REST OF THE CLASS UNTIL WE CAN GO BACK INSIDE.
AND NO MORE HIDE-AND-SEEK!
OH MAN, THAT WAS CLOSE!
WE'RE NOT OUT OF TROUBLE YET.

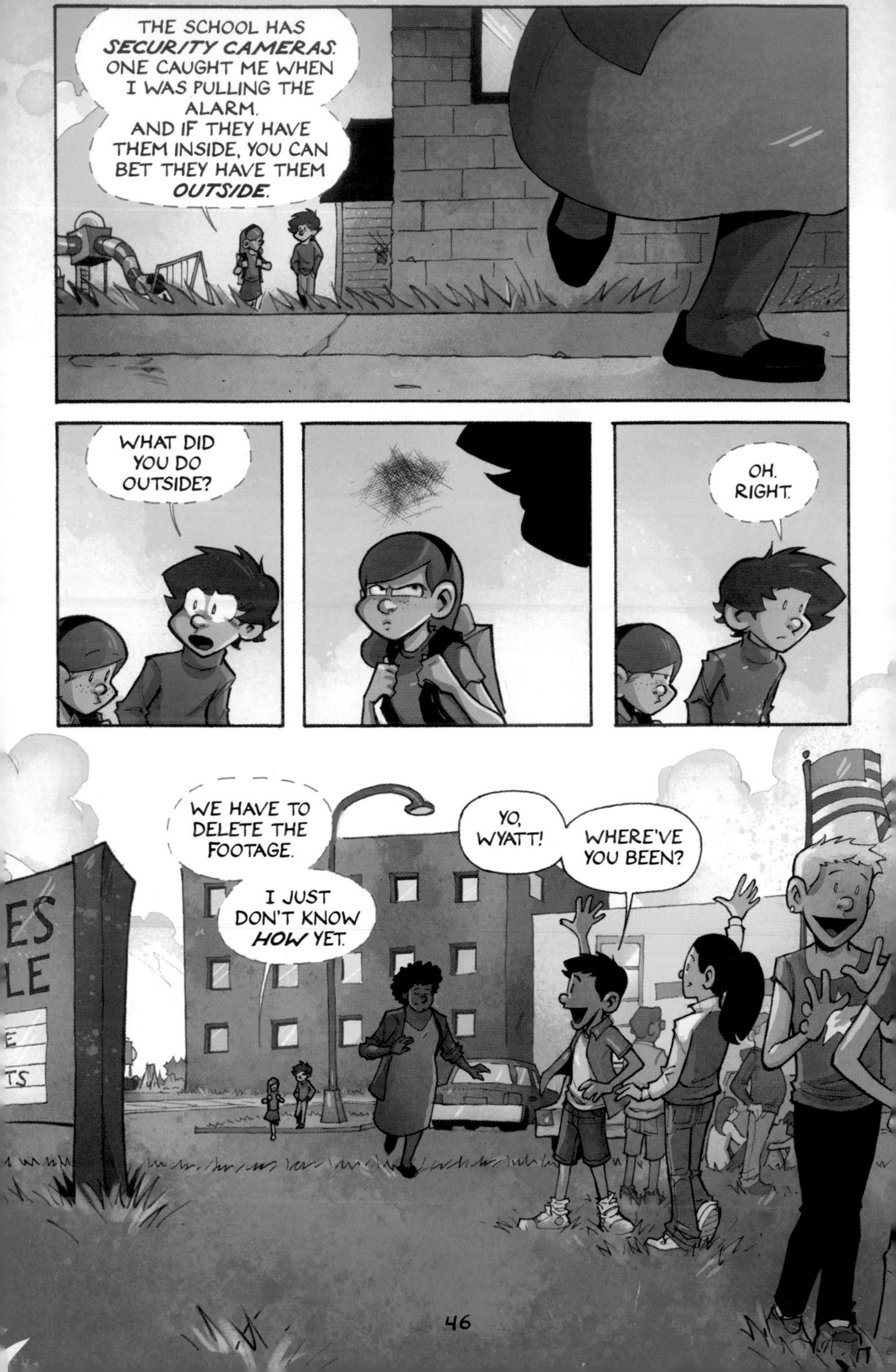
THE SCHOOL HAS SECURITY CAMERAS. ONE CAUGHT ME WHEN I WAS PULLING THE ALARM.
AND IF THEY HAVE THEM INSIDE, YOU CAN BET THEY HAVE THEM OUTSIDE.
WHAT DID YOU DO OUTSIDE?
OH. RIGHT.
WE HAVE TO DELETE THE FOOTAGE.
I JUST DON'T KNOW HOW YET.
YO, WYATT!
WHERE'VE YOU BEEN?

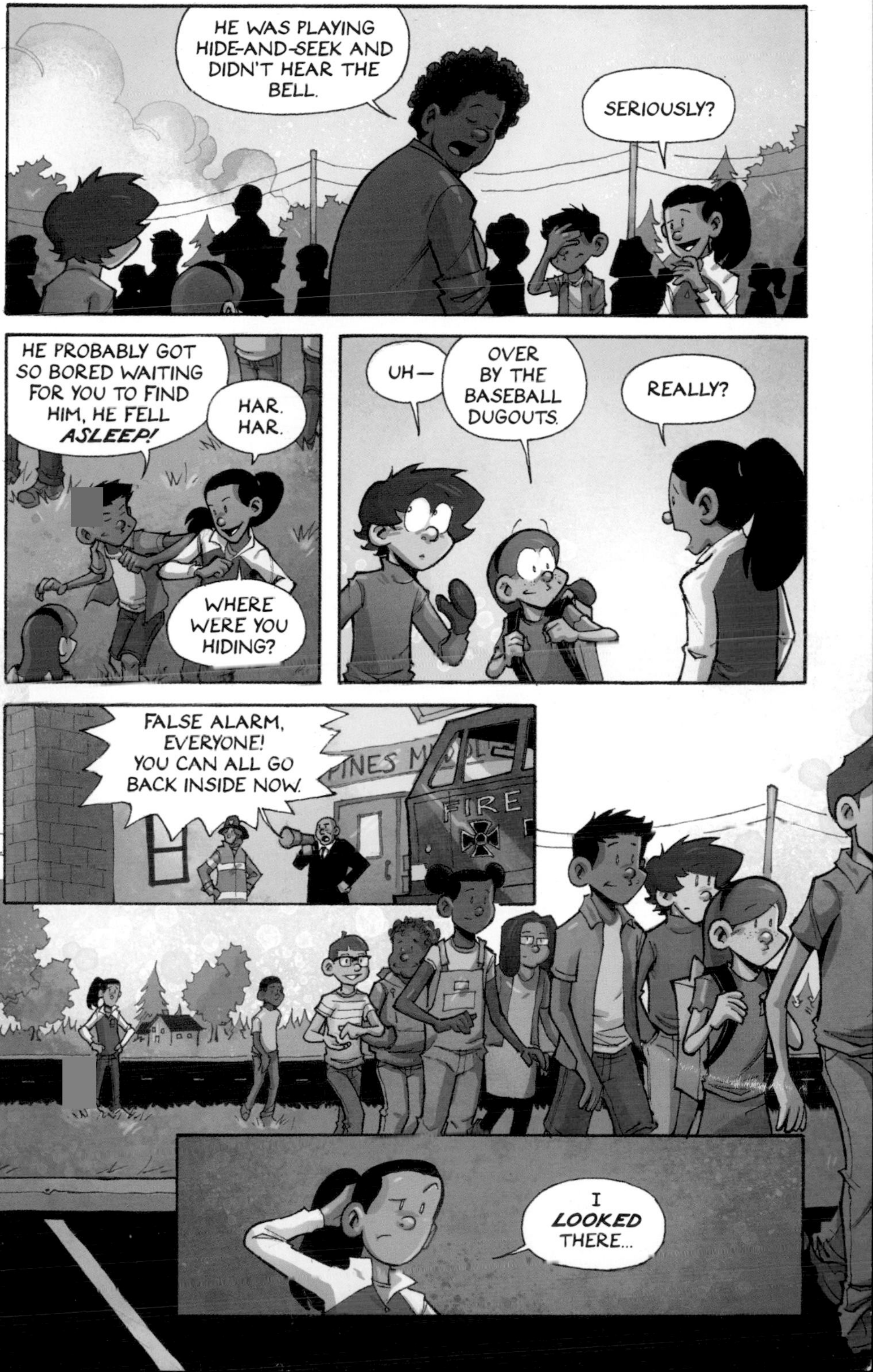
HE WAS PLAYING HIDE-AND-SEEK AND DIDN'T HEAR THE BELL.
SERIOUSLY?
HE PROBABLY GOT SO BORED WAITING FOR YOU TO FIND HIM, HE FELL *ASLEEP!*
HAR. HAR.
WHERE WERE YOU HIDING?
UH—
OVER BY THE BASEBALL DUGOUTS.
REALLY?
FALSE ALARM, EVERYONE! YOU CAN ALL GO BACK INSIDE NOW.
PINES M
FIRE
I *LOOKED* THERE...

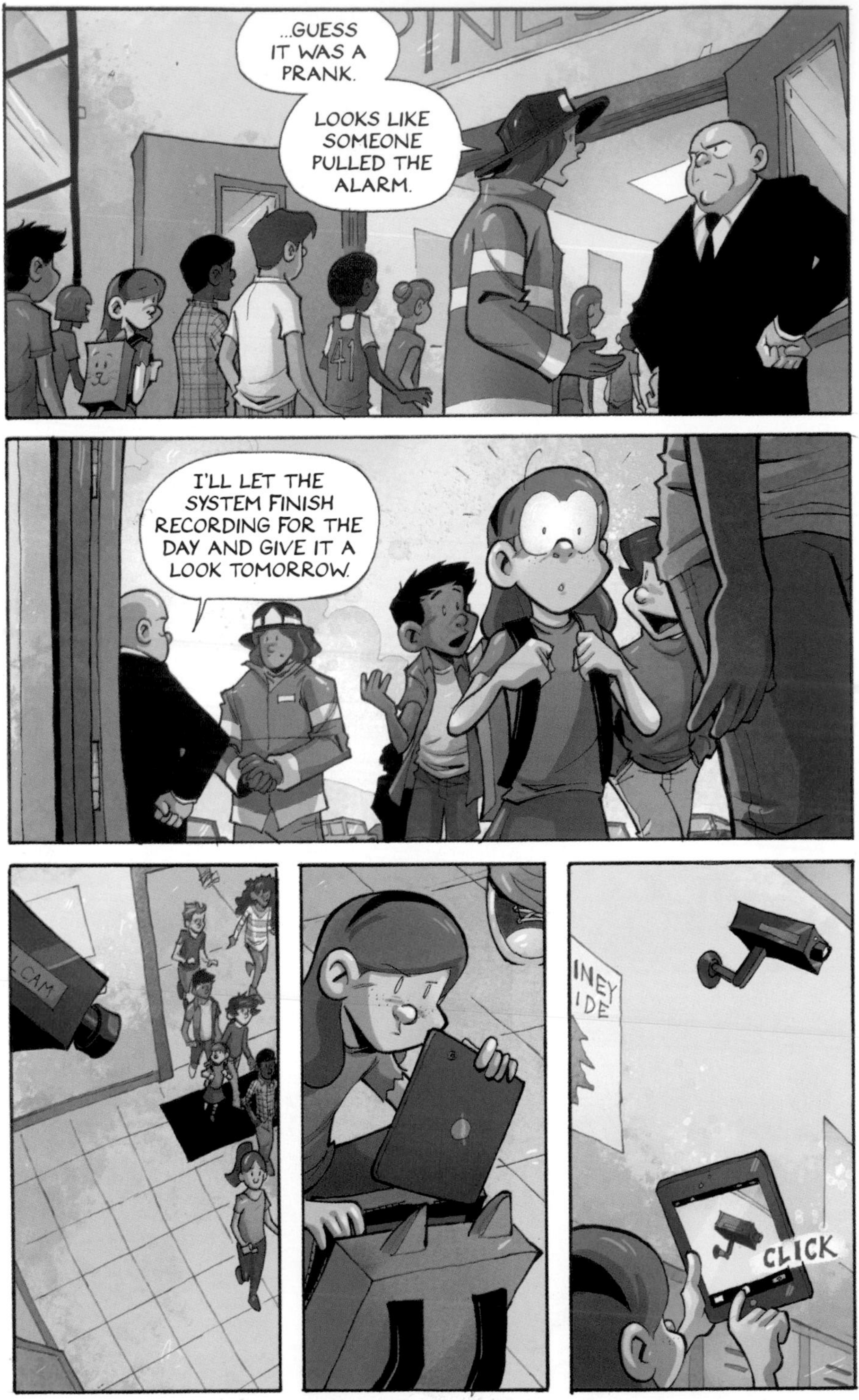
...GUESS IT WAS A PRANK.
LOOKS LIKE SOMEONE PULLED THE ALARM.
I'LL LET THE SYSTEM FINISH RECORDING FOR THE DAY AND GIVE IT A LOOK TOMORROW.
CLICK

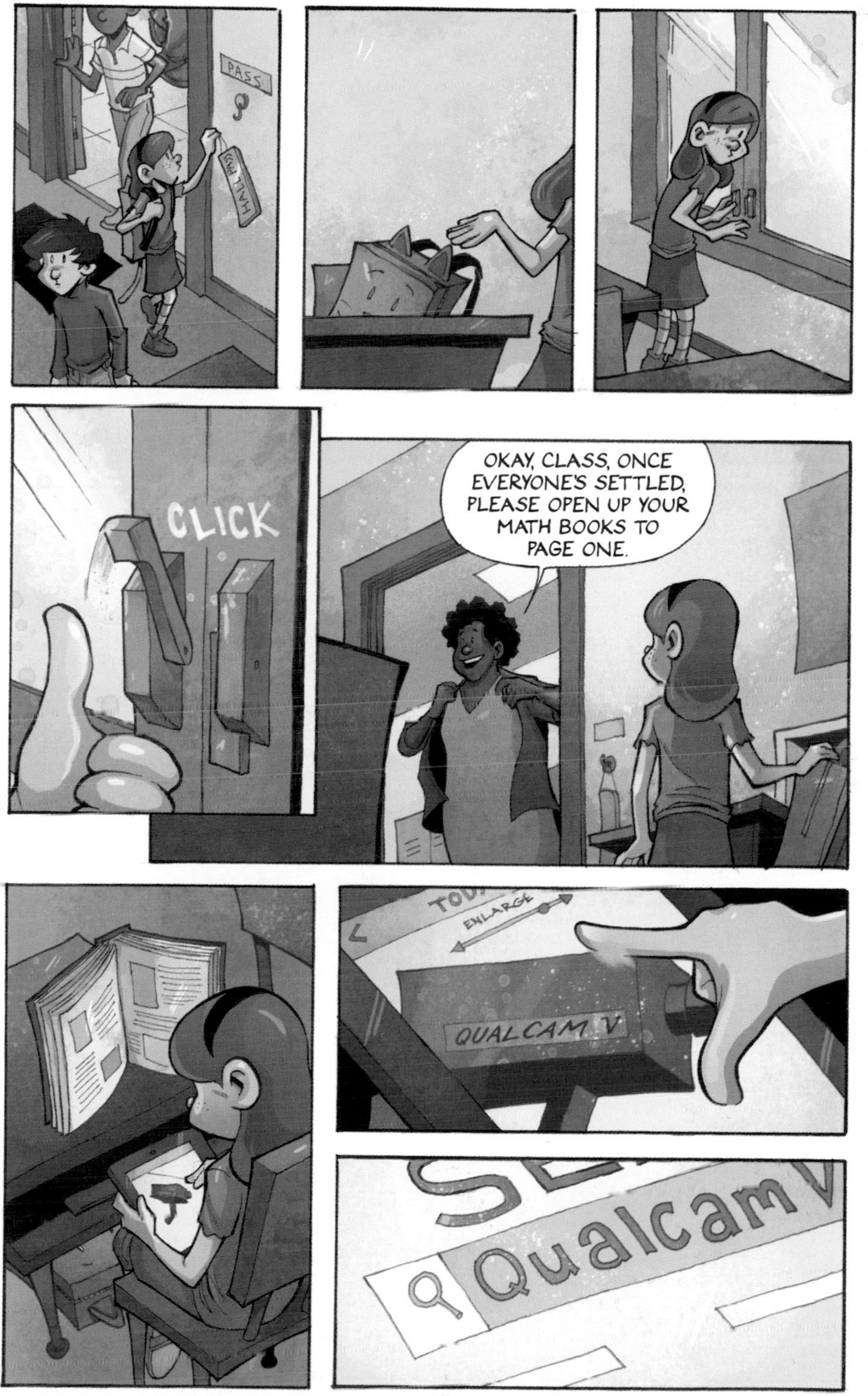
PASS
HALL PASS
CLICK
OKAY, CLASS, ONCE EVERYONE'S SETTLED, PLEASE OPEN UP YOUR MATH BOOKS TO PAGE ONE.
ENLARGE
QUALCAM V
Qualcam V

CHAPTER FOUR

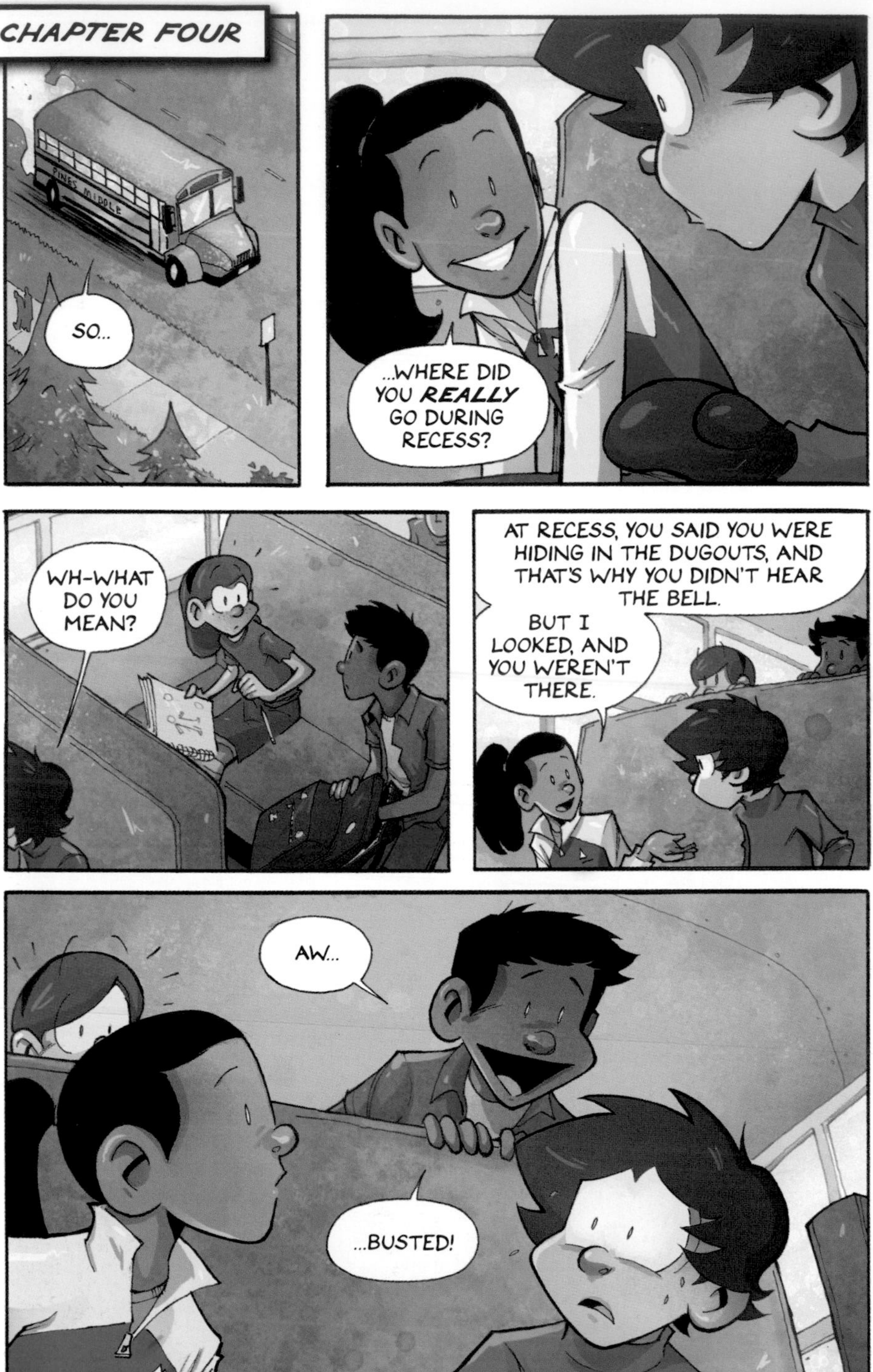
PINES MIDDLE
SO...
...WHERE DID YOU *REALLY* GO DURING RECESS?
WH-WHAT DO YOU MEAN?
AT RECESS, YOU SAID YOU WERE HIDING IN THE DUGOUTS, AND THAT'S WHY YOU DIDN'T HEAR THE BELL.
BUT I LOOKED, AND YOU WEREN'T THERE.
AW...
...BUSTED!

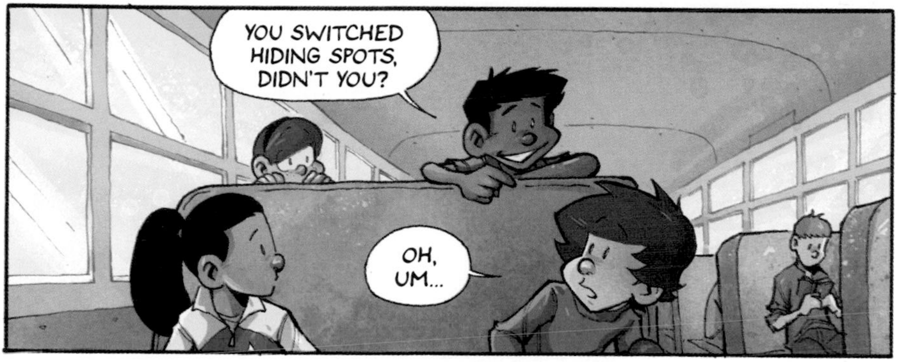
YOU SWITCHED HIDING SPOTS, DIDN'T YOU?
OH, UM...

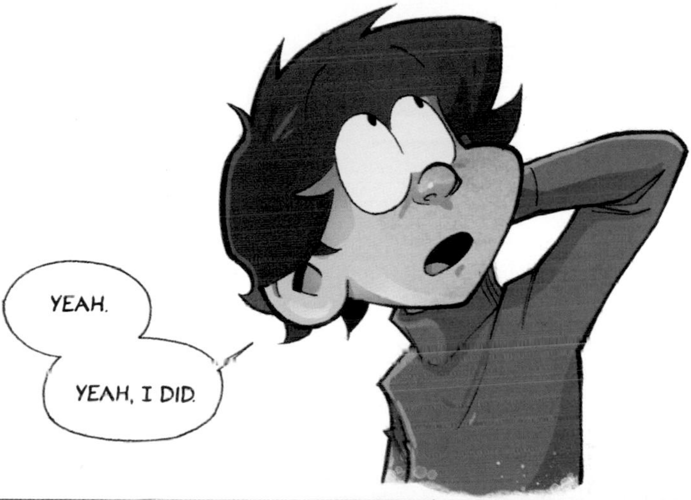
YEAH.
YEAH, I DID.

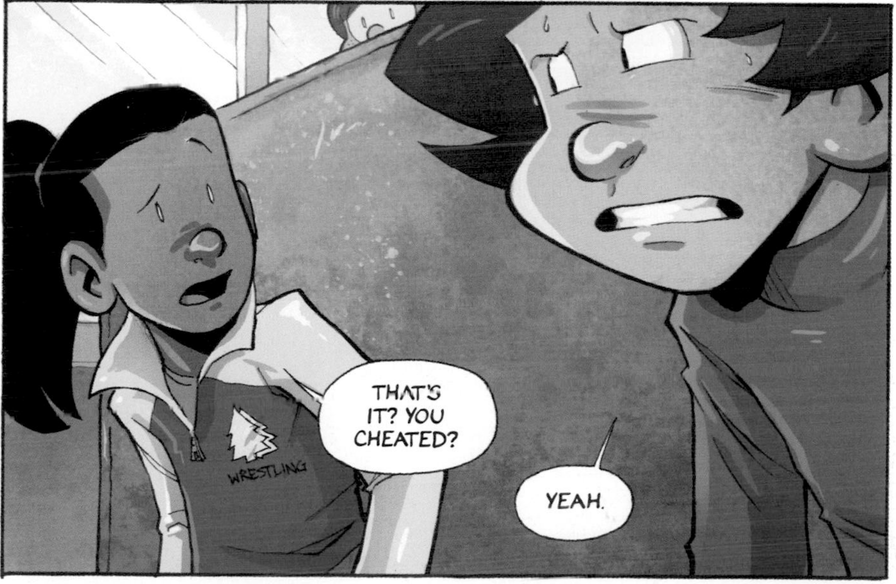
WRESTLING
THAT'S IT? YOU CHEATED?
YEAH.

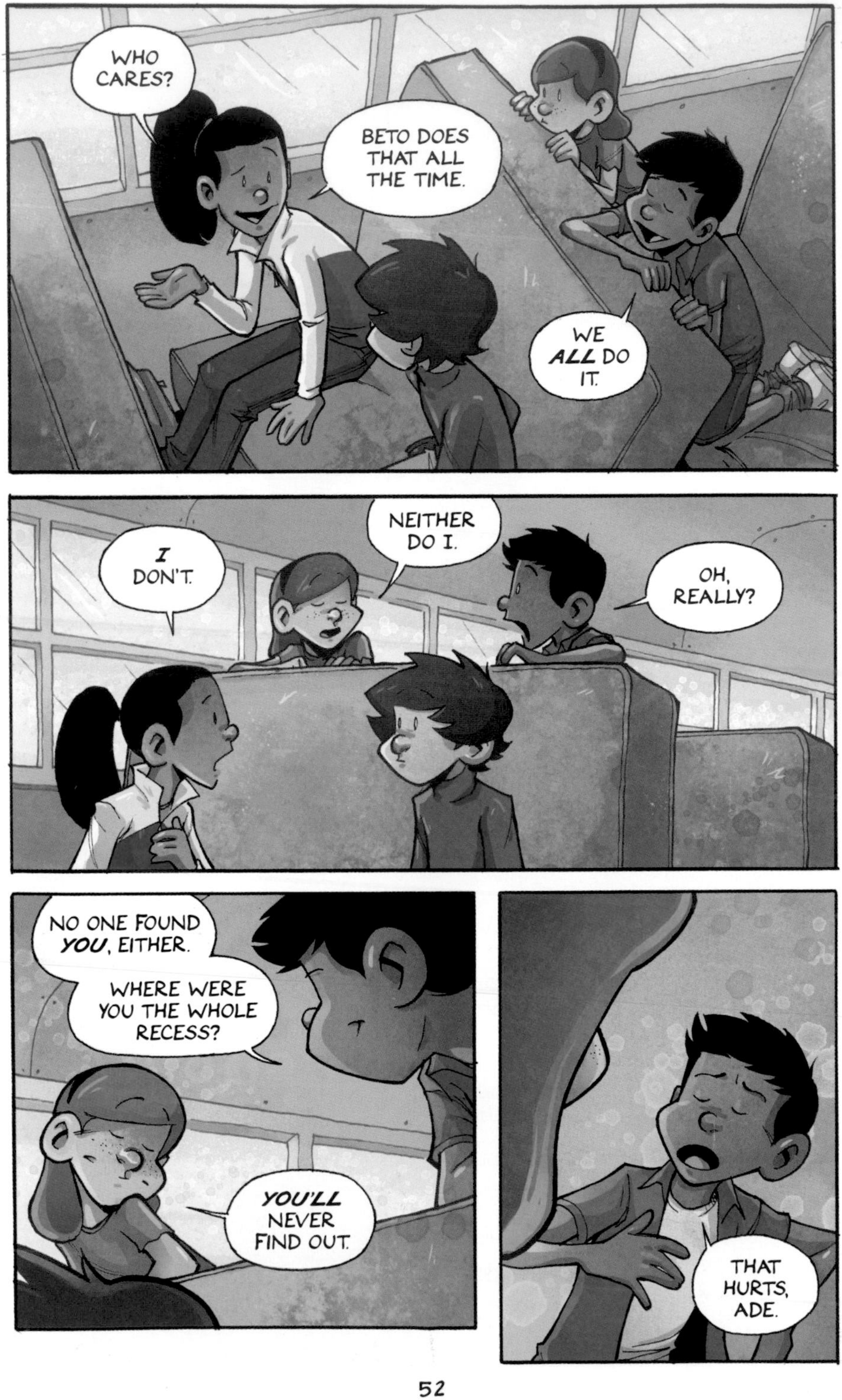
WHO CARES?
BETO DOES THAT ALL THE TIME.
WE ALL DO IT.
I DON'T.
NEITHER DO I.
OH, REALLY?
NO ONE FOUND YOU, EITHER.
WHERE WERE YOU THE WHOLE RECESS?
YOU'LL NEVER FIND OUT.
THAT HURTS, ADE.

IS THAT REALLY IT?

YEAH.

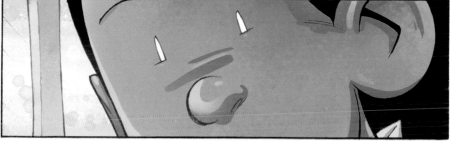

OKAY.

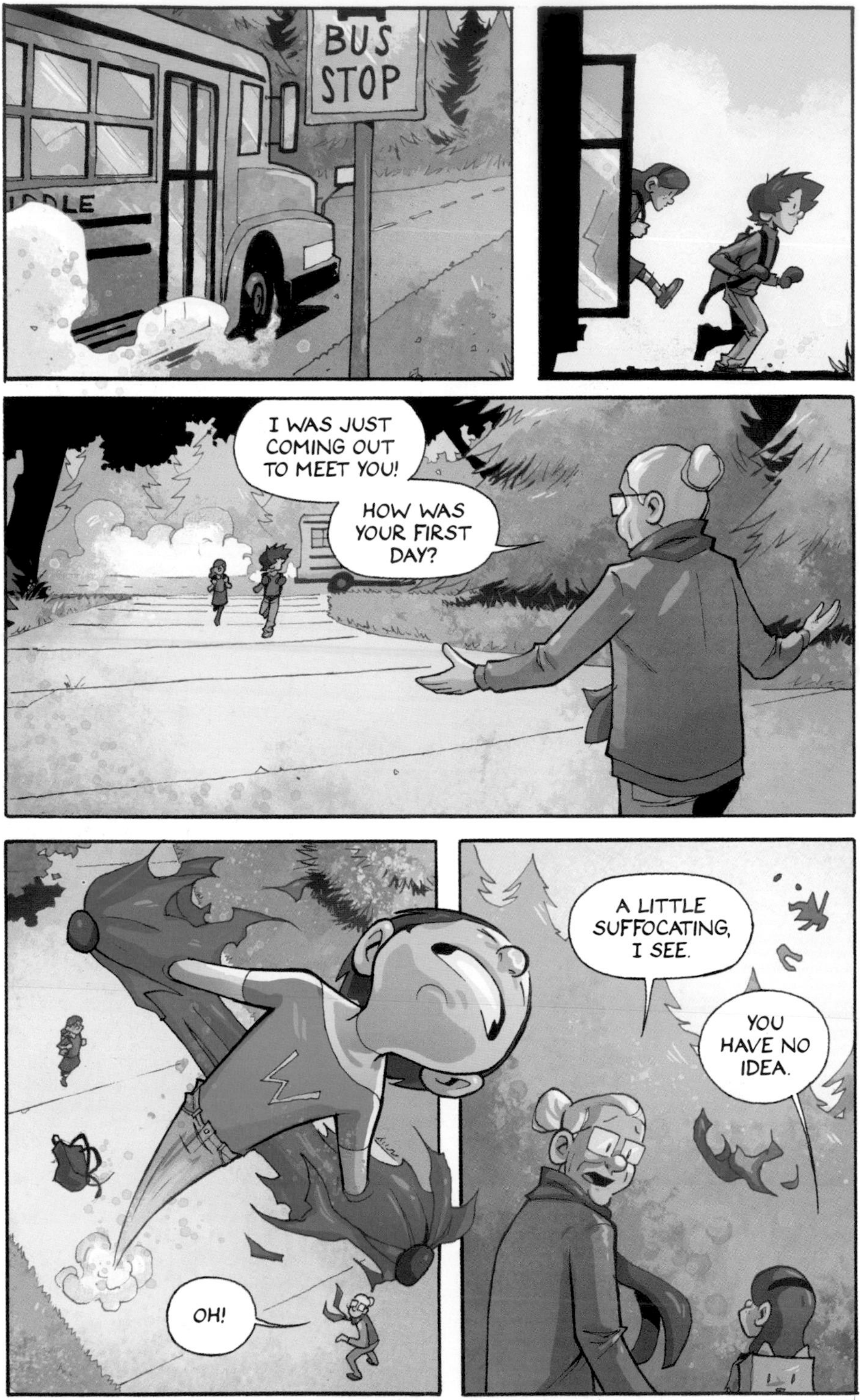
BUS STOP
IDDLE
I WAS JUST COMING OUT TO MEET YOU!
HOW WAS YOUR FIRST DAY?
A LITTLE SUFFOCATING, I SEE.
YOU HAVE NO IDEA.
OH!

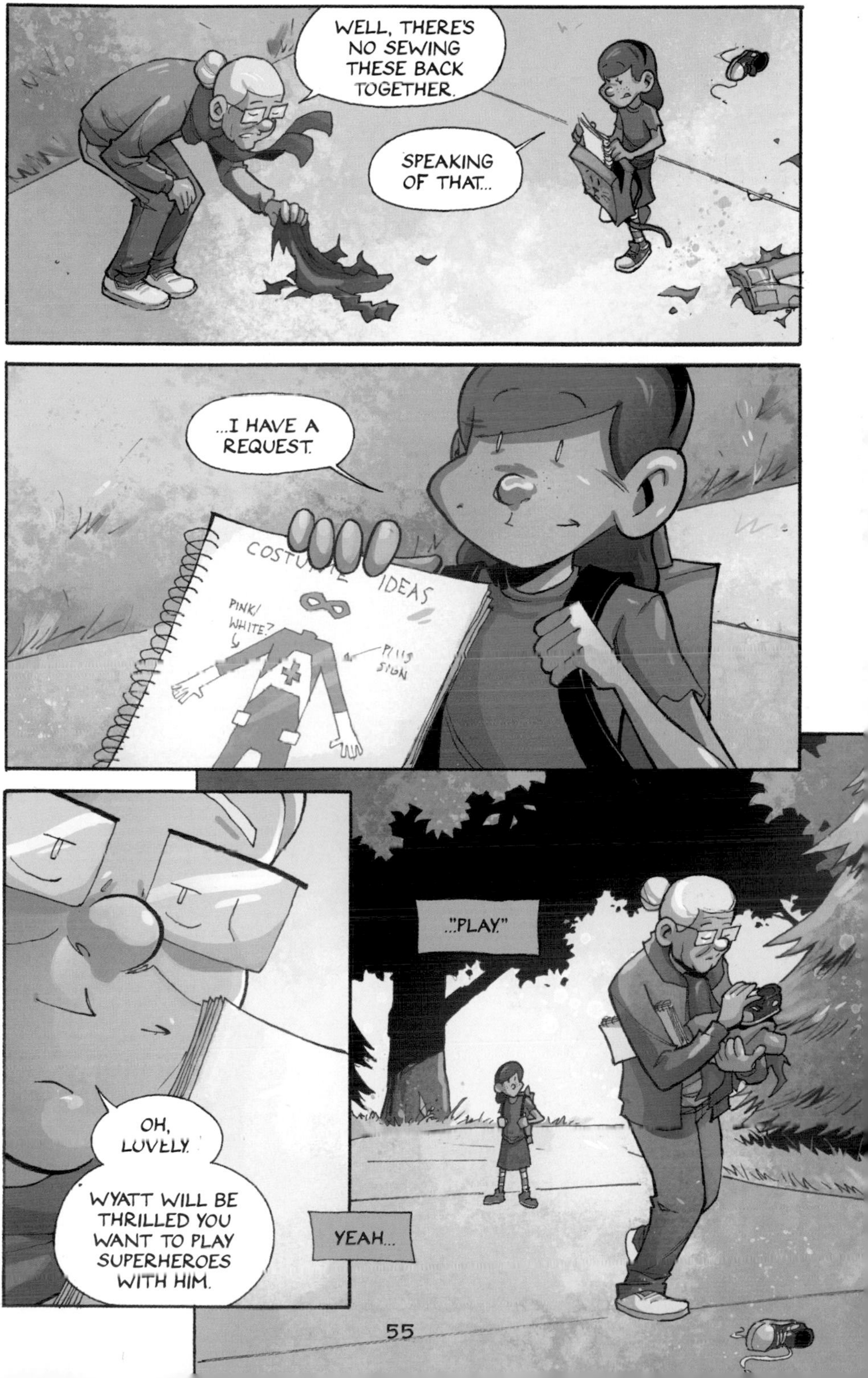
WELL, THERE'S NO SEWING THESE BACK TOGETHER.
SPEAKING OF THAT...
...I HAVE A REQUEST.
COSTUME IDEAS
PINK/ WHITE?
PLUS SIGN
OH, LOVELY.
WYATT WILL BE THRILLED YOU WANT TO PLAY SUPERHEROES WITH HIM.
..."PLAY."
YEAH...

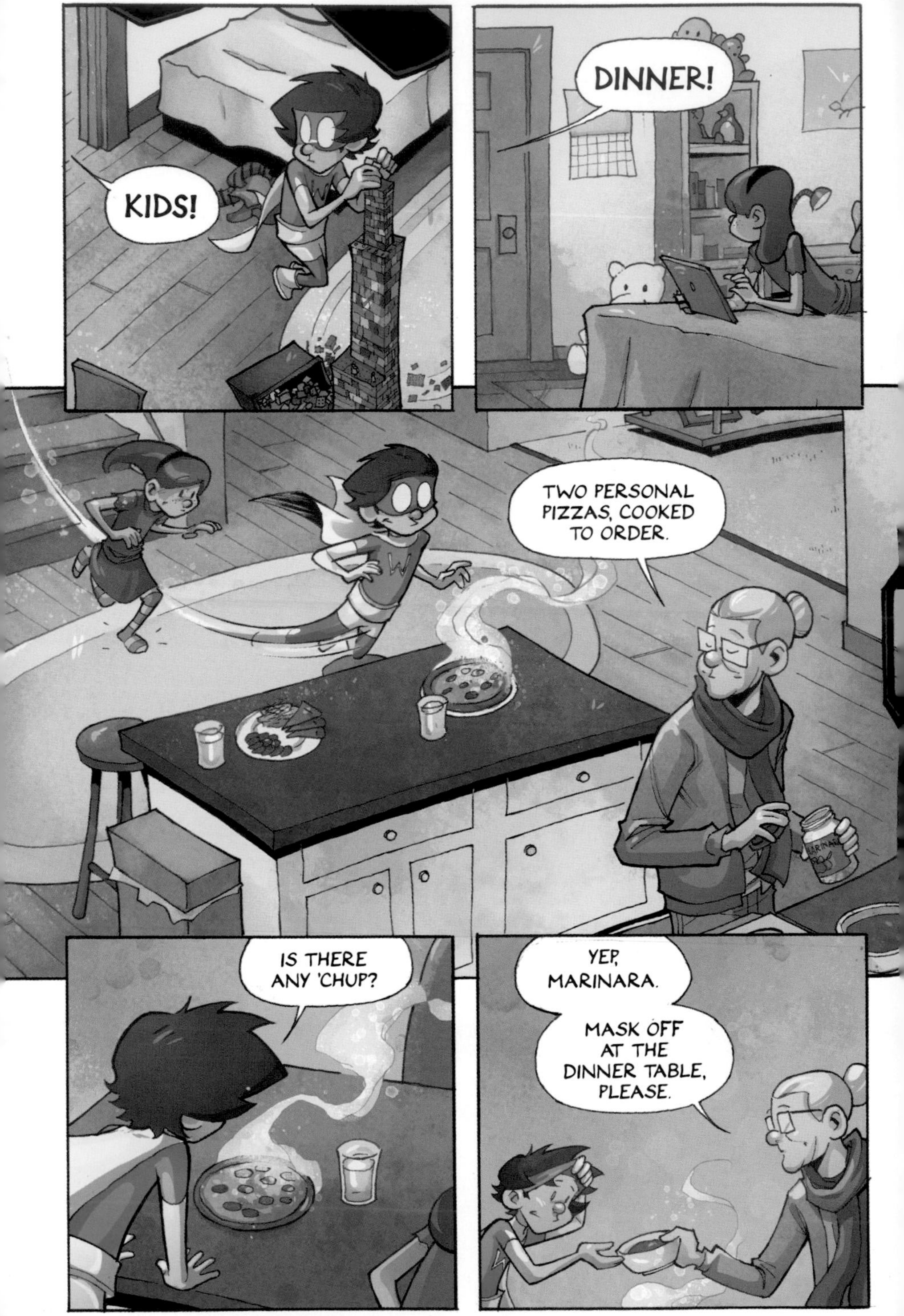
KIDS!
DINNER!
TWO PERSONAL PIZZAS, COOKED TO ORDER.
IS THERE ANY 'CHUP?
YEP, MARINARA.
MASK OFF AT THE DINNER TABLE, PLEASE.

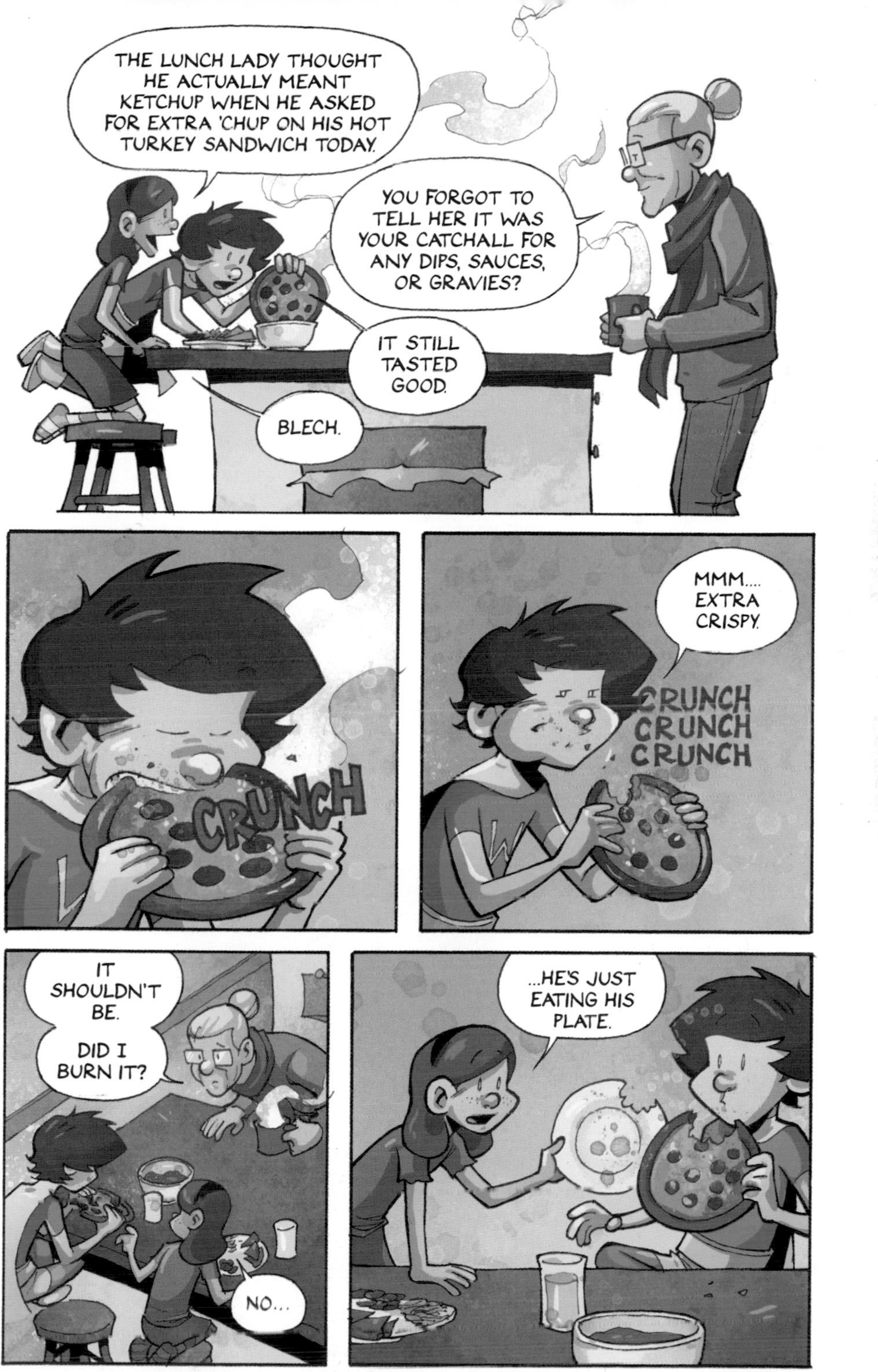
THE LUNCH LADY THOUGHT HE ACTUALLY MEANT KETCHUP WHEN HE ASKED FOR EXTRA 'CHUP ON HIS HOT TURKEY SANDWICH TODAY.
YOU FORGOT TO TELL HER IT WAS YOUR CATCHALL FOR ANY DIPS, SAUCES, OR GRAVIES?
IT STILL TASTED GOOD.
BLECH.
CRUNCH
MMM.... EXTRA CRISPY.
CRUNCH CRUNCH CRUNCH
IT SHOULDN'T BE.
DID I BURN IT?
NO...
...HE'S JUST EATING HIS PLATE.

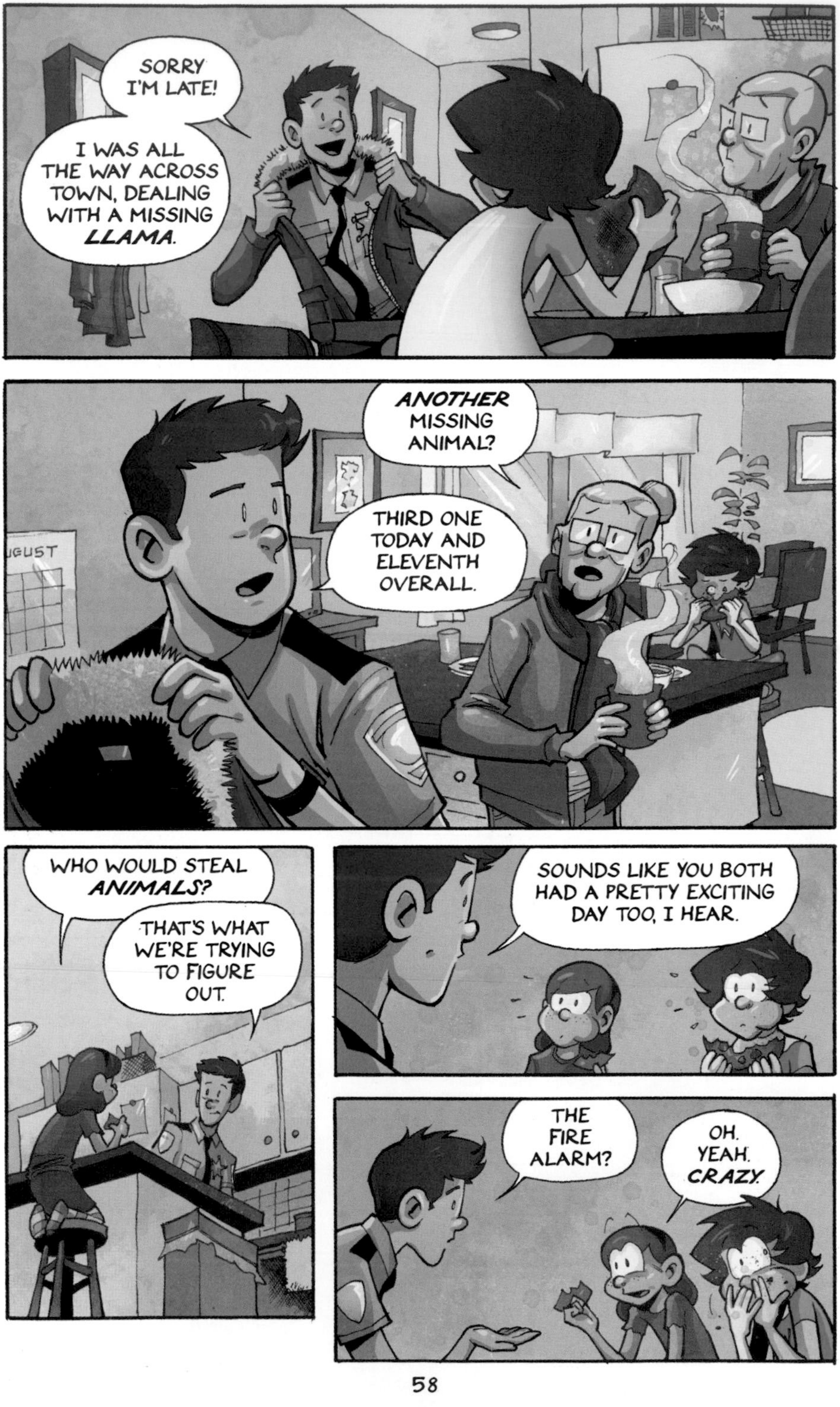
SORRY I'M LATE!
I WAS ALL THE WAY ACROSS TOWN, DEALING WITH A MISSING *LLAMA*.
UGUST
ANOTHER MISSING ANIMAL?
THIRD ONE TODAY AND ELEVENTH OVERALL.
WHO WOULD STEAL *ANIMALS?*
THAT'S WHAT WE'RE TRYING TO FIGURE OUT.
SOUNDS LIKE YOU BOTH HAD A PRETTY EXCITING DAY TOO, I HEAR.
THE FIRE ALARM?
OH. YEAH. *CRAZY.*

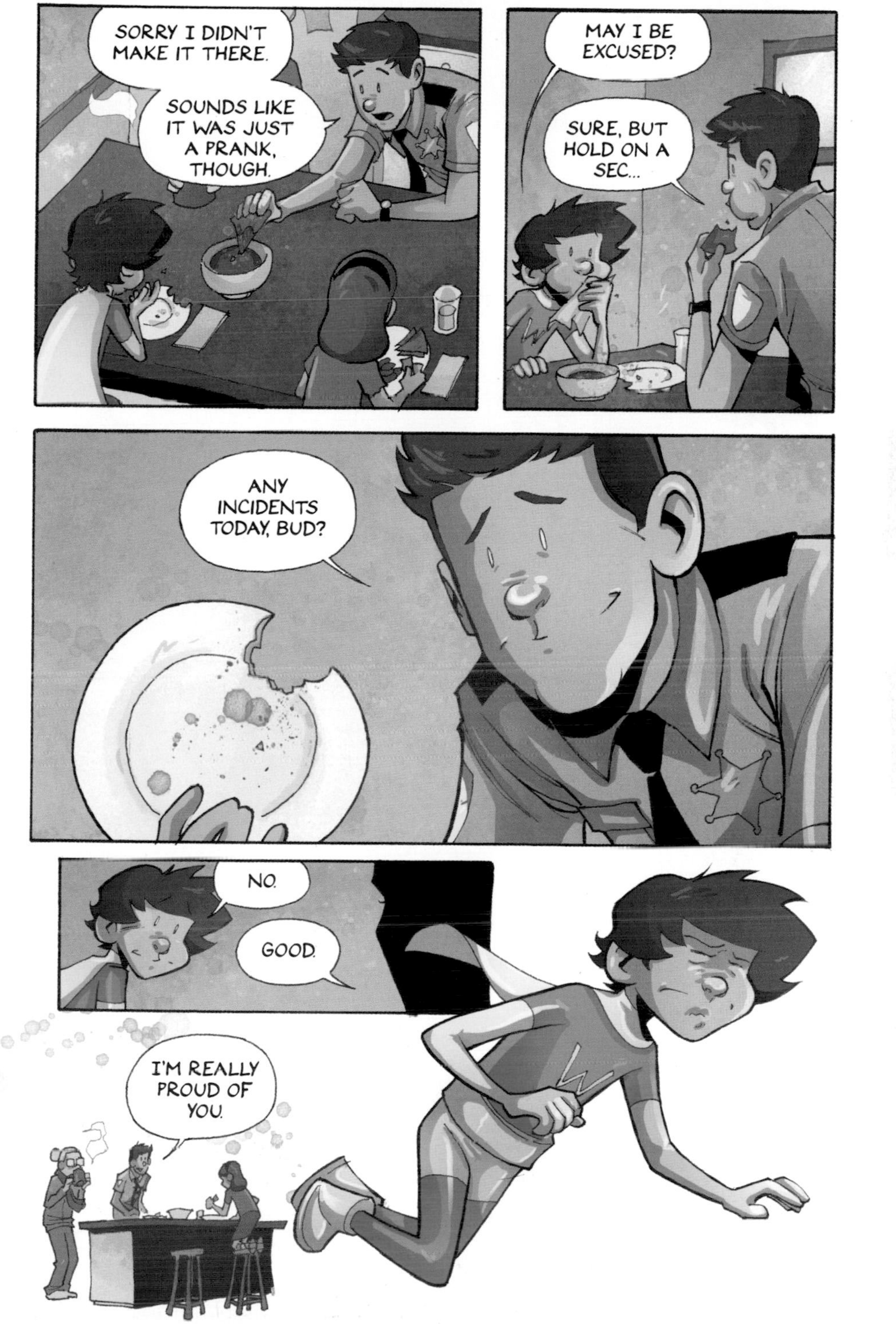
SORRY I DIDN'T MAKE IT THERE.
SOUNDS LIKE IT WAS JUST A PRANK, THOUGH.
MAY I BE EXCUSED?
SURE, BUT HOLD ON A SEC...
ANY INCIDENTS TODAY, BUD?
NO.
GOOD.
I'M REALLY PROUD OF YOU.

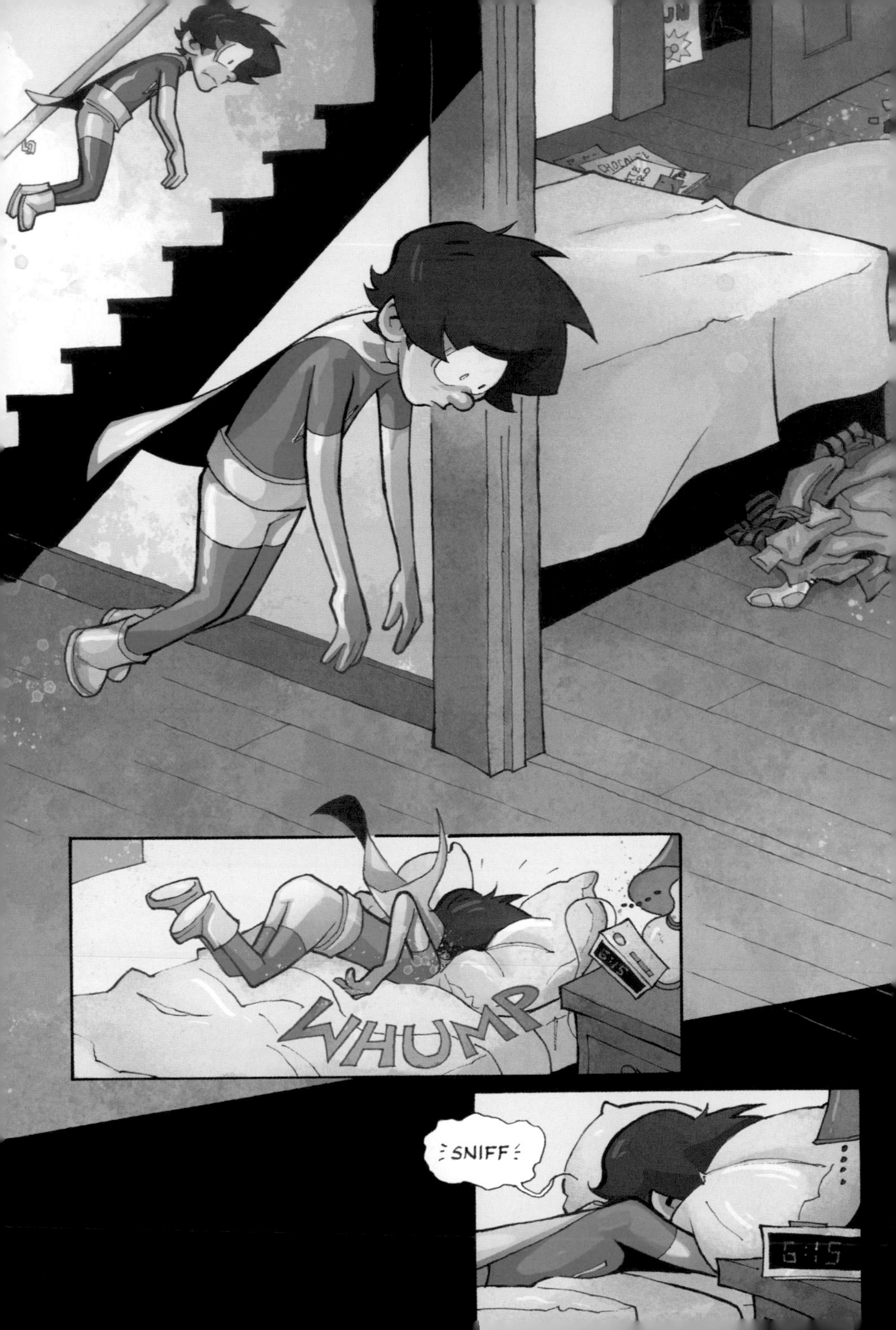

WHUMP
SNIFF

CHAPTER FIVE

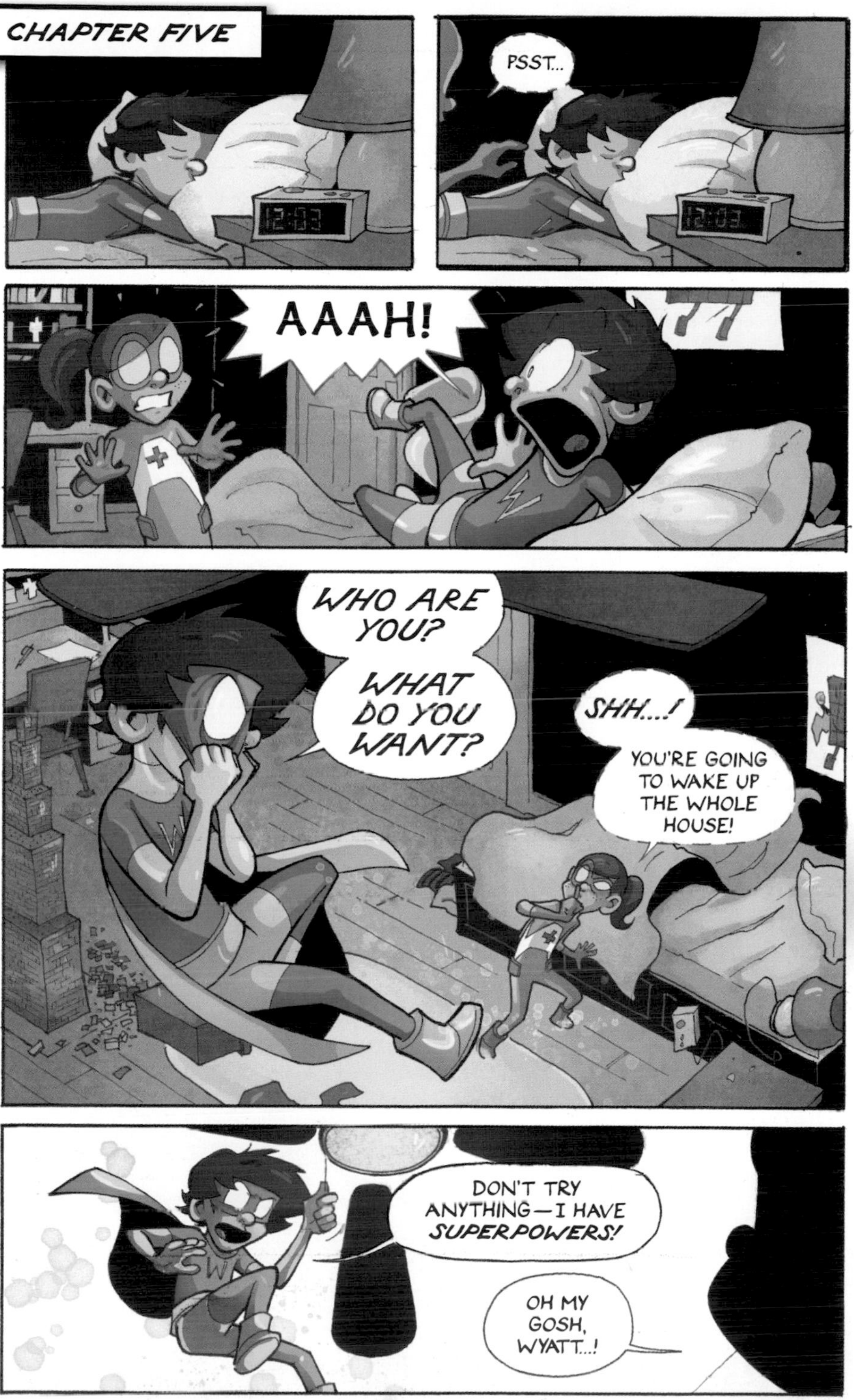

PSST...
AAAH!
WHO ARE YOU?
WHAT DO YOU WANT?
SHH...!
YOU'RE GOING TO WAKE UP THE WHOLE HOUSE!
DON'T TRY ANYTHING—I HAVE *SUPERPOWERS!*
OH MY GOSH, WYATT...!

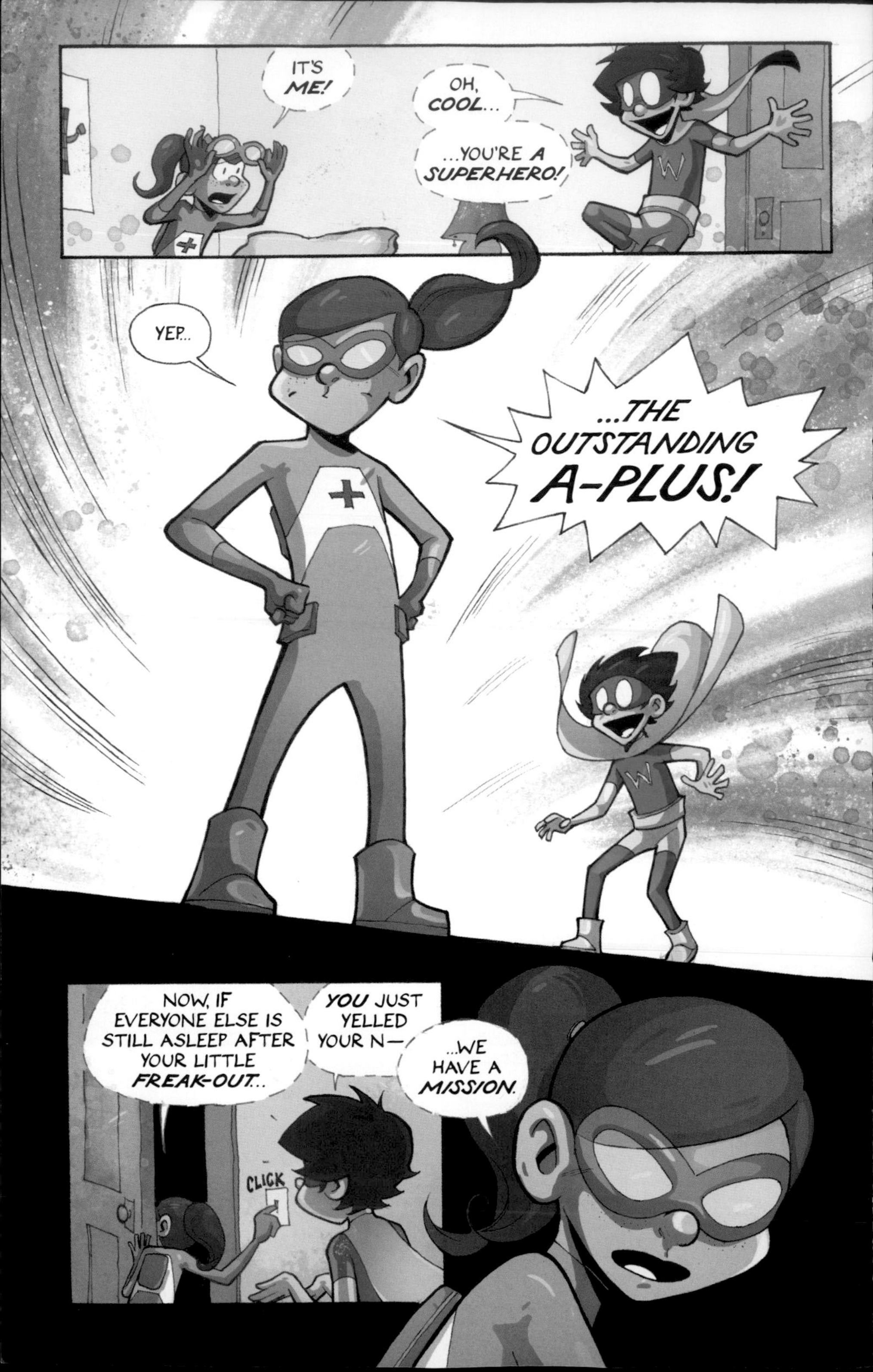
IT'S ME!
OH, COOL...
...YOU'RE A SUPERHERO!
YEP...
...THE OUTSTANDING A-PLUS!
NOW, IF EVERYONE ELSE IS STILL ASLEEP AFTER YOUR LITTLE FREAK-OUT...
YOU JUST YELLED YOUR N—
...WE HAVE A MISSION.
CLICK

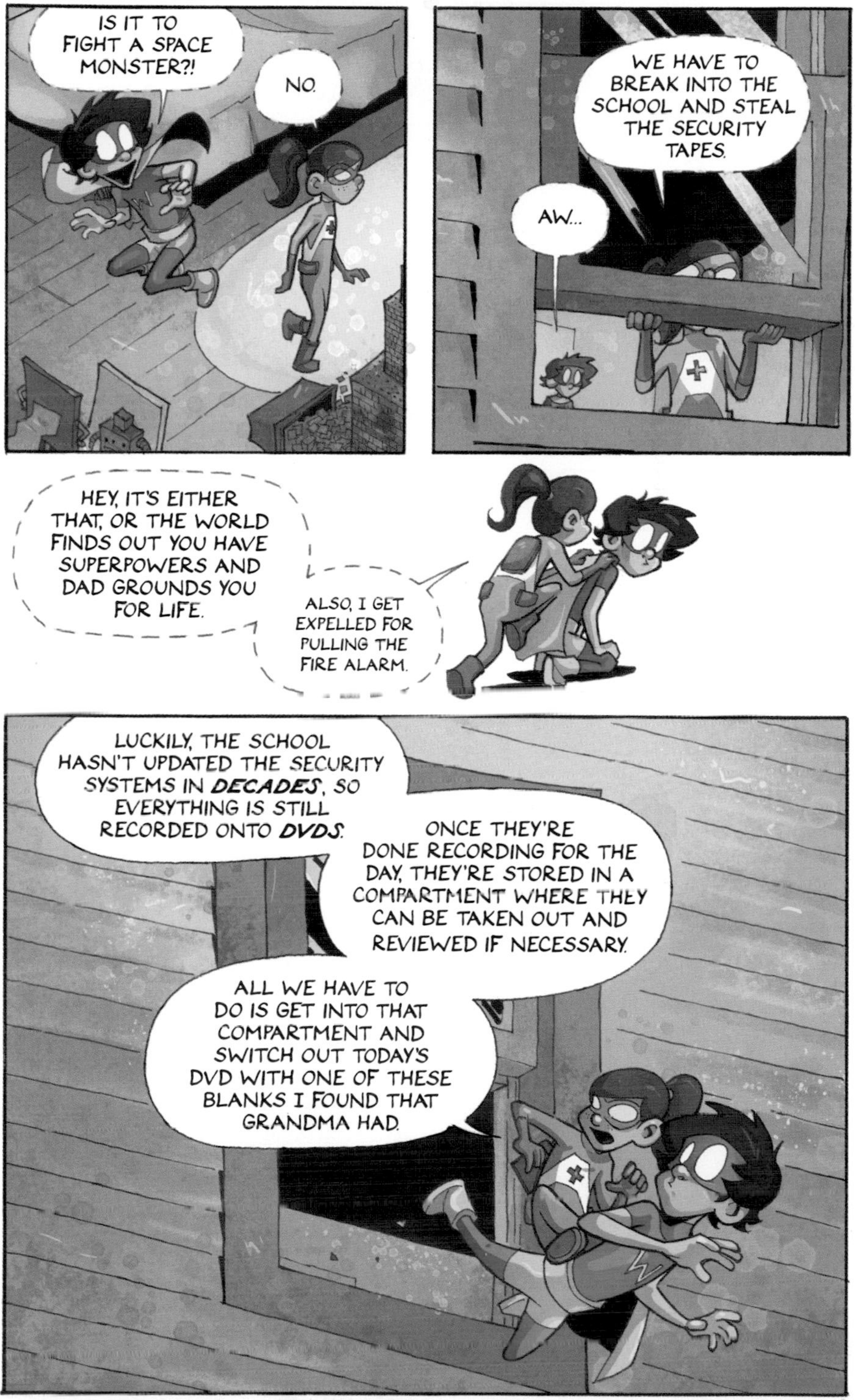
IS IT TO FIGHT A SPACE MONSTER?!
NO.
WE HAVE TO BREAK INTO THE SCHOOL AND STEAL THE SECURITY TAPES.
AW...
HEY, IT'S EITHER THAT, OR THE WORLD FINDS OUT YOU HAVE SUPERPOWERS AND DAD GROUNDS YOU FOR LIFE.
ALSO, I GET EXPELLED FOR PULLING THE FIRE ALARM.
LUCKILY, THE SCHOOL HASN'T UPDATED THE SECURITY SYSTEMS IN DECADES, SO EVERYTHING IS STILL RECORDED ONTO DVDS.
ONCE THEY'RE DONE RECORDING FOR THE DAY, THEY'RE STORED IN A COMPARTMENT WHERE THEY CAN BE TAKEN OUT AND REVIEWED IF NECESSARY.
ALL WE HAVE TO DO IS GET INTO THAT COMPARTMENT AND SWITCH OUT TODAY'S DVD WITH ONE OF THESE BLANKS I FOUND THAT GRANDMA HAD.

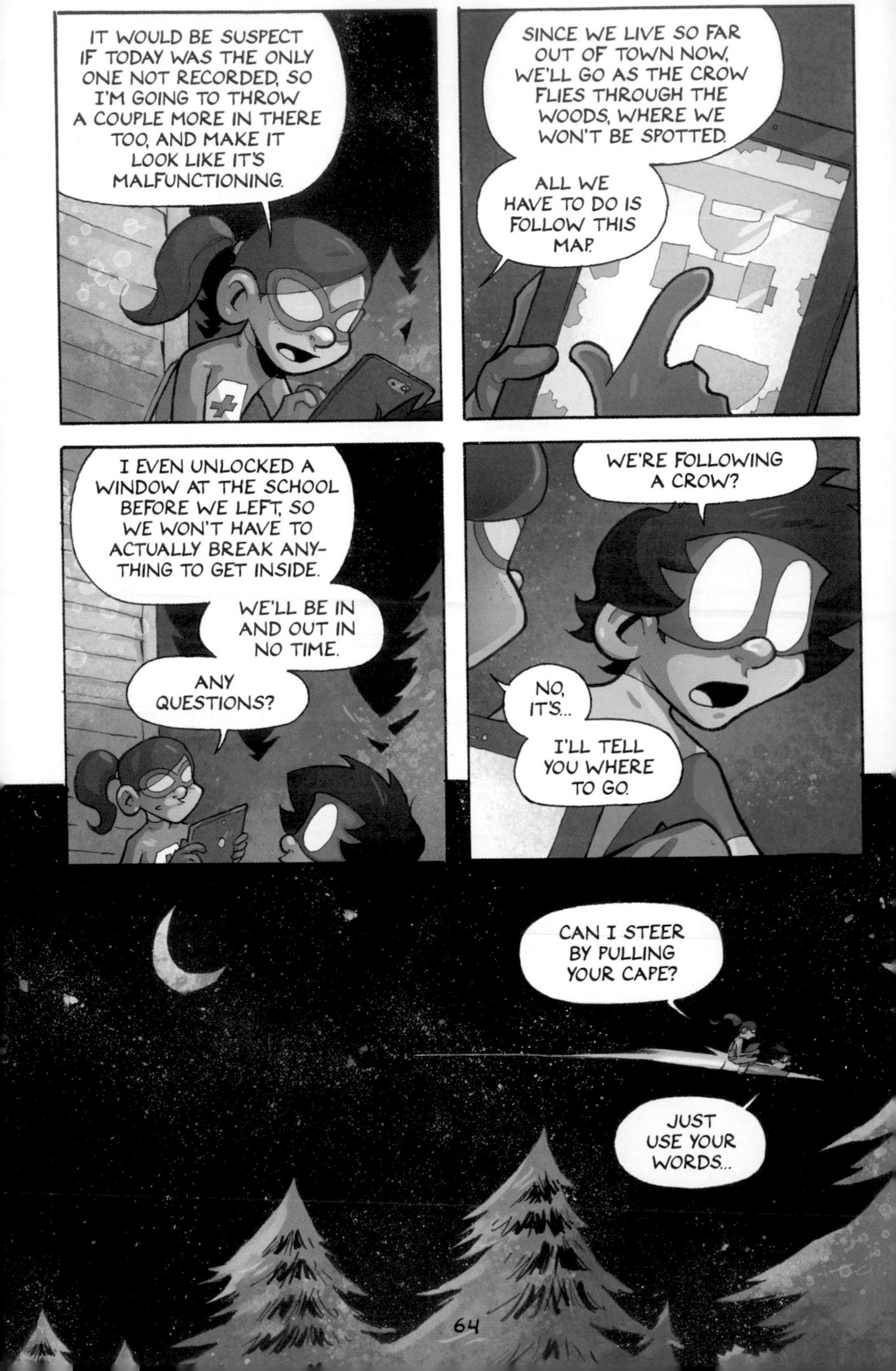
IT WOULD BE SUSPECT IF TODAY WAS THE ONLY ONE NOT RECORDED, SO I'M GOING TO THROW A COUPLE MORE IN THERE TOO, AND MAKE IT LOOK LIKE IT'S MALFUNCTIONING.
SINCE WE LIVE SO FAR OUT OF TOWN NOW, WE'LL GO AS THE CROW FLIES THROUGH THE WOODS, WHERE WE WON'T BE SPOTTED.
ALL WE HAVE TO DO IS FOLLOW THIS MAP.
I EVEN UNLOCKED A WINDOW AT THE SCHOOL BEFORE WE LEFT, SO WE WON'T HAVE TO ACTUALLY BREAK ANY-THING TO GET INSIDE.
WE'LL BE IN AND OUT IN NO TIME.
ANY QUESTIONS?
WE'RE FOLLOWING A CROW?
NO, IT'S...
I'LL TELL YOU WHERE TO GO.
CAN I STEER BY PULLING YOUR CAPE?
JUST USE YOUR WORDS...

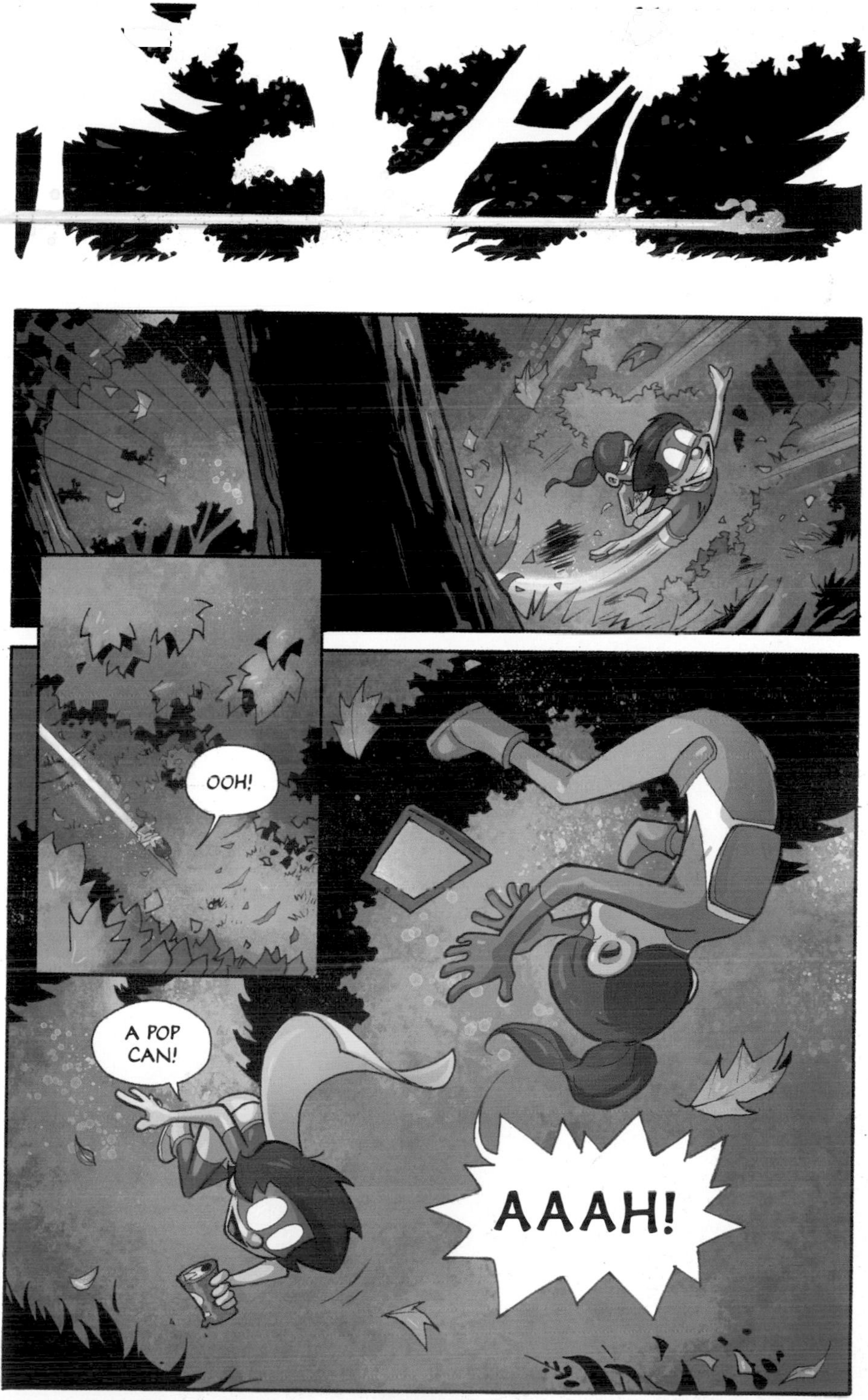
OOH!
A POP CAN!
AAAH!

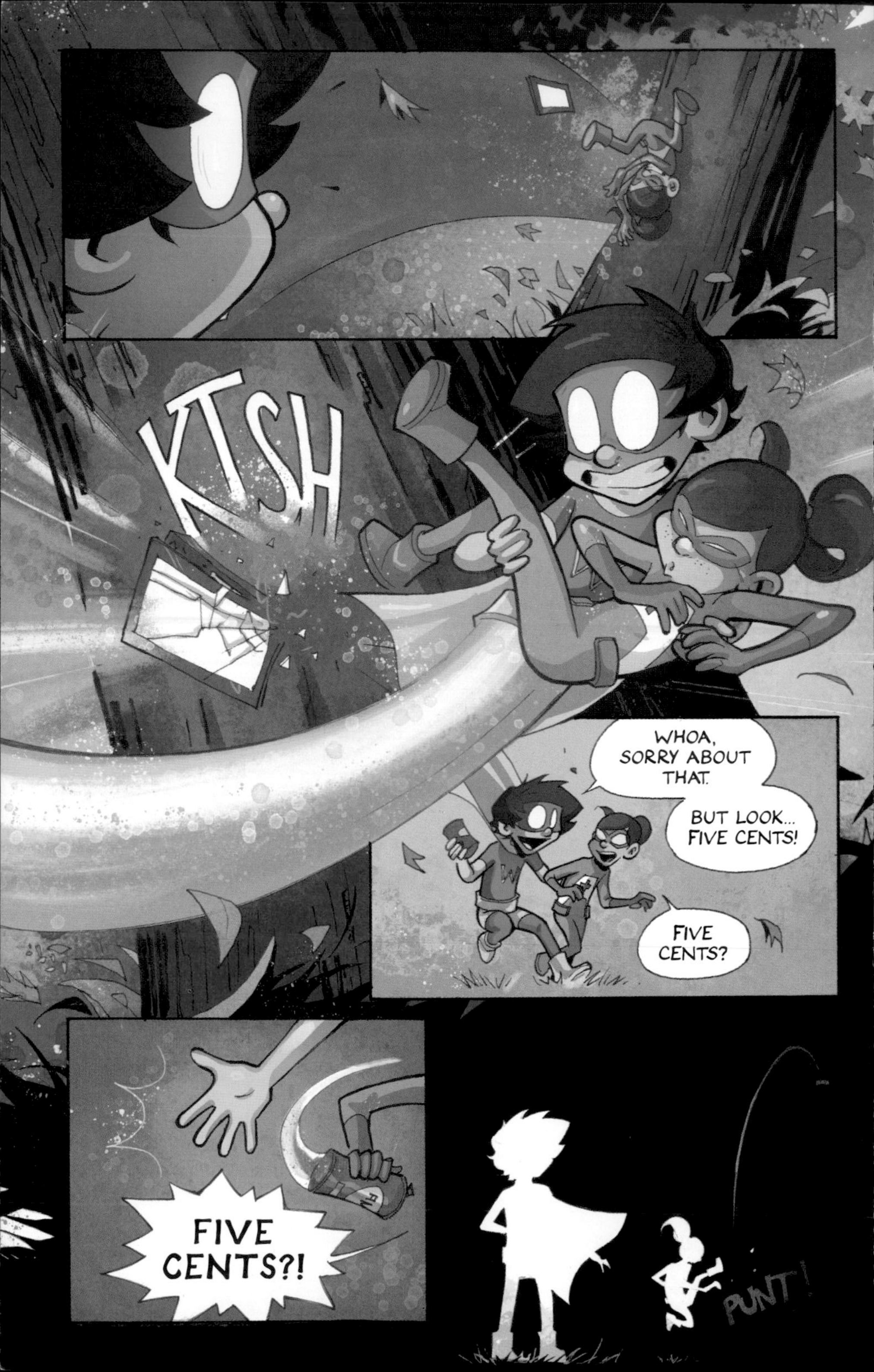
KTSH
WHOA, SORRY ABOUT THAT.
BUT LOOK... FIVE CENTS!
FIVE CENTS?
FIVE CENTS?!
PUNT!

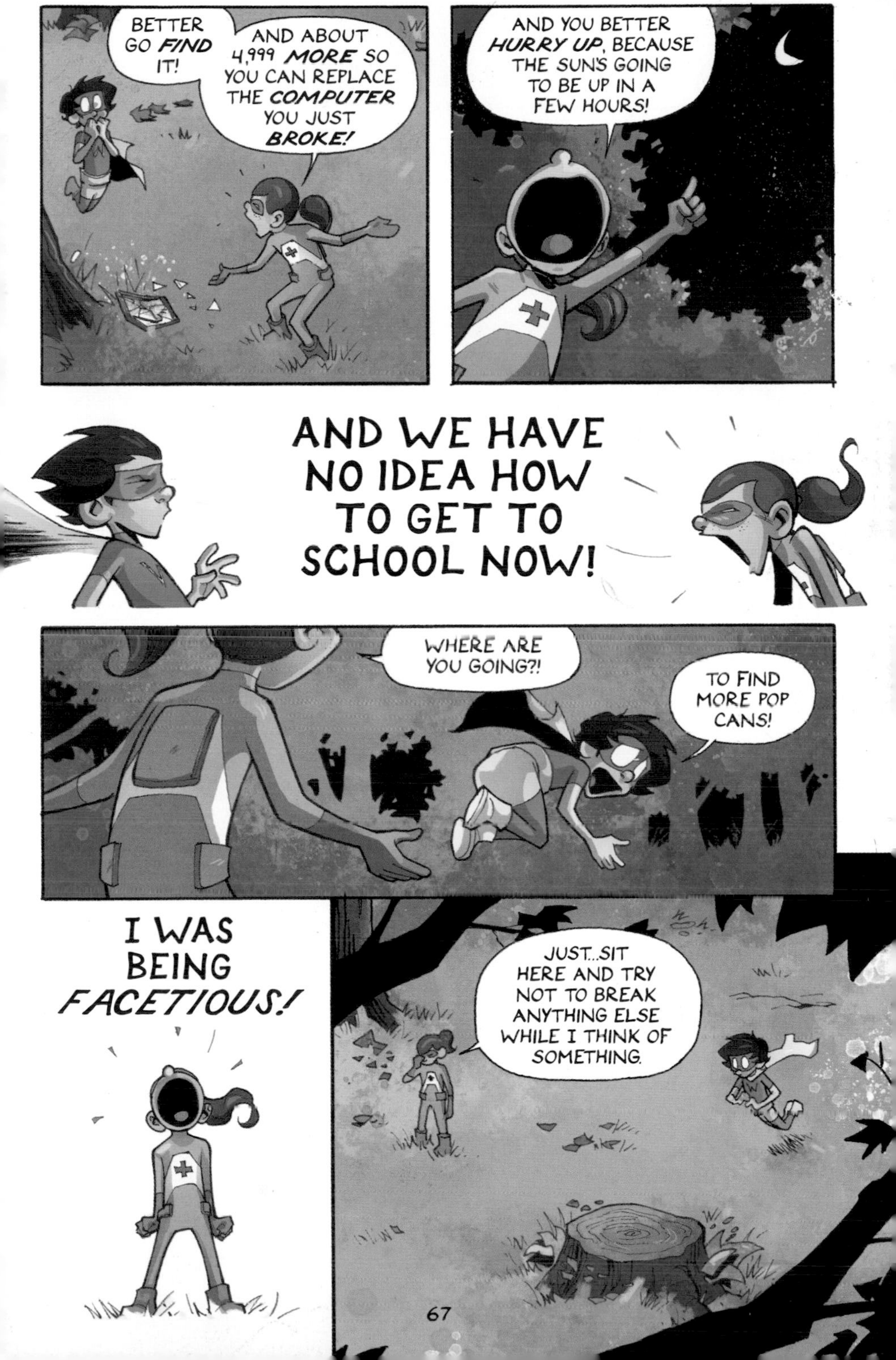
BETTER GO FIND IT!
AND ABOUT 4,999 MORE SO YOU CAN REPLACE THE COMPUTER YOU JUST BROKE!
AND YOU BETTER HURRY UP, BECAUSE THE SUN'S GOING TO BE UP IN A FEW HOURS!
AND WE HAVE NO IDEA HOW TO GET TO SCHOOL NOW!
WHERE ARE YOU GOING?!
TO FIND MORE POP CANS!
I WAS BEING FACETIOUS!
JUST...SIT HERE AND TRY NOT TO BREAK ANYTHING ELSE WHILE I THINK OF SOMETHING.

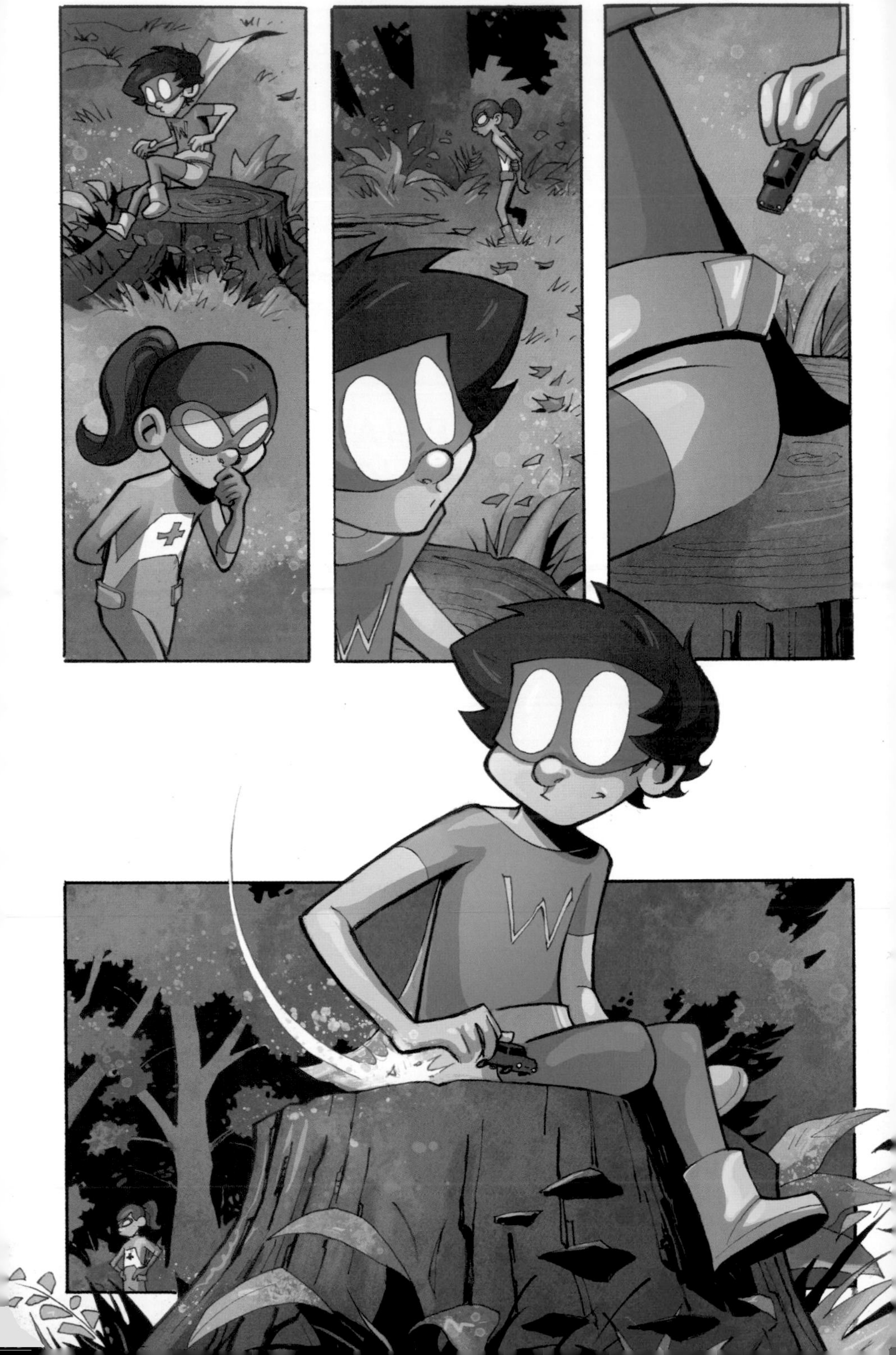

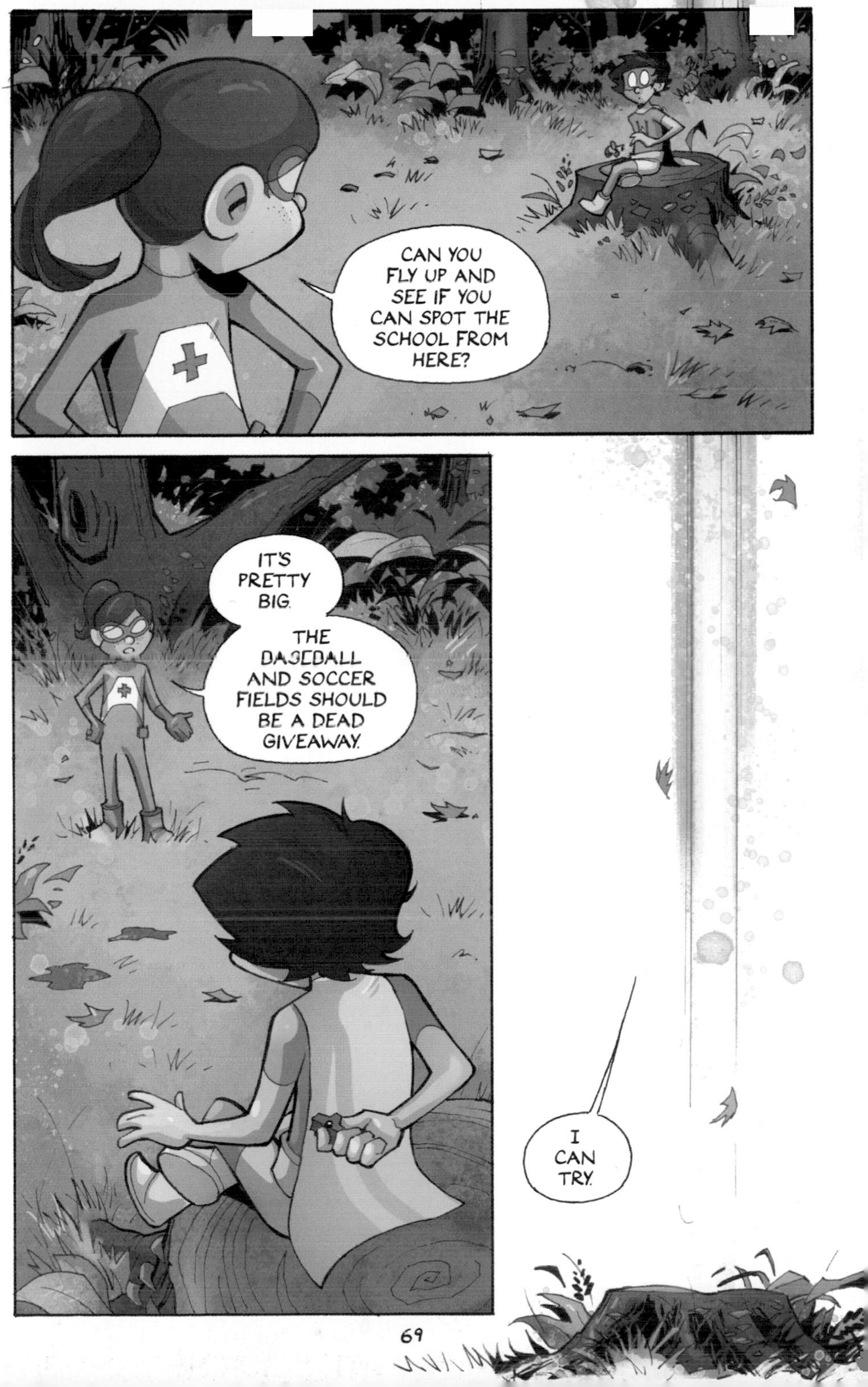
CAN YOU FLY UP AND SEE IF YOU CAN SPOT THE SCHOOL FROM HERE?
IT'S PRETTY BIG.
THE BASEBALL AND SOCCER FIELDS SHOULD BE A DEAD GIVEAWAY.
I CAN TRY.

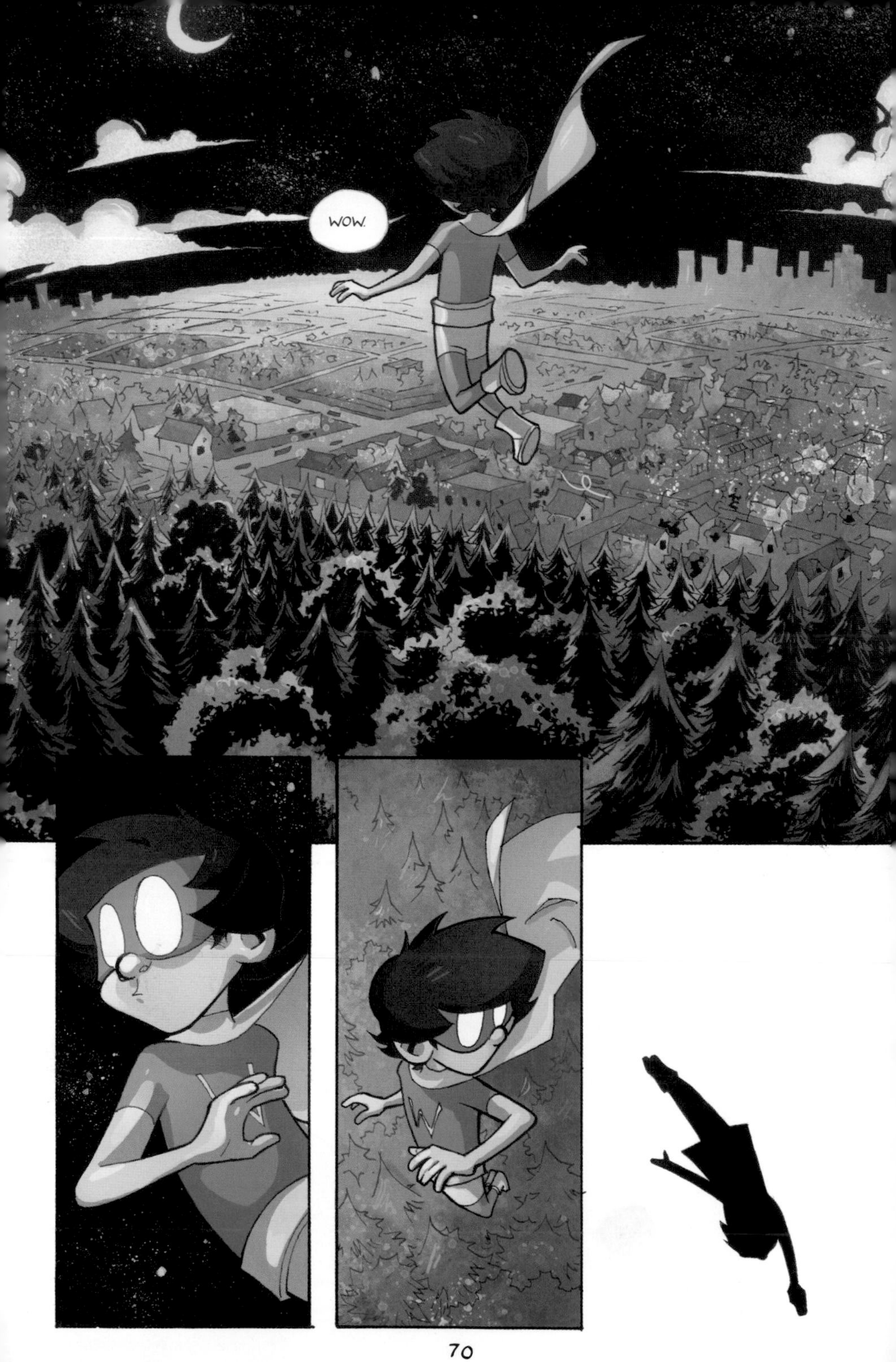
WOW.

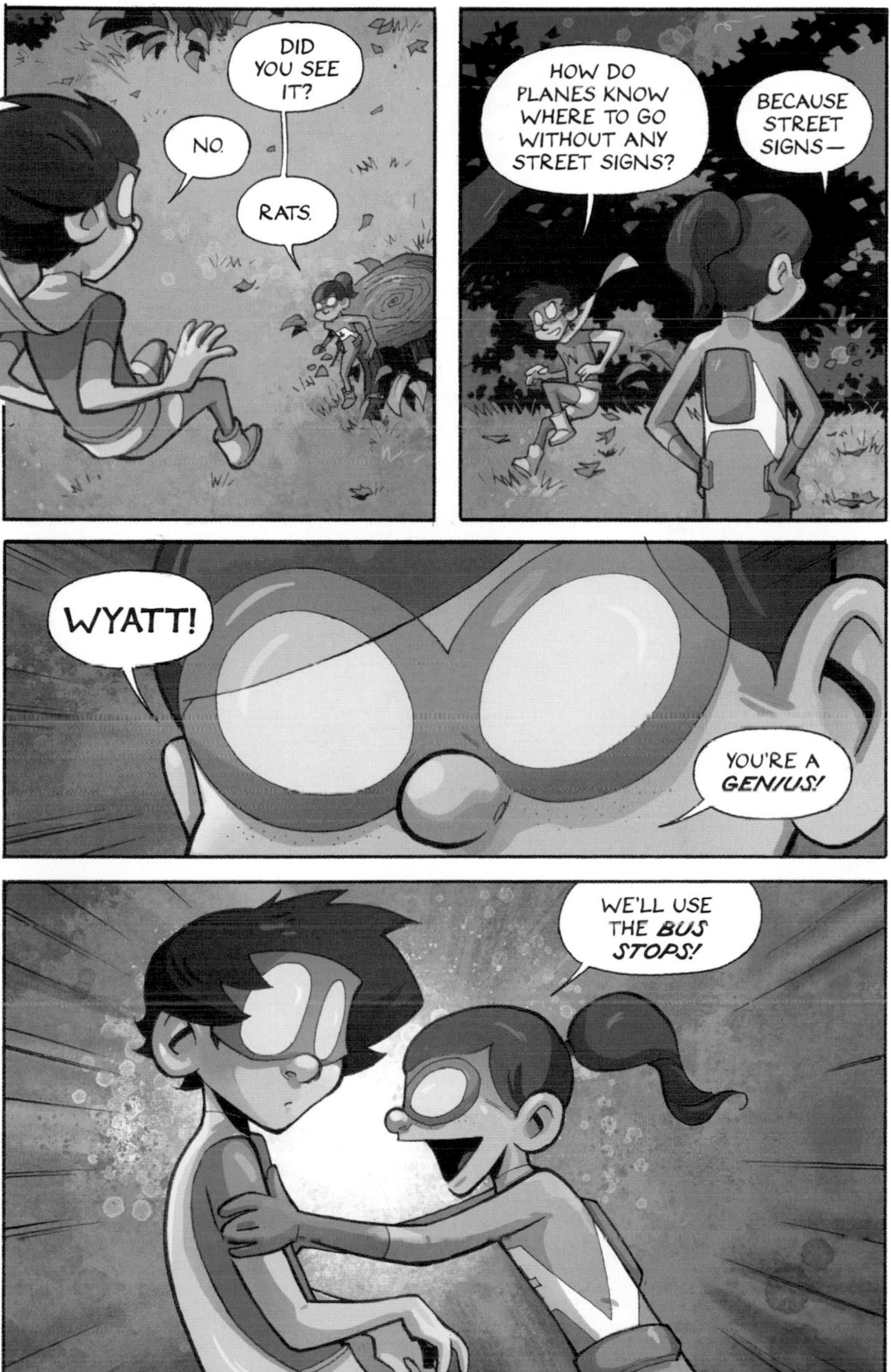
DID YOU SEE IT?
NO.
RATS.
HOW DO PLANES KNOW WHERE TO GO WITHOUT ANY STREET SIGNS?
BECAUSE STREET SIGNS—
WYATT!
YOU'RE A *GENIUS!*
WE'LL USE THE *BUS STOPS!*

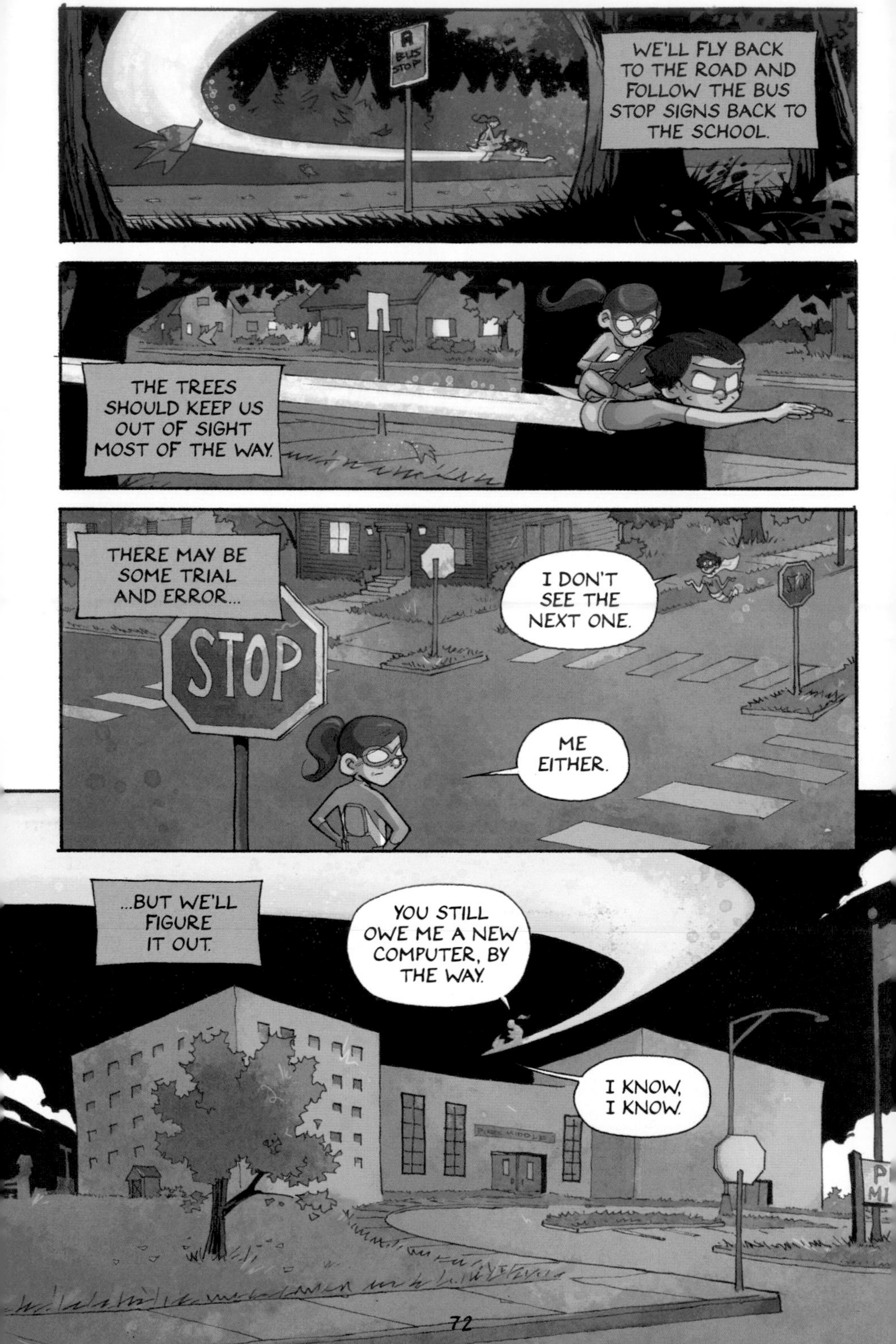
BUS STOP
WE'LL FLY BACK TO THE ROAD AND FOLLOW THE BUS STOP SIGNS BACK TO THE SCHOOL.
THE TREES SHOULD KEEP US OUT OF SIGHT MOST OF THE WAY.
THERE MAY BE SOME TRIAL AND ERROR...
STOP
I DON'T SEE THE NEXT ONE.
ME EITHER.
...BUT WE'LL FIGURE IT OUT.
YOU STILL OWE ME A NEW COMPUTER, BY THE WAY.
I KNOW, I KNOW.

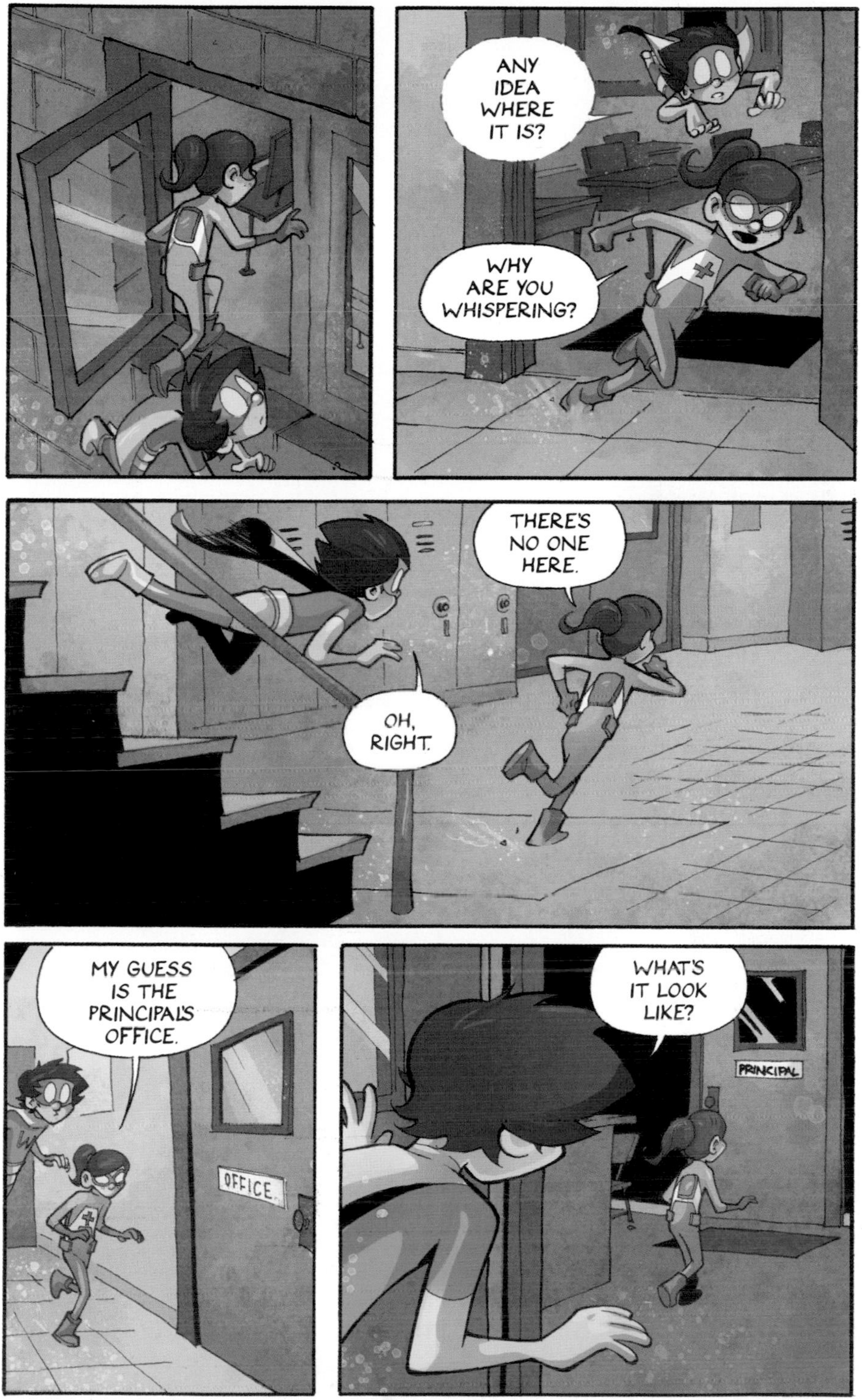
ANY IDEA WHERE IT IS?
WHY ARE YOU WHISPERING?
THERE'S NO ONE HERE.
OH, RIGHT.
MY GUESS IS THE PRINCIPAL'S OFFICE.
OFFICE
WHAT'S IT LOOK LIKE?
PRINCIPAL

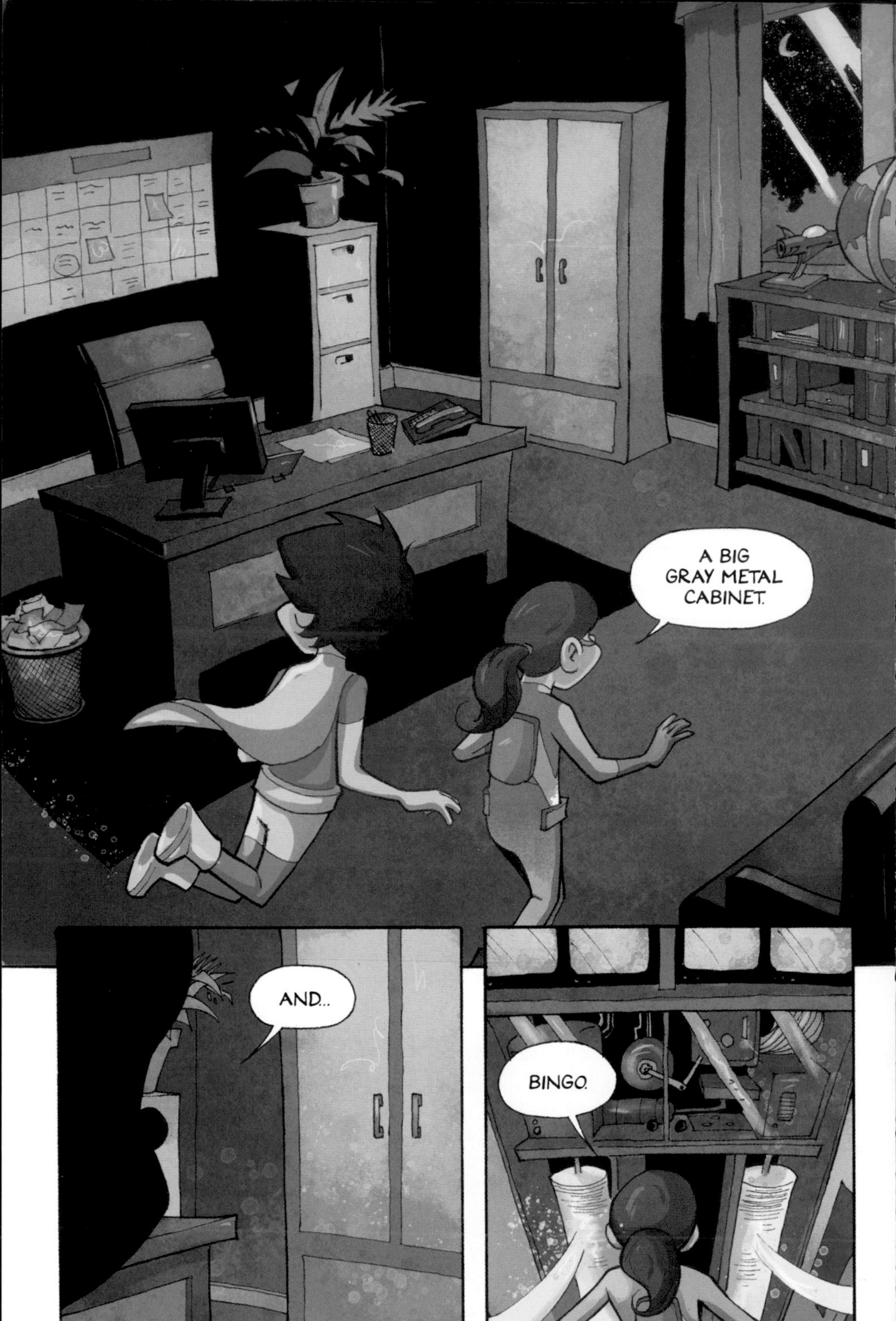
A BIG GRAY METAL CABINET.
AND...
BINGO.

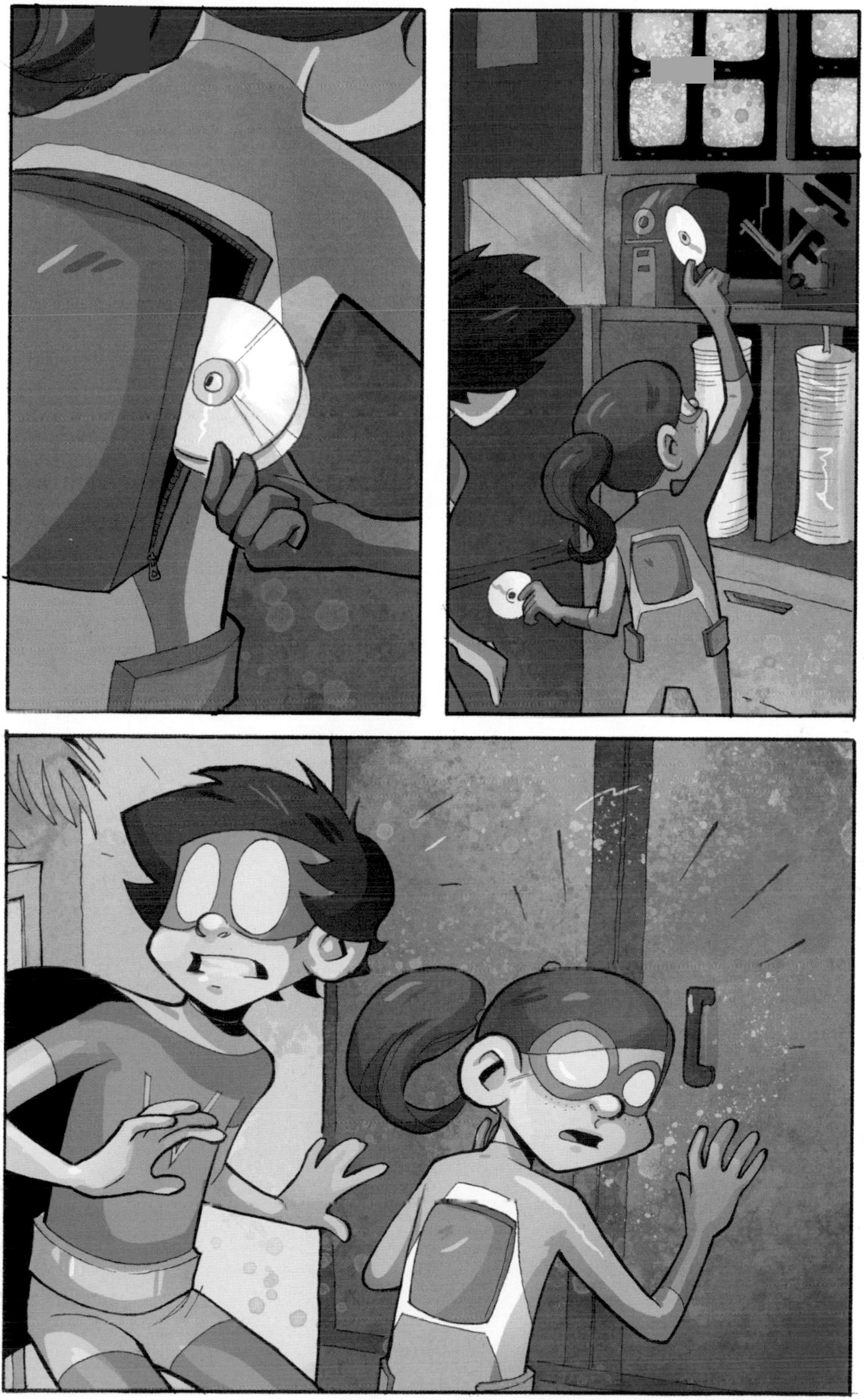
[redacted]

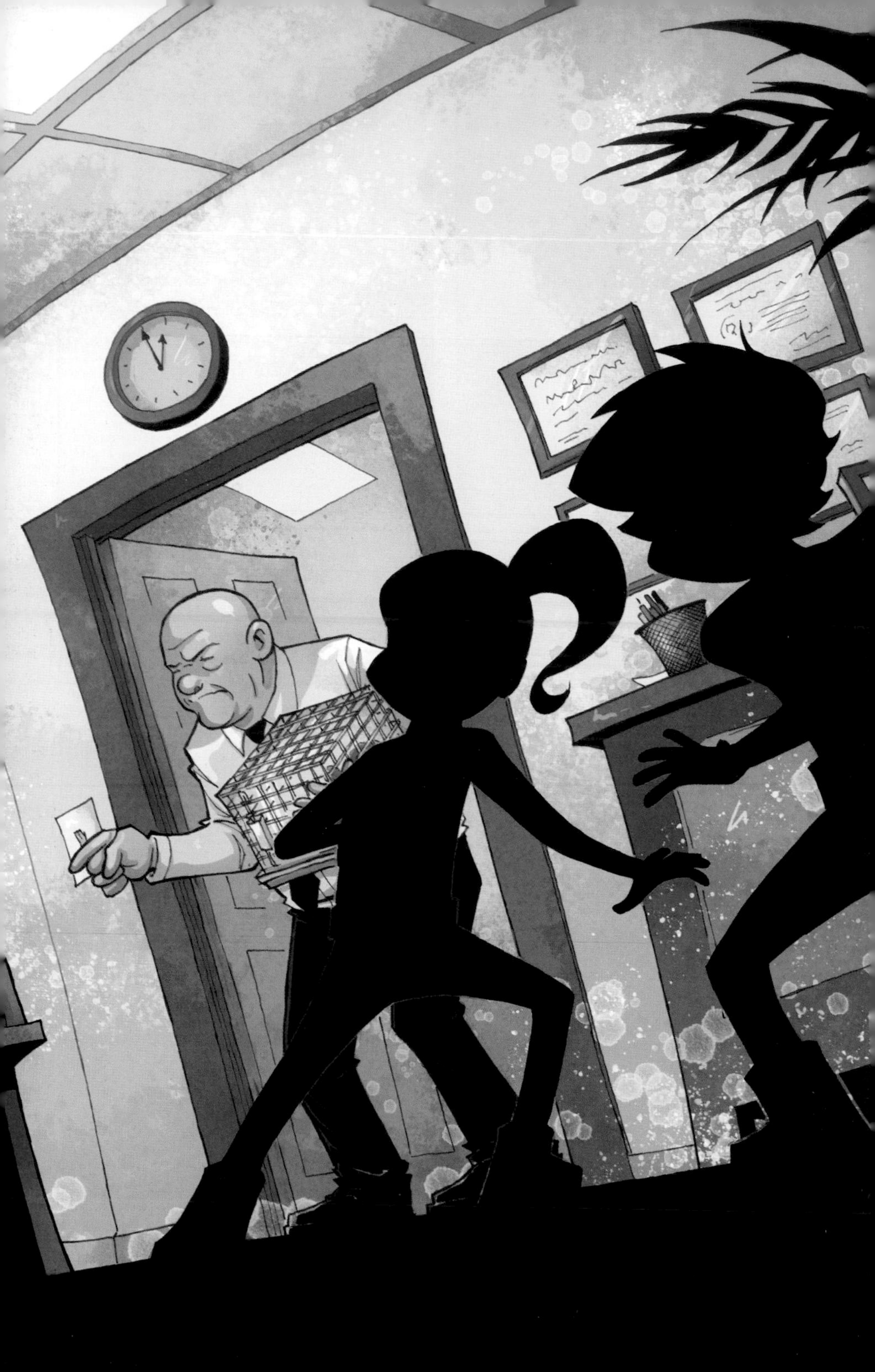

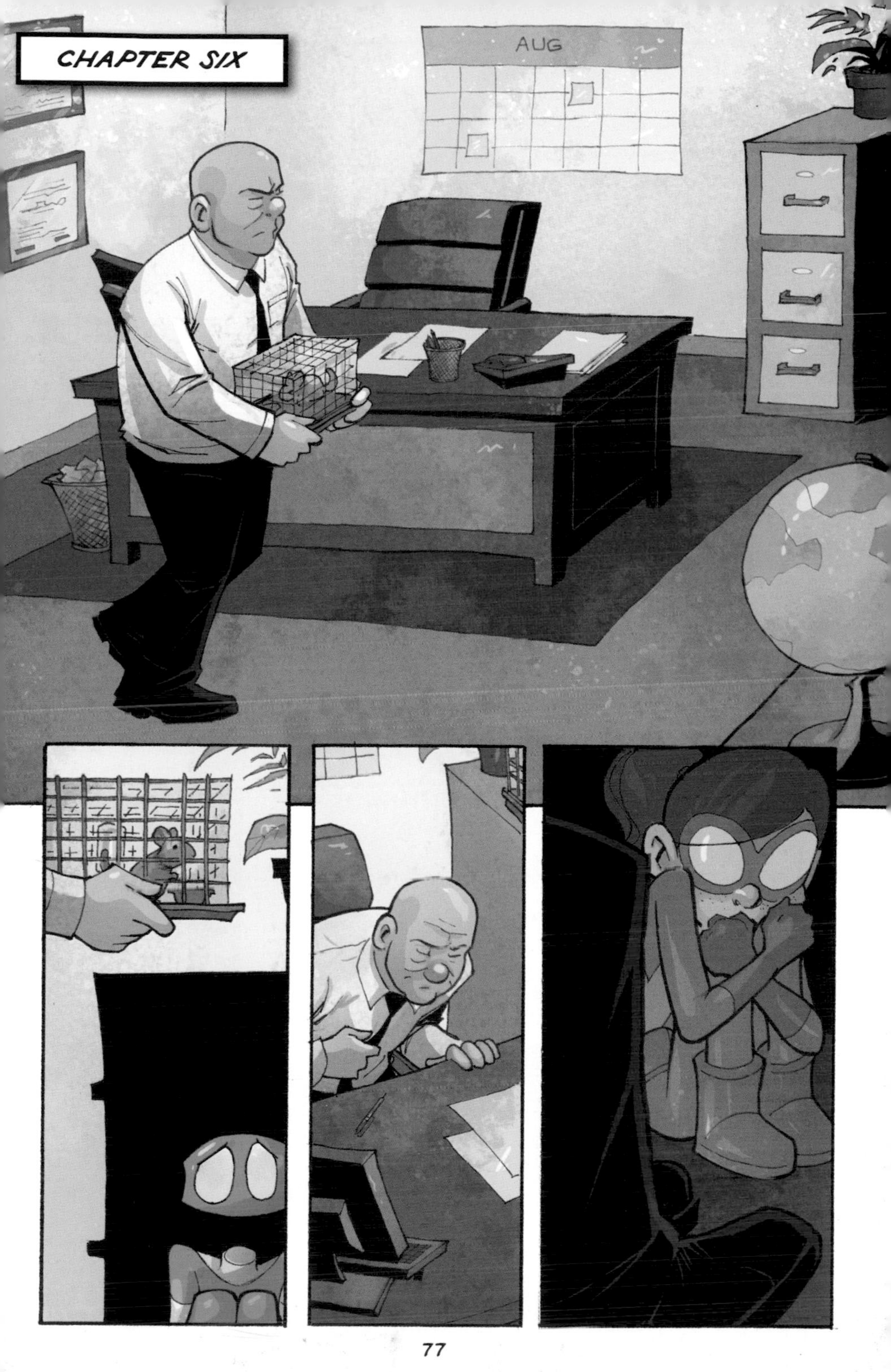
CHAPTER SIX
AUG

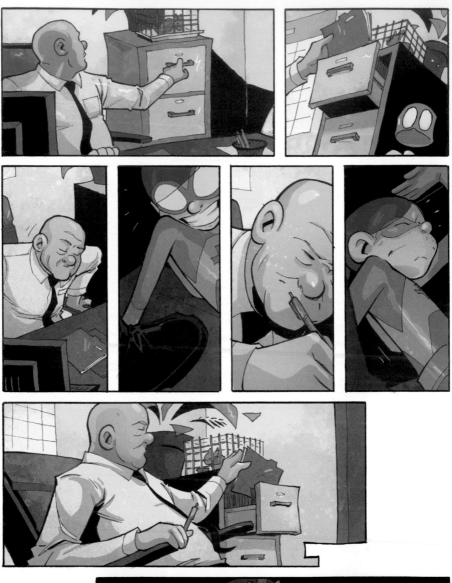

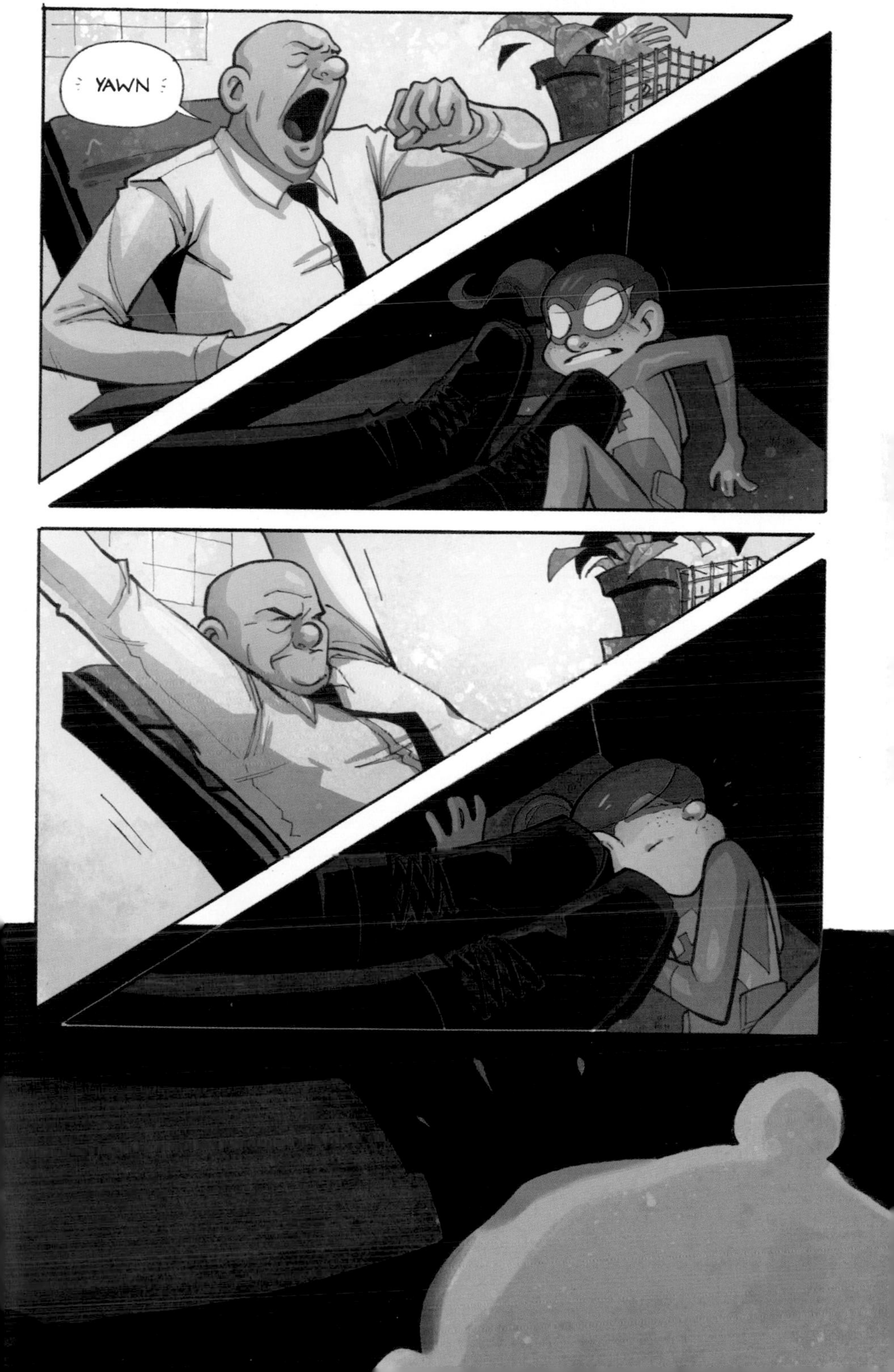
YAWN

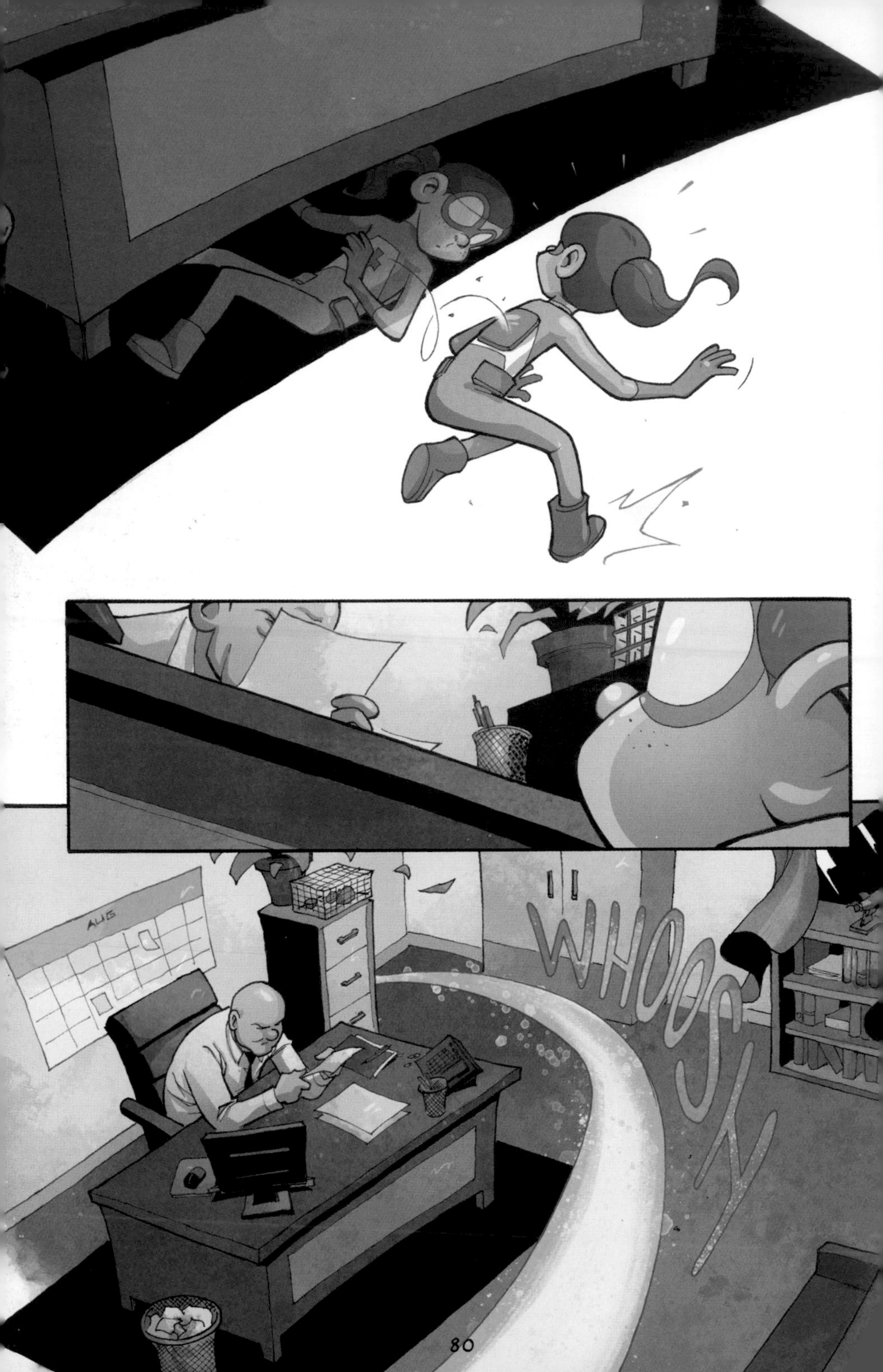
AUG
WHOOSH

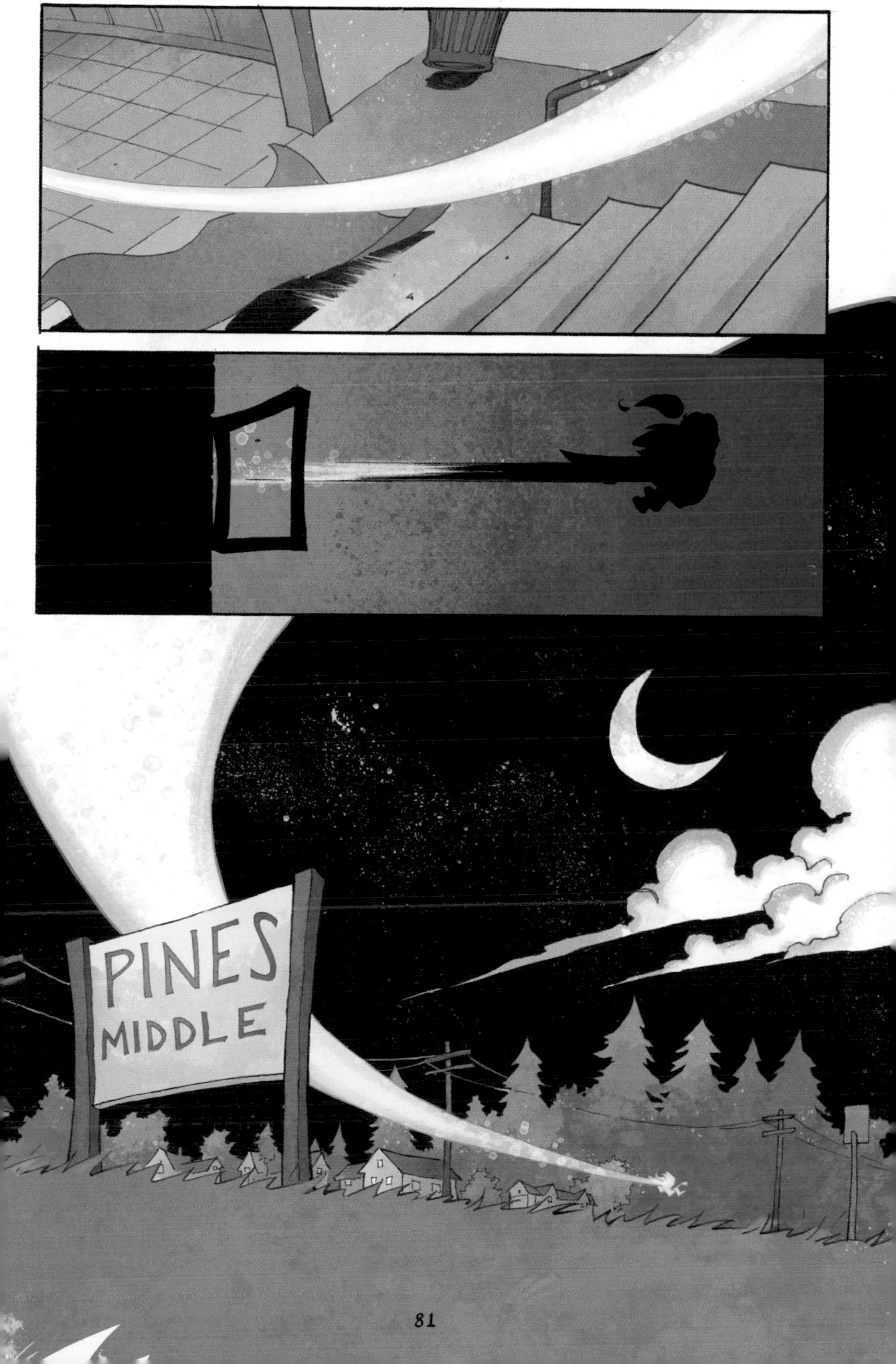
PINES
MIDDLE

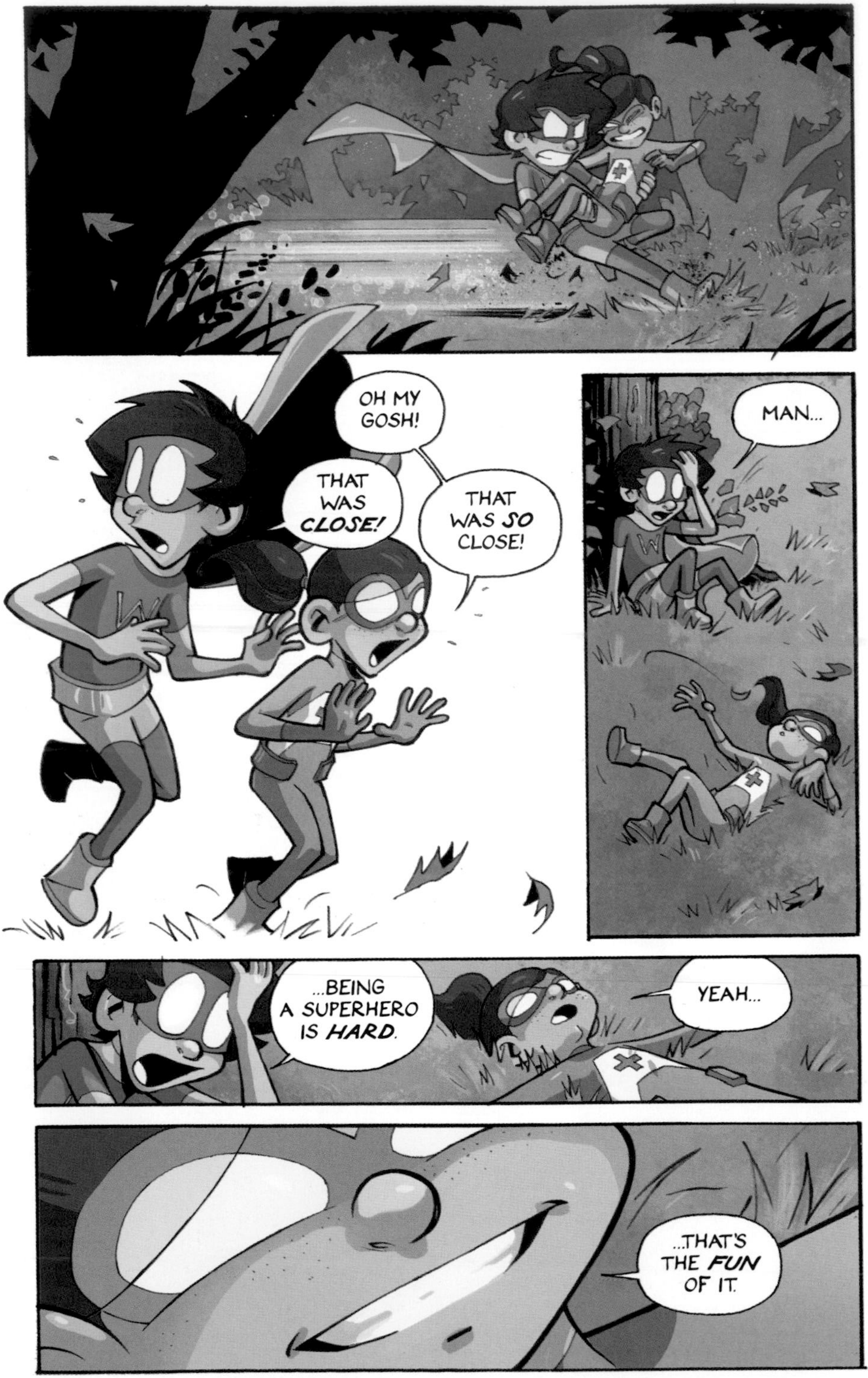
OH MY GOSH!
THAT WAS *CLOSE!*
THAT WAS *SO* CLOSE!
MAN...
...BEING A SUPERHERO IS *HARD*.
YEAH...
...THAT'S THE *FUN* OF IT.

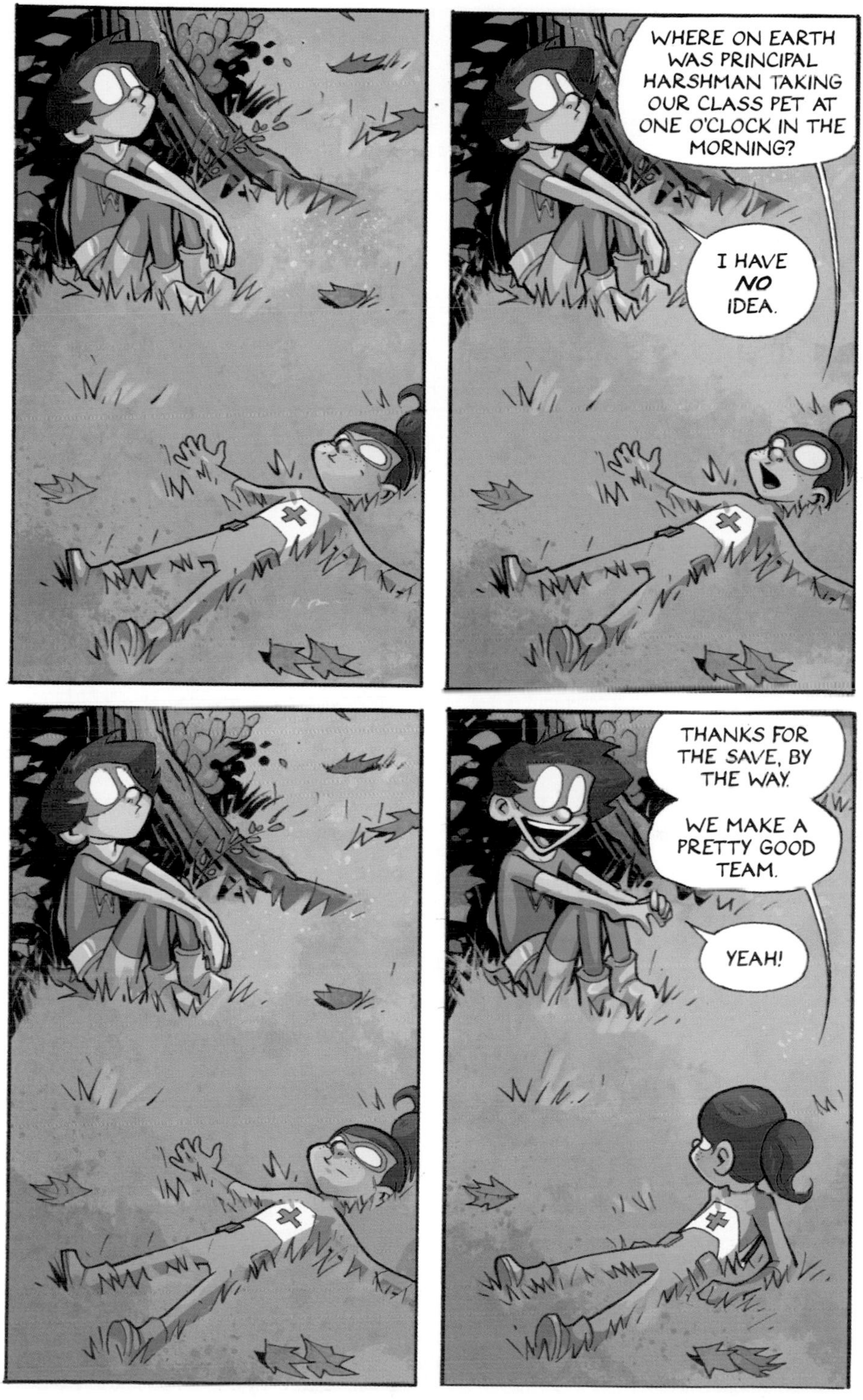
WHERE ON EARTH WAS PRINCIPAL HARSHMAN TAKING OUR CLASS PET AT ONE O'CLOCK IN THE MORNING?
I HAVE *NO* IDEA.
THANKS FOR THE SAVE, BY THE WAY.
WE MAKE A PRETTY GOOD TEAM.
YEAH!

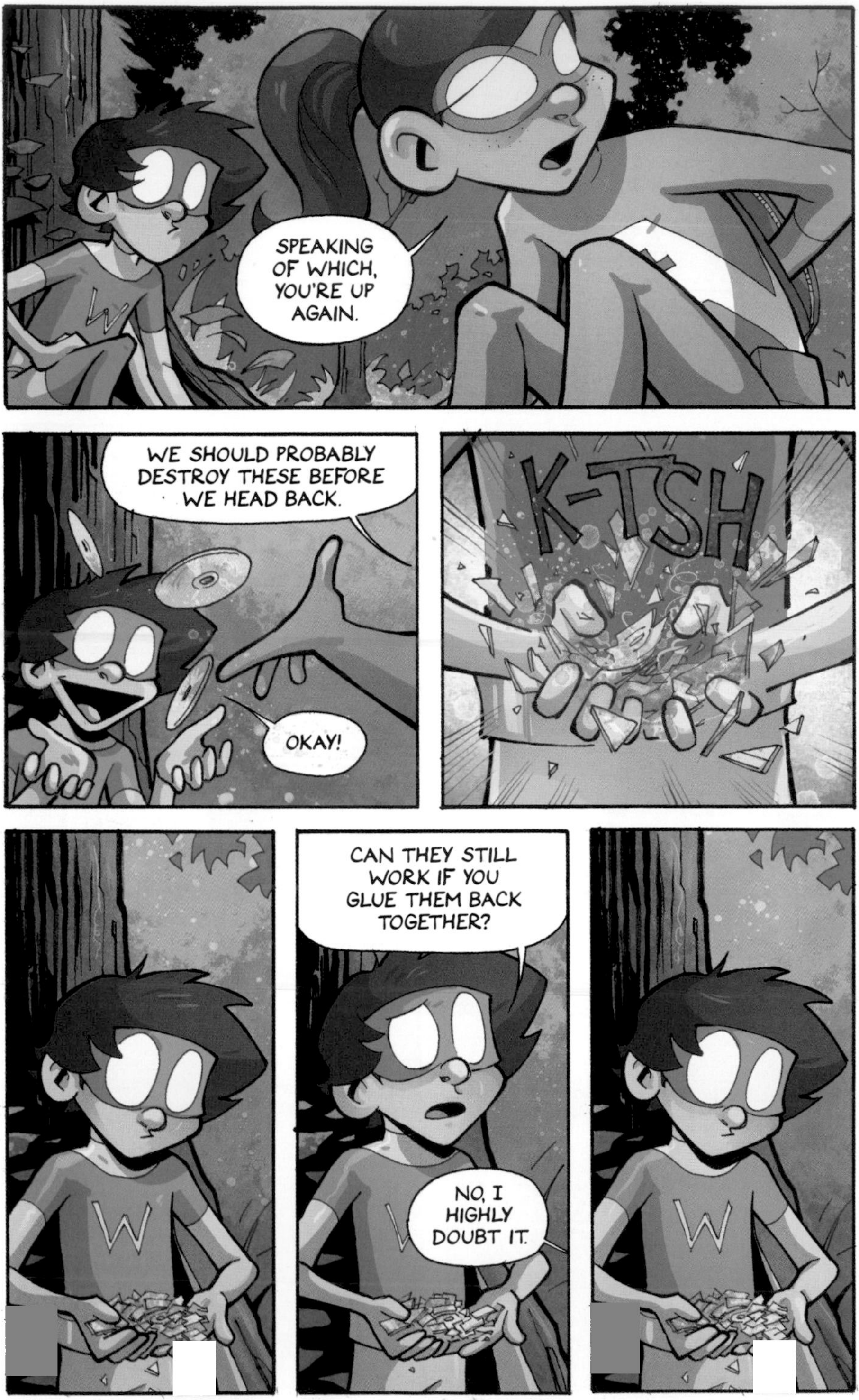
SPEAKING OF WHICH, YOU'RE UP AGAIN.
WE SHOULD PROBABLY DESTROY THESE BEFORE WE HEAD BACK.
OKAY!
K-TSH
CAN THEY STILL WORK IF YOU GLUE THEM BACK TOGETHER?
NO, I HIGHLY DOUBT IT.

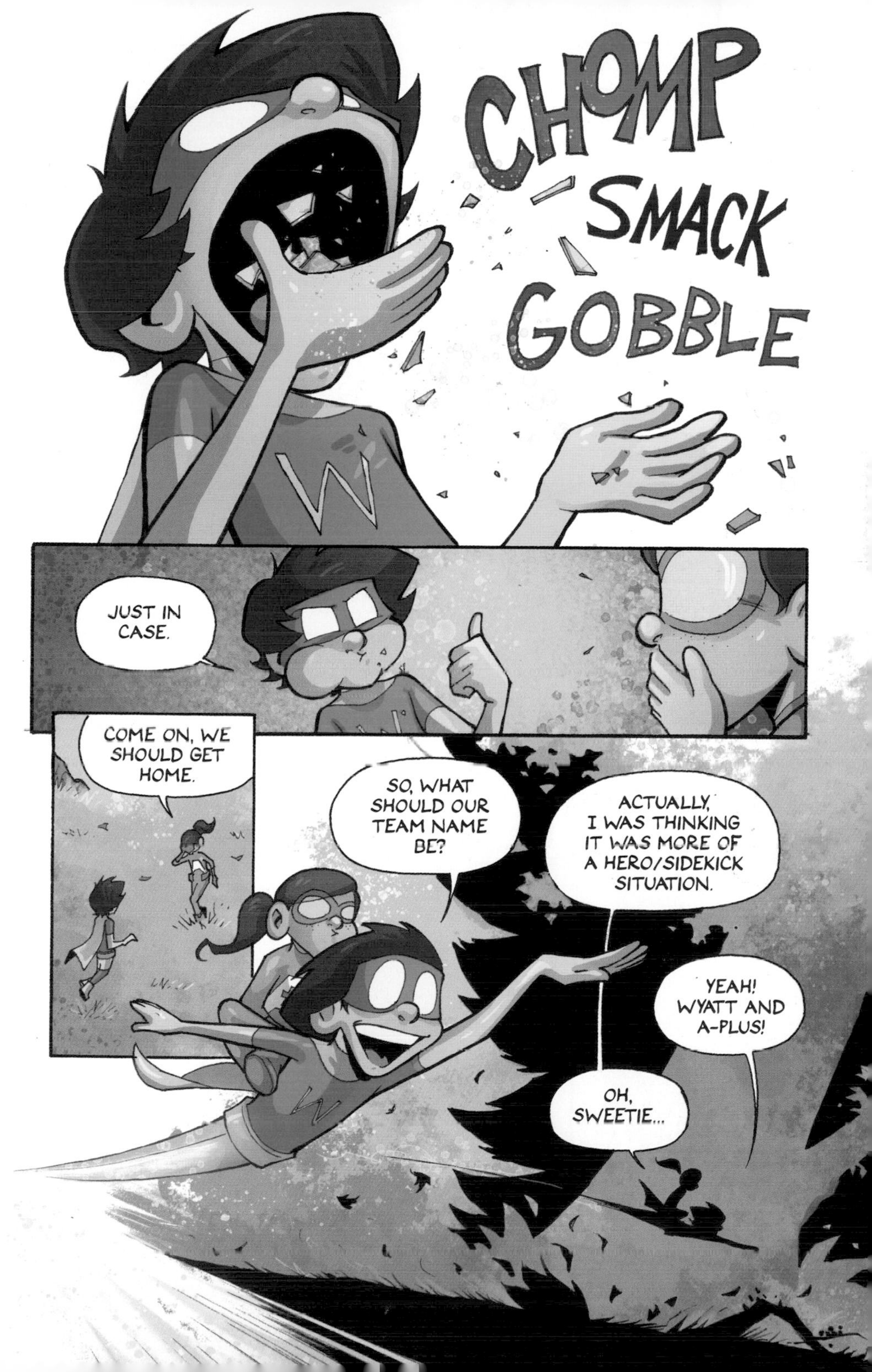
CHOMP
SMACK
GOBBLE
JUST IN CASE.
COME ON, WE SHOULD GET HOME.
SO, WHAT SHOULD OUR TEAM NAME BE?
ACTUALLY, I WAS THINKING IT WAS MORE OF A HERO/SIDEKICK SITUATION.
YEAH! WYATT AND A-PLUS!
OH, SWEETIE...

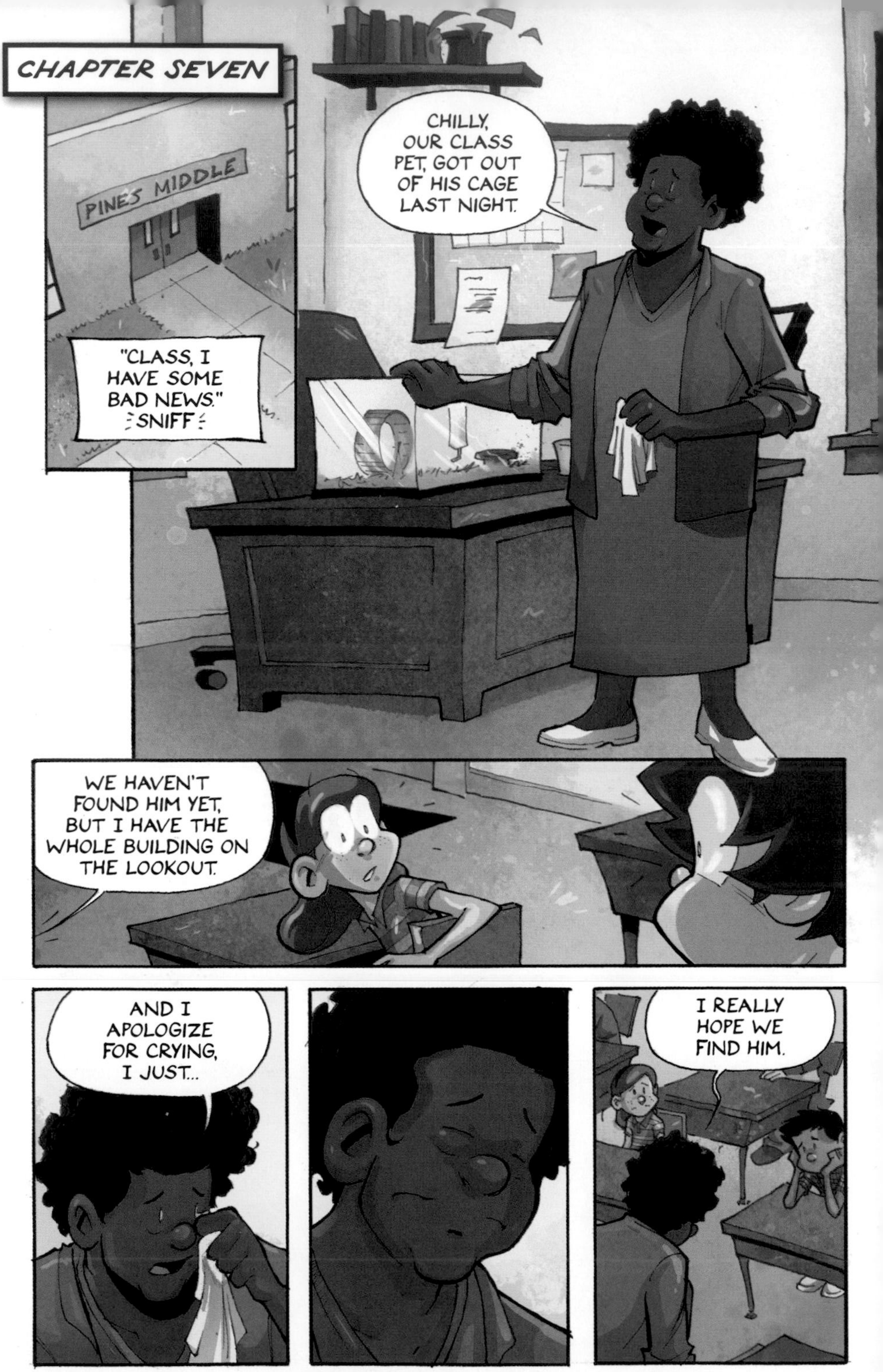
CHAPTER SEVEN
PINES MIDDLE
"CLASS, I HAVE SOME BAD NEWS."
SNIFF
CHILLY, OUR CLASS PET, GOT OUT OF HIS CAGE LAST NIGHT.
WE HAVEN'T FOUND HIM YET, BUT I HAVE THE WHOLE BUILDING ON THE LOOKOUT.
AND I APOLOGIZE FOR CRYING, I JUST...
I REALLY HOPE WE FIND HIM.

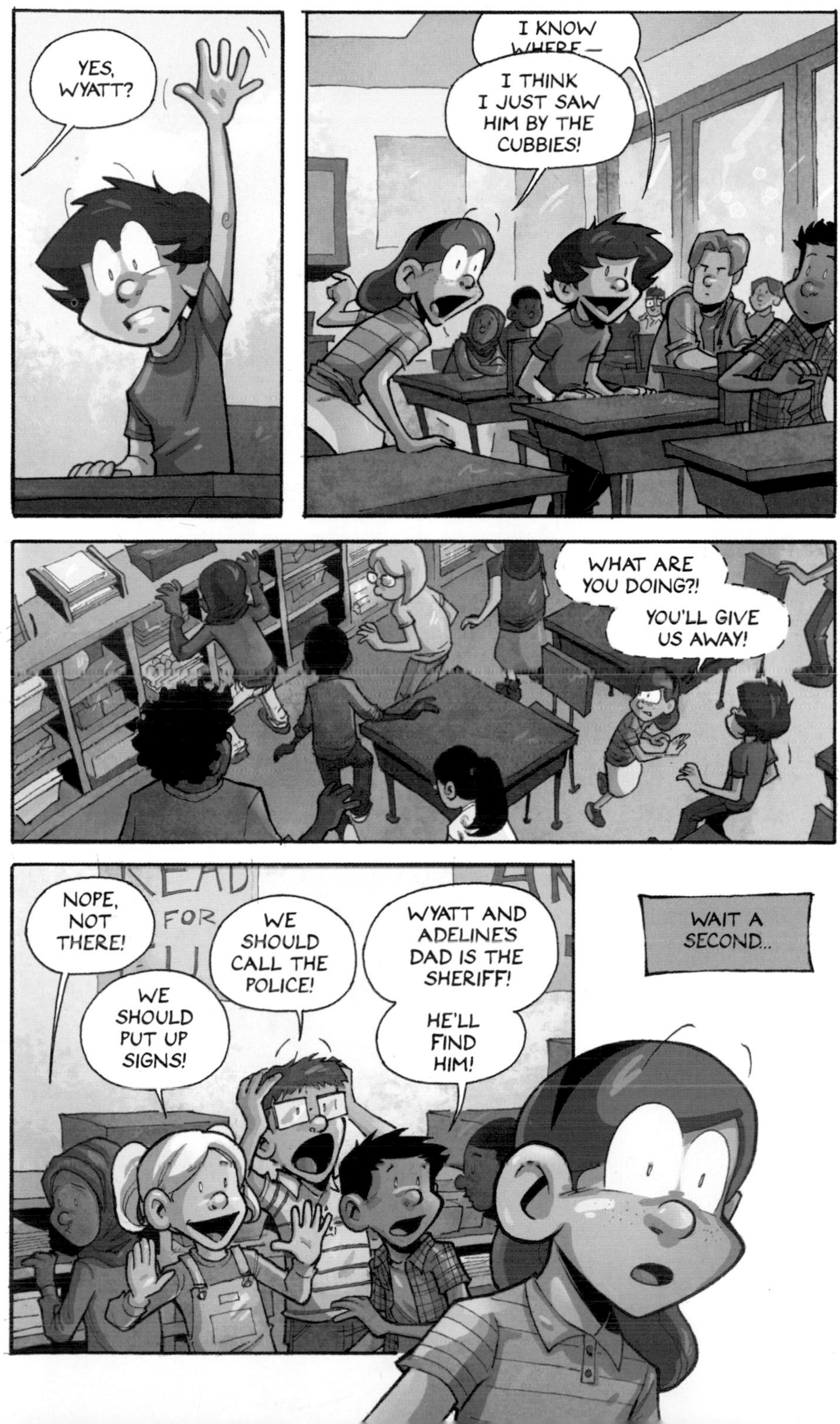
YES, WYATT?
I KNOW WHERE—
I THINK I JUST SAW HIM BY THE CUBBIES!
WHAT ARE YOU DOING?!
YOU'LL GIVE US AWAY!
READ FOR
NOPE, NOT THERE!
WE SHOULD PUT UP SIGNS!
WE SHOULD CALL THE POLICE!
WYATT AND ADELINE'S DAD IS THE SHERIFF!
HE'LL FIND HIM!
WAIT A SECOND...

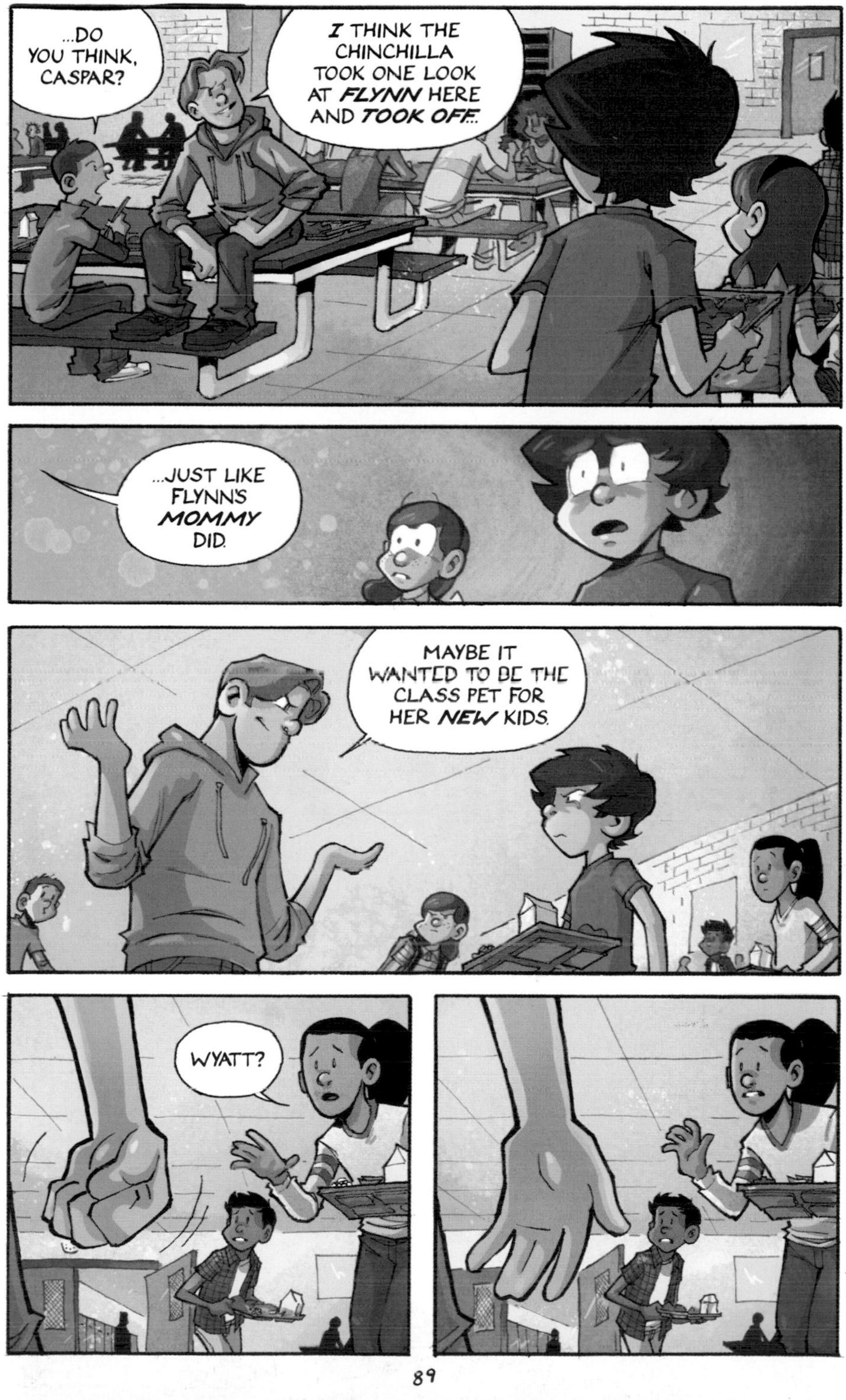
...DO YOU THINK, CASPAR?
I THINK THE CHINCHILLA TOOK ONE LOOK AT FLYNN HERE AND TOOK OFF...
...JUST LIKE FLYNN'S MOMMY DID.
MAYBE IT WANTED TO BE THE CLASS PET FOR HER NEW KIDS.
WYATT?

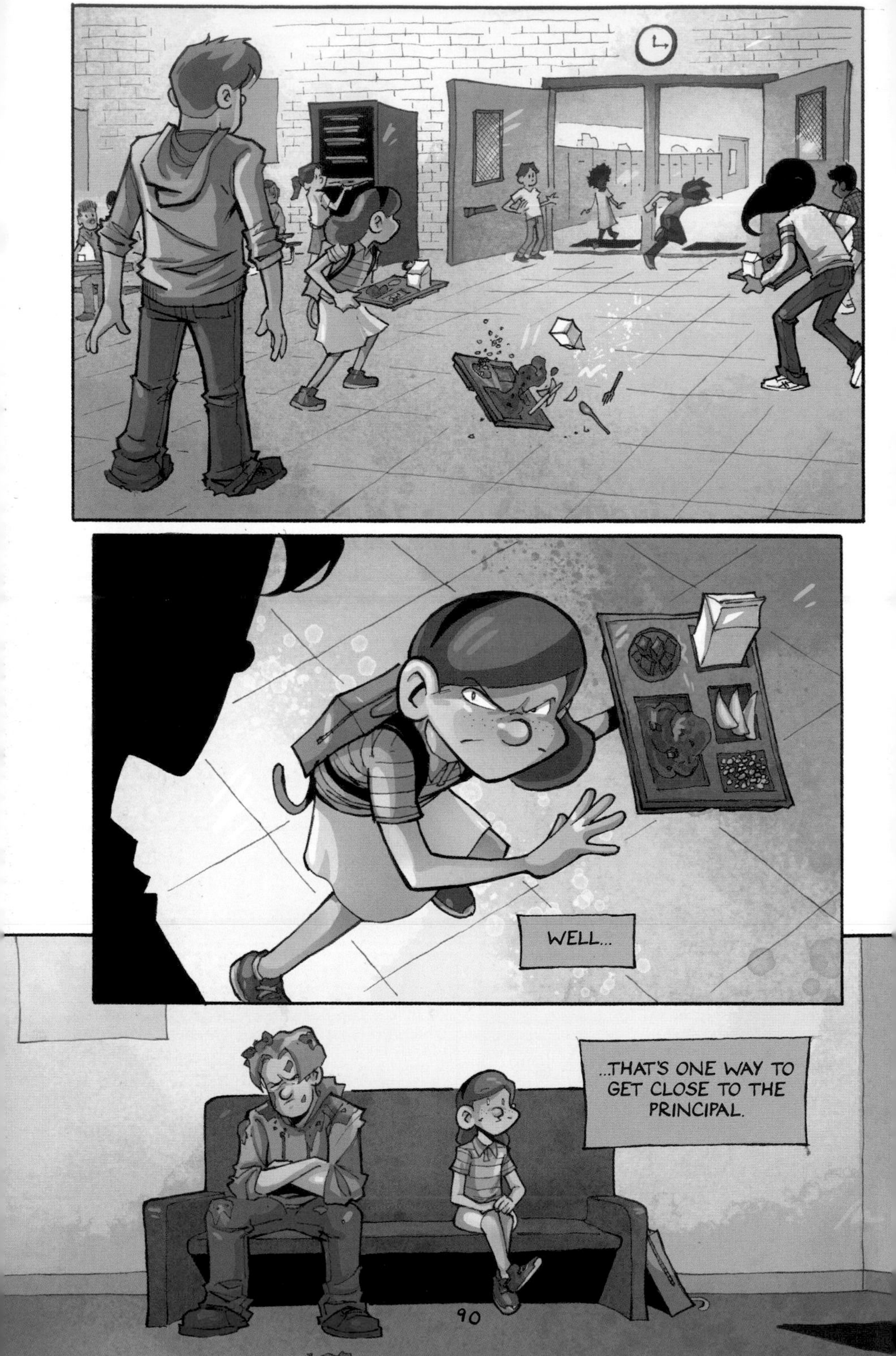
WELL...
...THAT'S ONE WAY TO GET CLOSE TO THE PRINCIPAL.

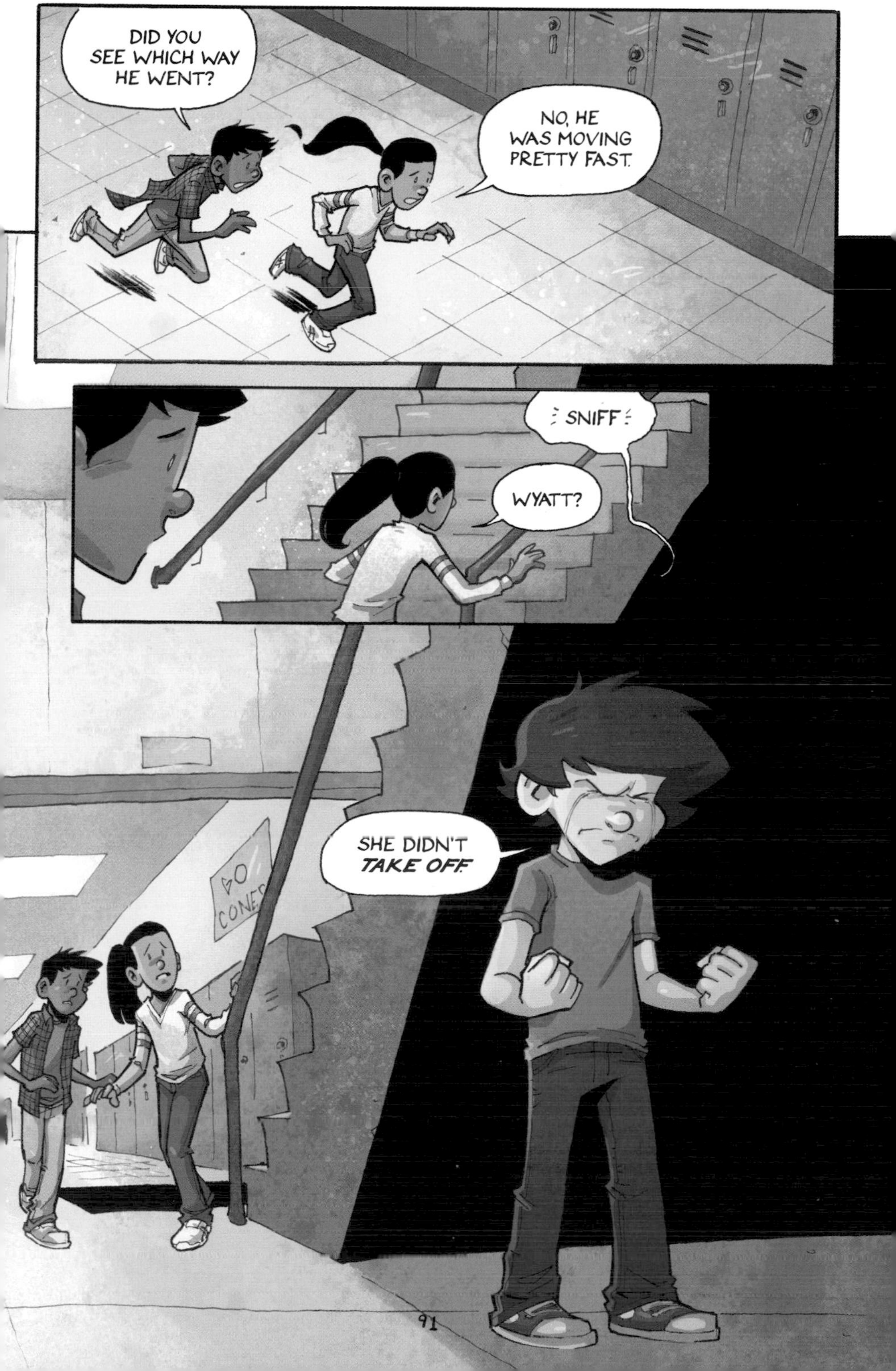
DID YOU SEE WHICH WAY HE WENT?
NO, HE WAS MOVING PRETTY FAST.
SNIFF
WYATT?
GO CONES
SHE DIDN'T *TAKE OFF*.

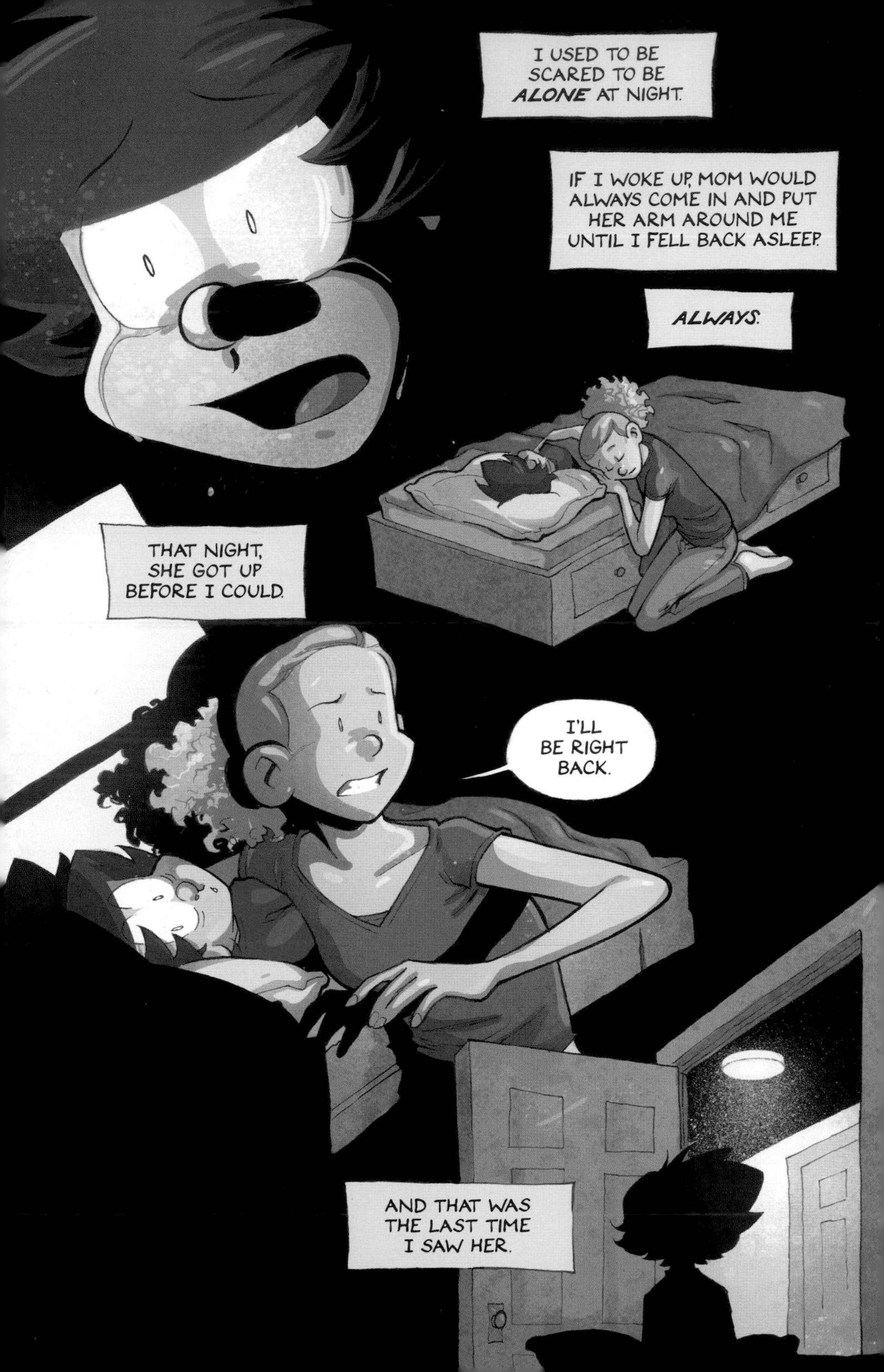
I USED TO BE SCARED TO BE ALONE AT NIGHT.
IF I WOKE UP, MOM WOULD ALWAYS COME IN AND PUT HER ARM AROUND ME UNTIL I FELL BACK ASLEEP.
ALWAYS.
THAT NIGHT, SHE GOT UP BEFORE I COULD.
I'LL BE RIGHT BACK.
AND THAT WAS THE LAST TIME I SAW HER.

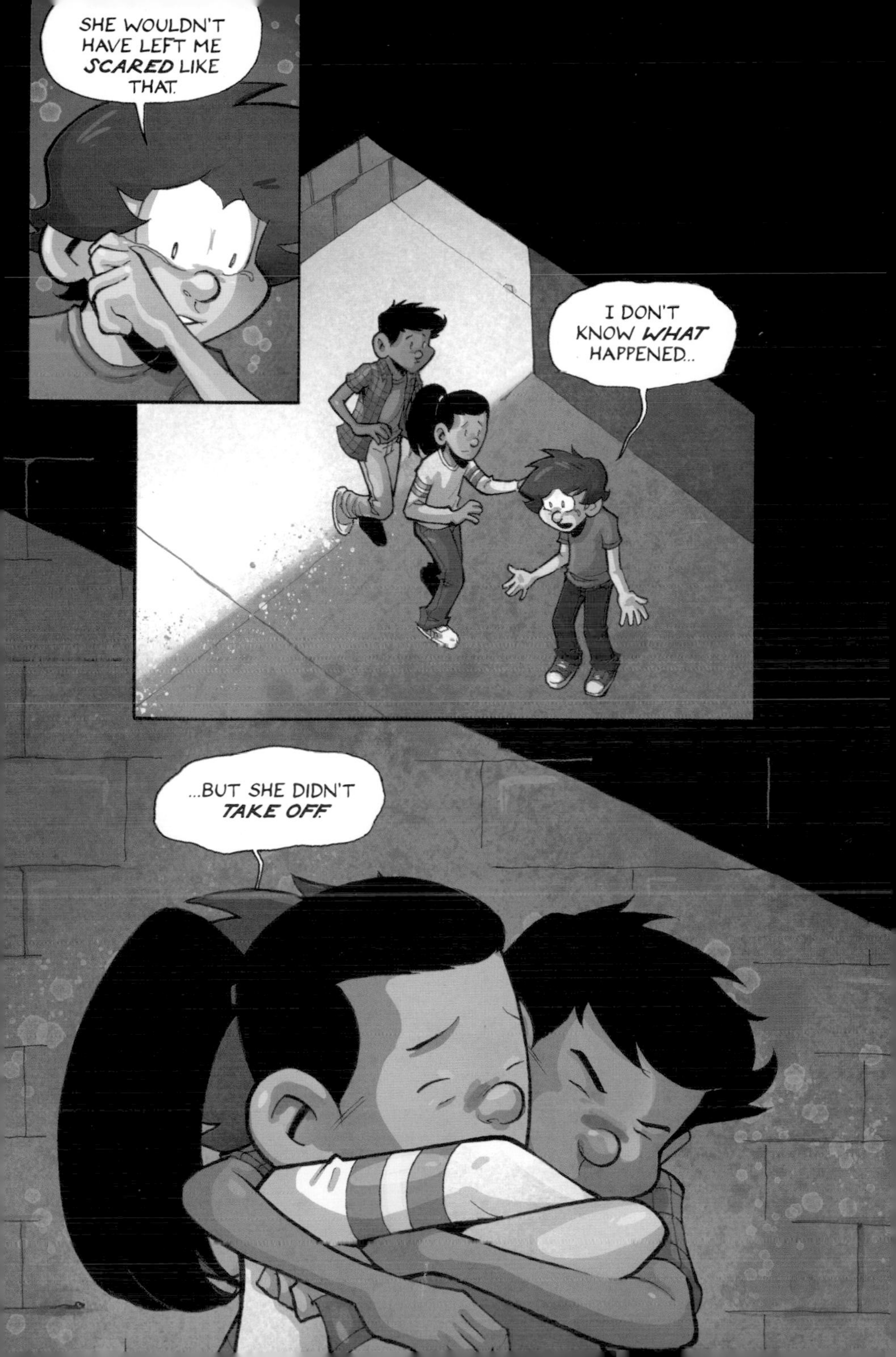
SHE WOULDN'T HAVE LEFT ME SCARED LIKE THAT.
I DON'T KNOW WHAT HAPPENED...
...BUT SHE DIDN'T TAKE OFF.

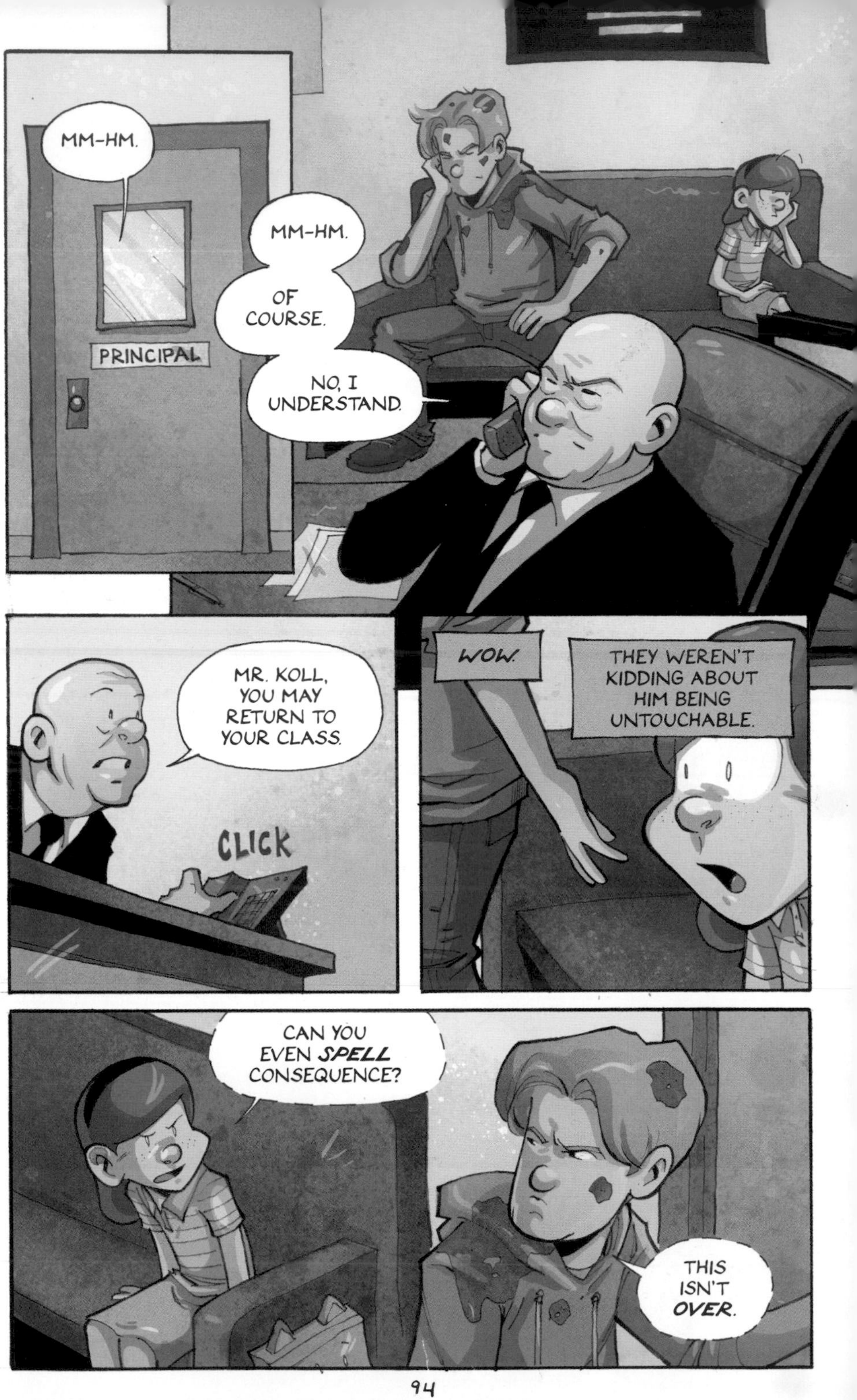
PRINCIPAL
MM-HM.
MM-HM.
OF COURSE.
NO, I UNDERSTAND.
MR. KOLL, YOU MAY RETURN TO YOUR CLASS.
CLICK
WOW.
THEY WEREN'T KIDDING ABOUT HIM BEING UNTOUCHABLE.
CAN YOU EVEN *SPELL* CONSEQUENCE?
THIS ISN'T *OVER*.

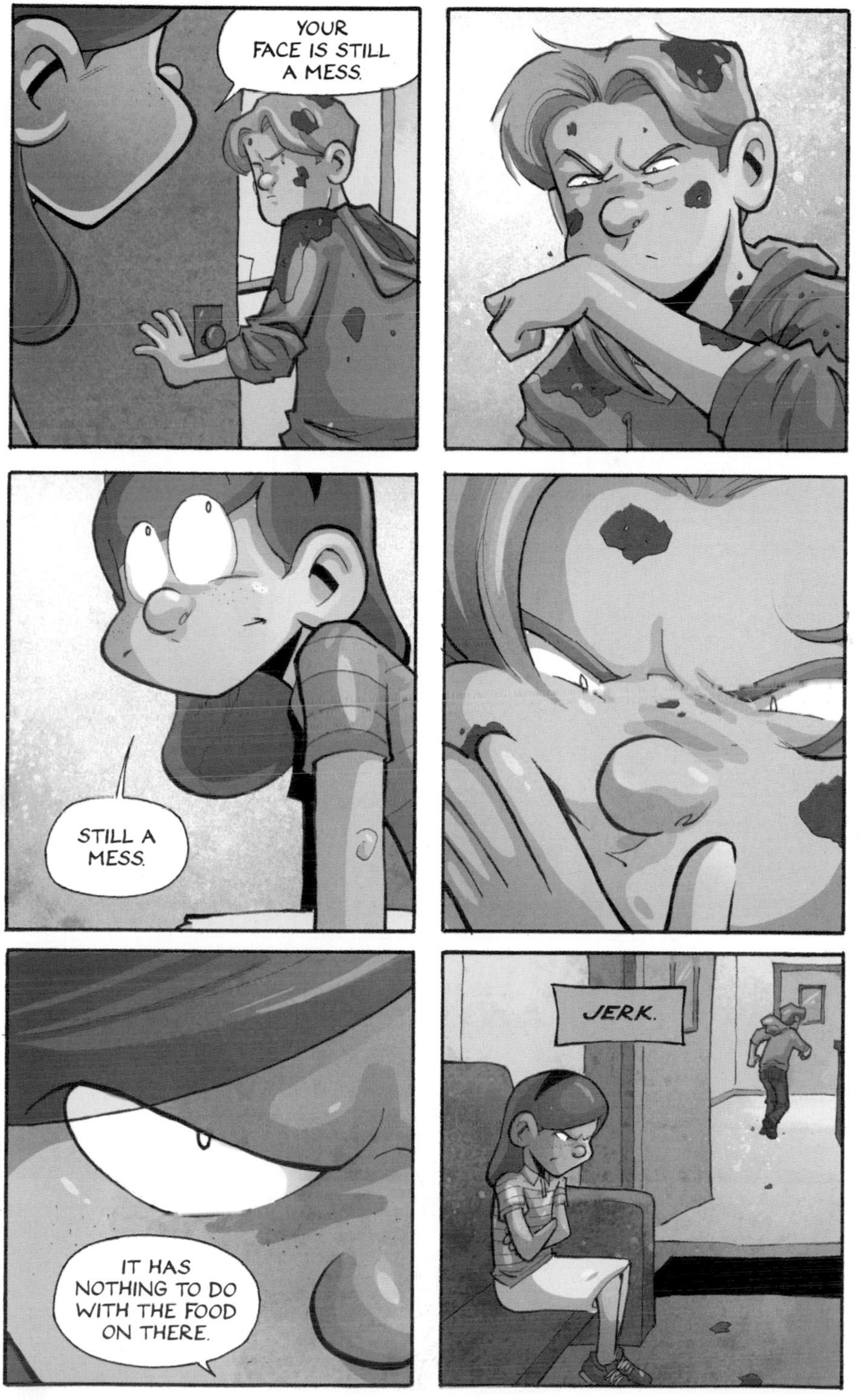
YOUR FACE IS STILL A MESS.
STILL A MESS.
IT HAS NOTHING TO DO WITH THE FOOD ON THERE.
JERK.

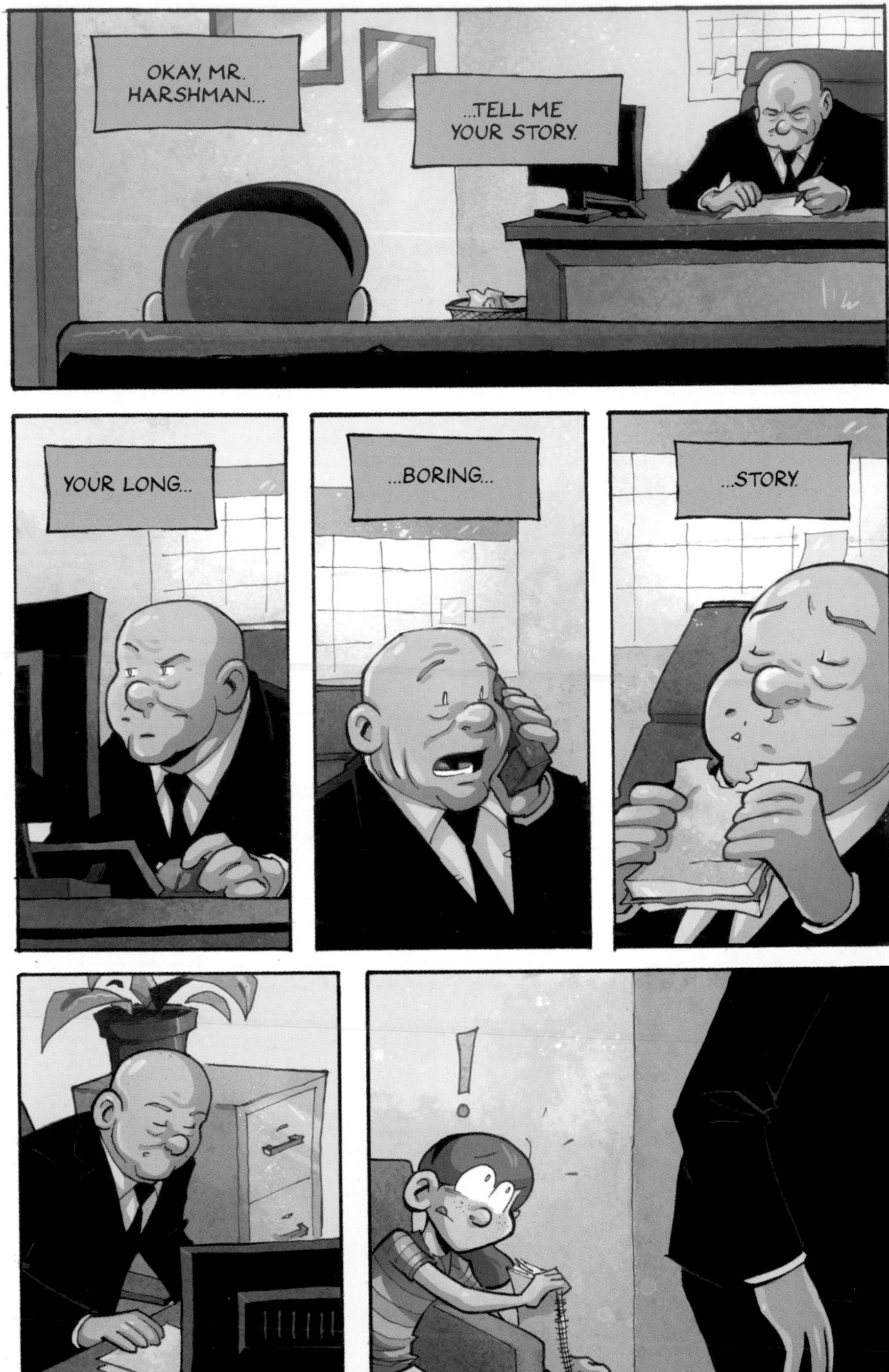
OKAY, MR. HARSHMAN...
...TELL ME YOUR STORY.
YOUR LONG...
...BORING...
...STORY.
!

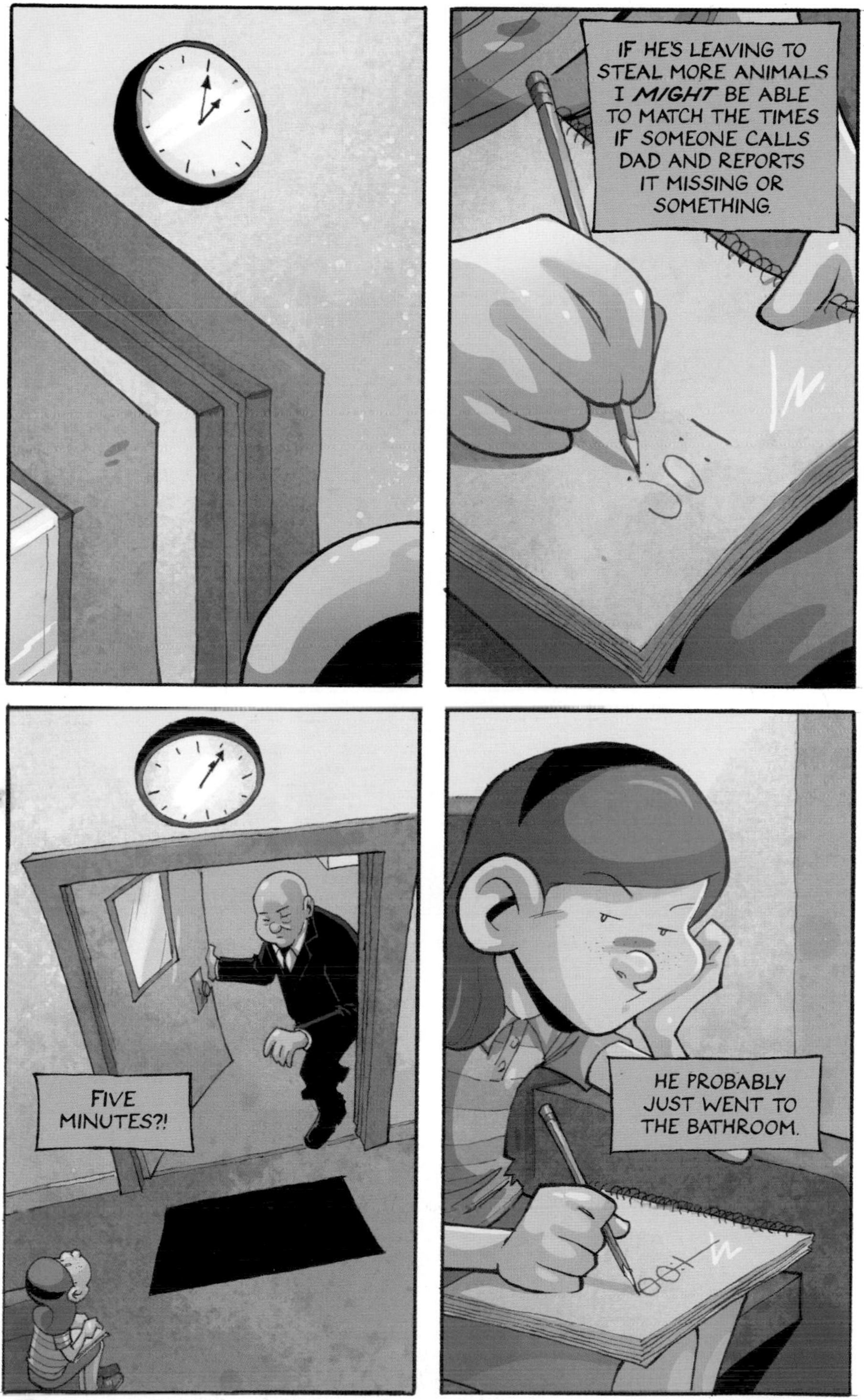
IF HE'S LEAVING TO STEAL MORE ANIMALS I *MIGHT* BE ABLE TO MATCH THE TIMES IF SOMEONE CALLS DAD AND REPORTS IT MISSING OR SOMETHING.
FIVE MINUTES?!
HE PROBABLY JUST WENT TO THE BATHROOM.

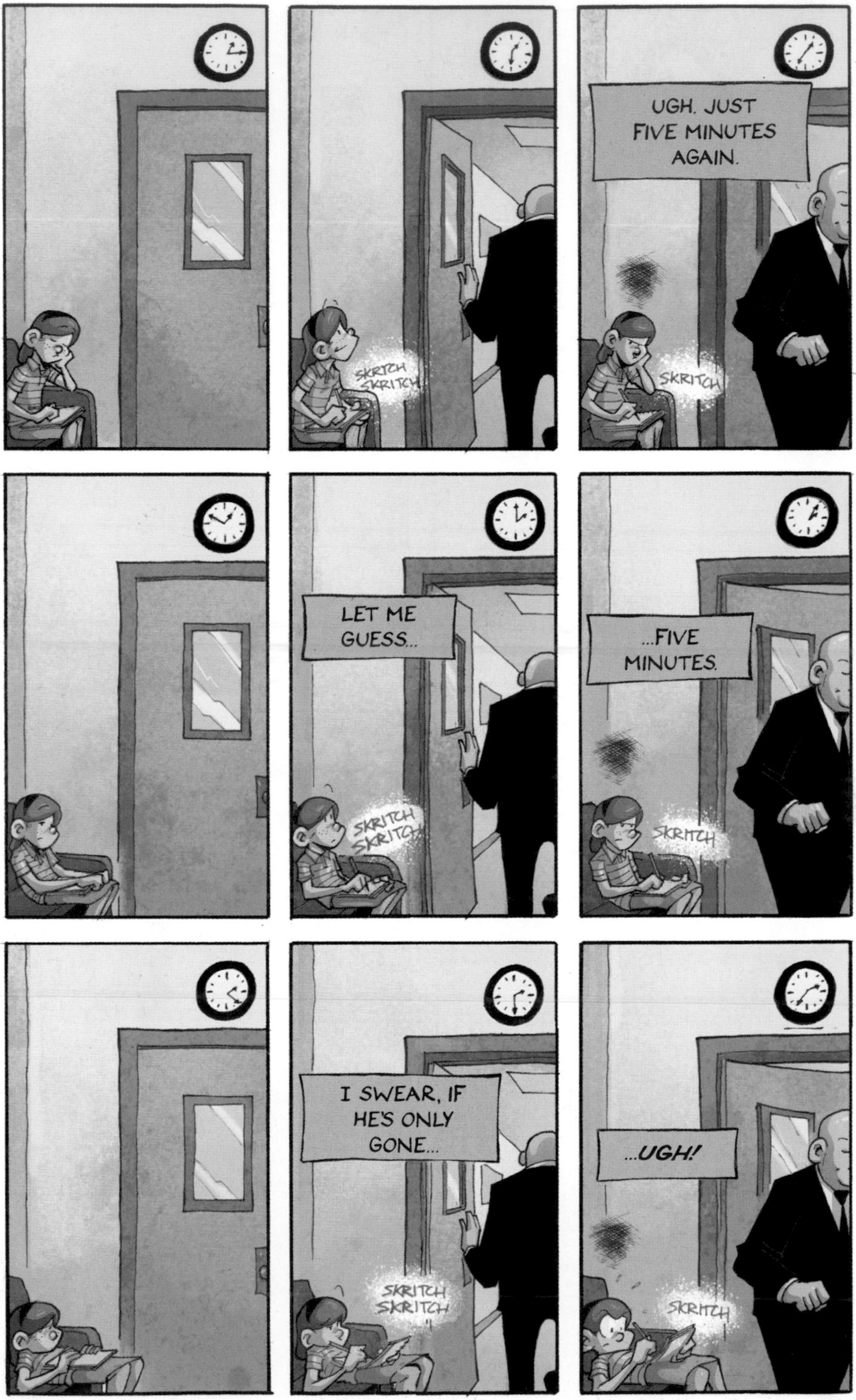
SKRITCH SKRITCH
UGH. JUST FIVE MINUTES AGAIN.
SKRITCH
LET ME GUESS...
SKRITCH SKRITCH
...FIVE MINUTES.
SKRITCH
I SWEAR, IF HE'S ONLY GONE...
SKRITCH SKRITCH
...UGH!
SKRITCH

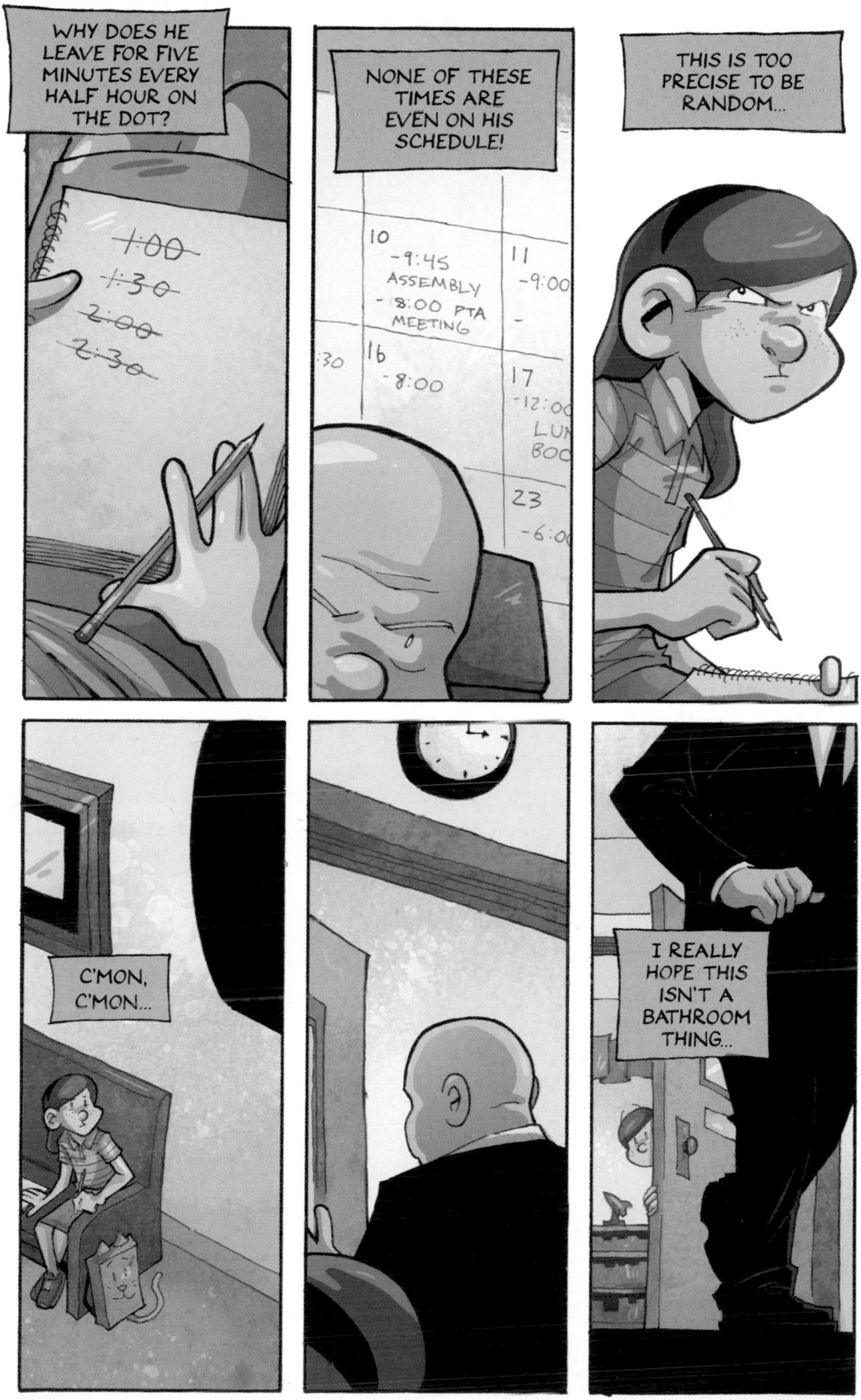
WHY DOES HE LEAVE FOR FIVE MINUTES EVERY HALF HOUR ON THE DOT?
1:00
1:30
2:00
2:30
NONE OF THESE TIMES ARE EVEN ON HIS SCHEDULE!
10
-9:45
ASSEMBLY
-8:00 PTA MEETING
11
-9:00
16
-8:00
17
23
THIS IS TOO PRECISE TO BE RANDOM...
C'MON, C'MON...
I REALLY HOPE THIS ISN'T A BATHROOM THING...

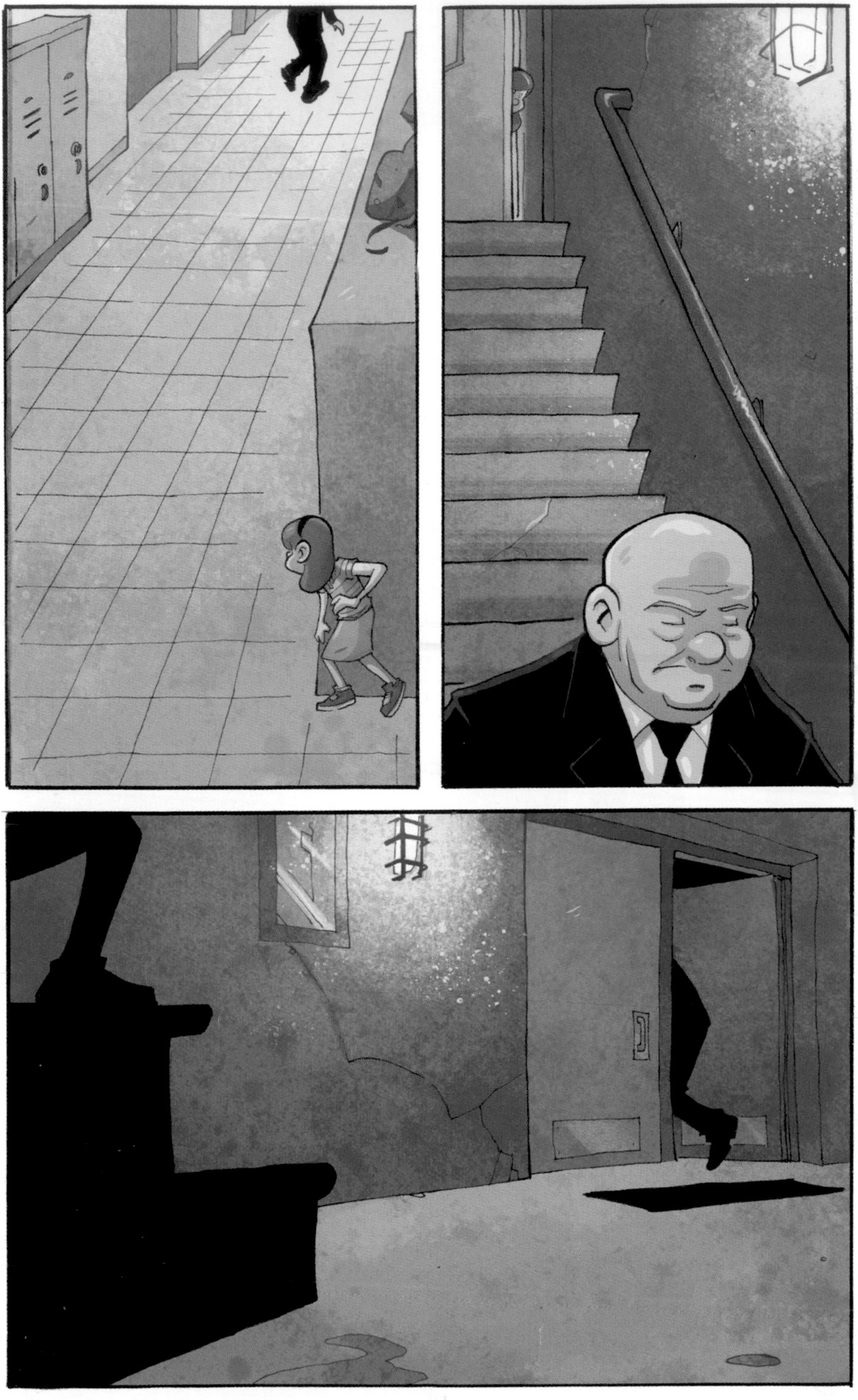

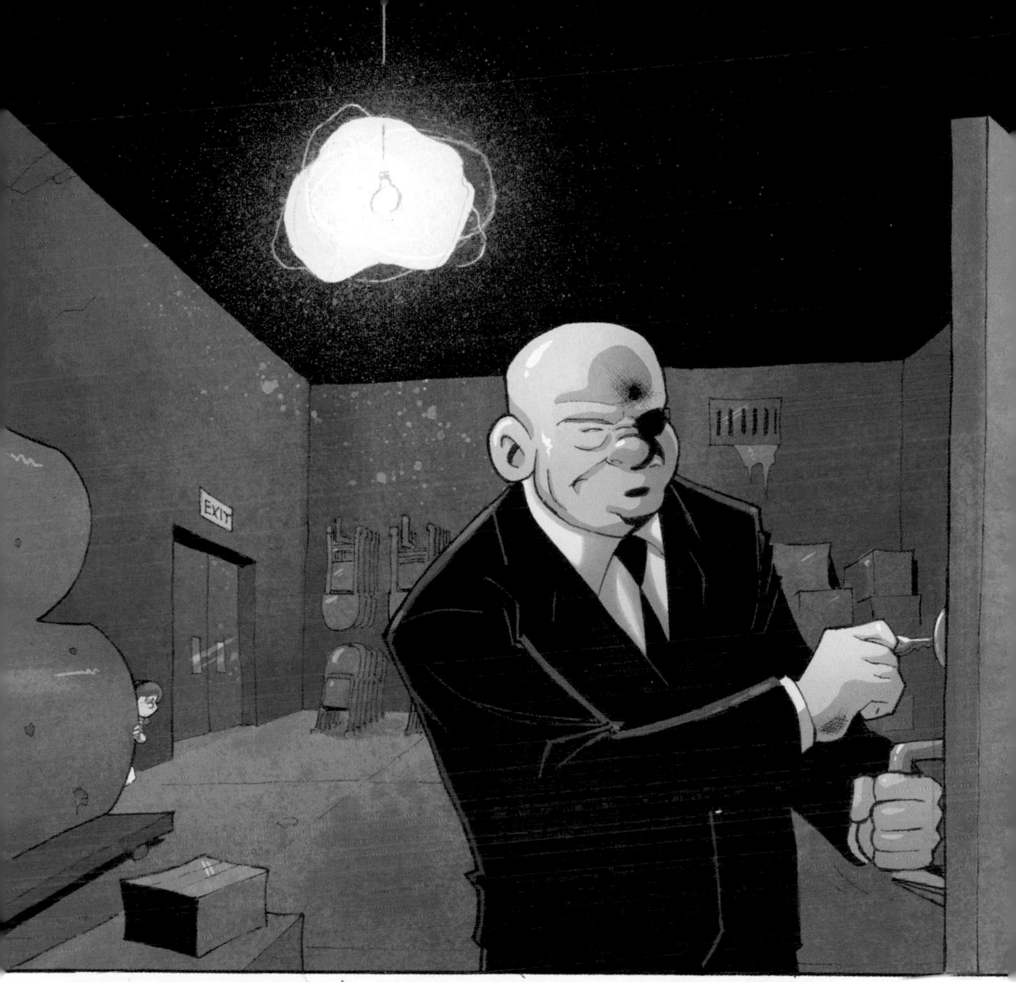
EXIT

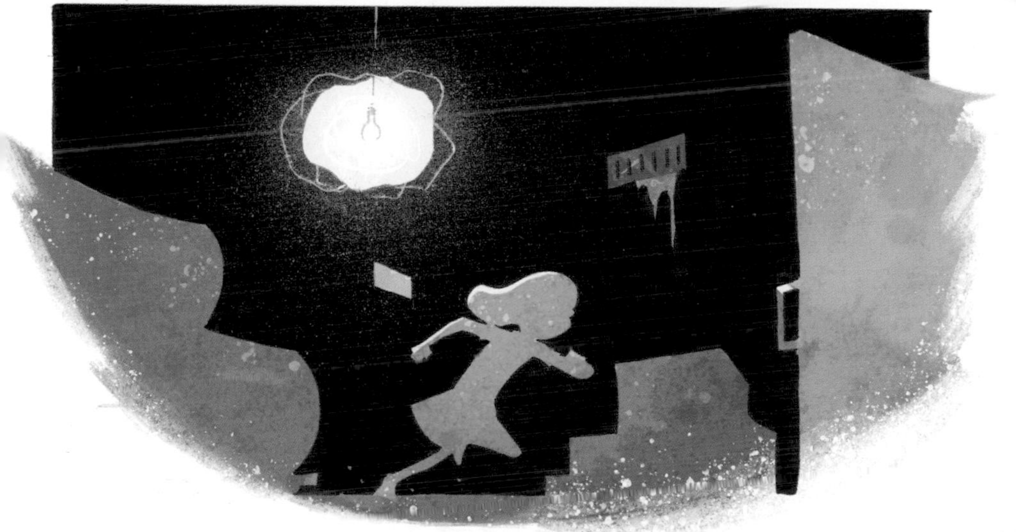

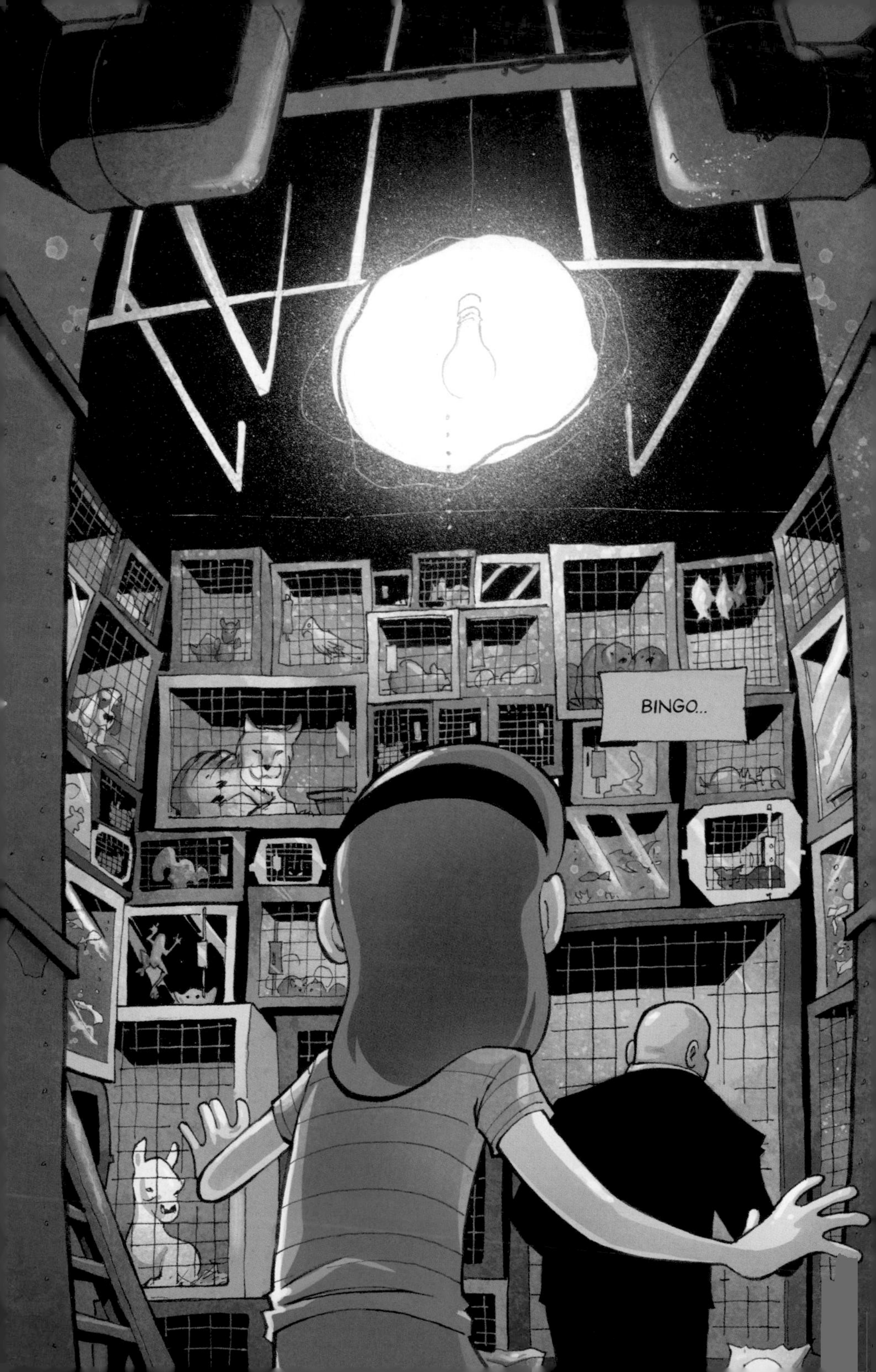
BINGO...

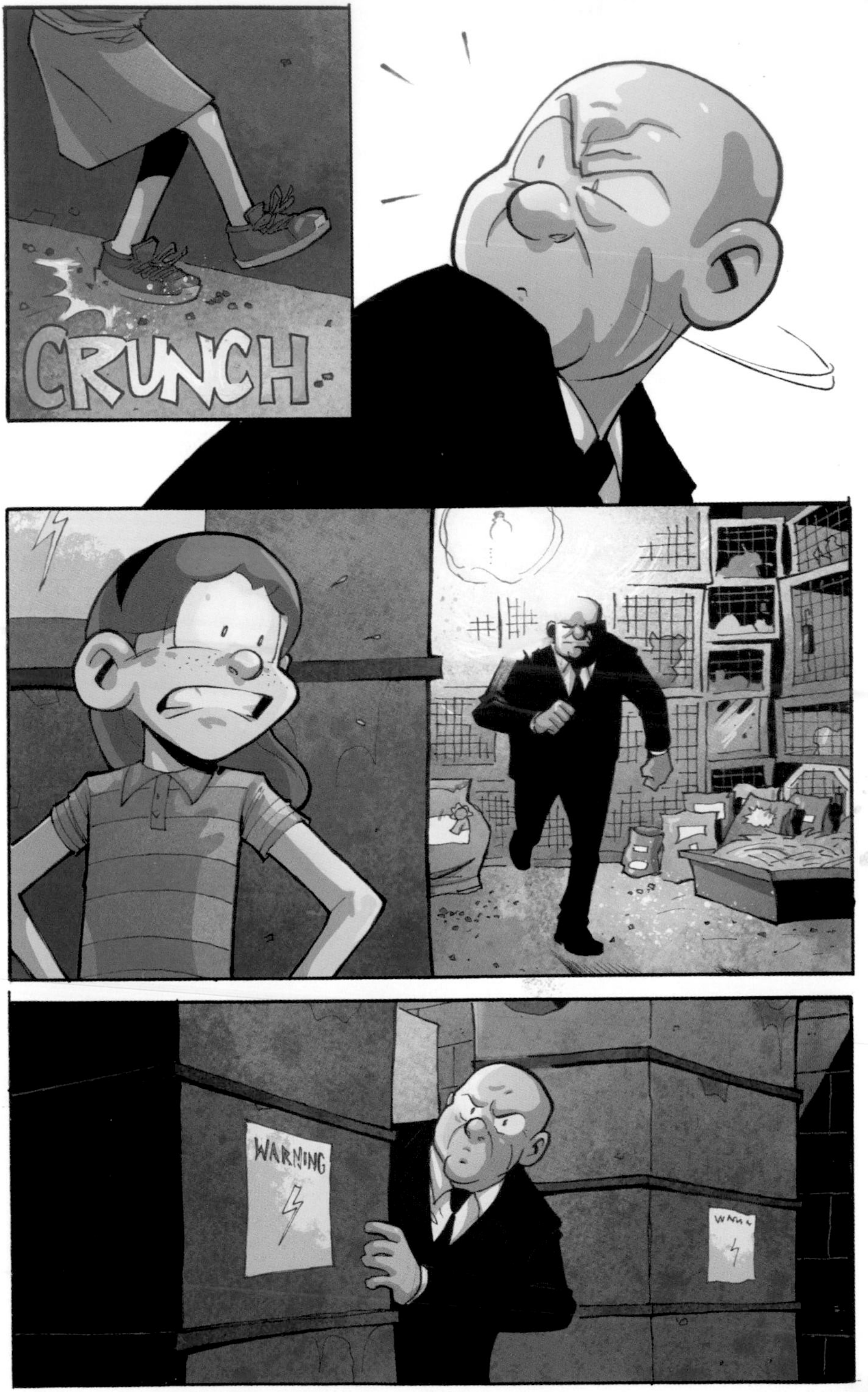
CRUNCH
WARNING

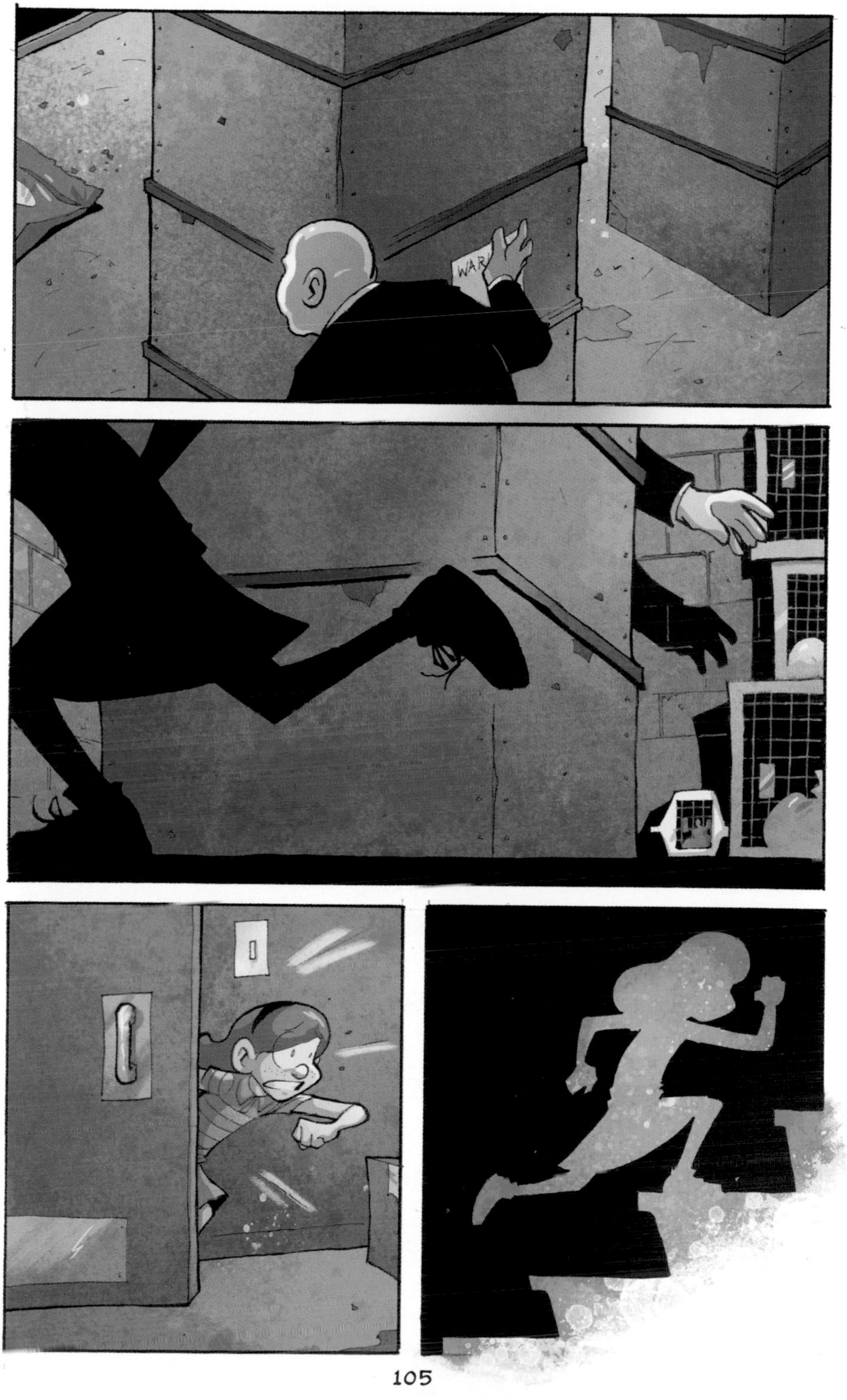
WAR

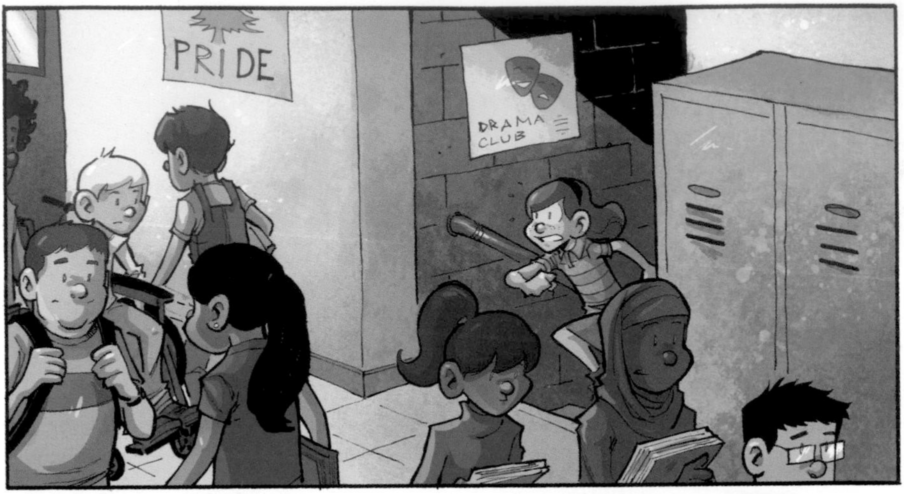
PRIDE
DRAMA CLUB

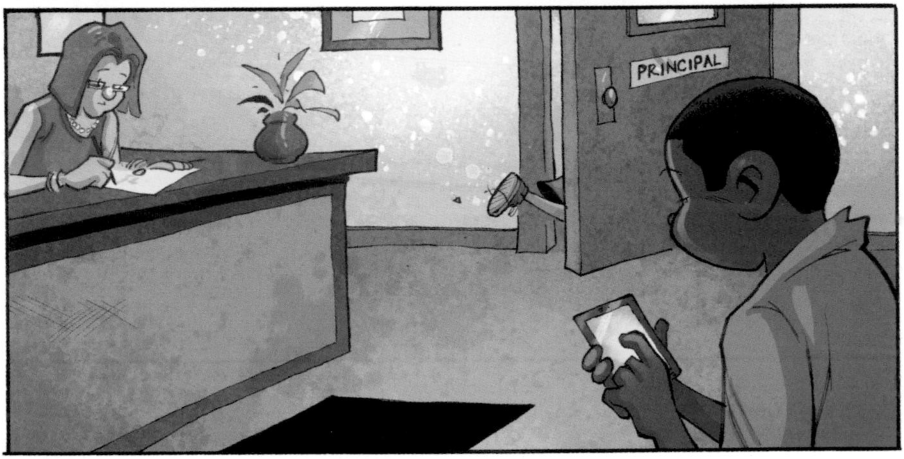
PRINCIPAL

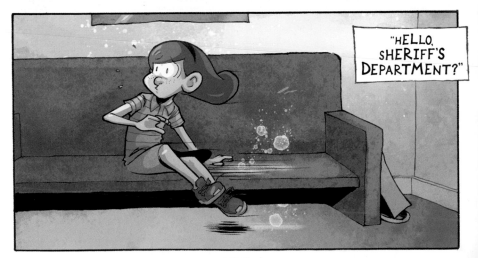

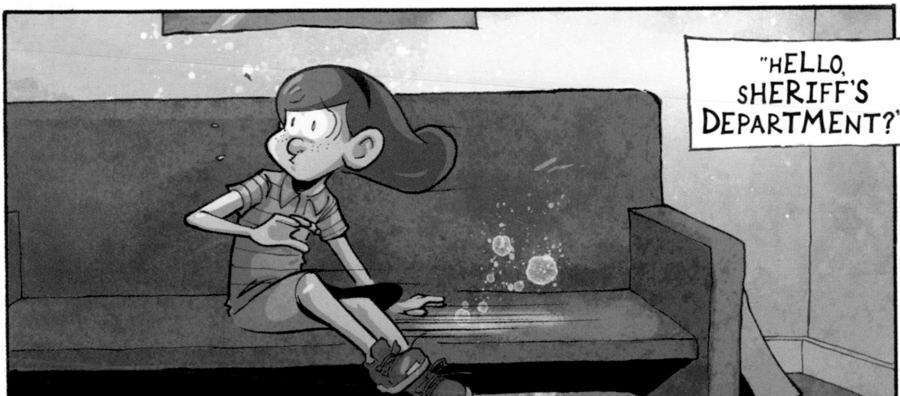
"HELLO, SHERIFF'S DEPARTMENT?"

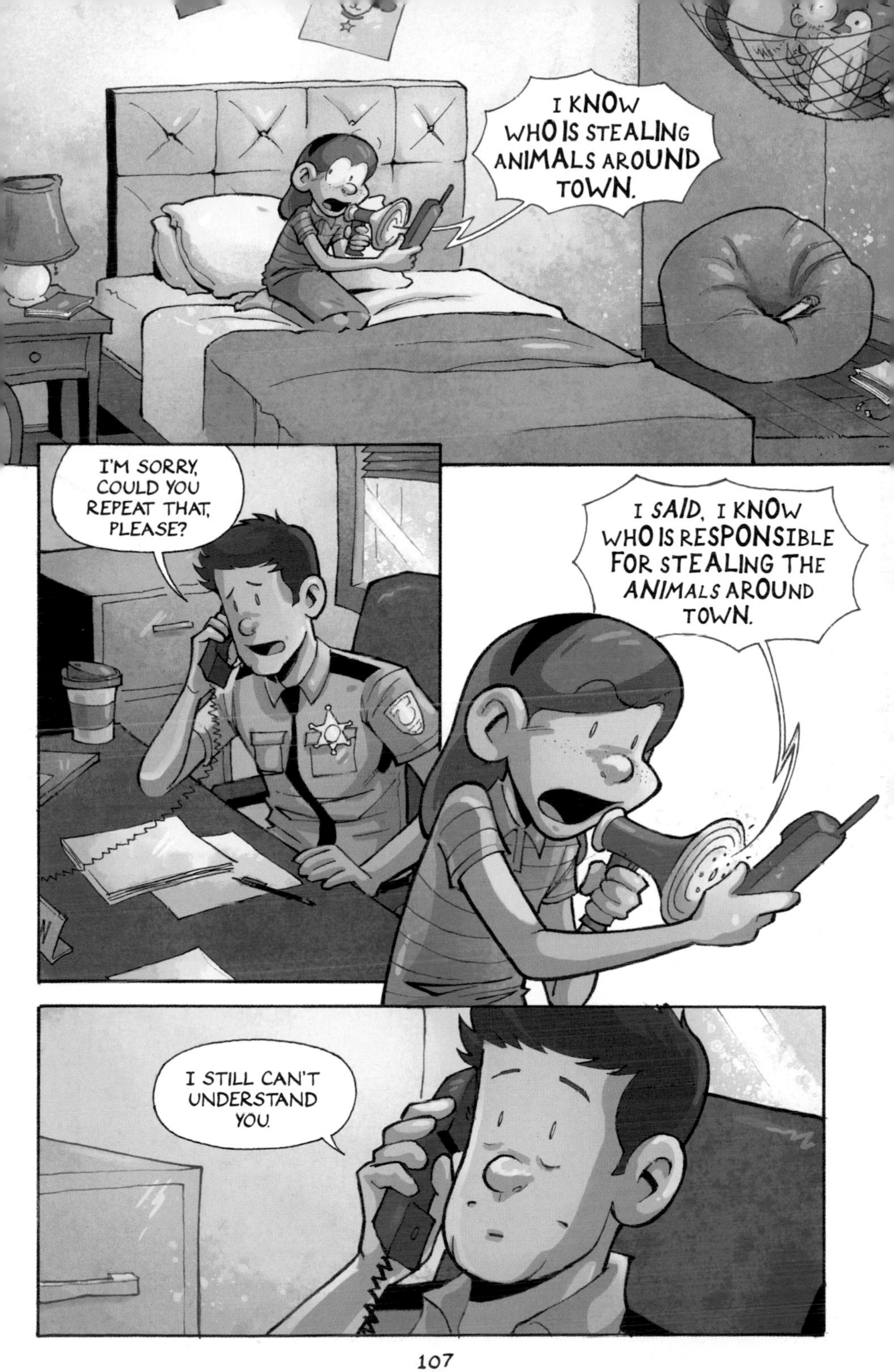
I KNOW WHO IS STEALING ANIMALS AROUND TOWN.
I'M SORRY, COULD YOU REPEAT THAT, PLEASE?
I SAID, I KNOW WHO IS RESPONSIBLE FOR STEALING THE ANIMALS AROUND TOWN.
I STILL CAN'T UNDERSTAND YOU.

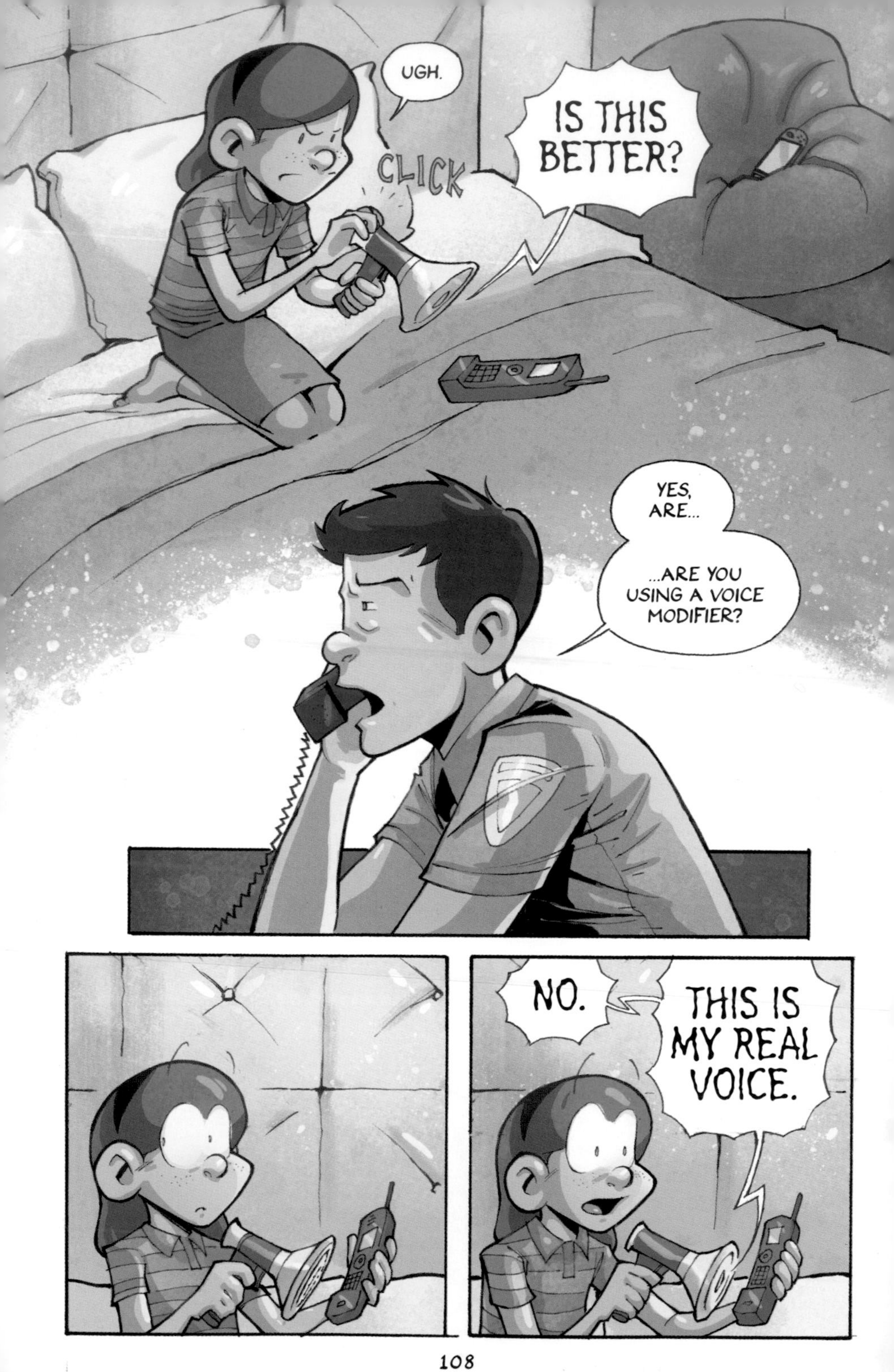
UGH.
CLICK
IS THIS BETTER?
YES, ARE...
...ARE YOU USING A VOICE MODIFIER?
NO.
THIS IS MY REAL VOICE.

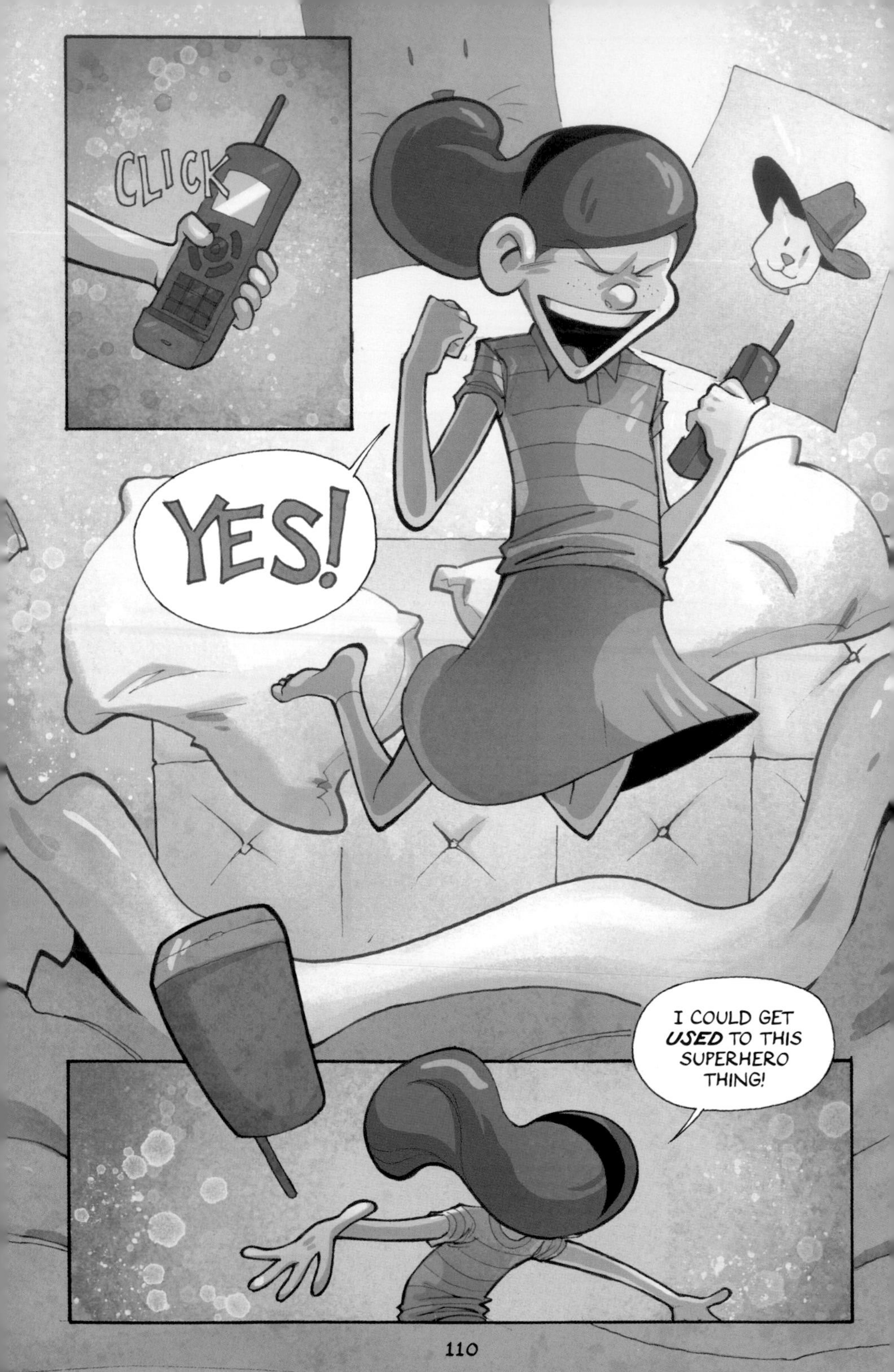
CLICK
YES!
I COULD GET *USED* TO THIS SUPERHERO THING!

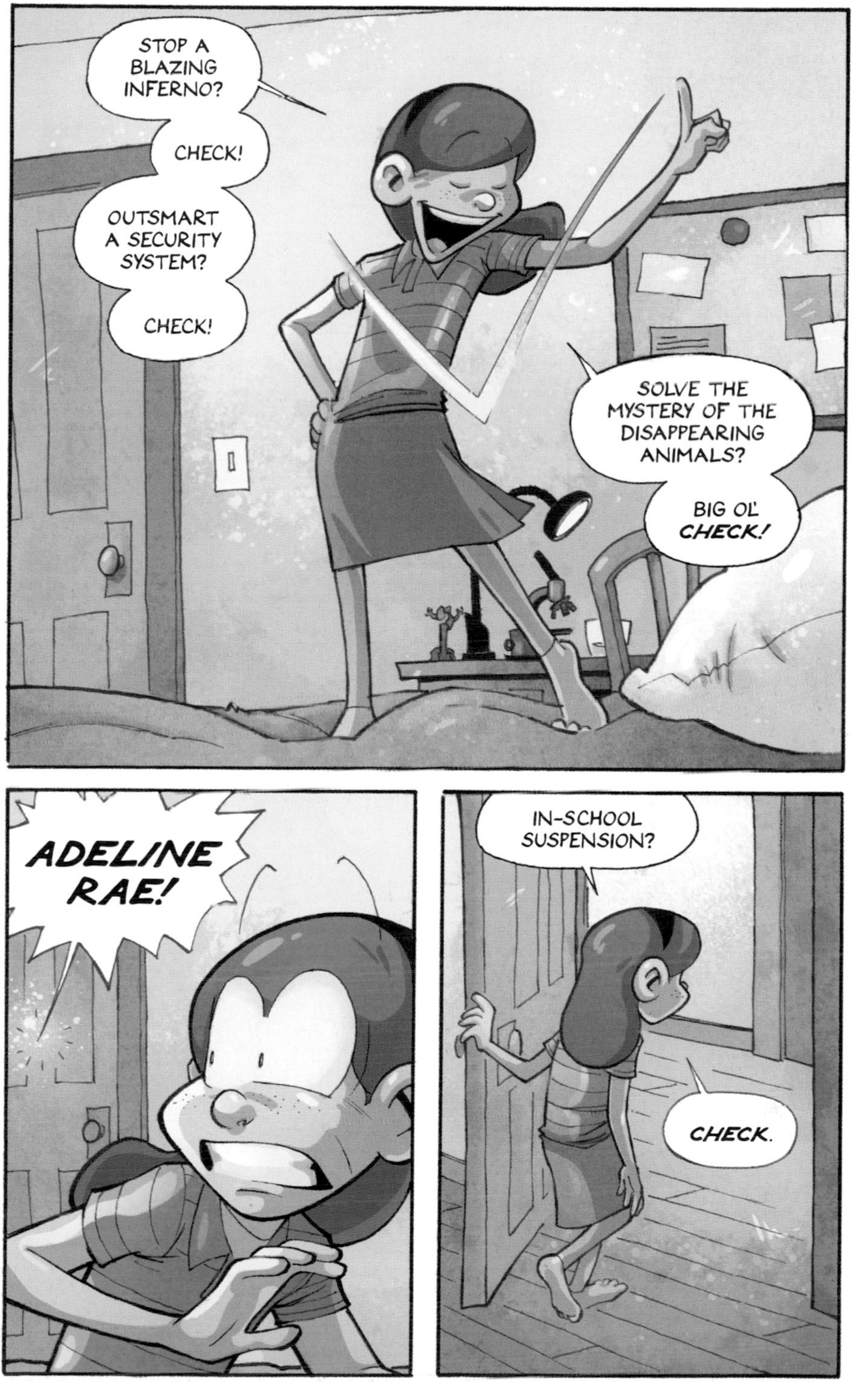
STOP A BLAZING INFERNO?
CHECK!
OUTSMART A SECURITY SYSTEM?
CHECK!
SOLVE THE MYSTERY OF THE DISAPPEARING ANIMALS?
BIG OL' *CHECK!*
ADELINE RAE!
IN-SCHOOL SUSPENSION?
CHECK.

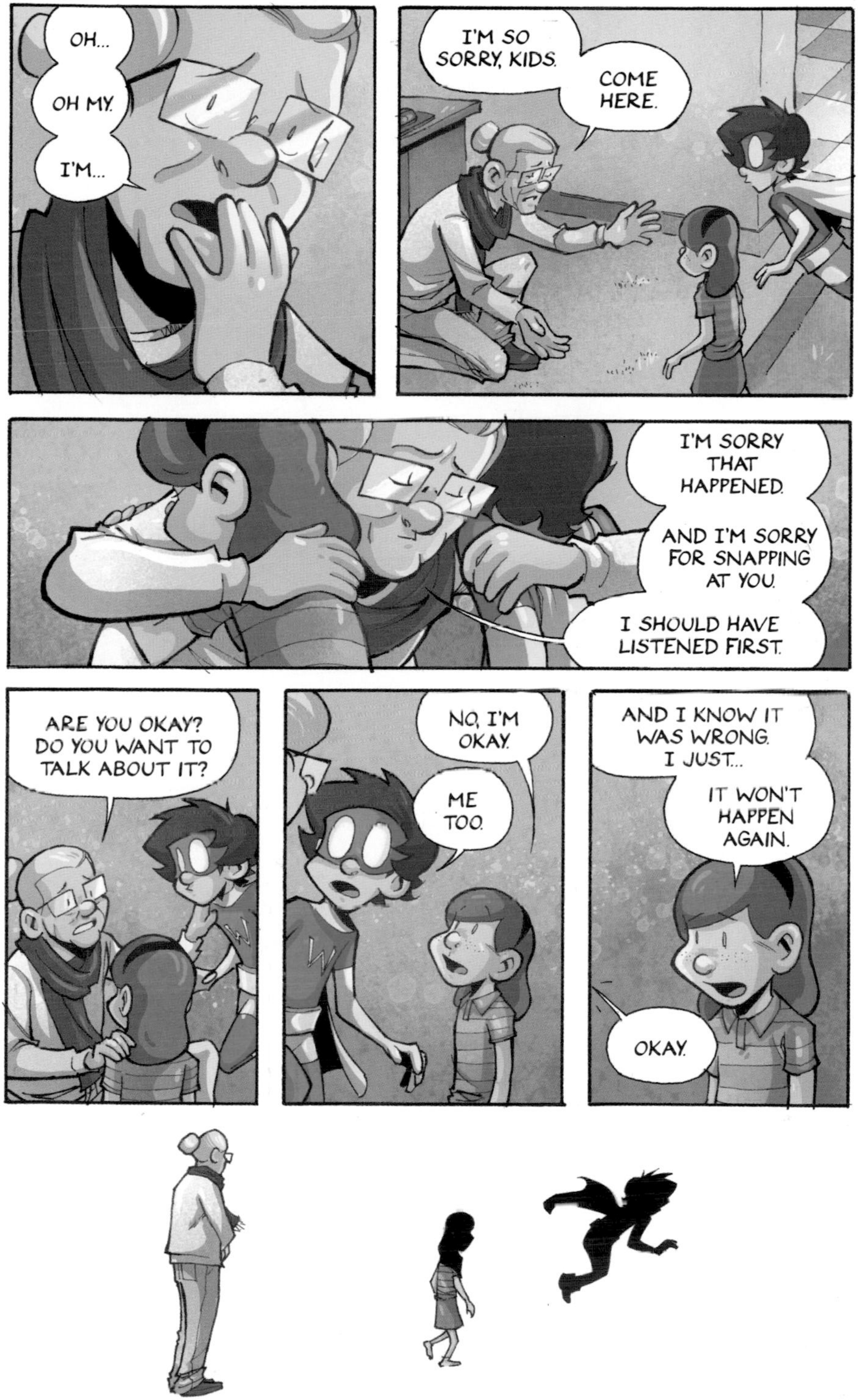
OH...
OH MY.
I'M...
I'M SO SORRY, KIDS.
COME HERE.
I'M SORRY THAT HAPPENED.
AND I'M SORRY FOR SNAPPING AT YOU.
I SHOULD HAVE LISTENED FIRST.
ARE YOU OKAY? DO YOU WANT TO TALK ABOUT IT?
NO, I'M OKAY.
ME TOO.
AND I KNOW IT WAS WRONG. I JUST...
IT WON'T HAPPEN AGAIN.
OKAY.

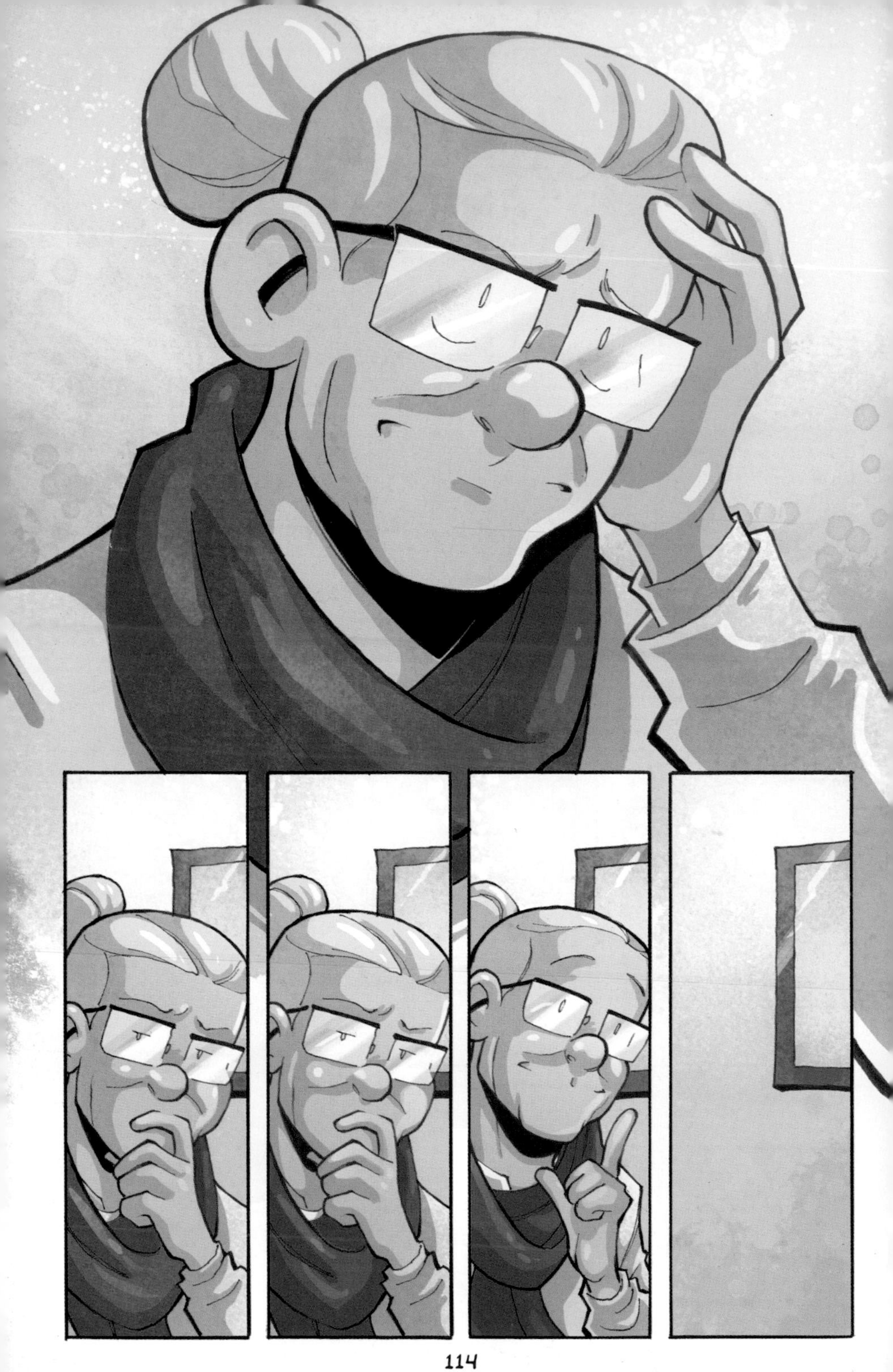

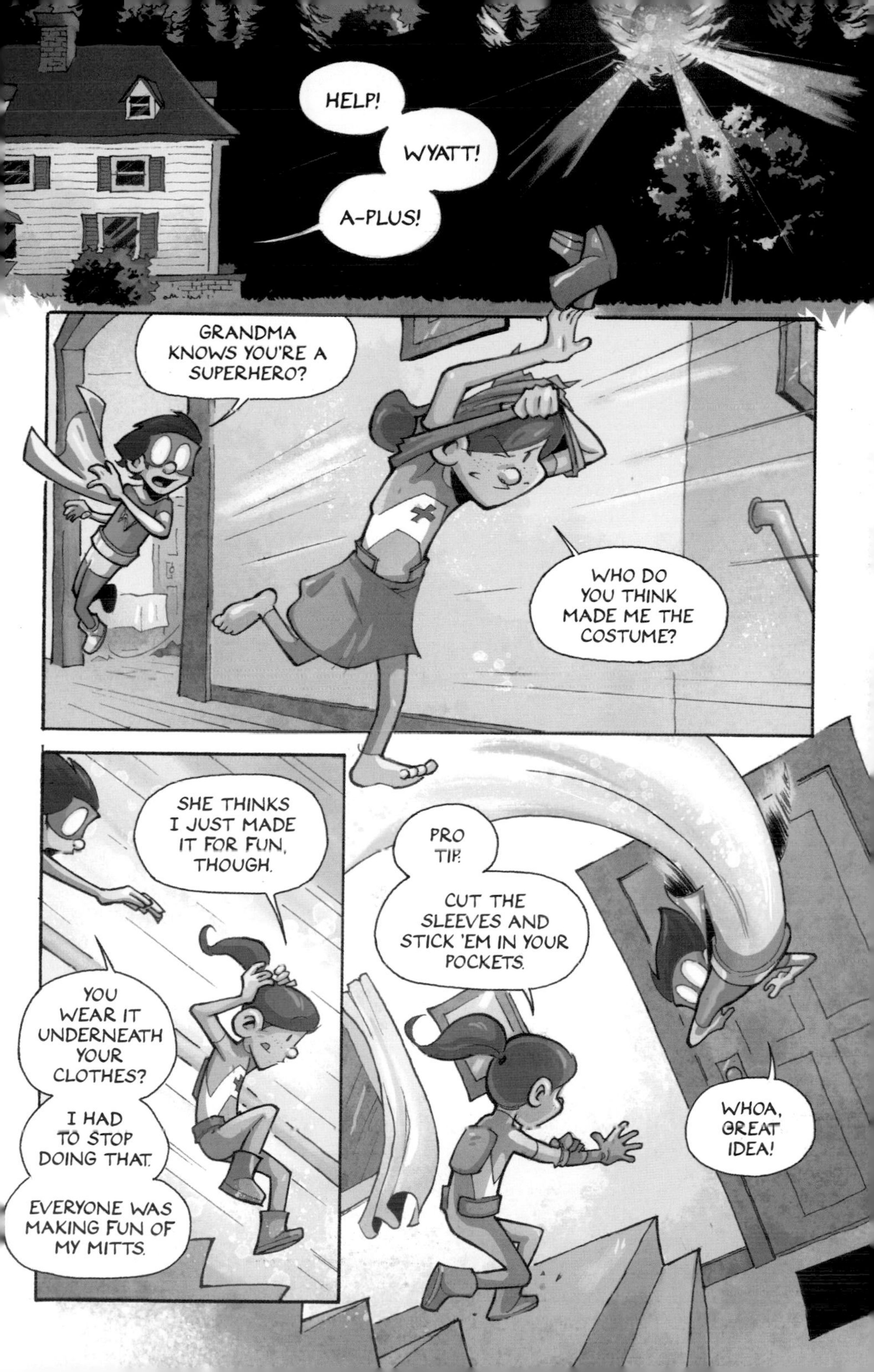
HELP!
WYATT!
A-PLUS!
GRANDMA KNOWS YOU'RE A SUPERHERO?
WHO DO YOU THINK MADE ME THE COSTUME?
SHE THINKS I JUST MADE IT FOR FUN, THOUGH.
YOU WEAR IT UNDERNEATH YOUR CLOTHES?
I HAD TO STOP DOING THAT.
EVERYONE WAS MAKING FUN OF MY MITTS.
PRO TIP.
CUT THE SLEEVES AND STICK 'EM IN YOUR POCKETS.
WHOA, GREAT IDEA!

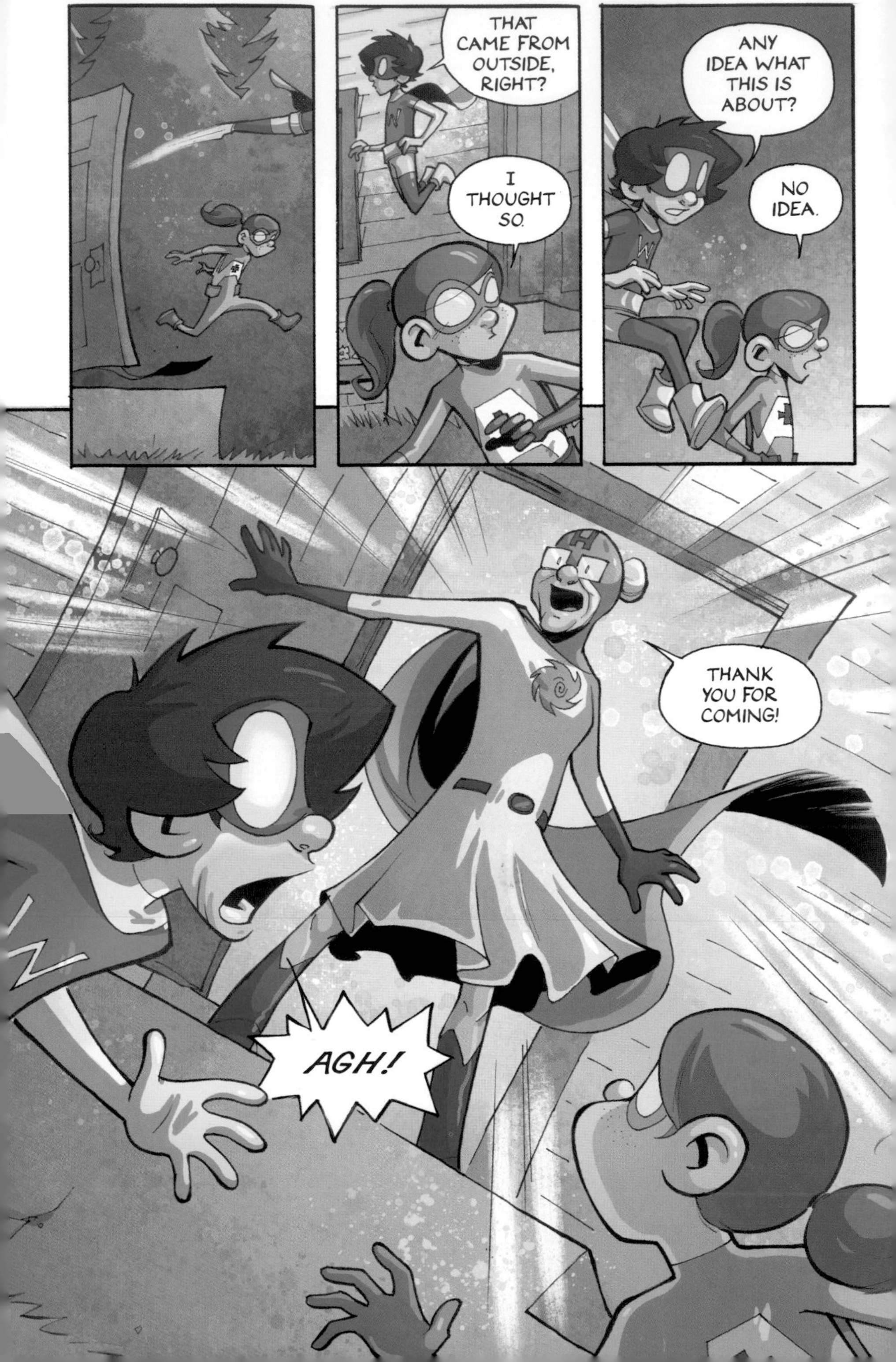

THAT CAME FROM OUTSIDE, RIGHT?
I THOUGHT SO.
ANY IDEA WHAT THIS IS ABOUT?
NO IDEA.
THANK YOU FOR COMING!
AGH!

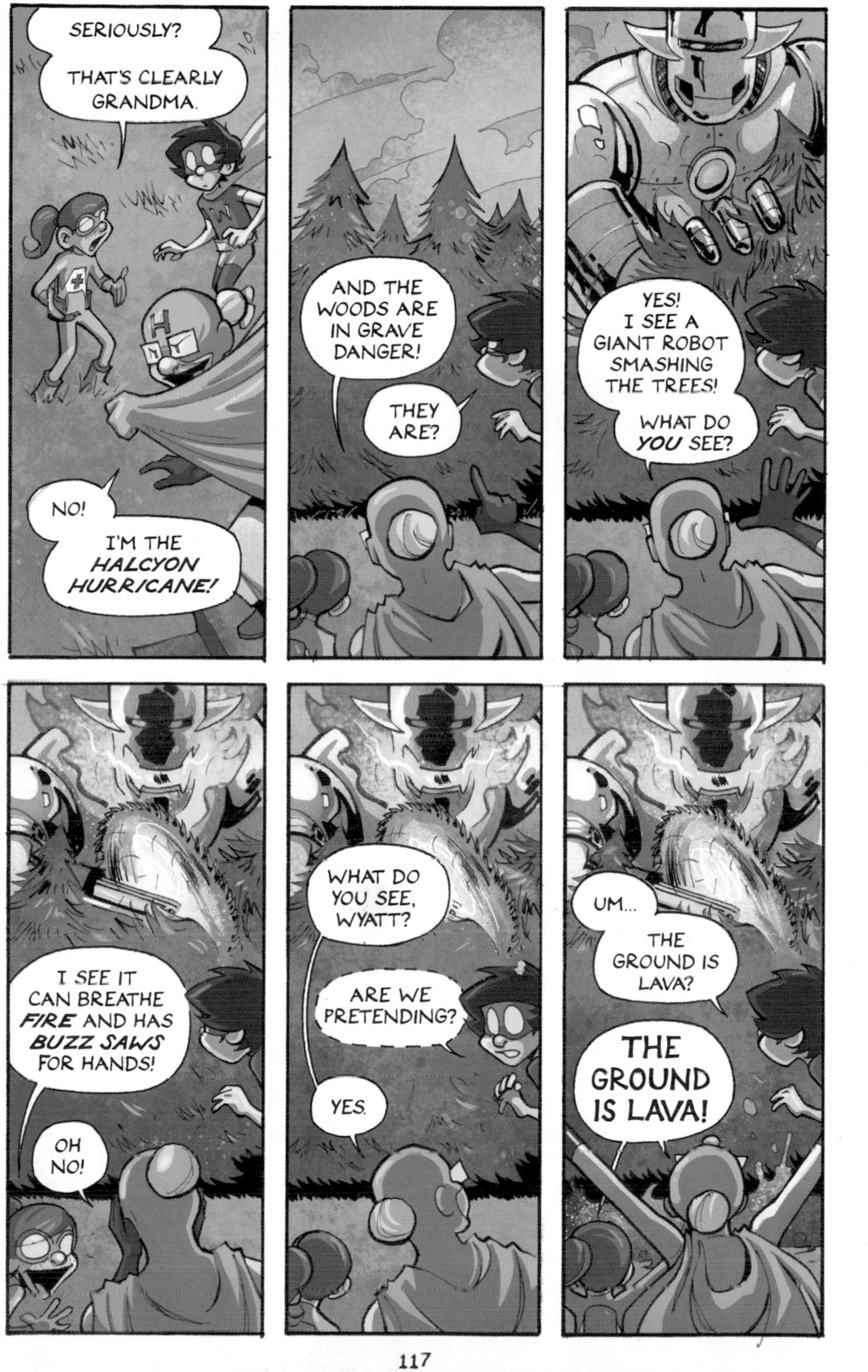
SERIOUSLY? THAT'S CLEARLY GRANDMA.
NO! I'M THE *HALCYON HURRICANE!*
AND THE WOODS ARE IN GRAVE DANGER!
THEY ARE?
YES! I SEE A GIANT ROBOT SMASHING THE TREES!
WHAT DO *YOU* SEE?
I SEE IT CAN BREATHE *FIRE* AND HAS *BUZZ SAWS* FOR HANDS!
OH NO!
WHAT DO YOU SEE, WYATT?
ARE WE PRETENDING?
YES.
UM...
THE GROUND IS LAVA?
THE GROUND IS LAVA!

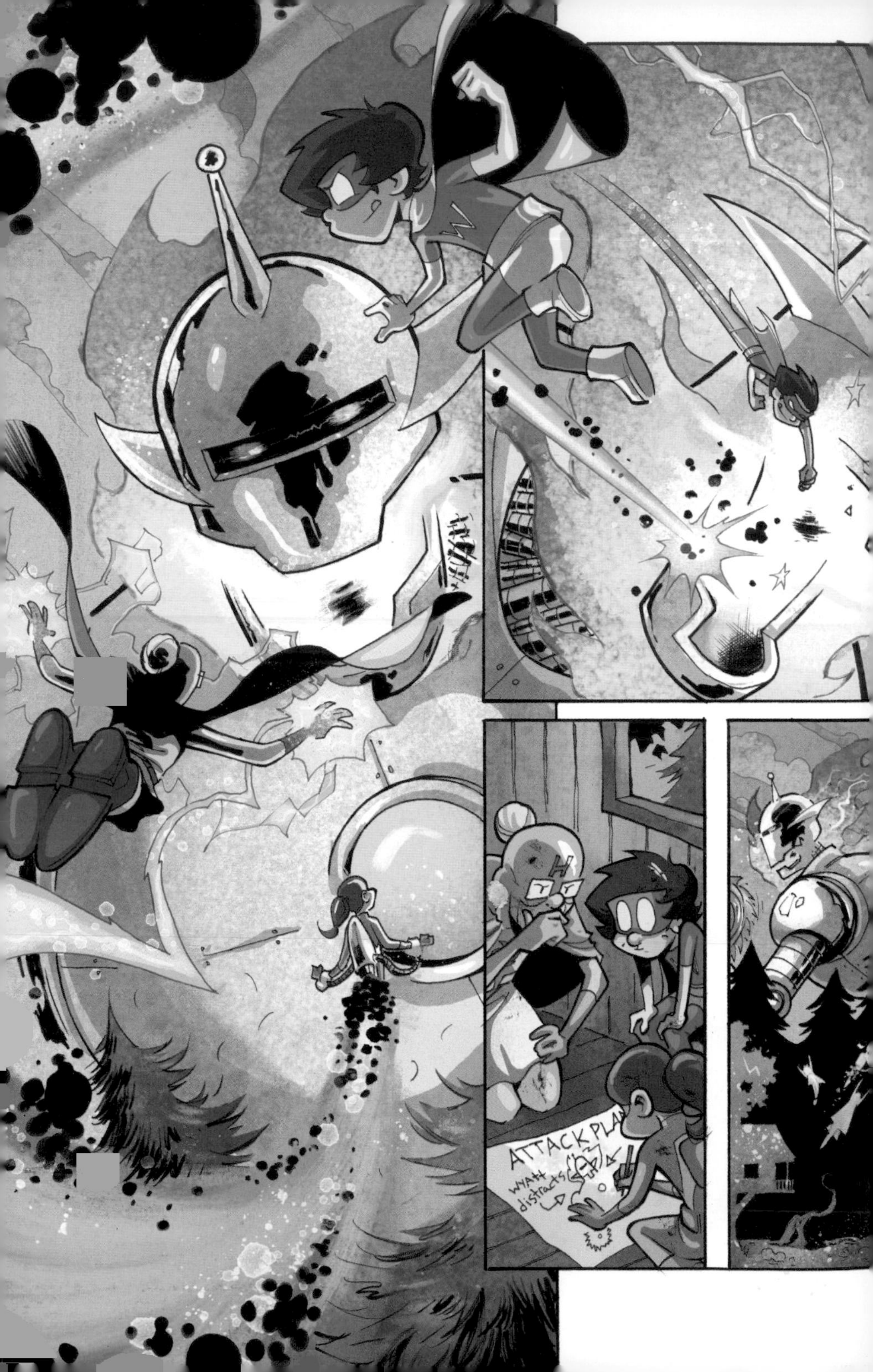
ATTACK PLA
wyatt distracts

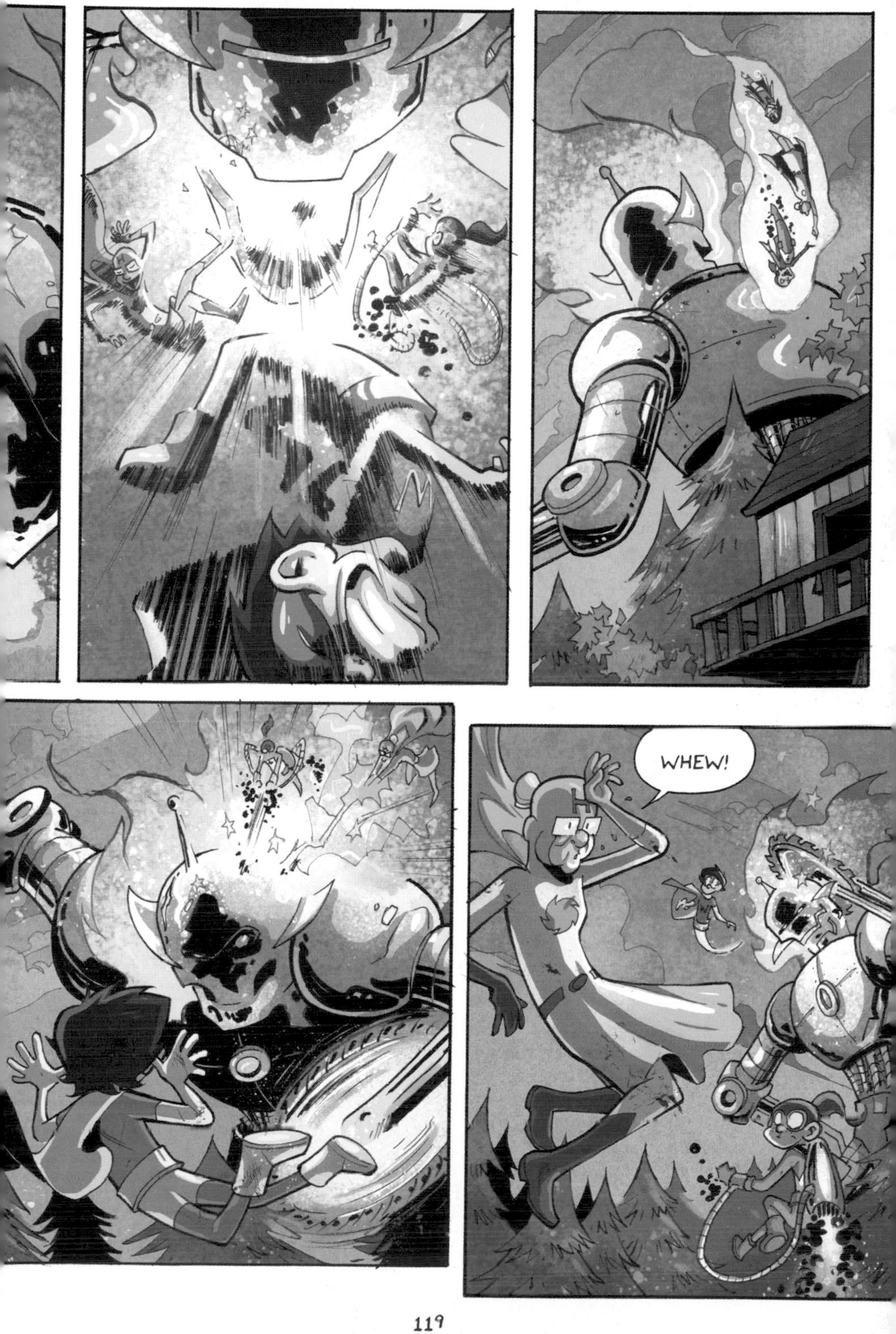
WHEW!

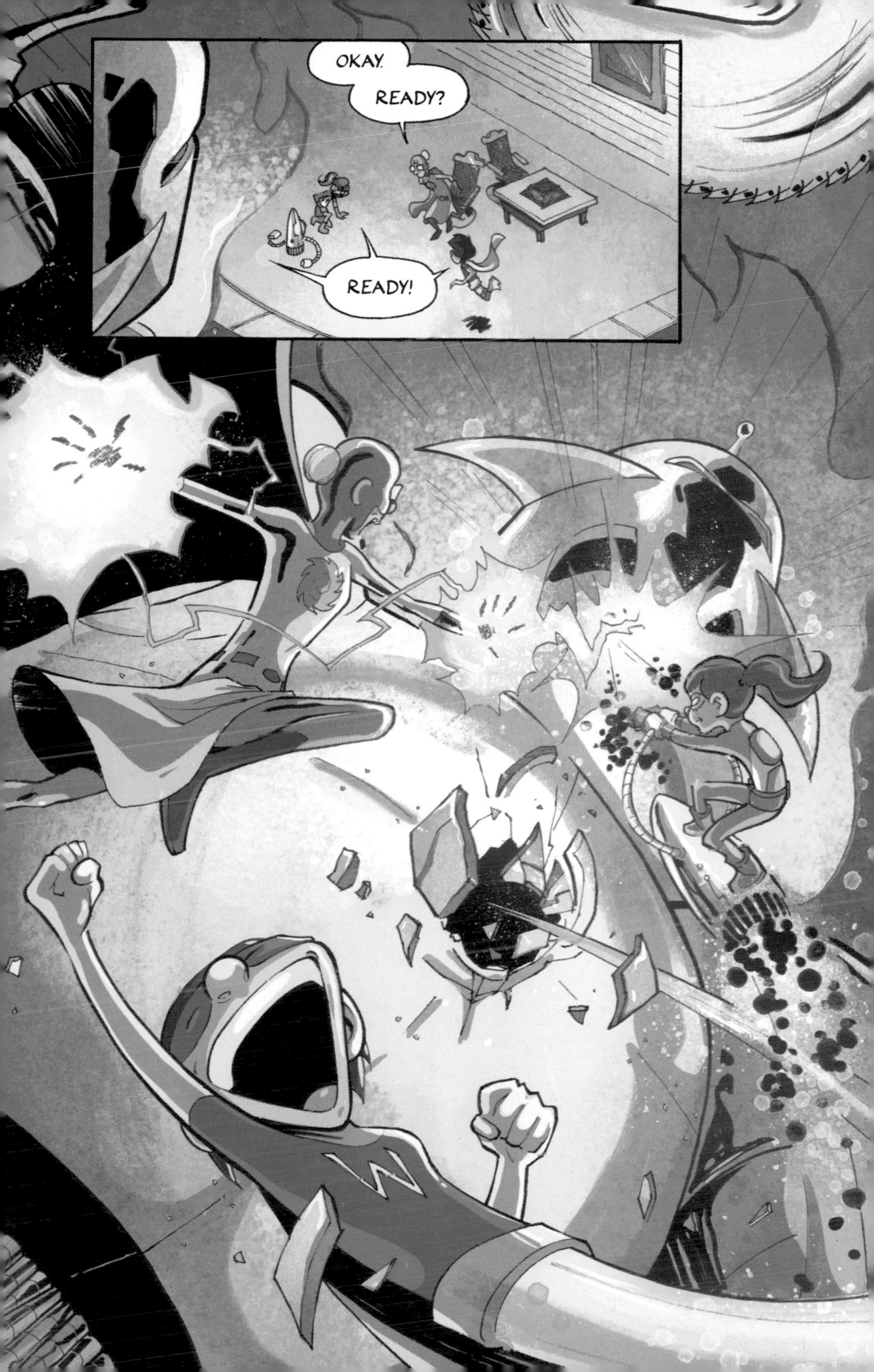
OKAY.
READY?
READY!

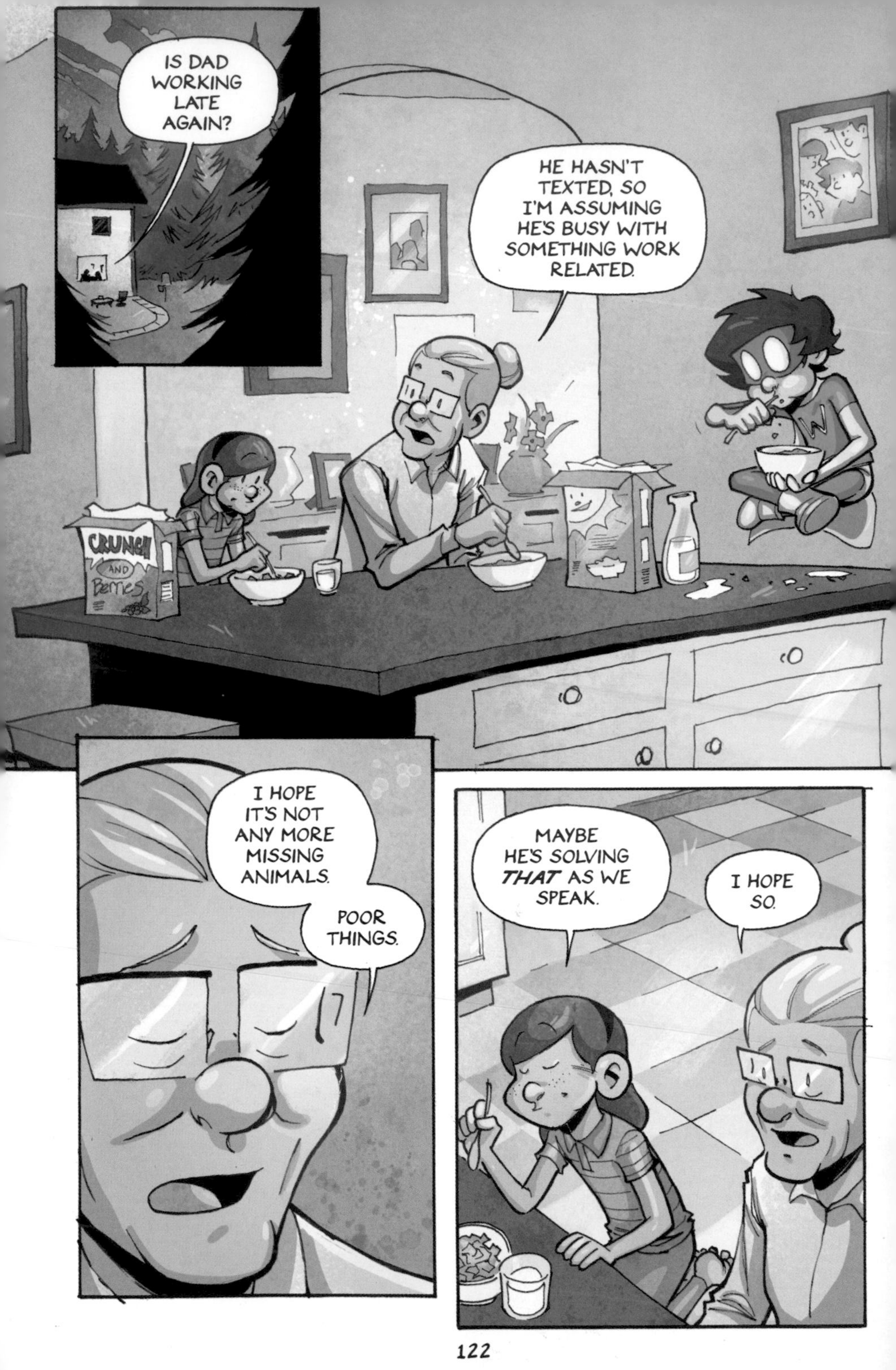
IS DAD WORKING LATE AGAIN?
HE HASN'T TEXTED, SO I'M ASSUMING HE'S BUSY WITH SOMETHING WORK RELATED.
CRUNCH AND Berries
I HOPE IT'S NOT ANY MORE MISSING ANIMALS.
POOR THINGS.
MAYBE HE'S SOLVING *THAT* AS WE SPEAK.
I HOPE SO.

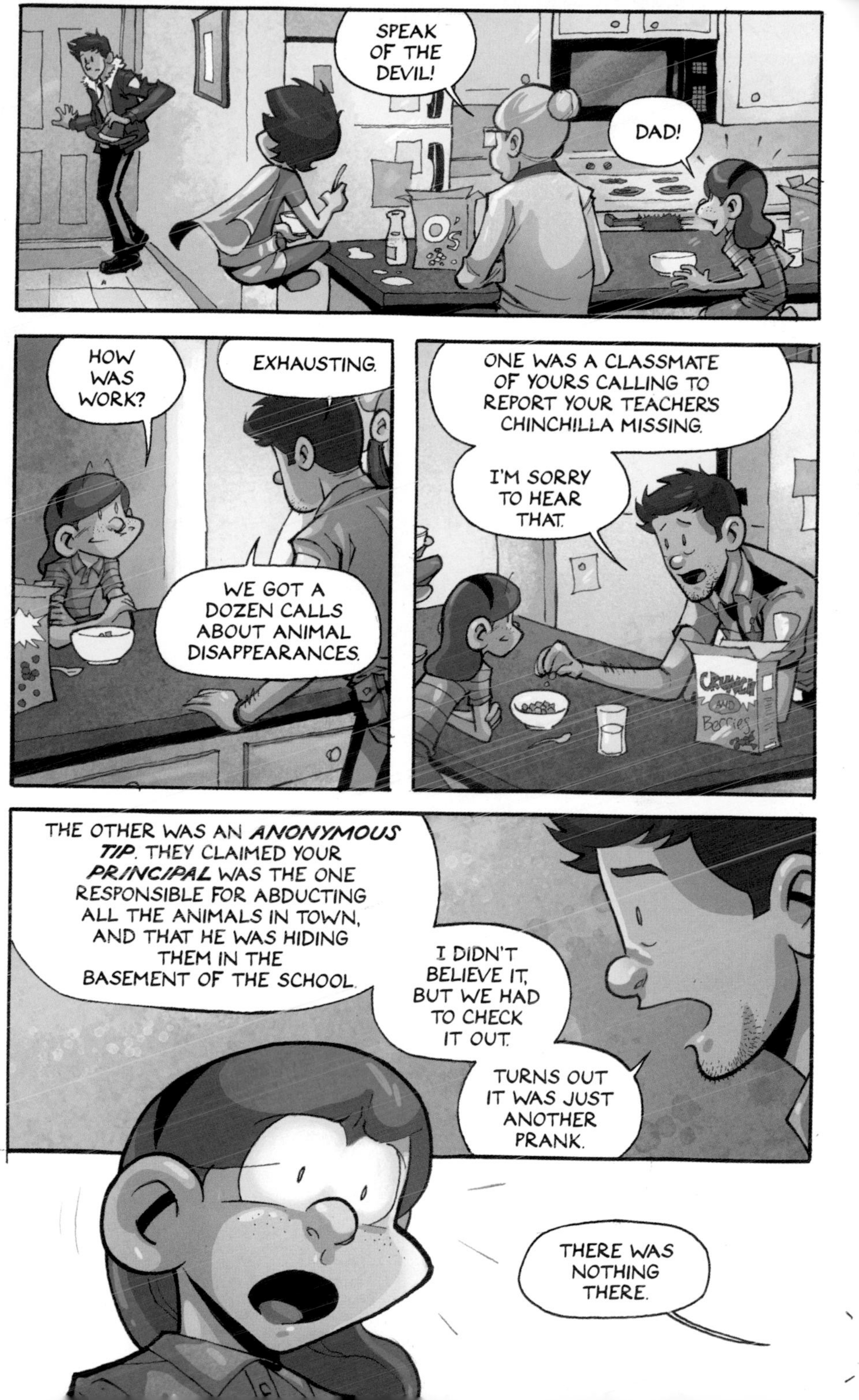
SPEAK OF THE DEVIL!
DAD!
HOW WAS WORK?
EXHAUSTING.
WE GOT A DOZEN CALLS ABOUT ANIMAL DISAPPEARANCES.
ONE WAS A CLASSMATE OF YOURS CALLING TO REPORT YOUR TEACHER'S CHINCHILLA MISSING.
I'M SORRY TO HEAR THAT.
O's
CRUNCH AND Berries
THE OTHER WAS AN *ANONYMOUS TIP*. THEY CLAIMED YOUR *PRINCIPAL* WAS THE ONE RESPONSIBLE FOR ABDUCTING ALL THE ANIMALS IN TOWN, AND THAT HE WAS HIDING THEM IN THE BASEMENT OF THE SCHOOL.
I DIDN'T BELIEVE IT, BUT WE HAD TO CHECK IT OUT.
TURNS OUT IT WAS JUST ANOTHER PRANK.
THERE WAS NOTHING THERE.

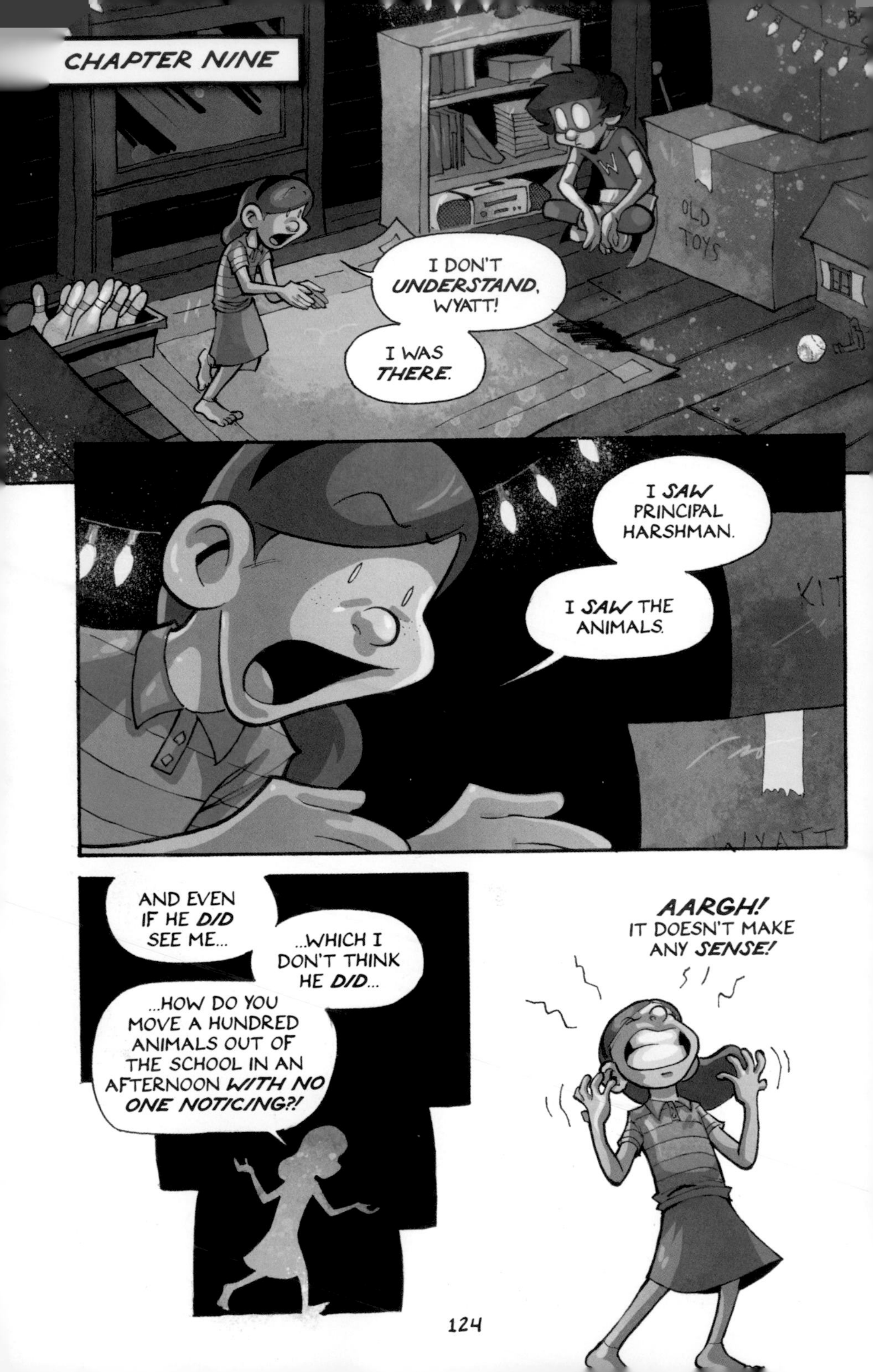
CHAPTER NINE
I DON'T UNDERSTAND, WYATT!
I WAS THERE.
OLD TOYS
I SAW PRINCIPAL HARSHMAN.
I SAW THE ANIMALS.
AND EVEN IF HE DID SEE ME...
...WHICH I DON'T THINK HE DID...
...HOW DO YOU MOVE A HUNDRED ANIMALS OUT OF THE SCHOOL IN AN AFTERNOON WITH NO ONE NOTICING?!
AARGH! IT DOESN'T MAKE ANY SENSE!

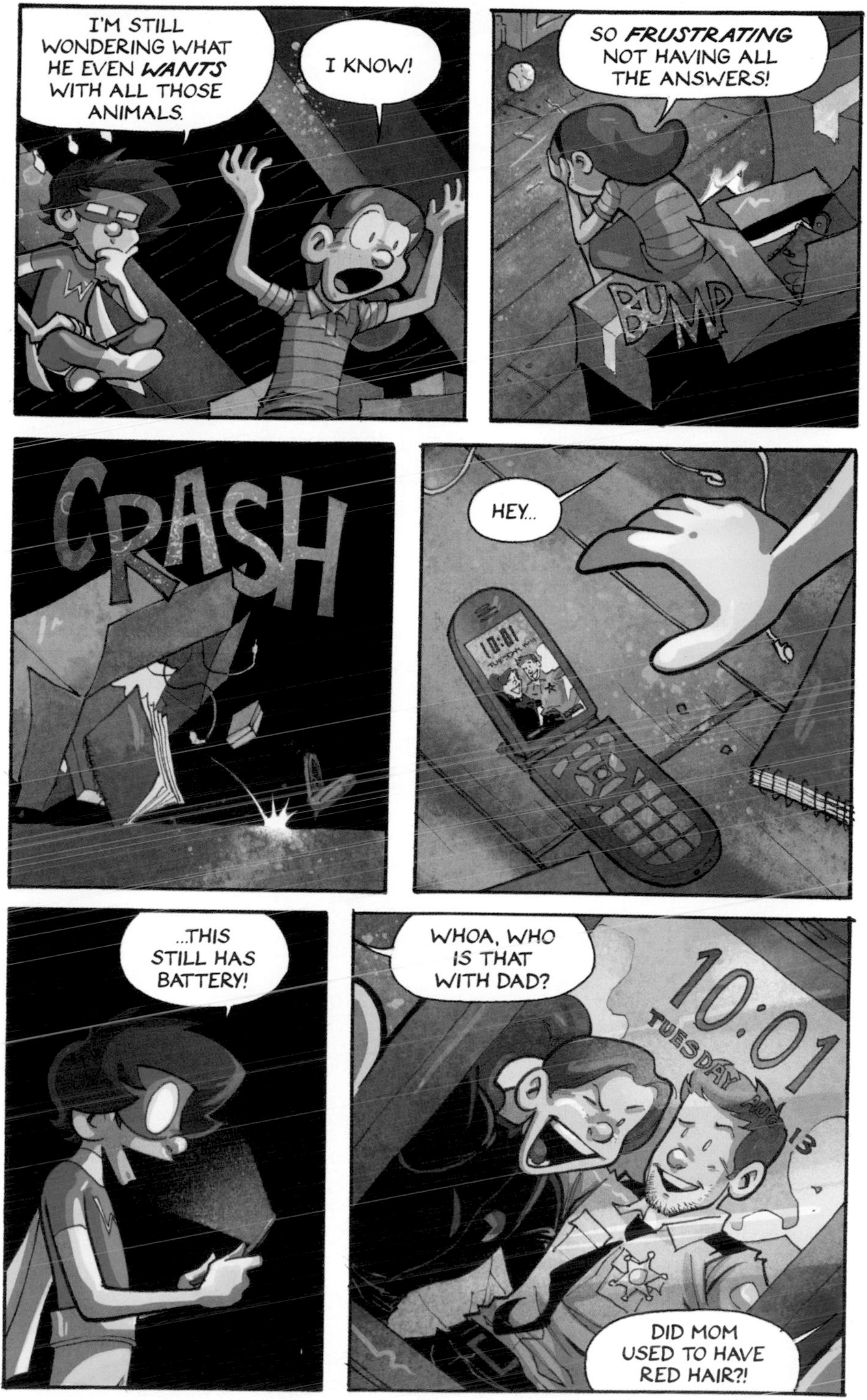
I'M STILL WONDERING WHAT HE EVEN *WANTS* WITH ALL THOSE ANIMALS.
I KNOW!
SO *FRUSTRATING* NOT HAVING ALL THE ANSWERS!
BUMP
CRASH
HEY...
...THIS STILL HAS BATTERY!
WHOA, WHO IS THAT WITH DAD?
10:01
TUESDAY AUG 13
DID MOM USED TO HAVE RED HAIR?!

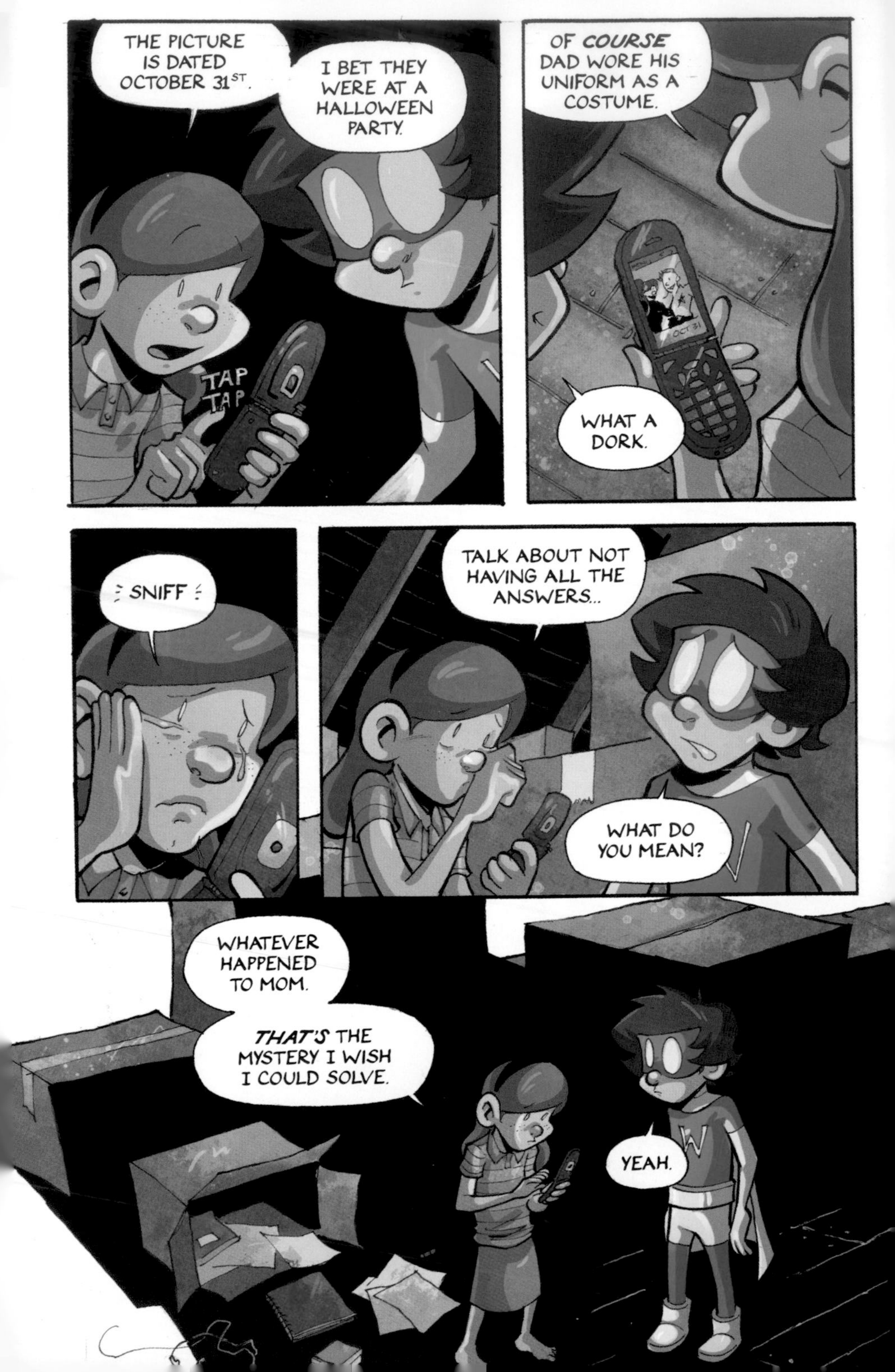
THE PICTURE IS DATED OCTOBER 31ST.
I BET THEY WERE AT A HALLOWEEN PARTY.
TAP TAP
OF COURSE DAD WORE HIS UNIFORM AS A COSTUME.
OCT 31
WHAT A DORK.
SNIFF
TALK ABOUT NOT HAVING ALL THE ANSWERS...
WHAT DO YOU MEAN?
WHATEVER HAPPENED TO MOM.
THAT'S THE MYSTERY I WISH I COULD SOLVE.
YEAH.

127

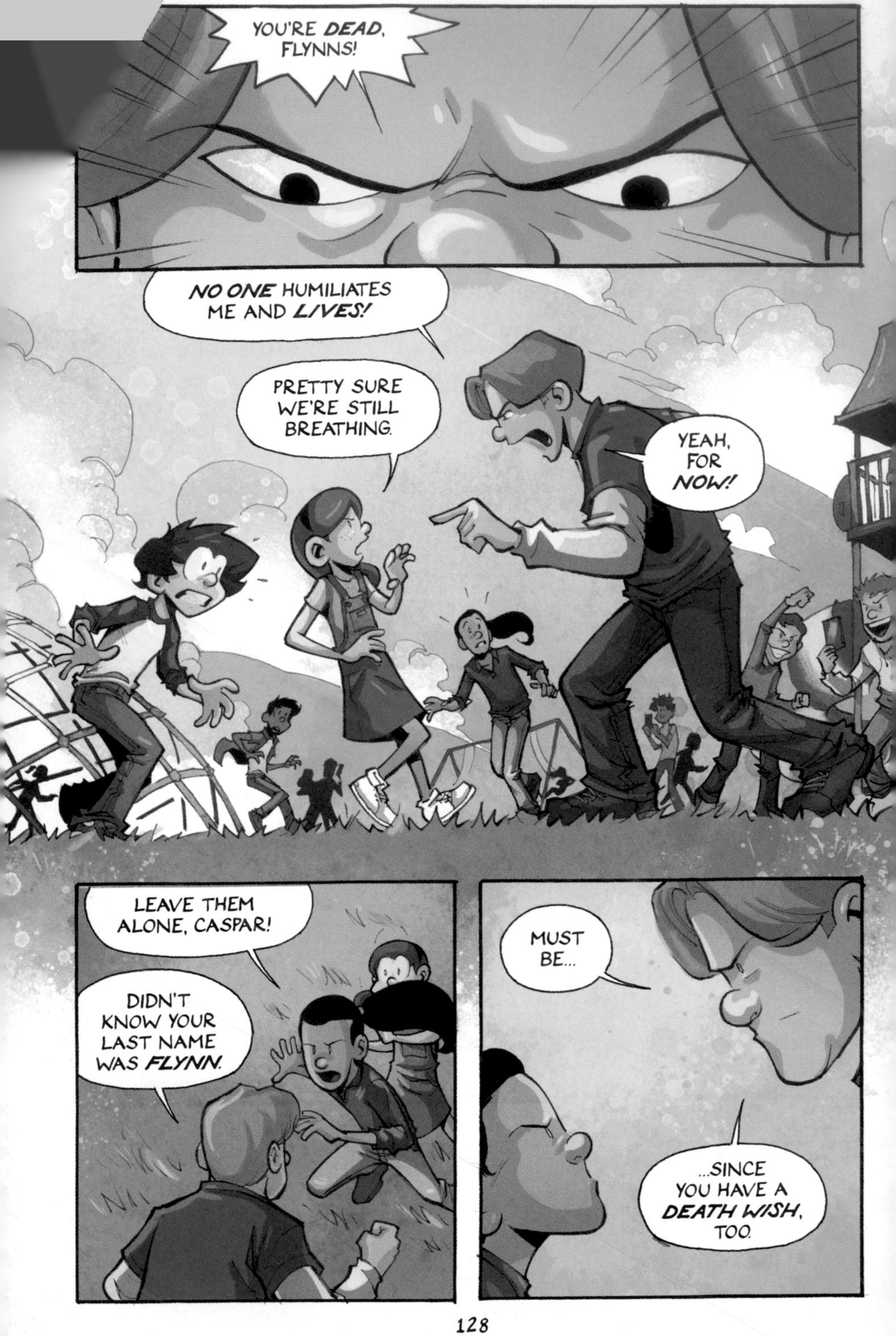
YOU'RE DEAD, FLYNNS!
NO ONE HUMILIATES ME AND LIVES!
PRETTY SURE WE'RE STILL BREATHING.
YEAH, FOR NOW!
LEAVE THEM ALONE, CASPAR!
DIDN'T KNOW YOUR LAST NAME WAS FLYNN.
MUST BE...
...SINCE YOU HAVE A DEATH WISH, TOO.

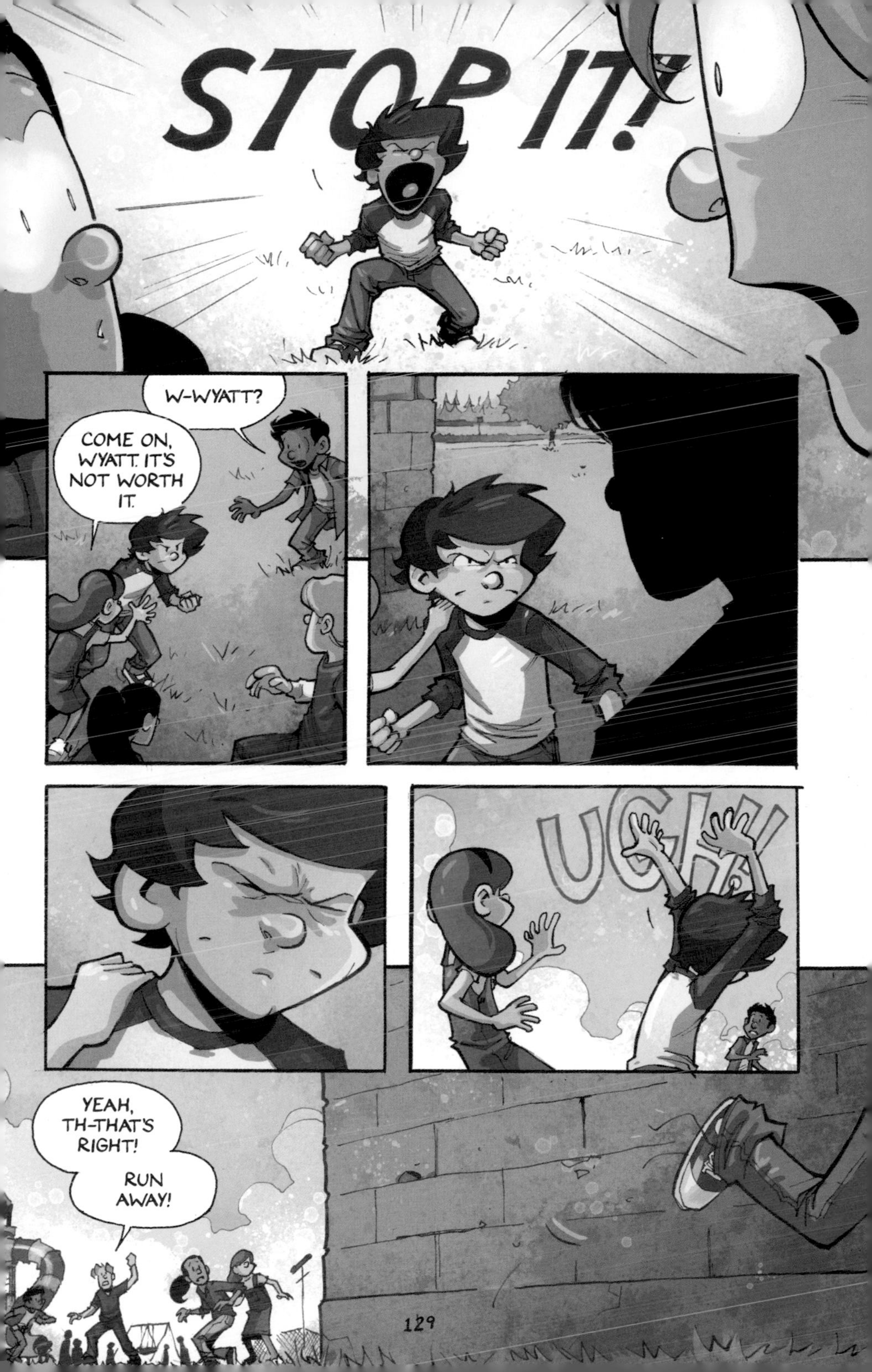
STOP IT!
W-WYATT?
COME ON, WYATT. IT'S NOT WORTH IT.
UGH!
YEAH, TH-THAT'S RIGHT!
RUN AWAY!

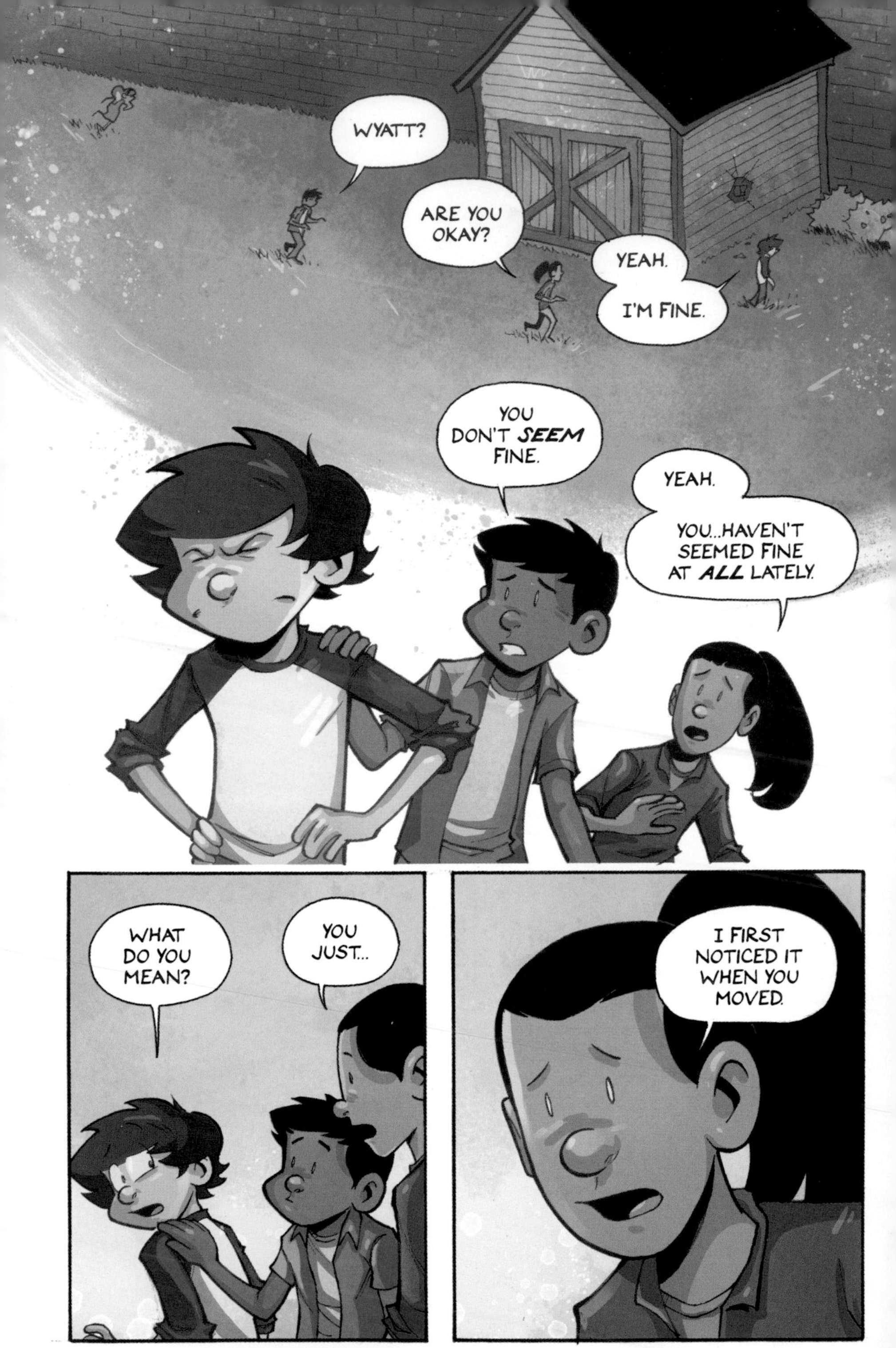
WYATT?
ARE YOU OKAY?
YEAH.
I'M FINE.
YOU DON'T SEEM FINE.
YEAH.
YOU...HAVEN'T SEEMED FINE AT ALL LATELY.
WHAT DO YOU MEAN?
YOU JUST...
I FIRST NOTICED IT WHEN YOU MOVED.

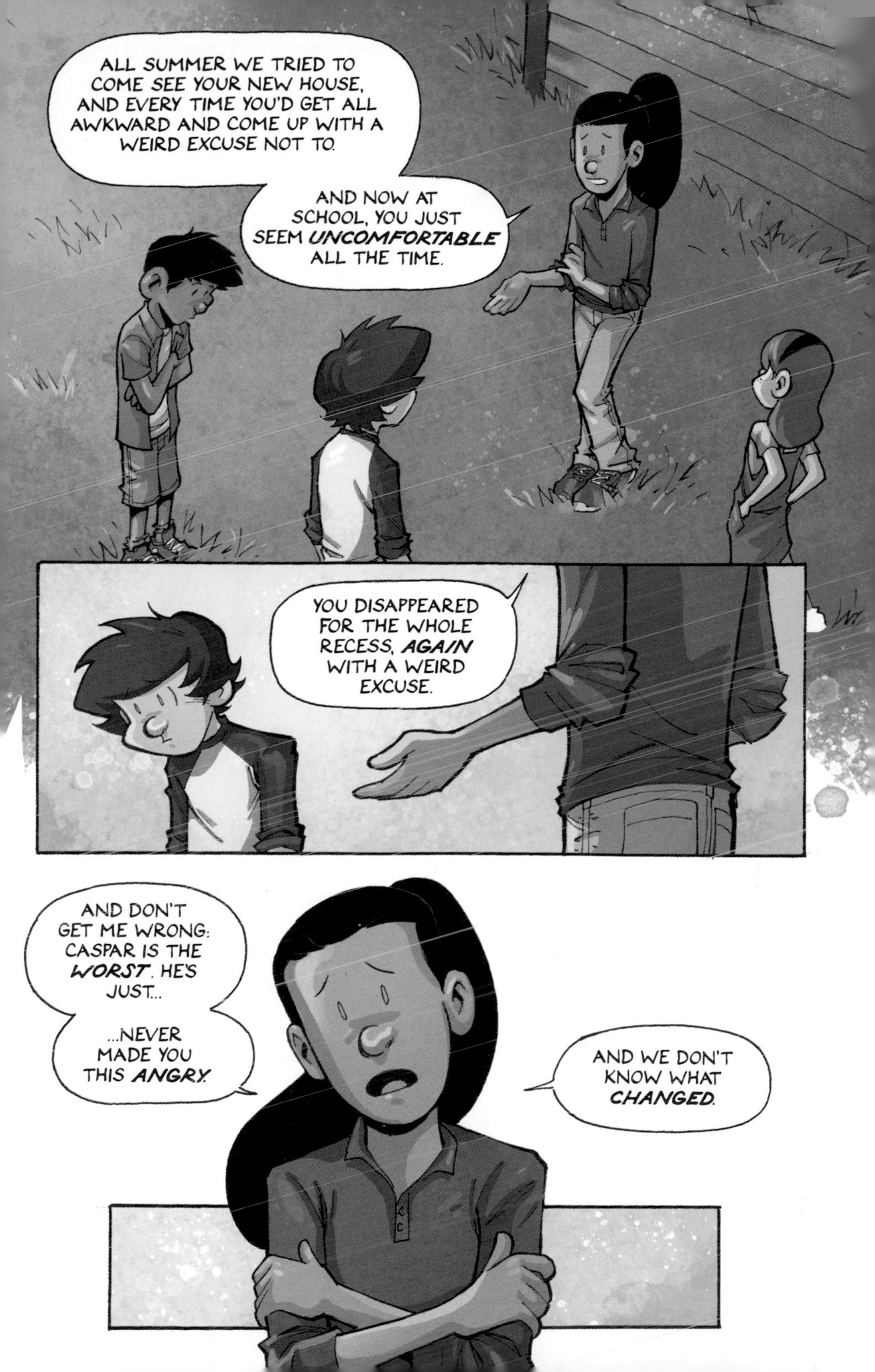
ALL SUMMER WE TRIED TO COME SEE YOUR NEW HOUSE, AND EVERY TIME YOU'D GET ALL AWKWARD AND COME UP WITH A WEIRD EXCUSE NOT TO.
AND NOW AT SCHOOL, YOU JUST SEEM *UNCOMFORTABLE* ALL THE TIME.
YOU DISAPPEARED FOR THE WHOLE RECESS, *AGAIN* WITH A WEIRD EXCUSE.
AND DON'T GET ME WRONG: CASPAR IS THE *WORST*. HE'S JUST...
...NEVER MADE YOU THIS *ANGRY*.
AND WE DON'T KNOW WHAT *CHANGED*.

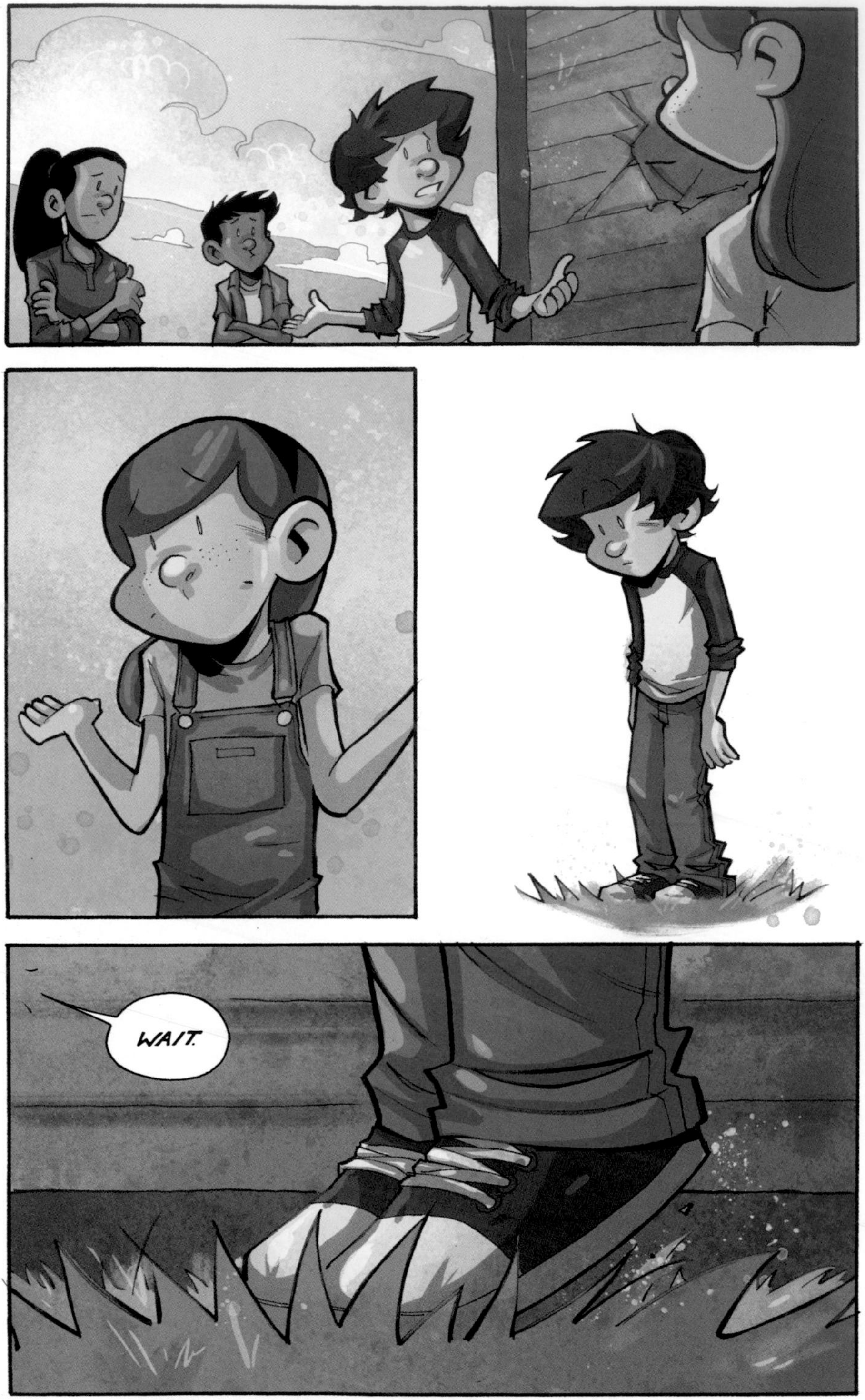
WAIT.

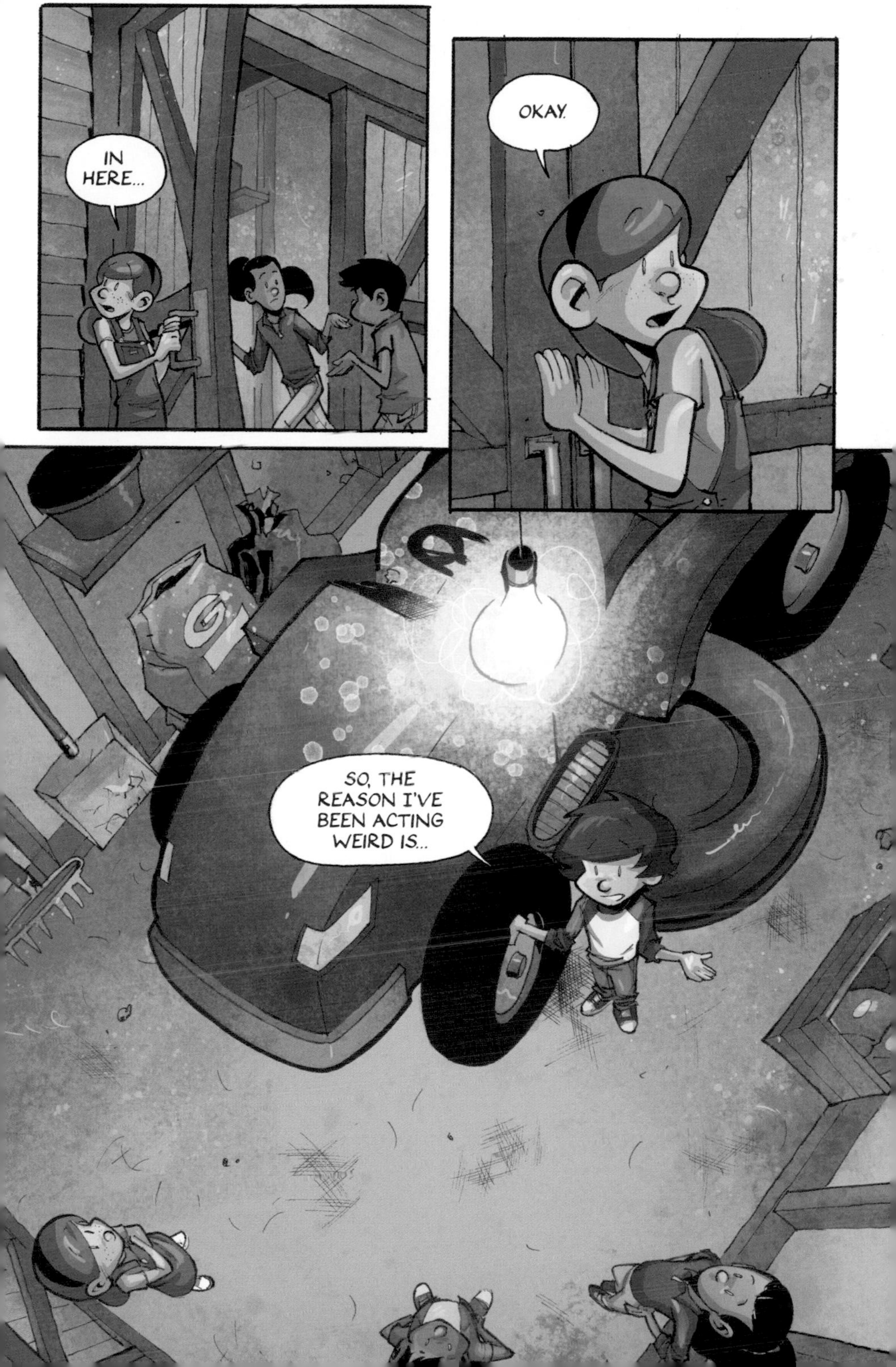
IN HERE...
OKAY.
SO, THE REASON I'VE BEEN ACTING WEIRD IS...

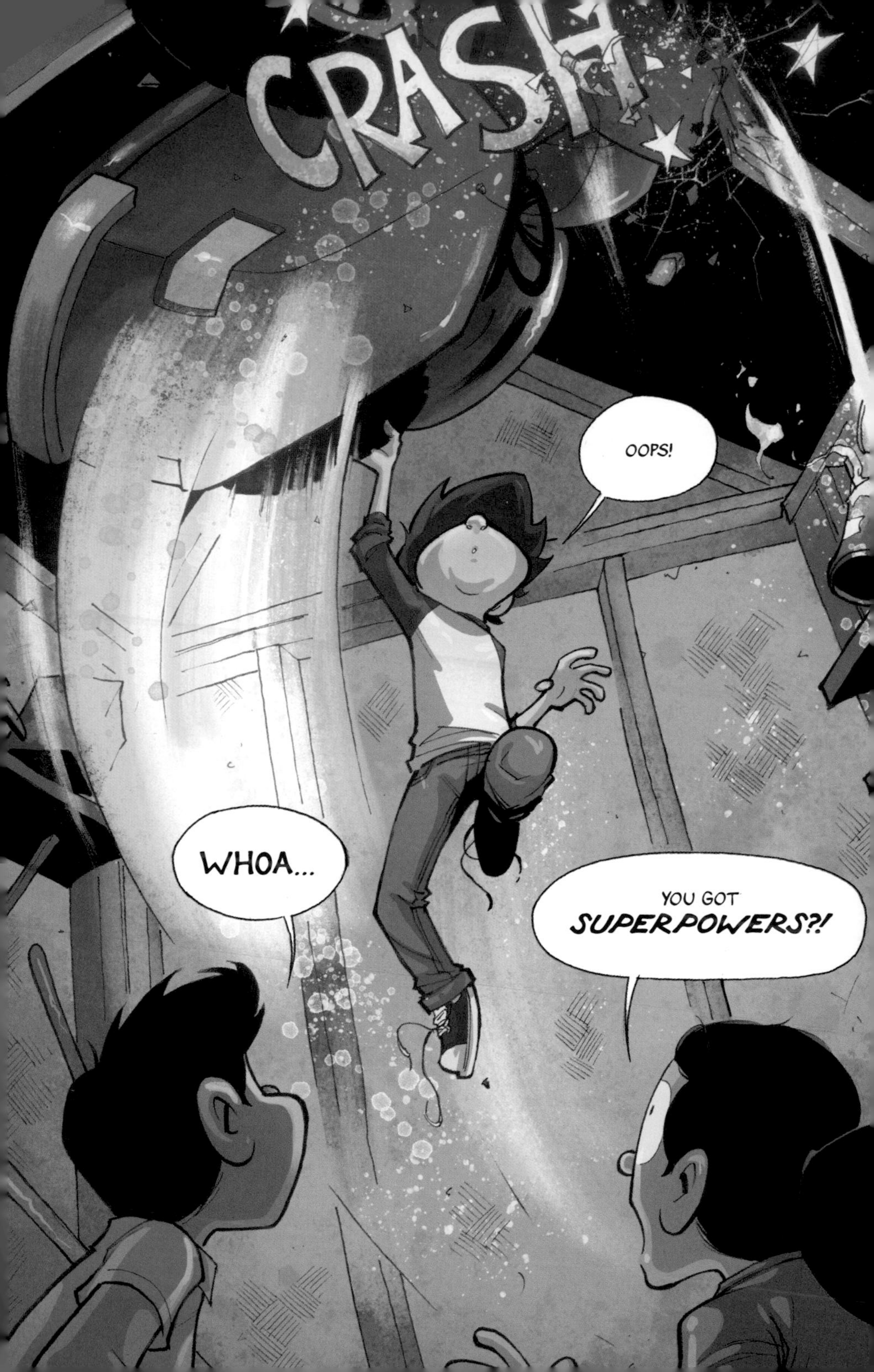
CRASH
OOPS!
WHOA...
YOU GOT SUPERPOWERS?!

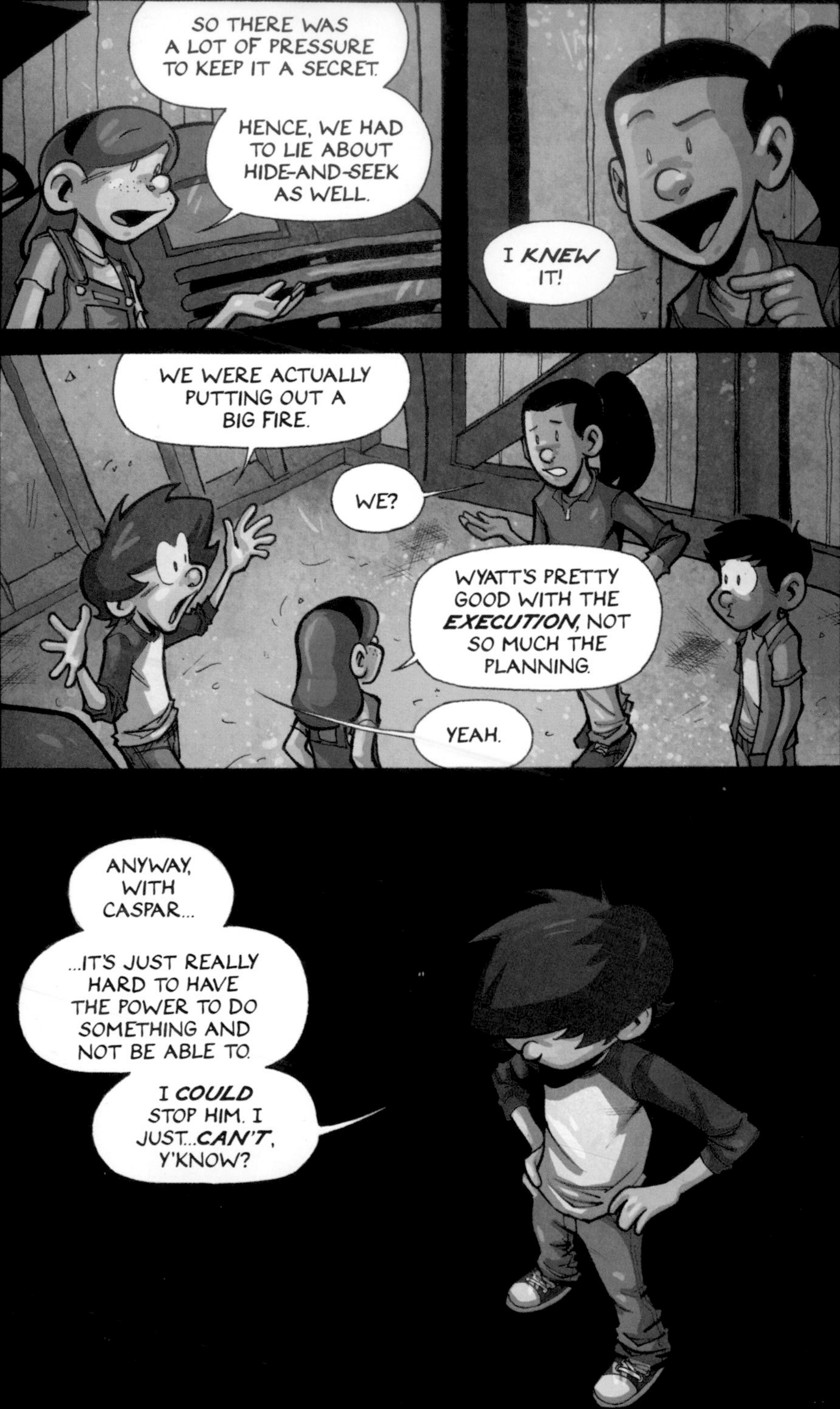
SO THERE WAS A LOT OF PRESSURE TO KEEP IT A SECRET.
HENCE, WE HAD TO LIE ABOUT HIDE-AND-SEEK AS WELL.
I *KNEW* IT!
WE WERE ACTUALLY PUTTING OUT A BIG FIRE.
WE?
WYATT'S PRETTY GOOD WITH THE ***EXECUTION***, NOT SO MUCH THE PLANNING.
YEAH.
ANYWAY, WITH CASPAR...
...IT'S JUST REALLY HARD TO HAVE THE POWER TO DO SOMETHING AND NOT BE ABLE TO.
I ***COULD*** STOP HIM. I JUST...***CAN'T***, Y'KNOW?

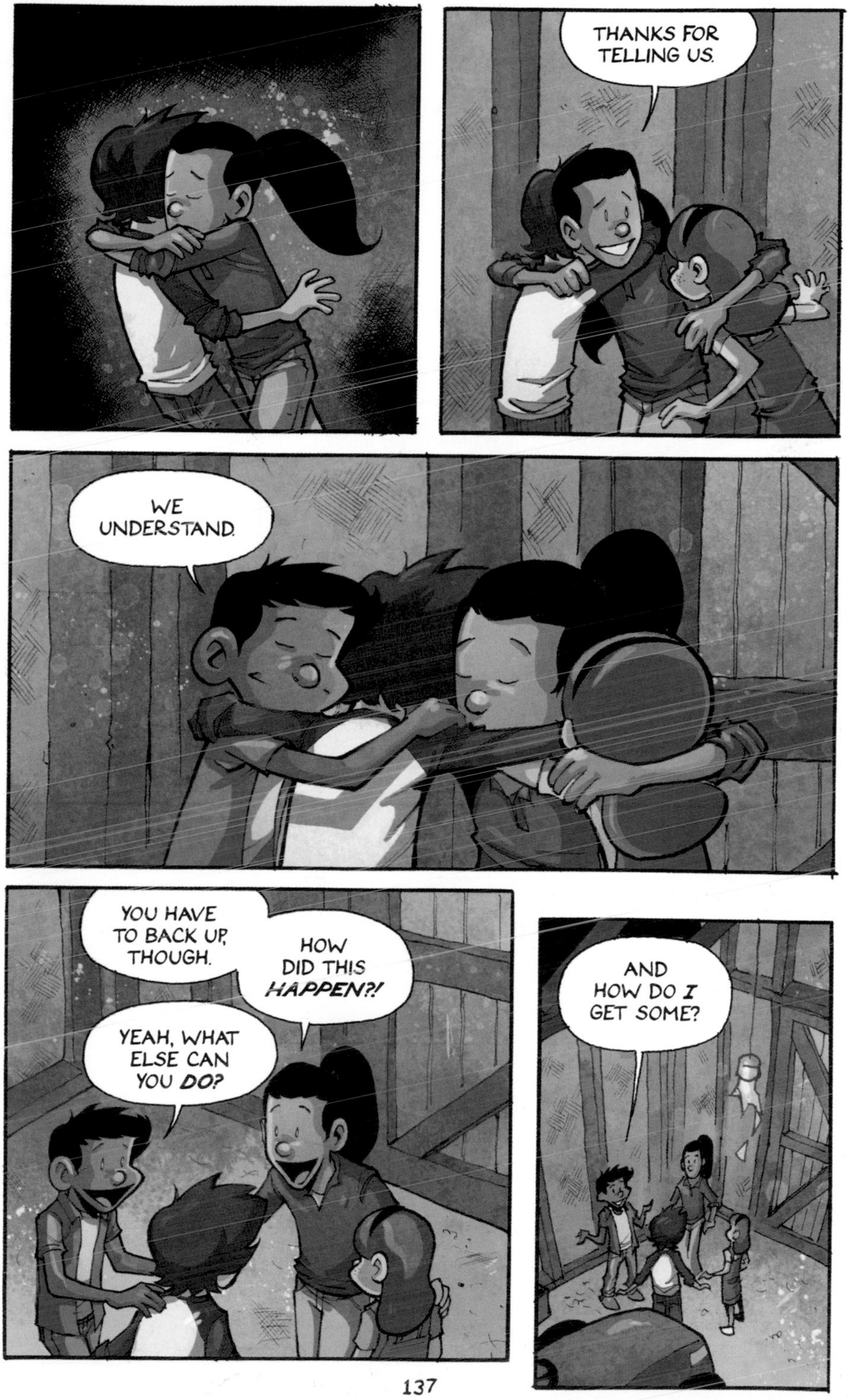
THANKS FOR TELLING US.
WE UNDERSTAND.
YOU HAVE TO BACK UP, THOUGH.
HOW DID THIS HAPPEN?!
YEAH, WHAT ELSE CAN YOU DO?
AND HOW DO I GET SOME?

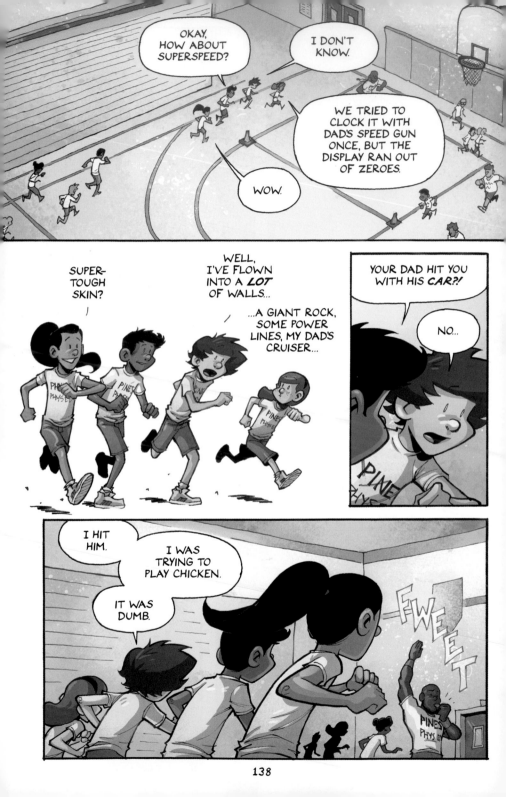

138

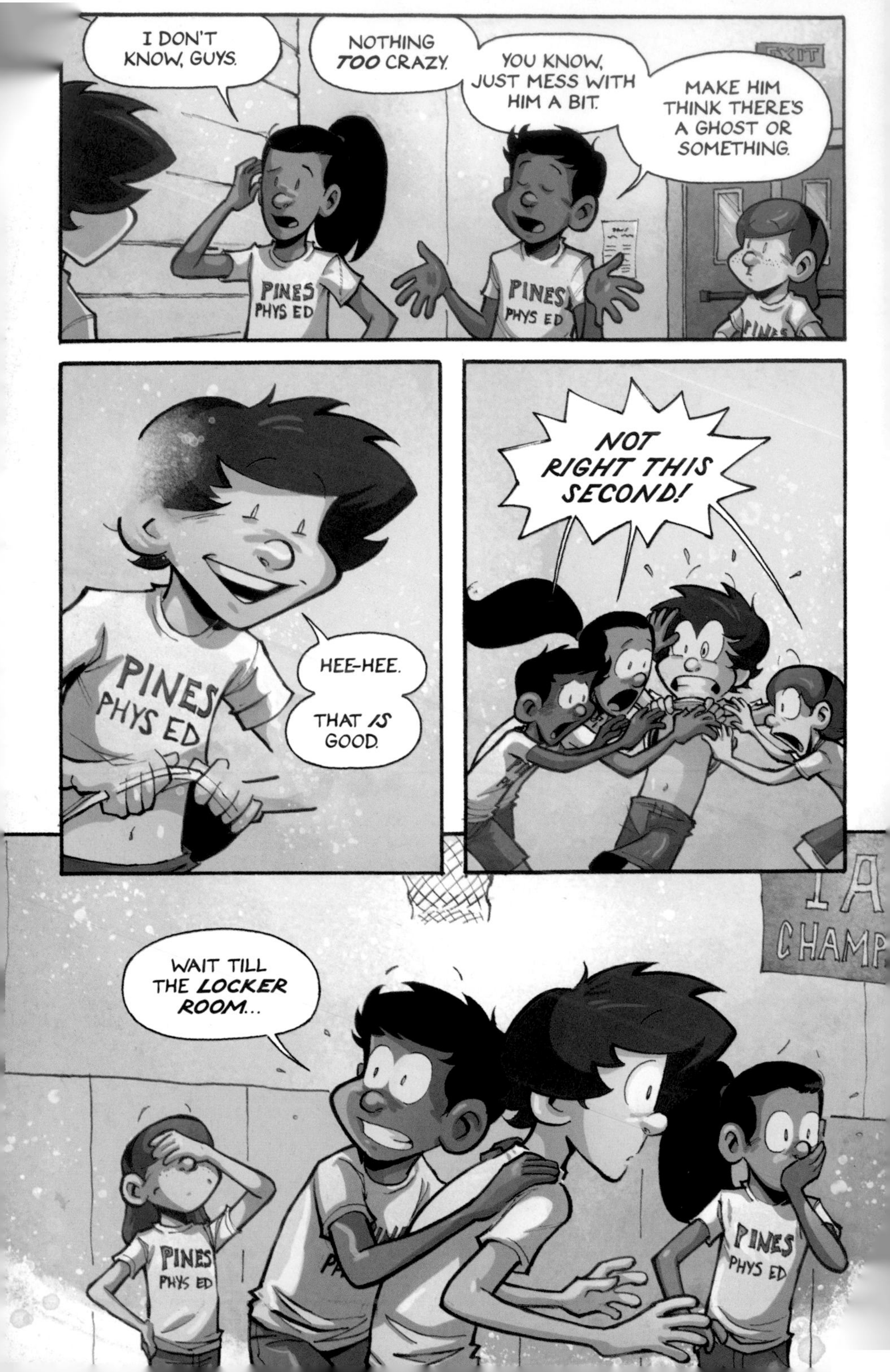
I DON'T KNOW, GUYS.
NOTHING *TOO* CRAZY.
YOU KNOW, JUST MESS WITH HIM A BIT.
MAKE HIM THINK THERE'S A GHOST OR SOMETHING.
EXIT
PINES PHYS ED
PINES PHYS ED
HEE-HEE.
THAT *IS* GOOD.
PINES PHYS ED
NOT RIGHT THIS SECOND!
1A CHAMP
WAIT TILL THE *LOCKER ROOM*...
PINES PHYS ED
PINES PHYS ED

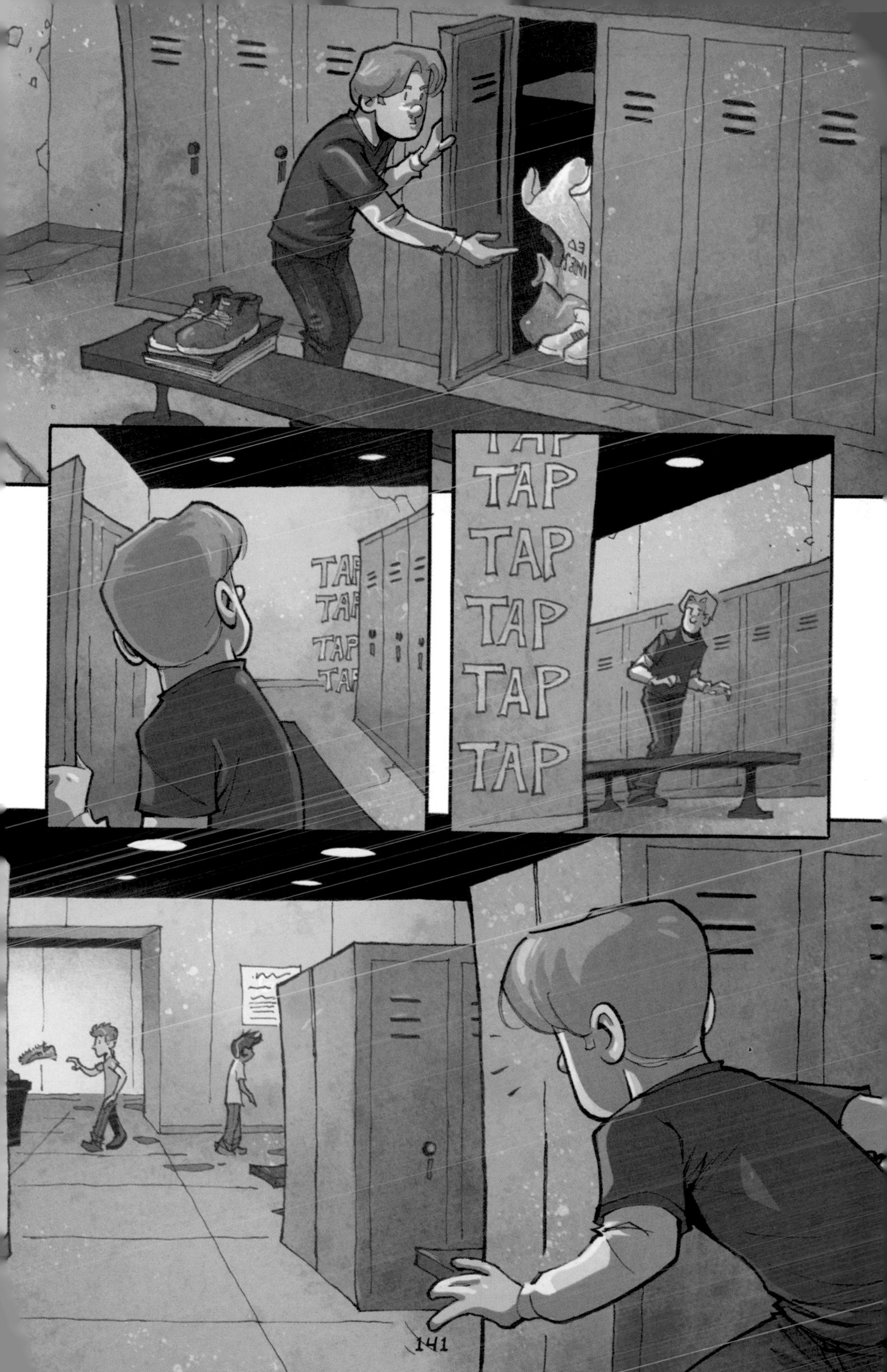
TAP
TAP
TAP
TAP
TAP
TAP
TAP
TAP
TAP
TAP

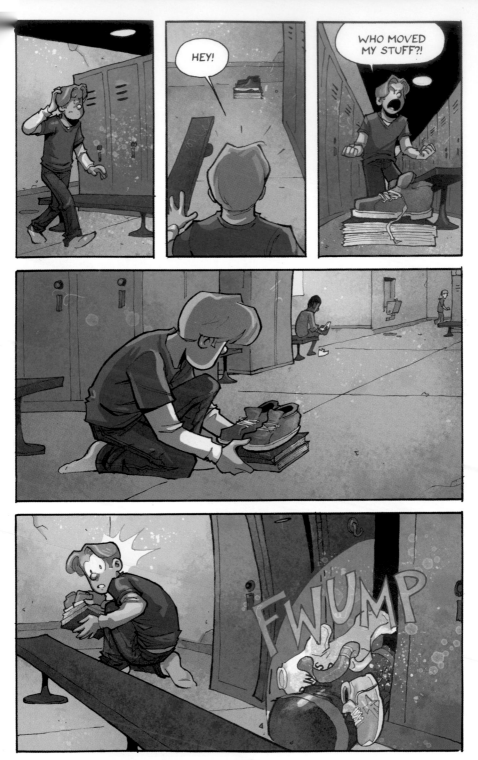

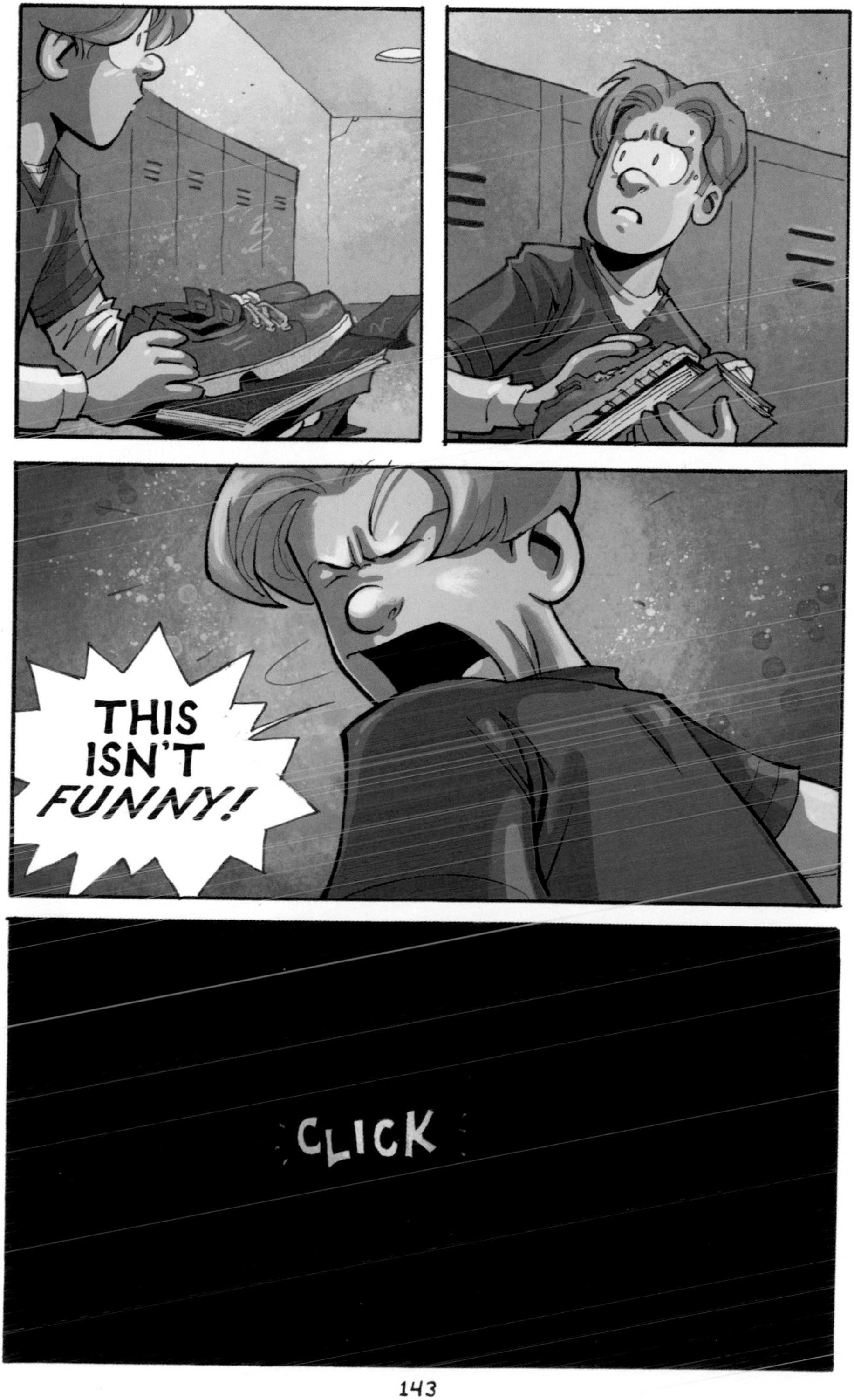
THIS ISN'T *FUNNY!*
CLICK

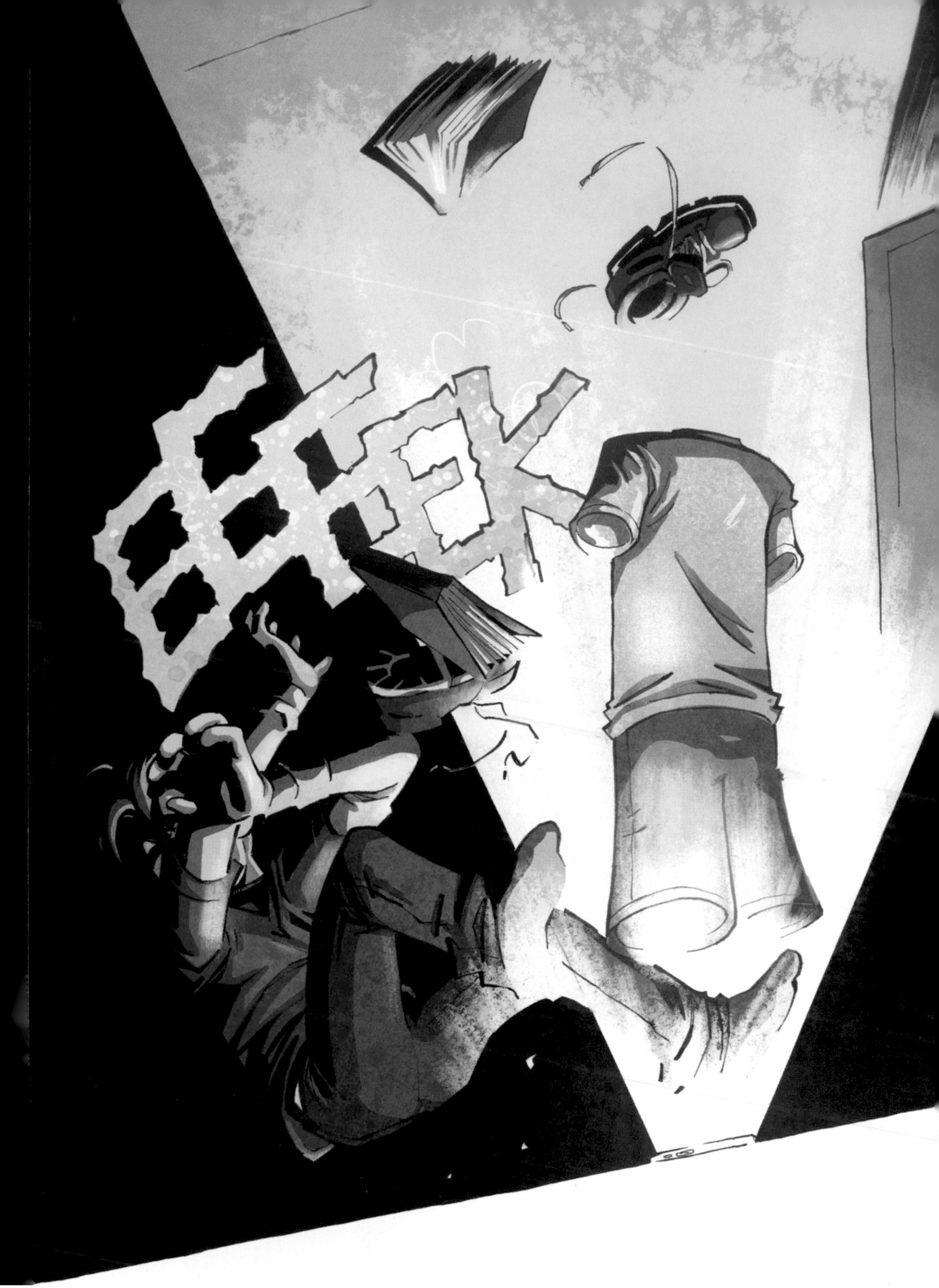

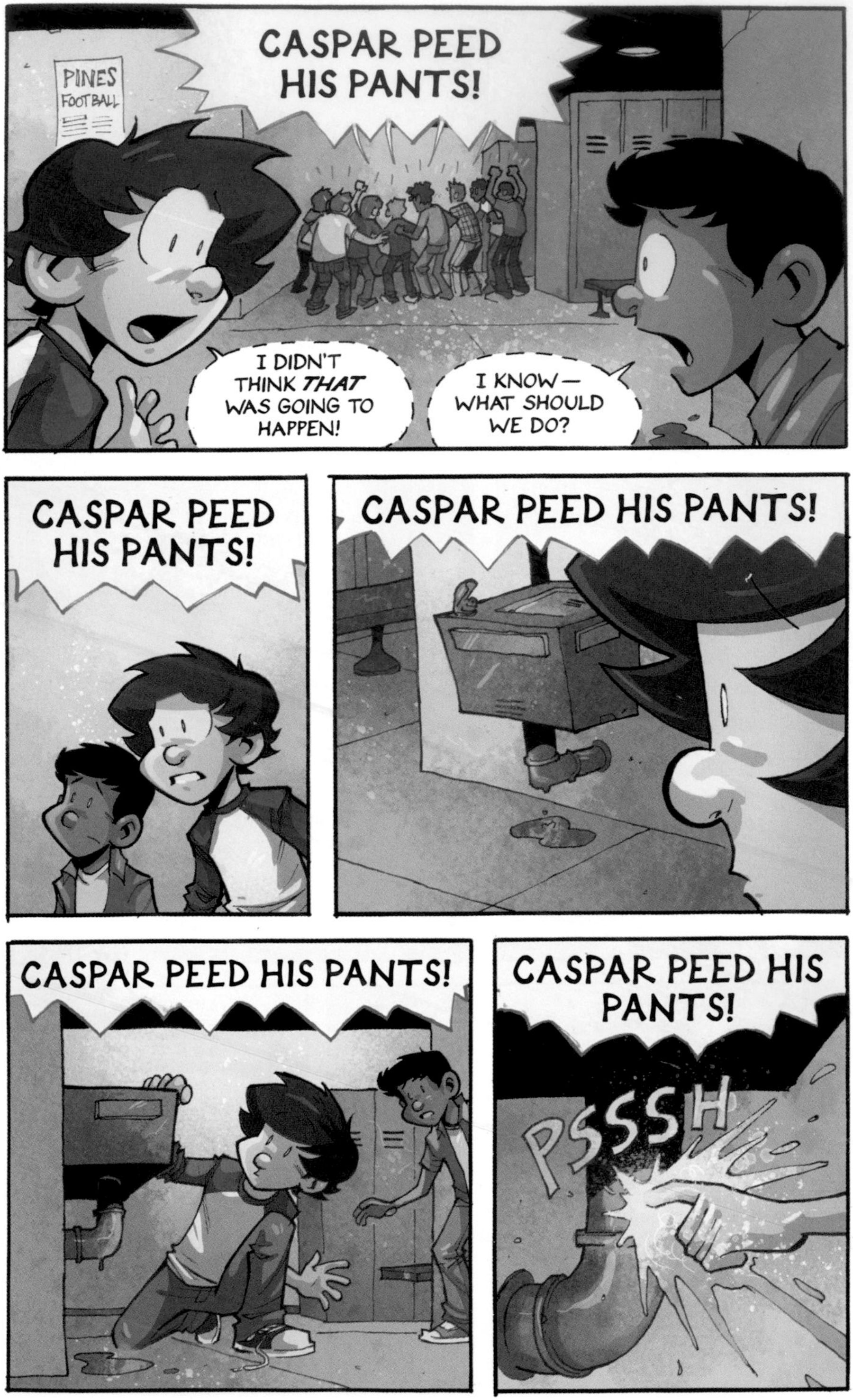

PINES FOOTBALL
CASPAR PEED HIS PANTS!
I DIDN'T THINK *THAT* WAS GOING TO HAPPEN!
I KNOW—WHAT SHOULD WE DO?
CASPAR PEED HIS PANTS!
CASPAR PEED HIS PANTS!
CASPAR PEED HIS PANTS!
CASPAR PEED HIS PANTS!
PSSSH

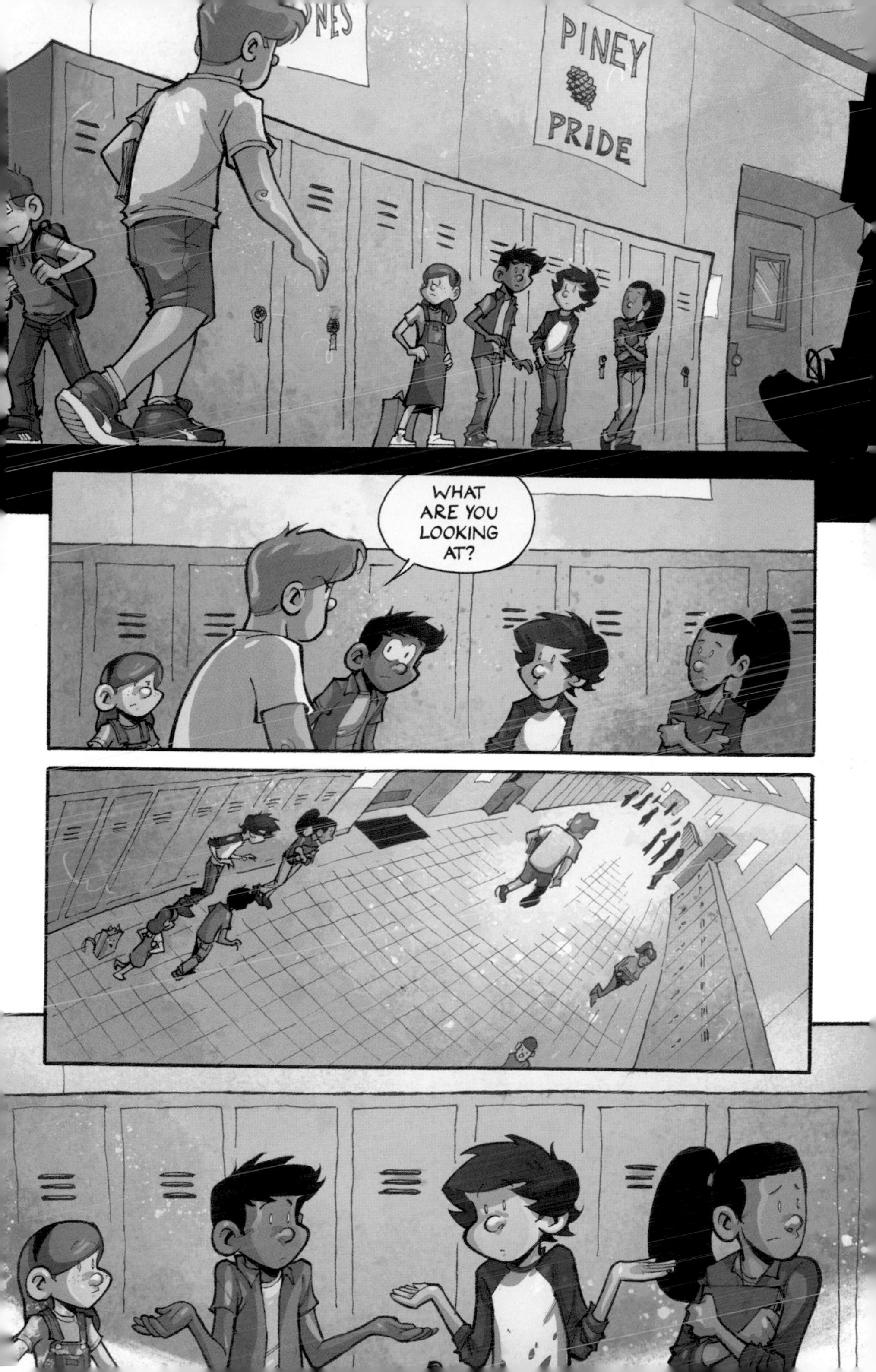
PINEY PRIDE
WHAT ARE YOU LOOKING AT?

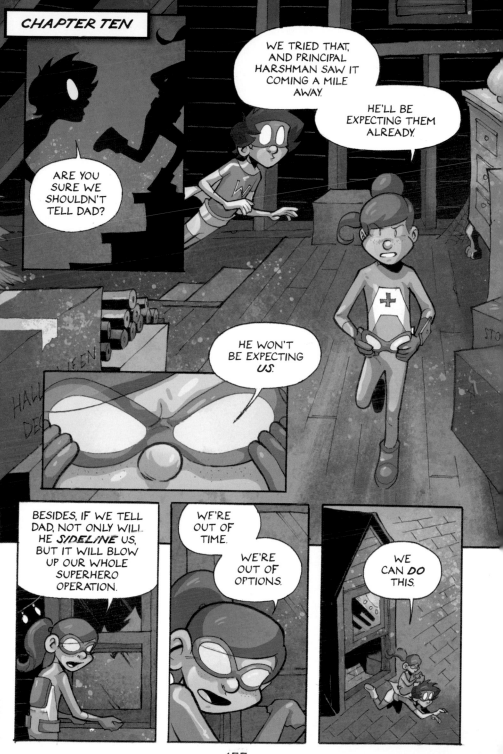

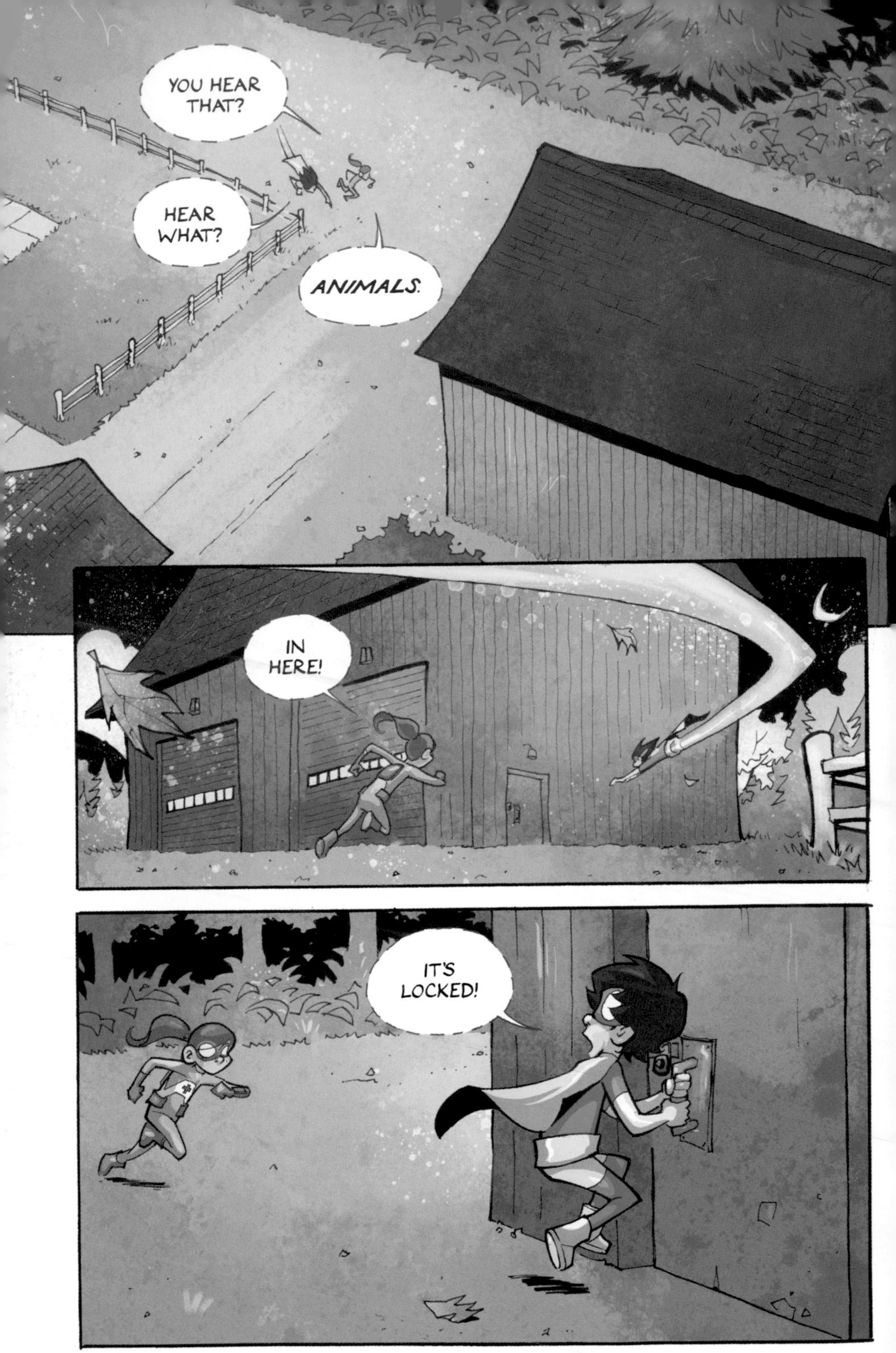
YOU HEAR THAT?
HEAR WHAT?
ANIMALS.
IN HERE!
IT'S LOCKED!

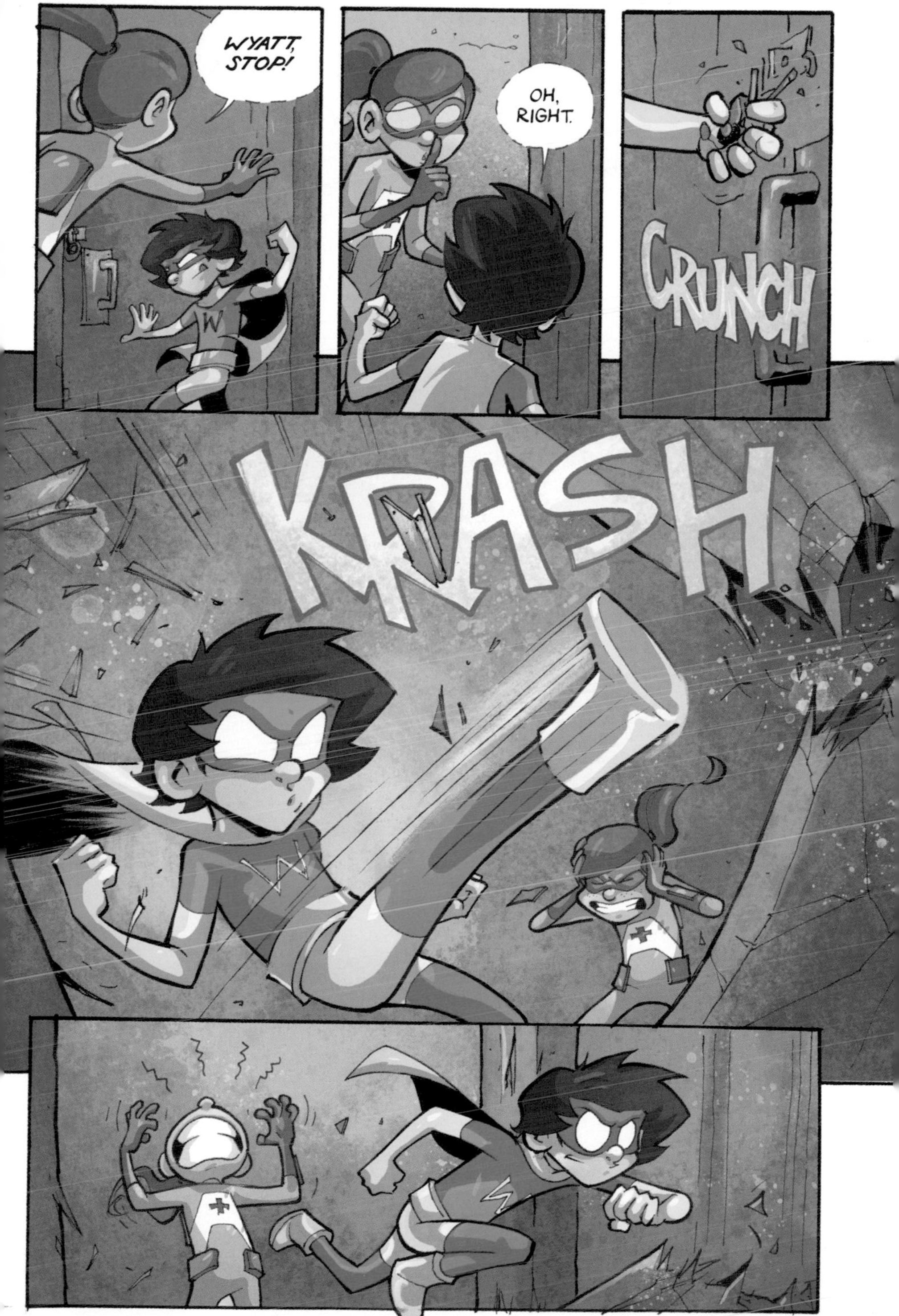
WYATT, STOP!
OH, RIGHT.
CRUNCH
KRASH

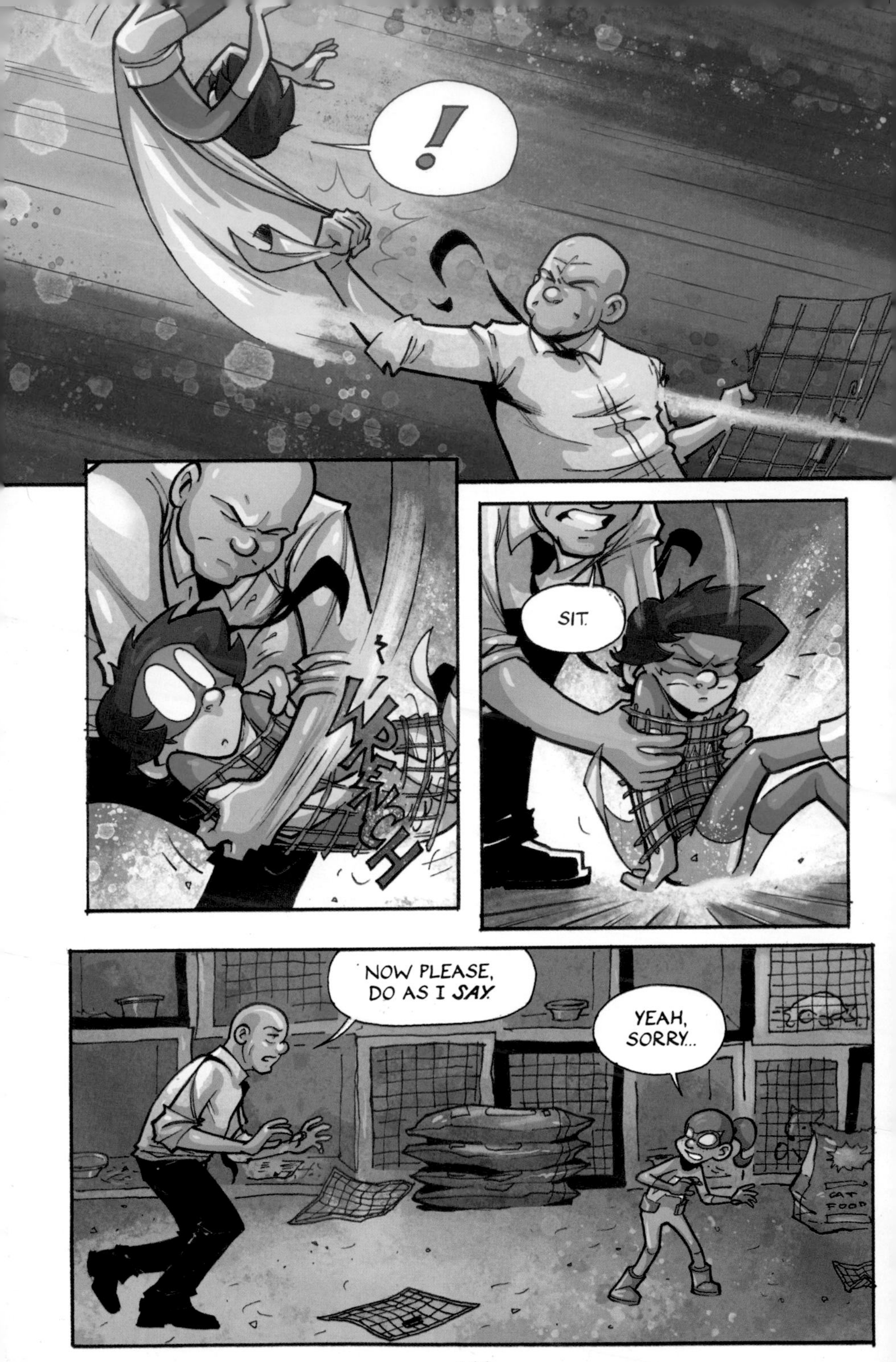
!
WRENCH
SIT.
NOW PLEASE, DO AS I SAY.
YEAH, SORRY...
CAT FOOD

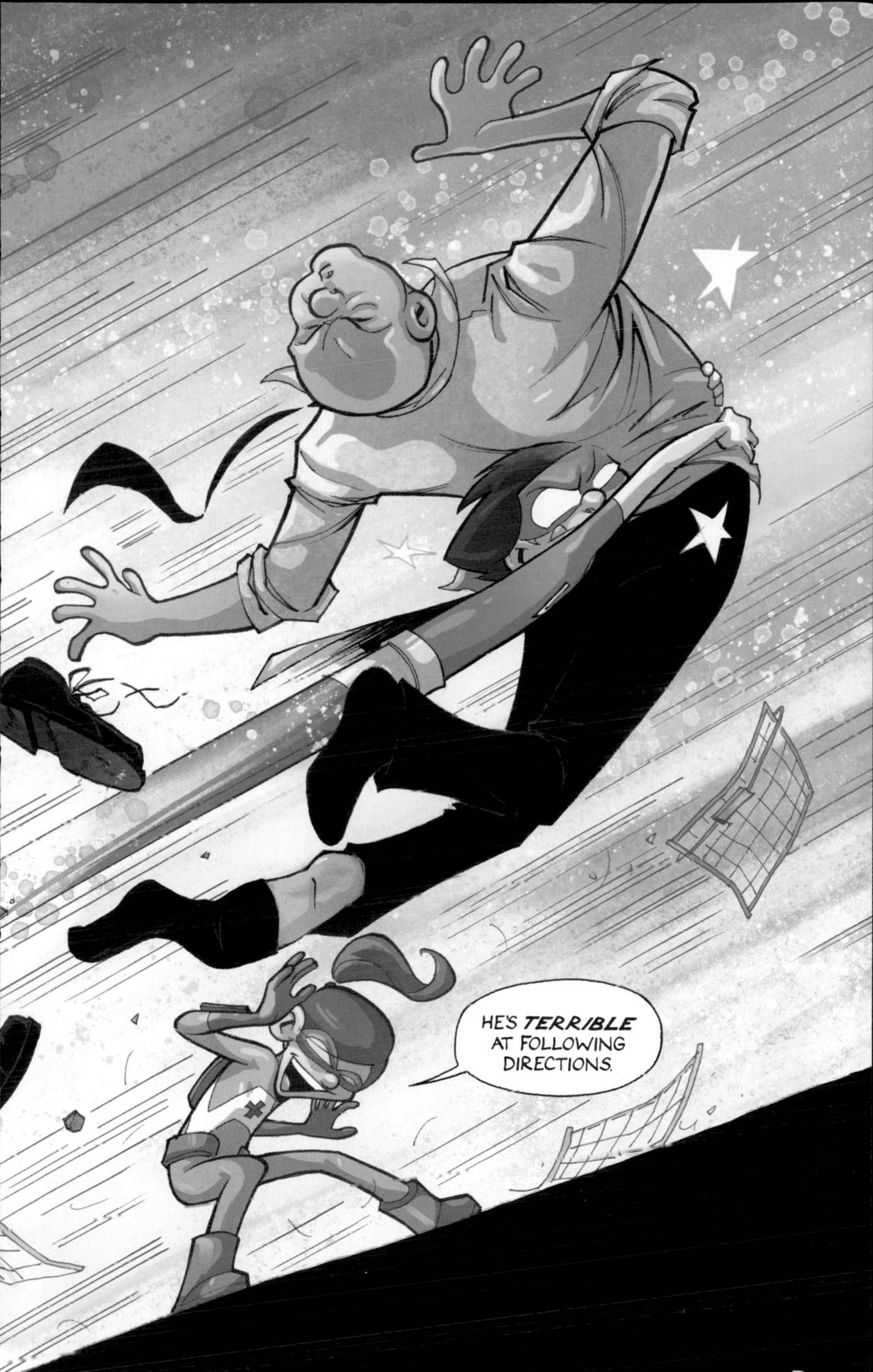
HE'S *TERRIBLE* AT FOLLOWING DIRECTIONS.

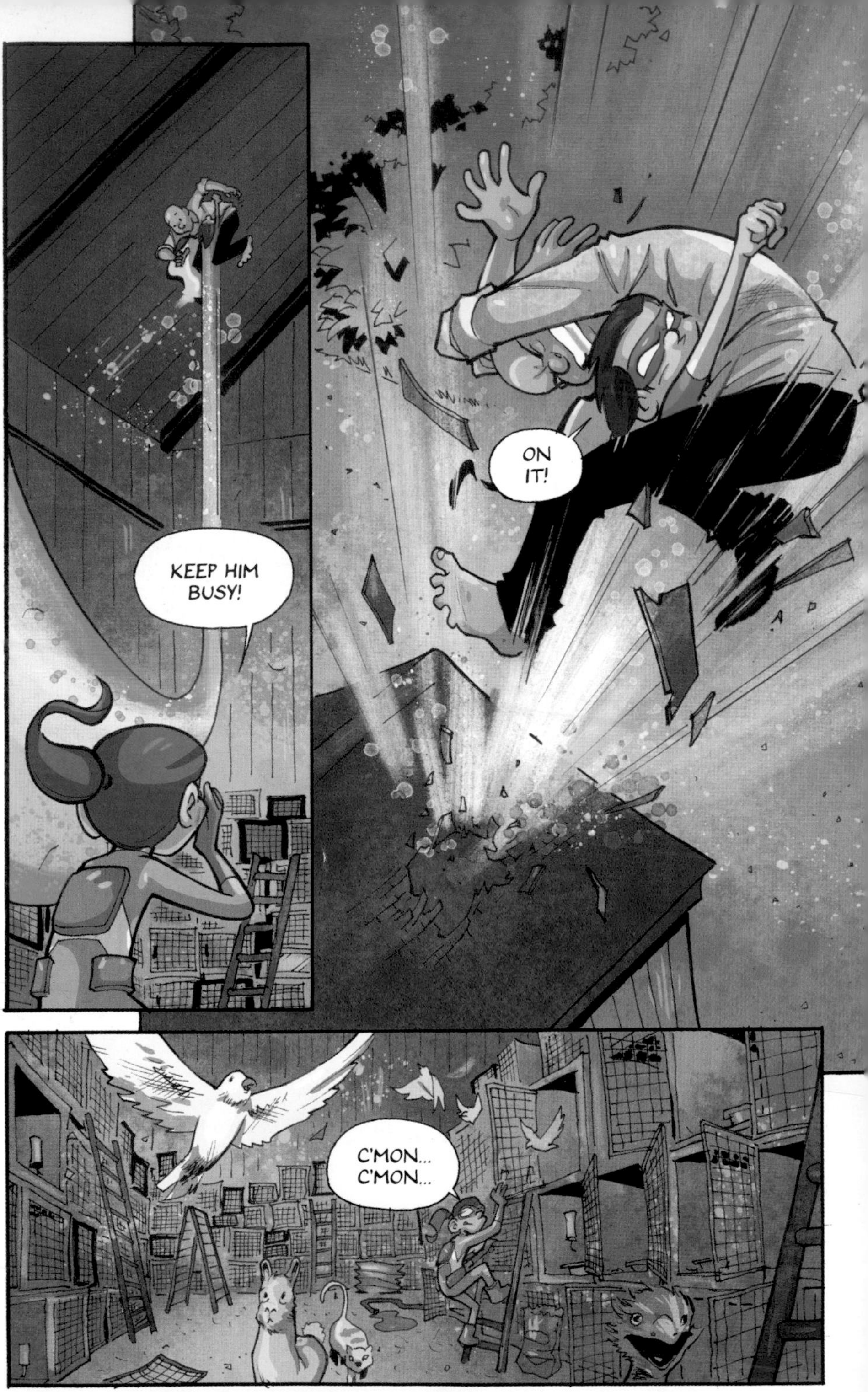
KEEP HIM BUSY!
ON IT!
C'MON... C'MON...

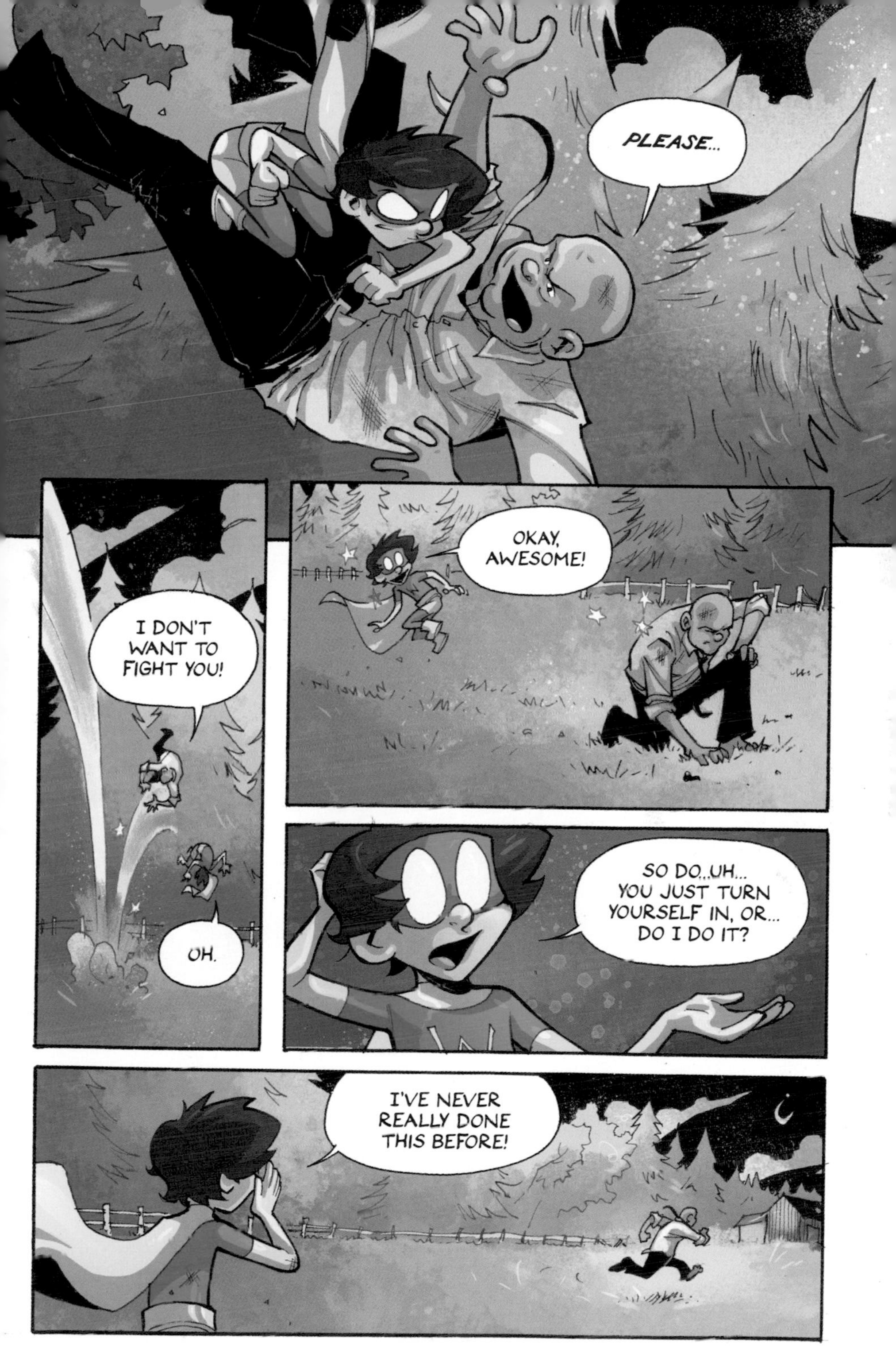
PLEASE...
I DON'T WANT TO FIGHT YOU!
OH.
OKAY, AWESOME!
SO DO...UH... YOU JUST TURN YOURSELF IN, OR... DO I DO IT?
I'VE NEVER REALLY DONE THIS BEFORE!

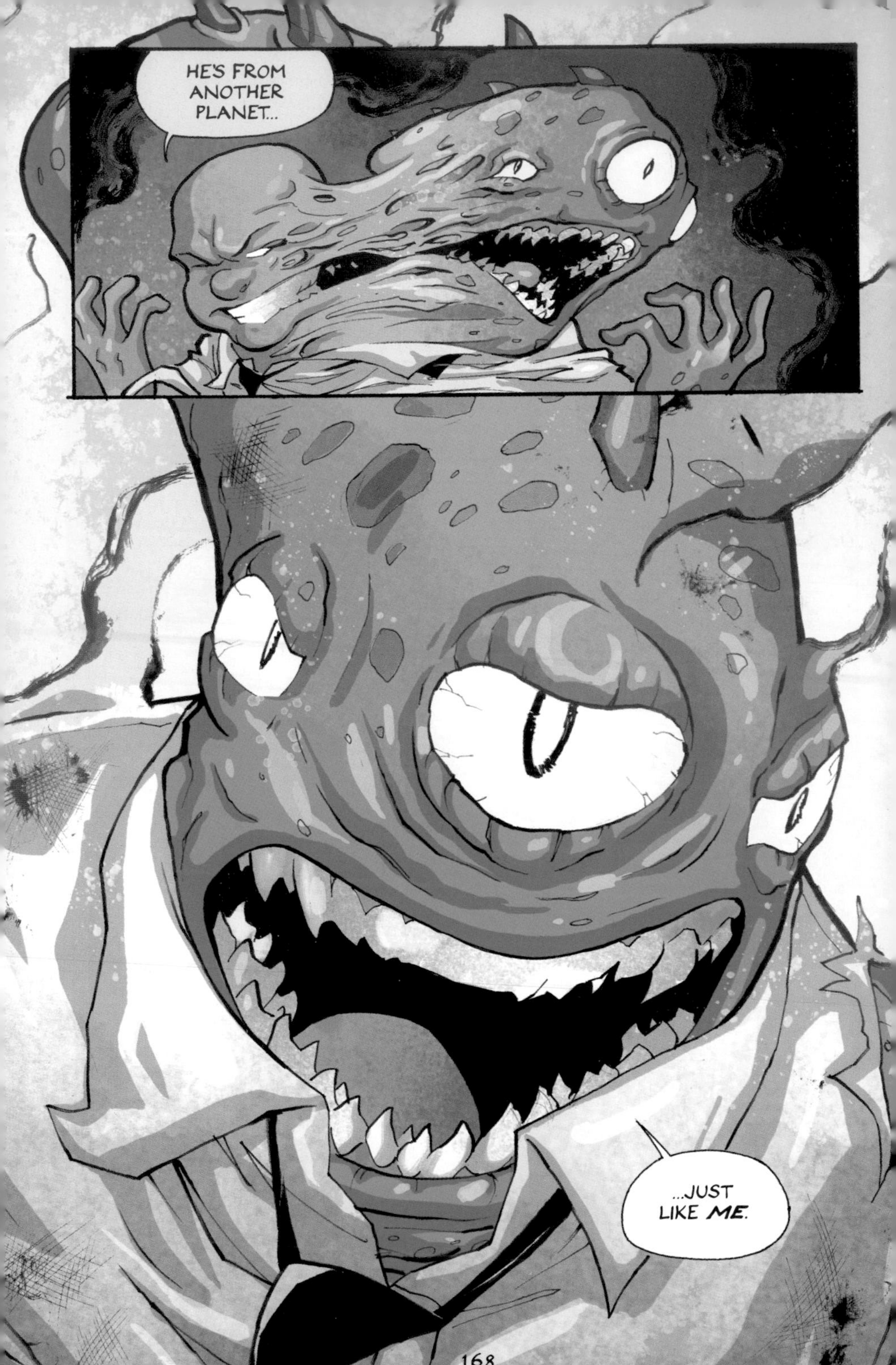
HE'S FROM ANOTHER PLANET...
...JUST LIKE ME.

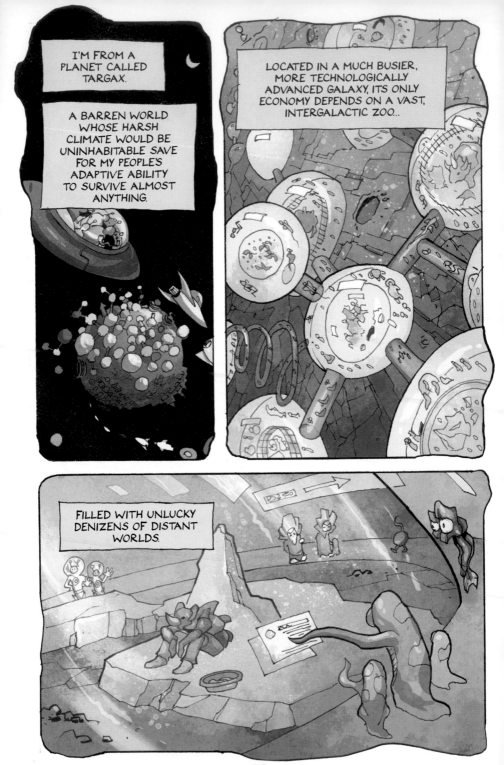

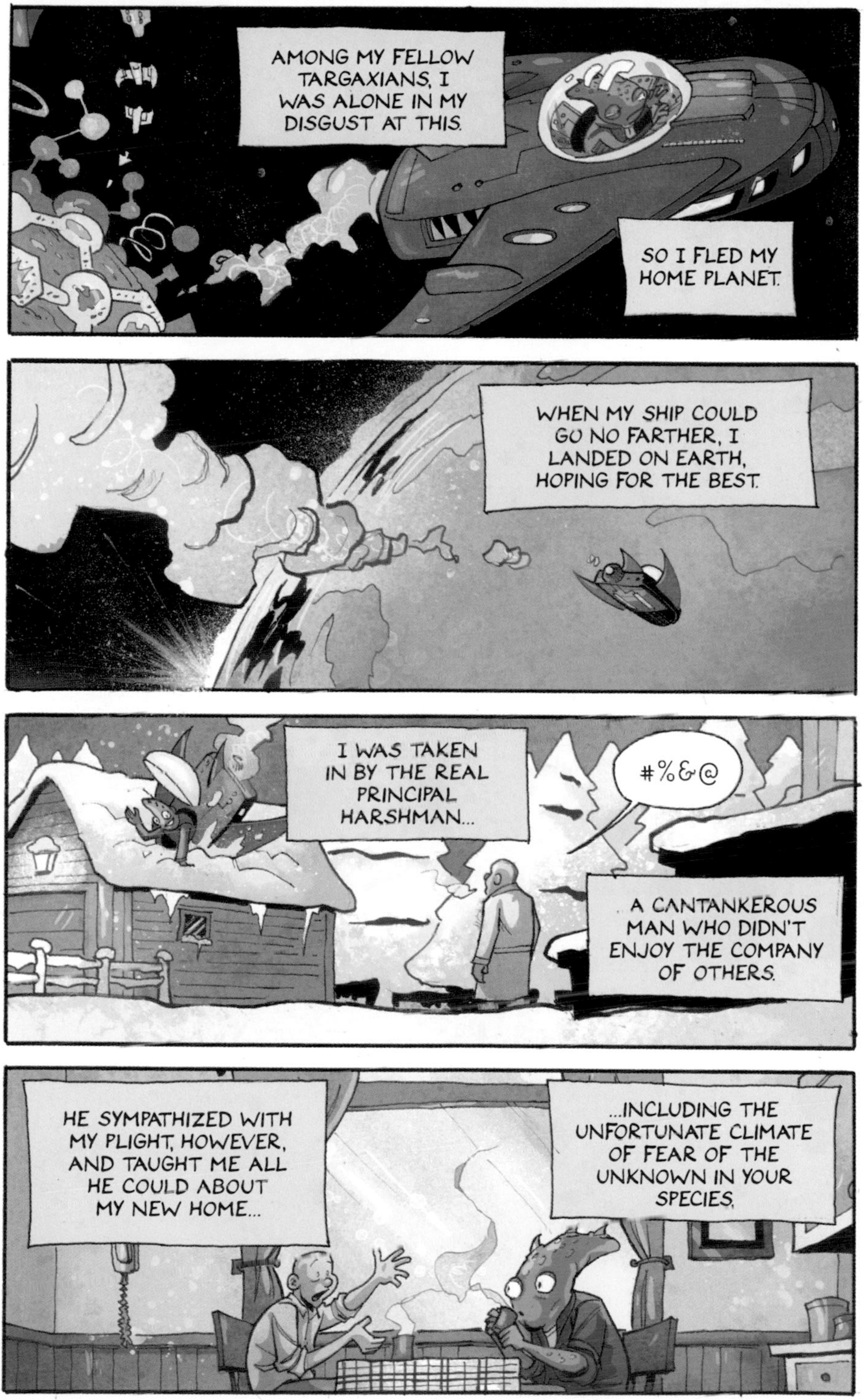
AMONG MY FELLOW TARGAXIANS, I WAS ALONE IN MY DISGUST AT THIS.
SO I FLED MY HOME PLANET.
WHEN MY SHIP COULD GO NO FARTHER, I LANDED ON EARTH, HOPING FOR THE BEST.
I WAS TAKEN IN BY THE REAL PRINCIPAL HARSHMAN...
#%&@
...A CANTANKEROUS MAN WHO DIDN'T ENJOY THE COMPANY OF OTHERS.
HE SYMPATHIZED WITH MY PLIGHT, HOWEVER, AND TAUGHT ME ALL HE COULD ABOUT MY NEW HOME...
...INCLUDING THE UNFORTUNATE CLIMATE OF FEAR OF THE UNKNOWN IN YOUR SPECIES.

173

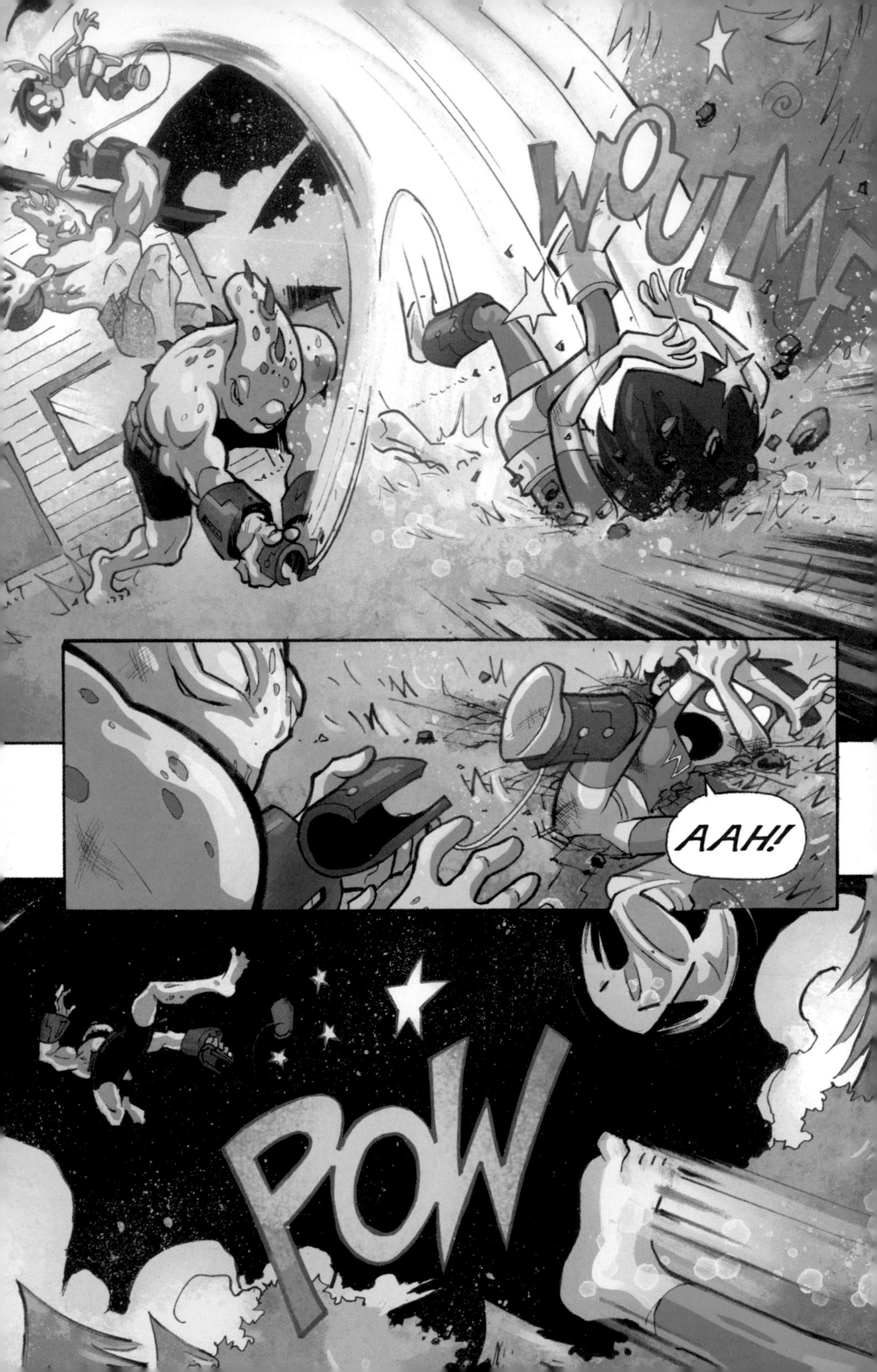
WOUMF
AAH!
POW

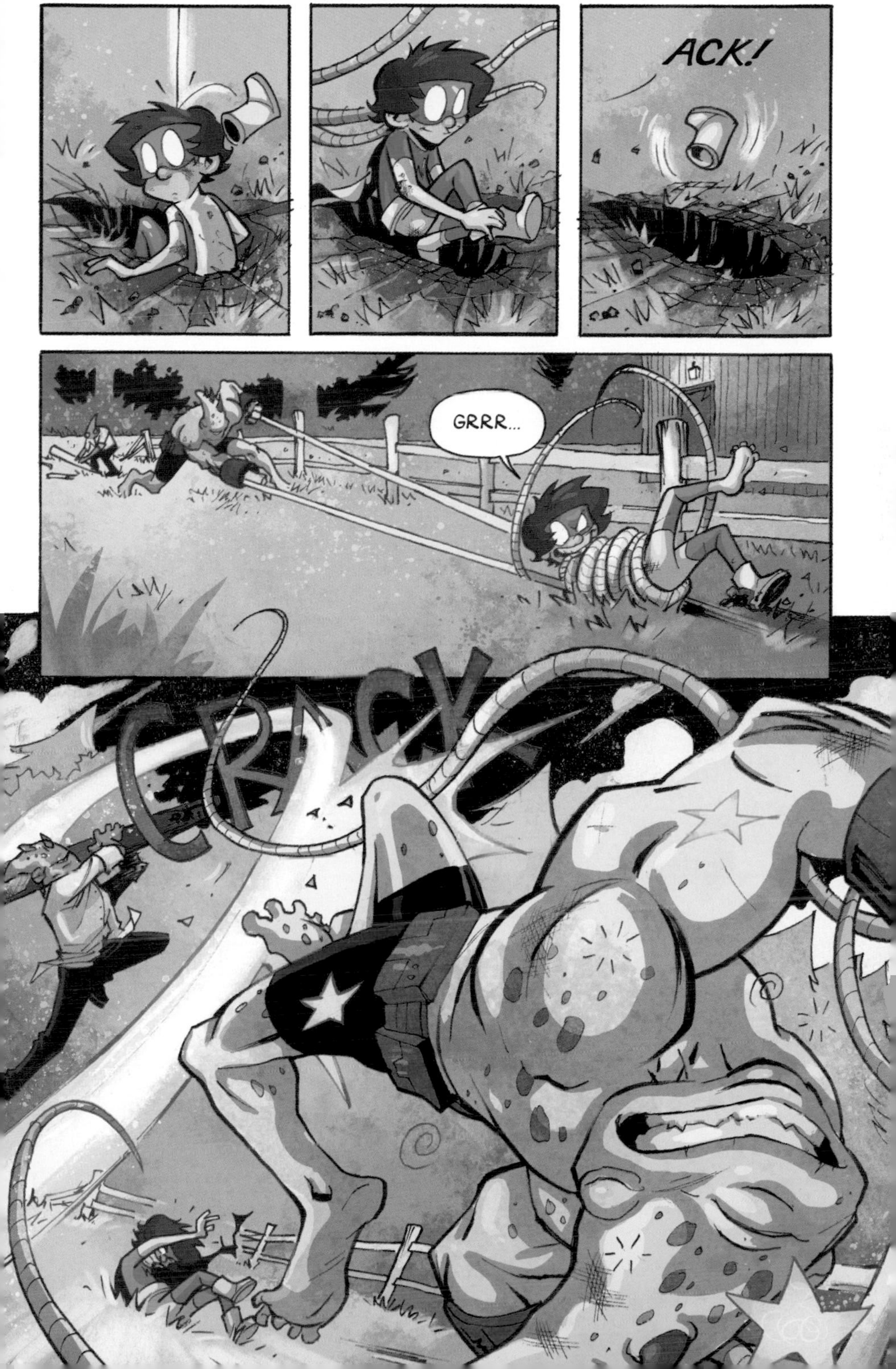
ACK!
GRRR...
CRACK

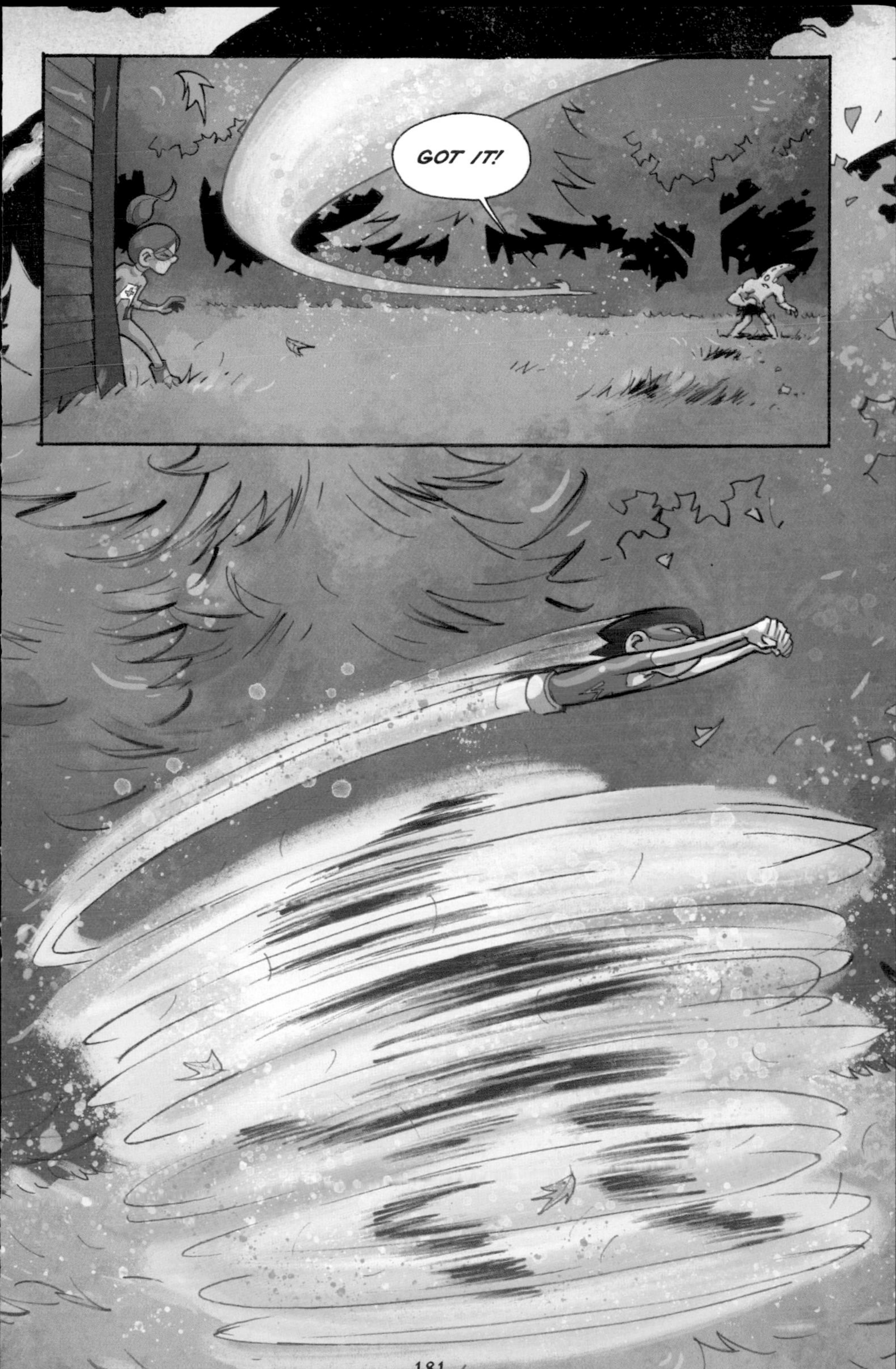
GOT IT!

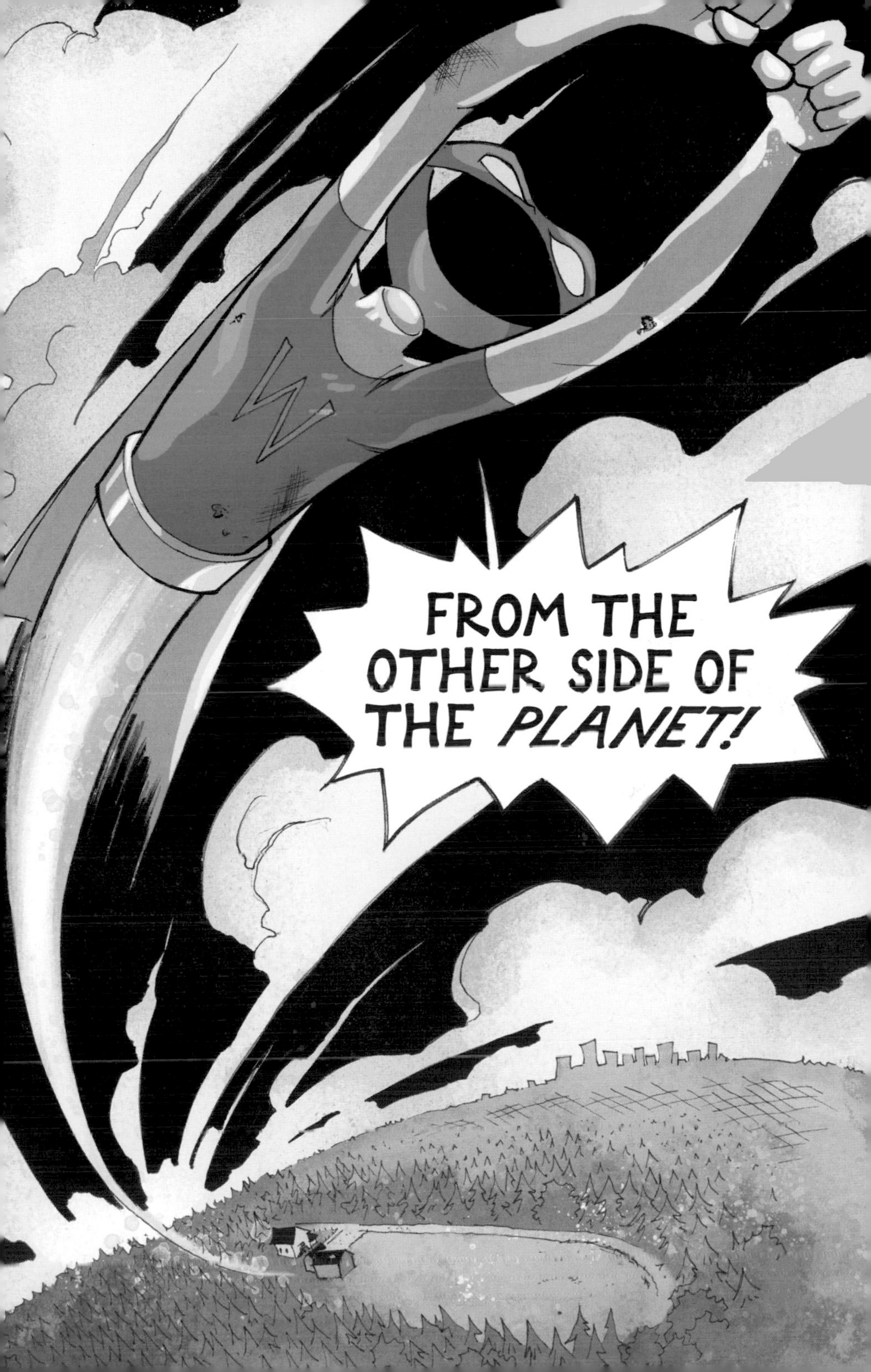
FROM THE OTHER SIDE OF THE *PLANET!*

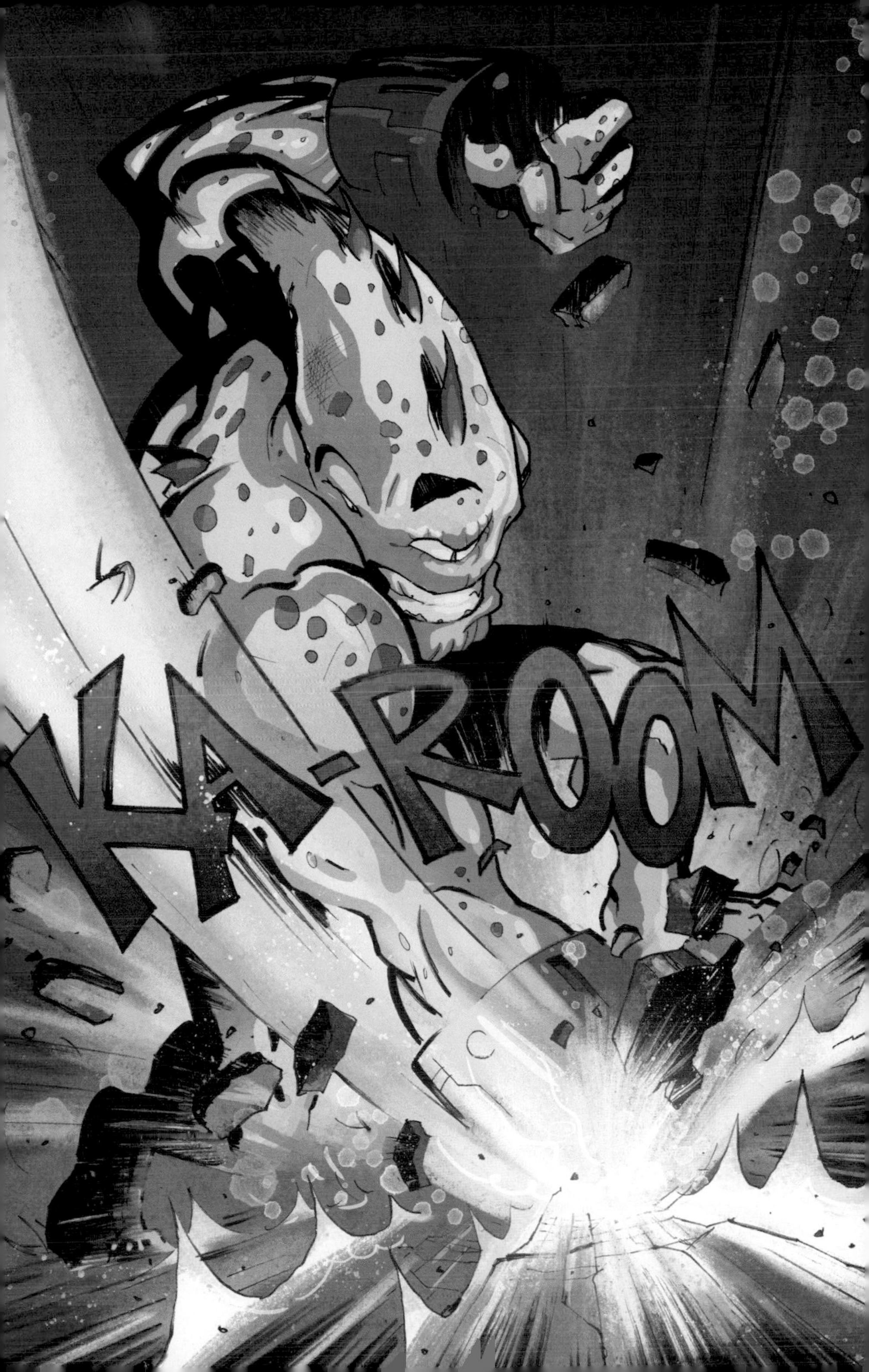
KA-ROOM

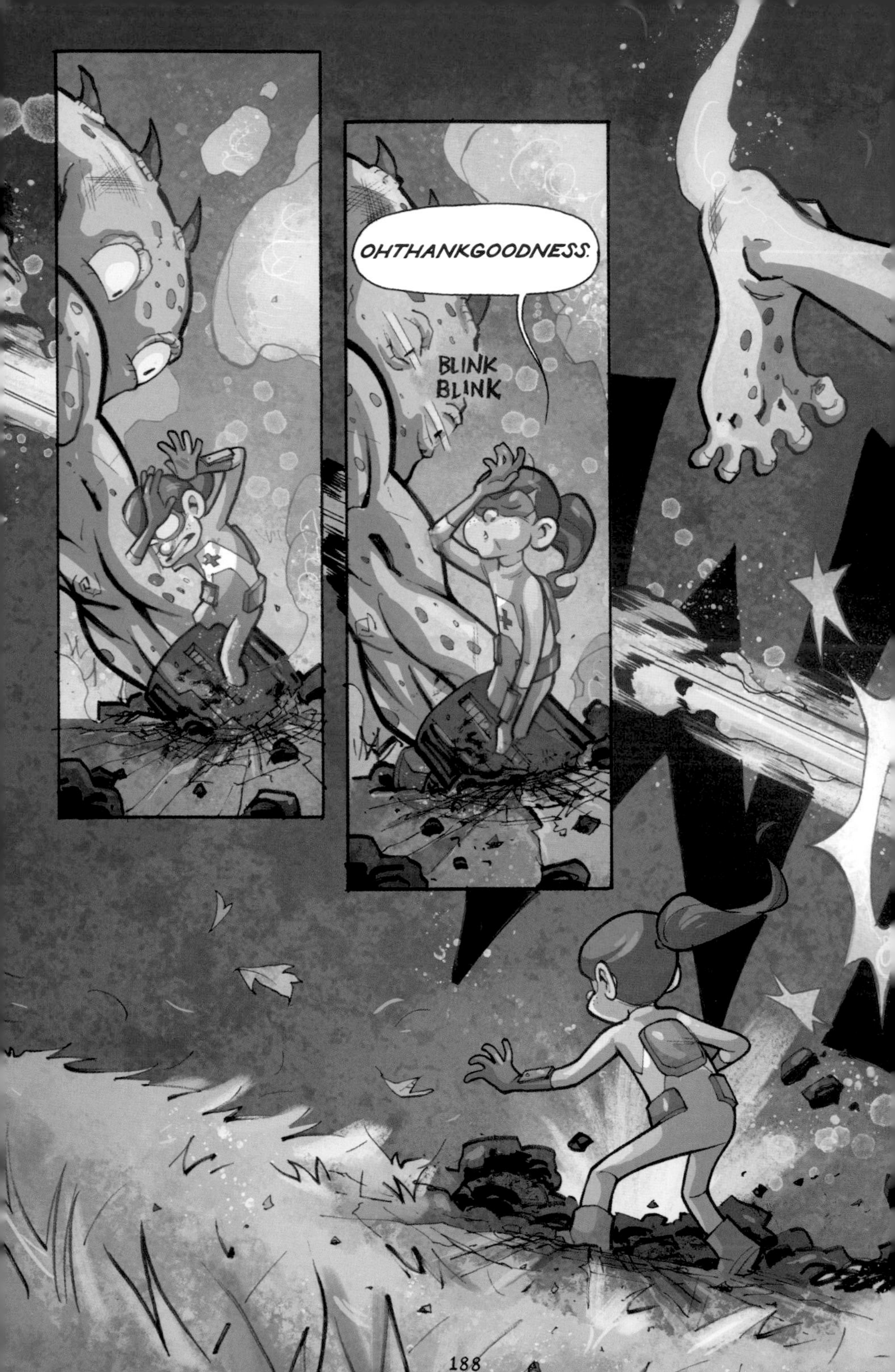
OHTHANKGOODNESS.
BLINK
BLINK

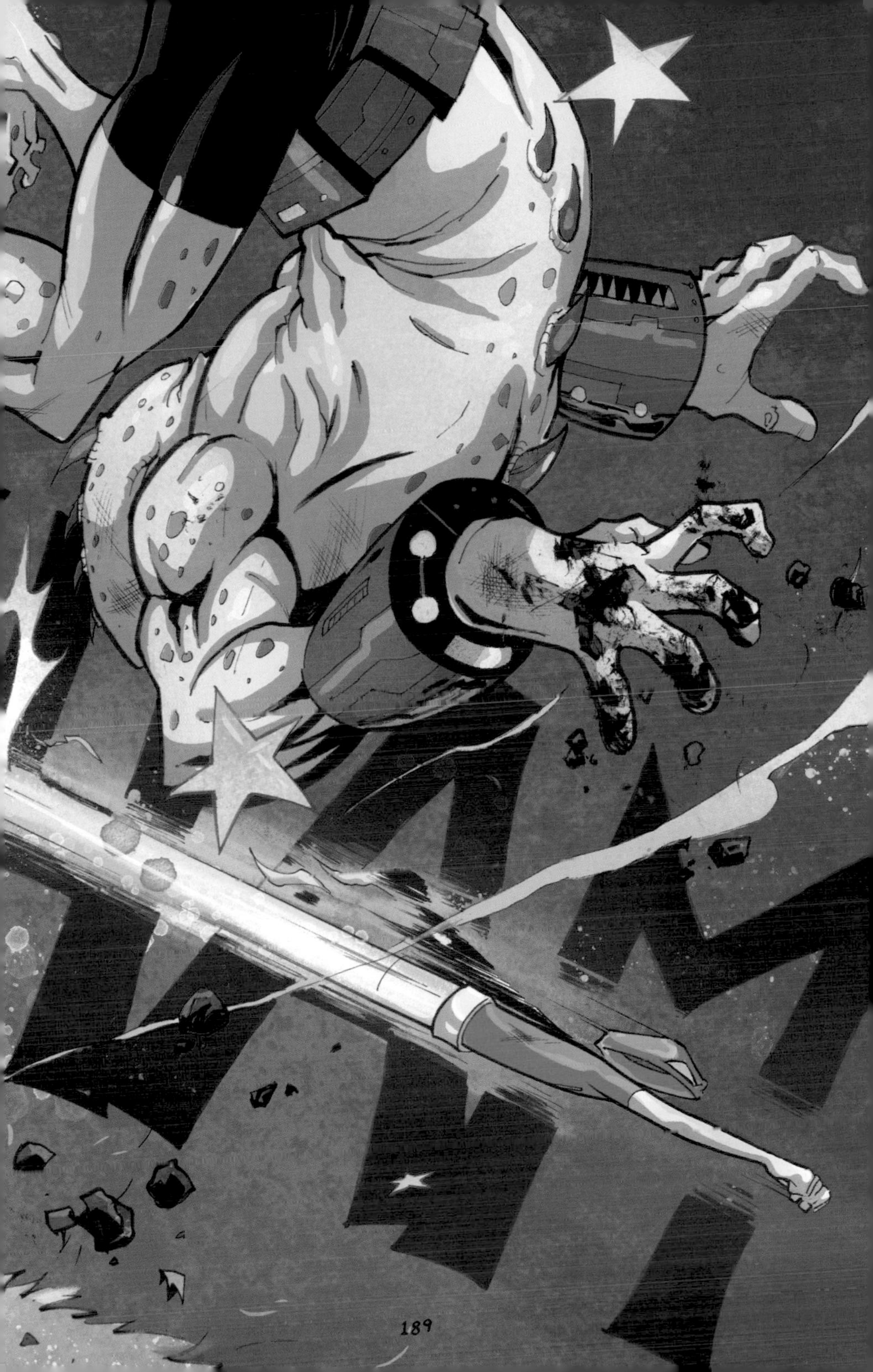

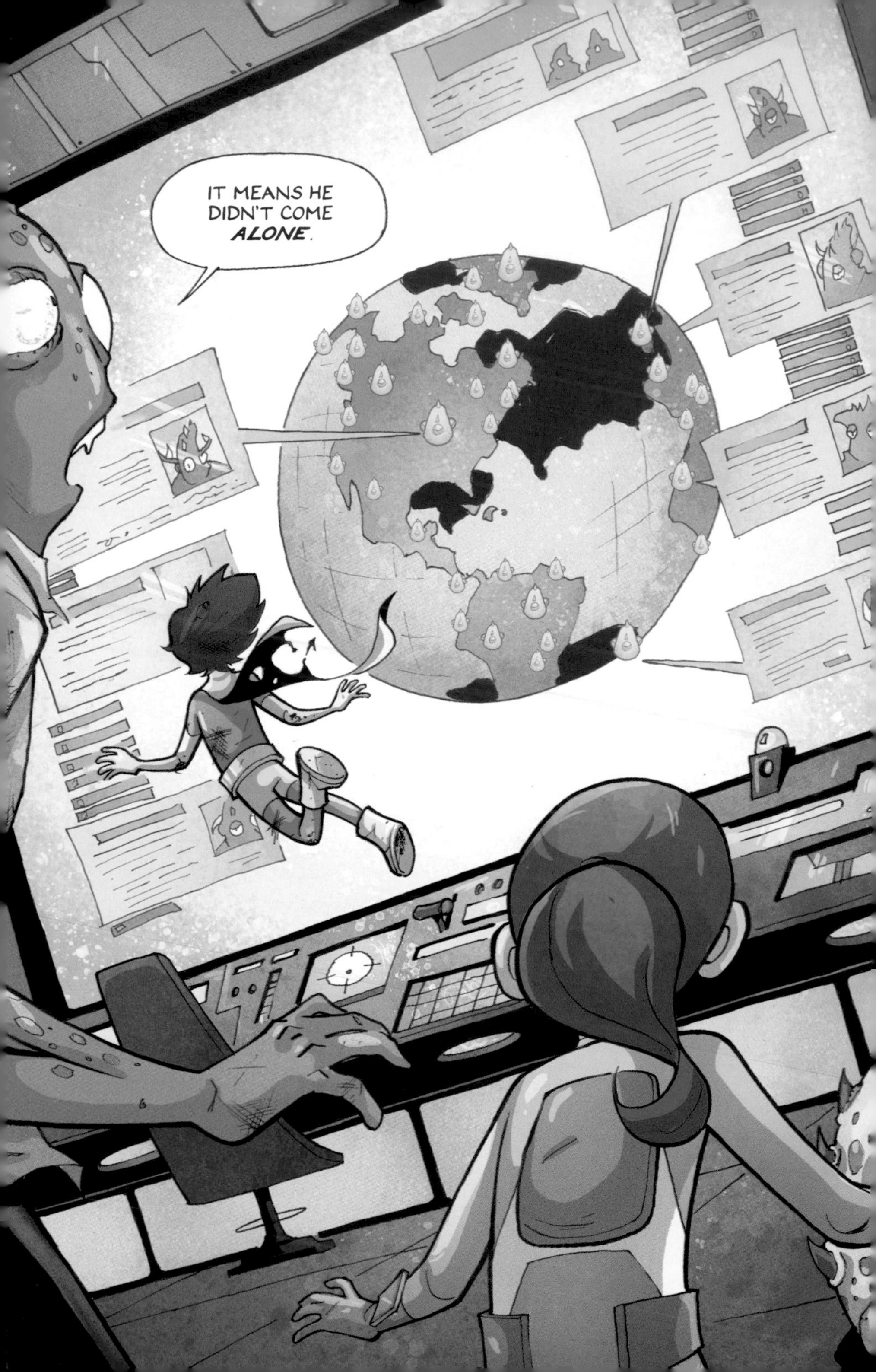
IT MEANS HE DIDN'T COME *ALONE*.

DING
SOMETHING FAR DIFFERENT FROM ANYTHING THEY'VE SEEN BEFORE.

FSSSSS

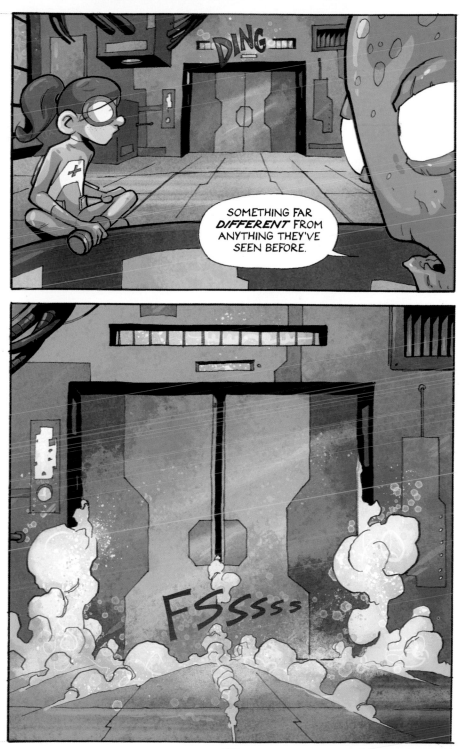

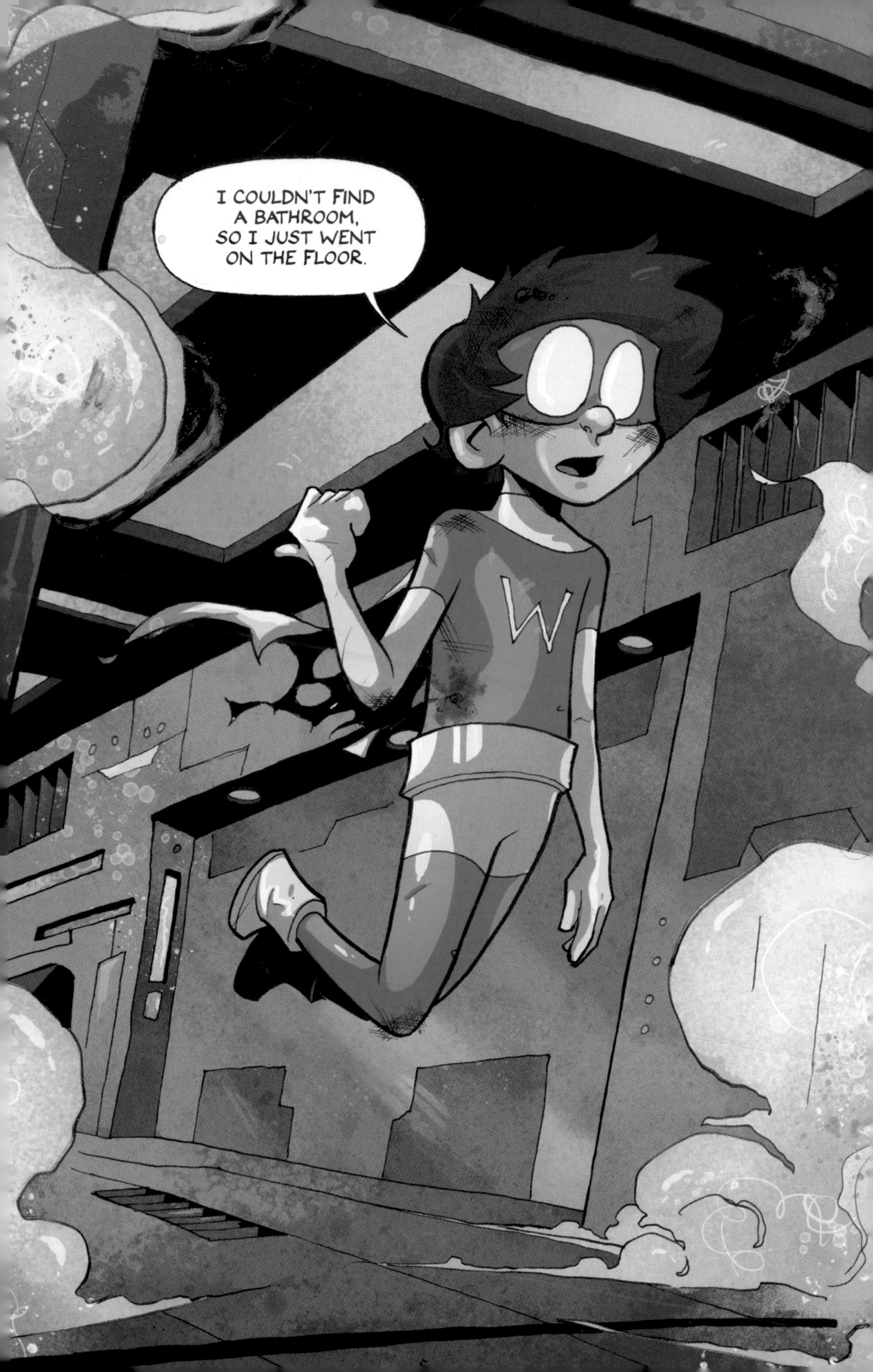
I COULDN'T FIND A BATHROOM, SO I JUST WENT ON THE FLOOR.

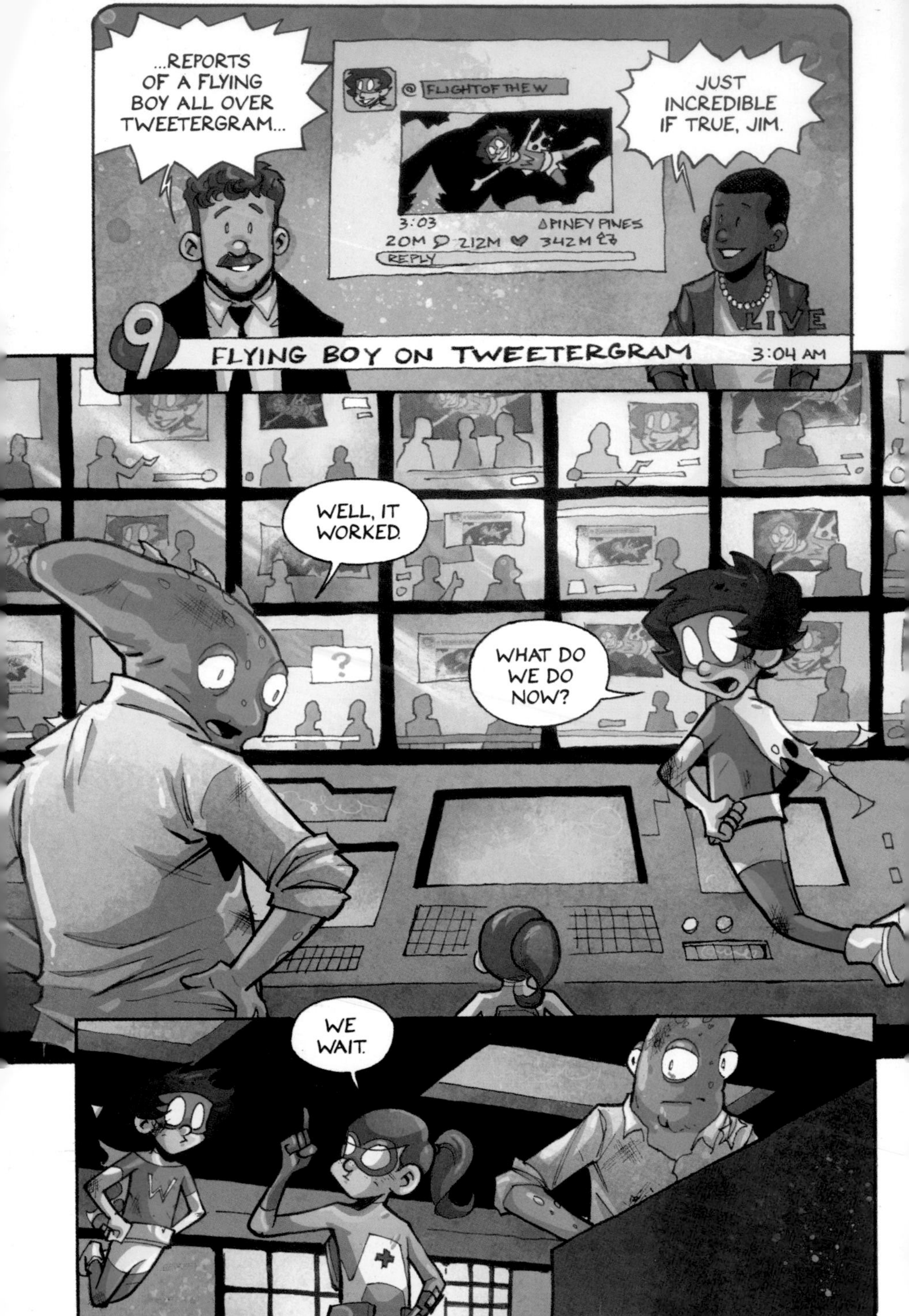
...REPORTS OF A FLYING BOY ALL OVER TWEETERGRAM...
@ FLIGHTOFTHEW
3:03
PINEY PINES
20M 212M 342M
REPLY
JUST INCREDIBLE IF TRUE, JIM.
LIVE
9
FLYING BOY ON TWEETERGRAM
3:04 AM
WELL, IT WORKED.
WHAT DO WE DO NOW?
WE WAIT.

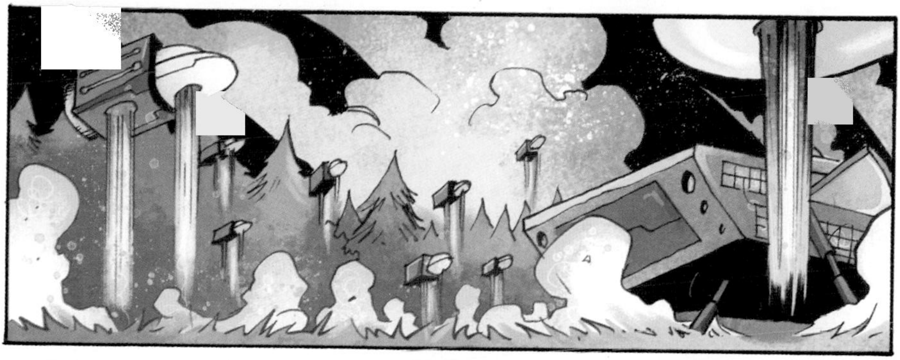

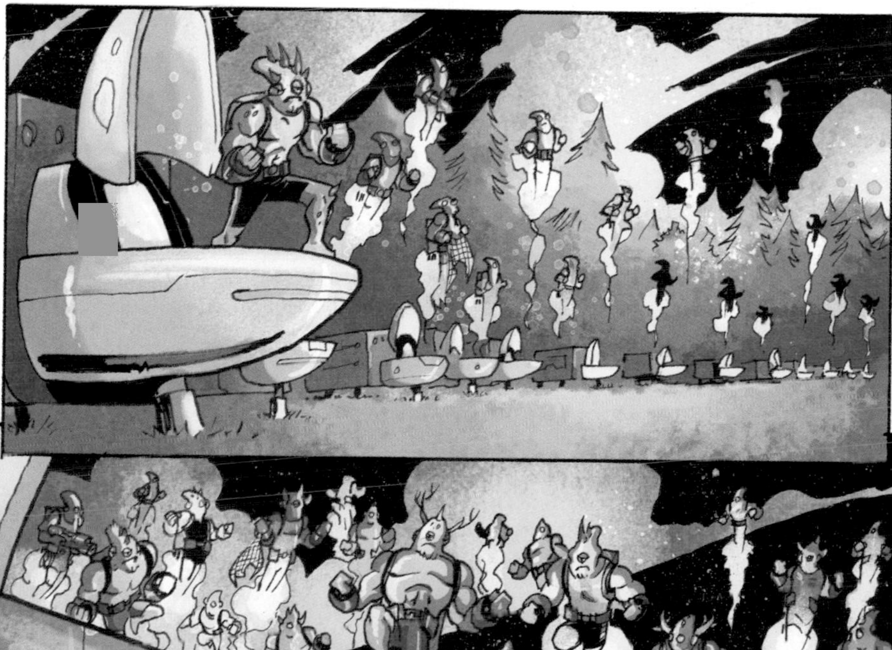

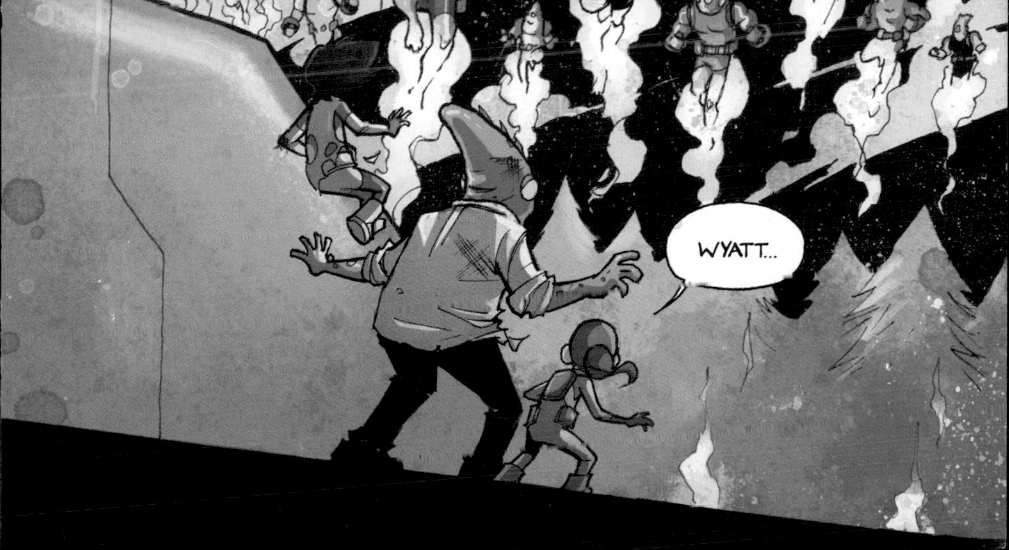
WYATT...

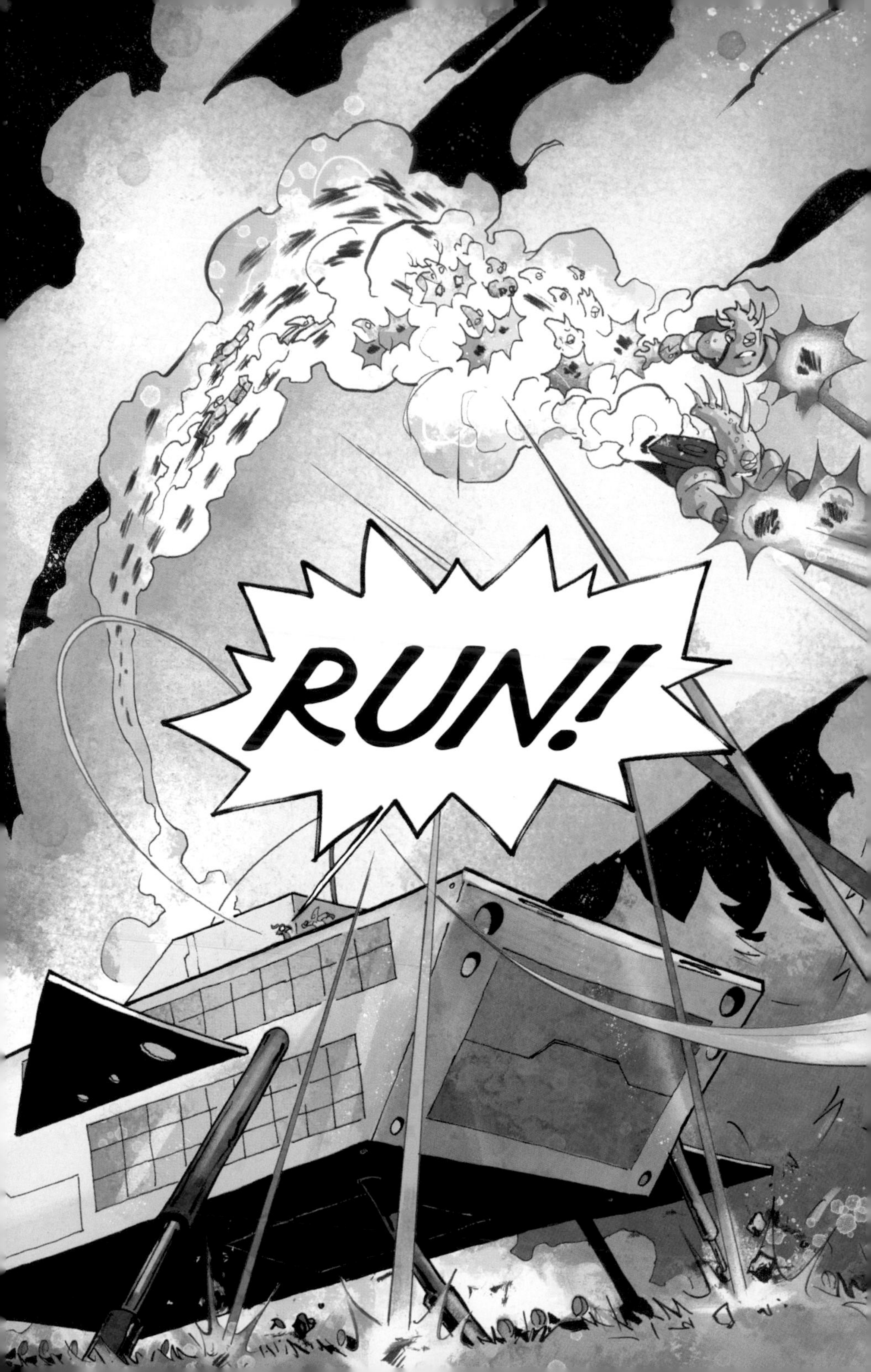
RUN!

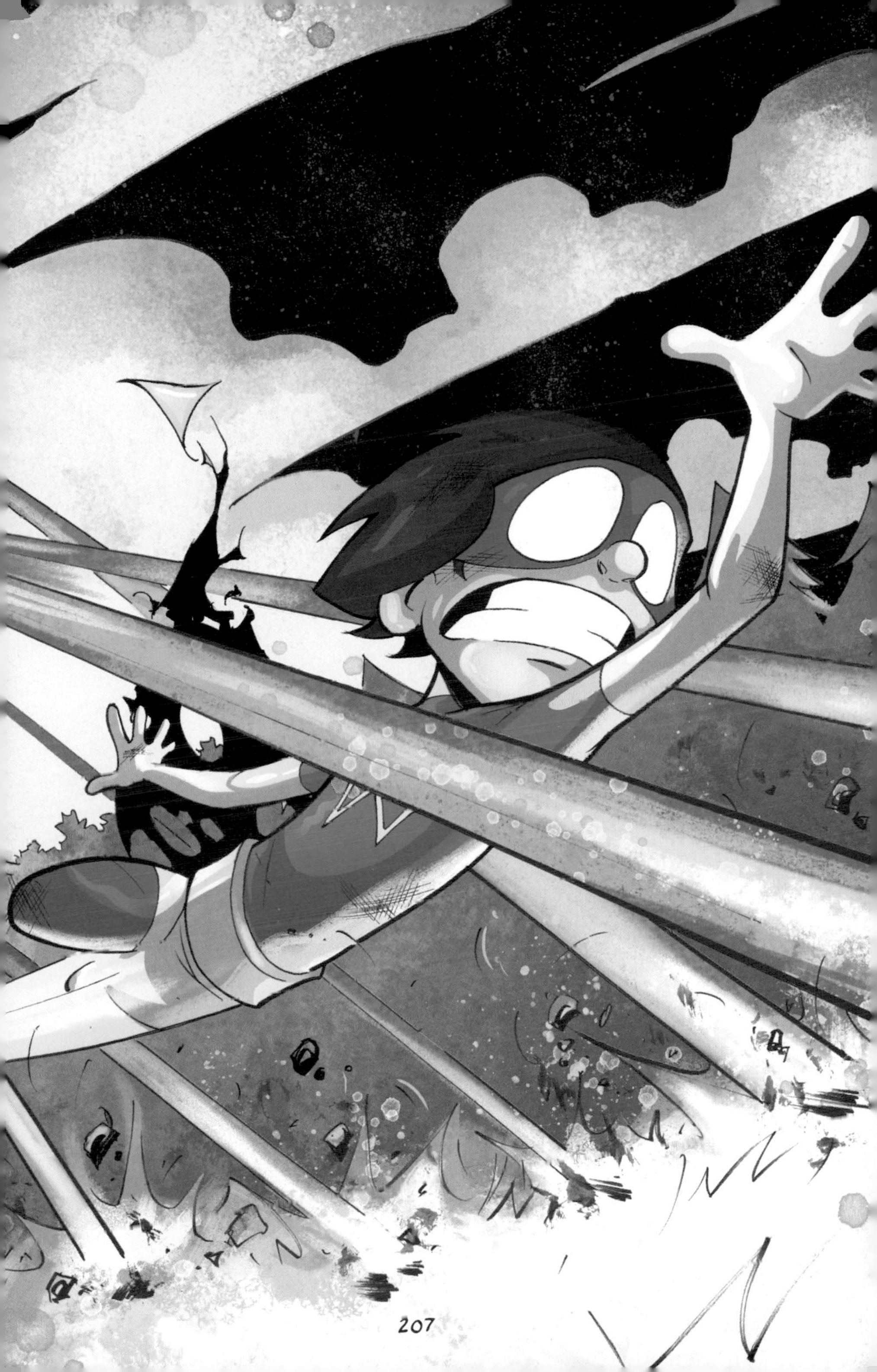

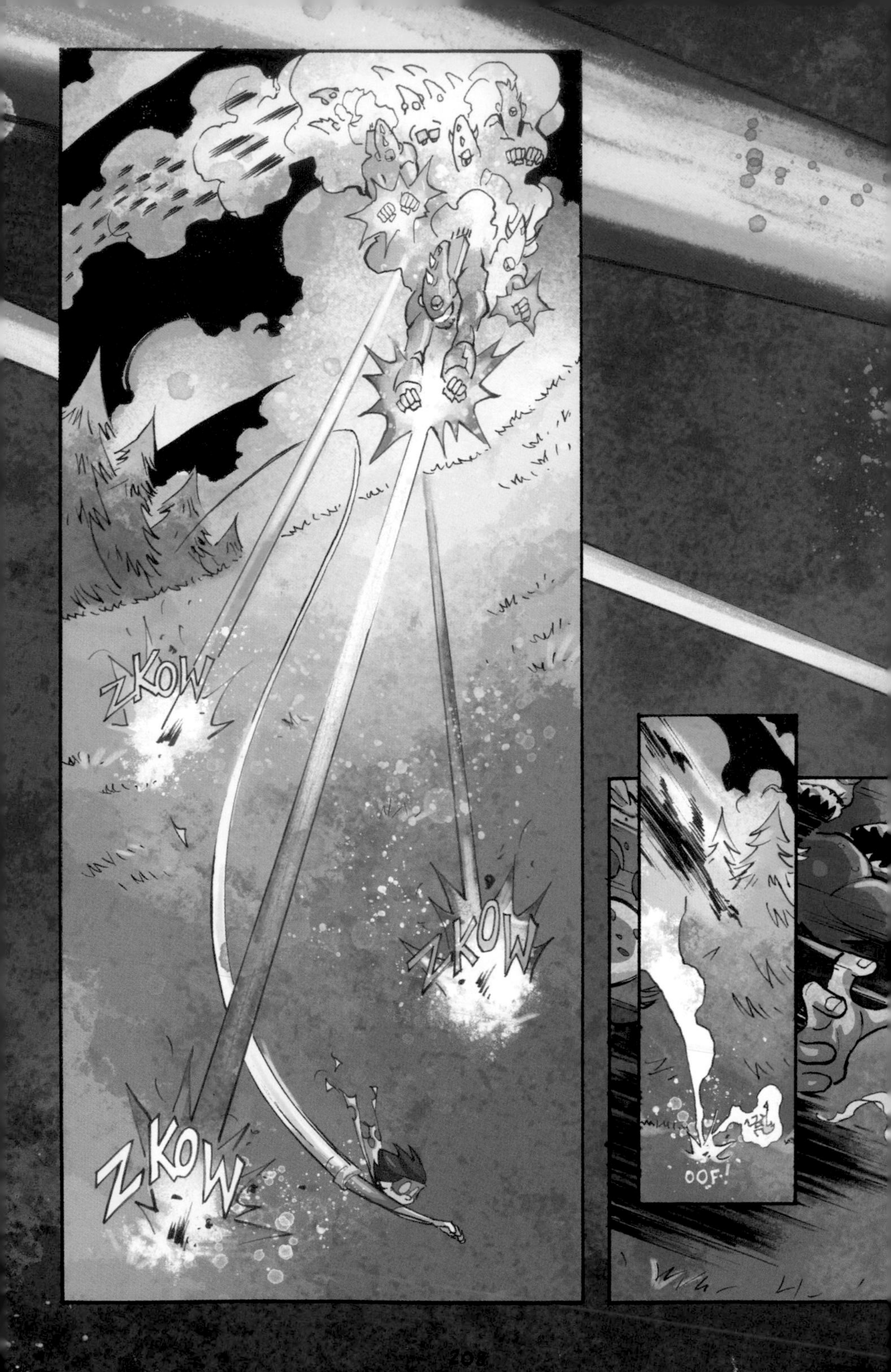
ZKOW
ZKOW
ZKOW
OOF!

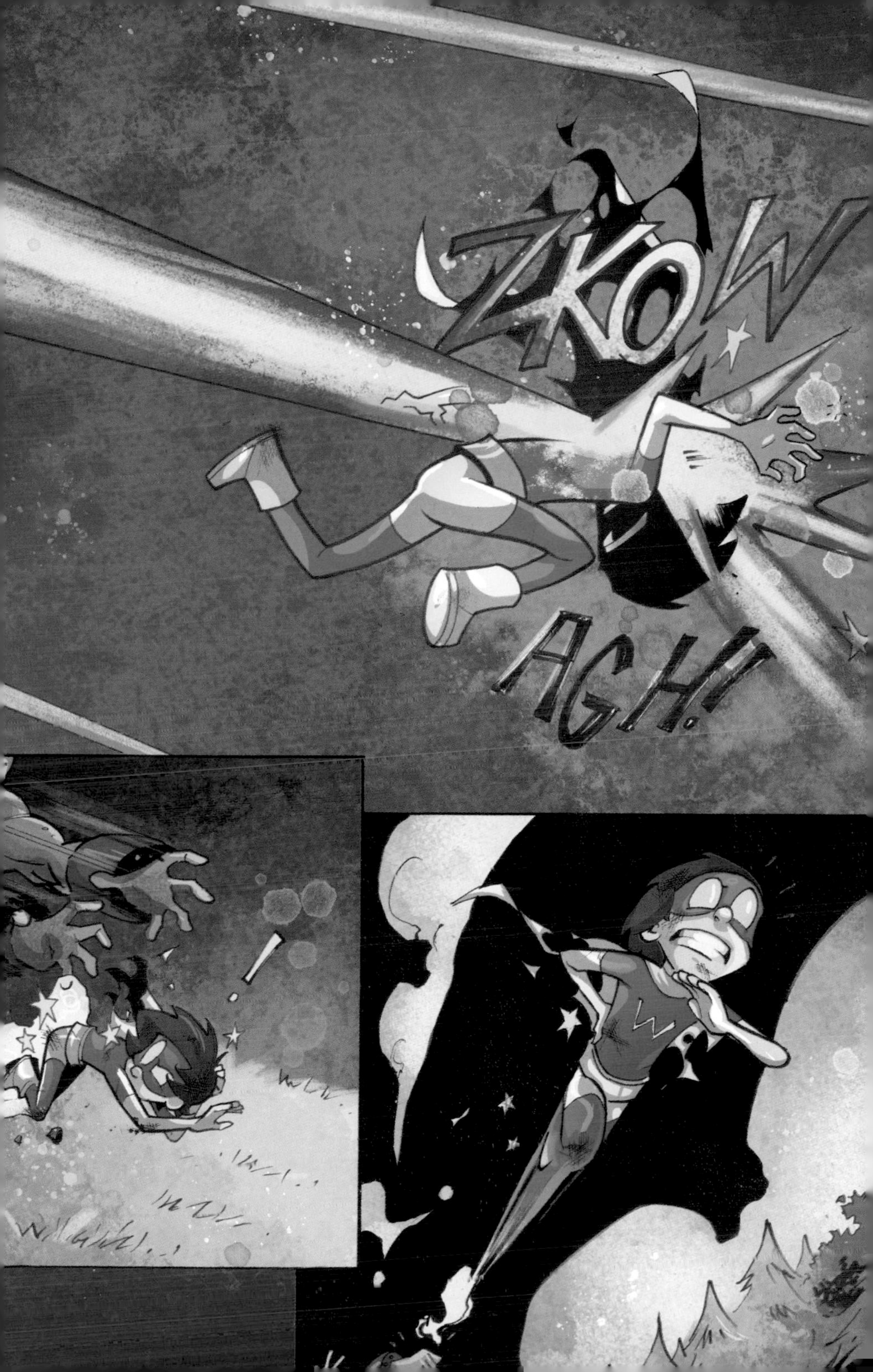

ZKOW
AGH!
!

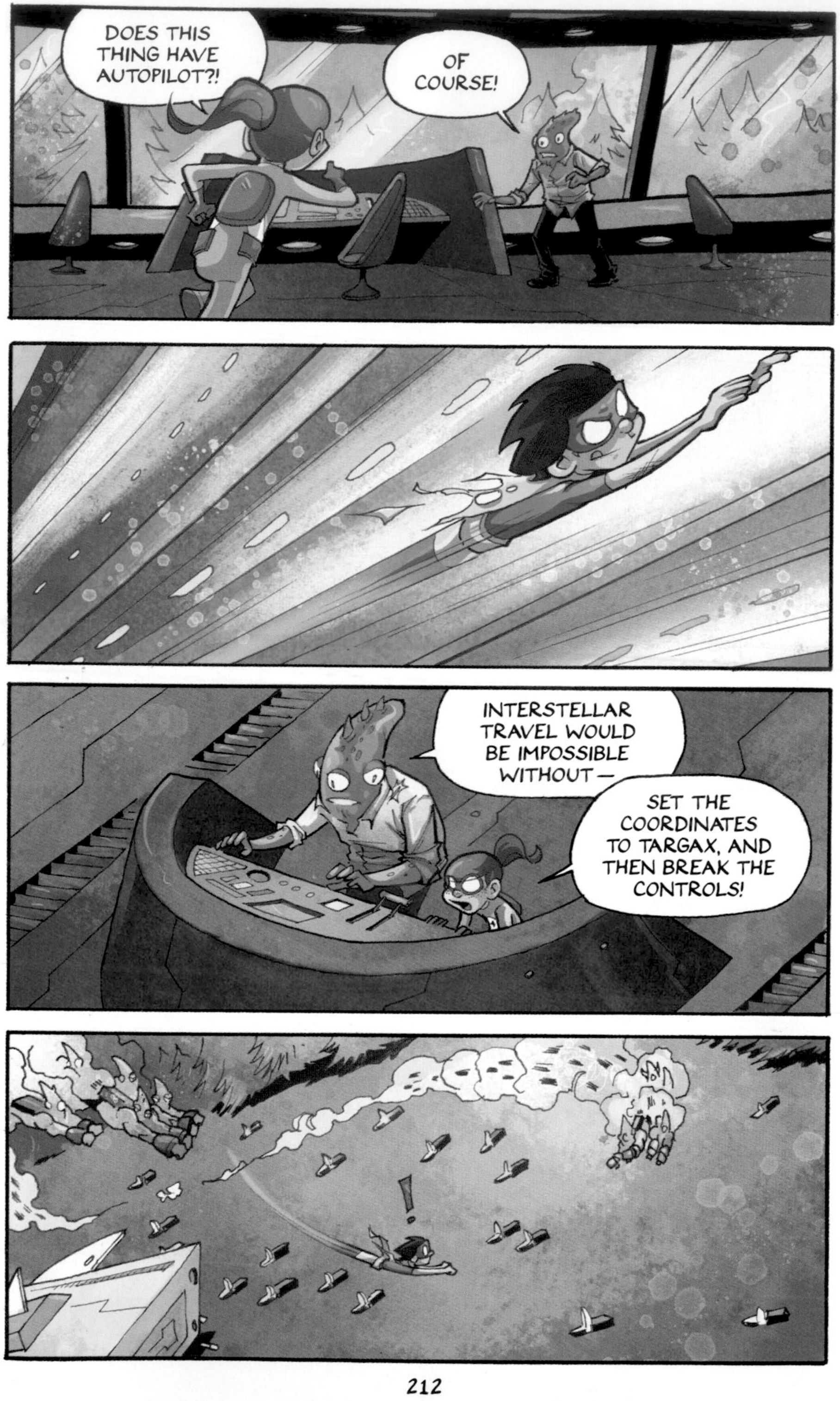
DOES THIS THING HAVE AUTOPILOT?!
OF COURSE!
INTERSTELLAR TRAVEL WOULD BE IMPOSSIBLE WITHOUT—
SET THE COORDINATES TO TARGAX, AND THEN BREAK THE CONTROLS!
!

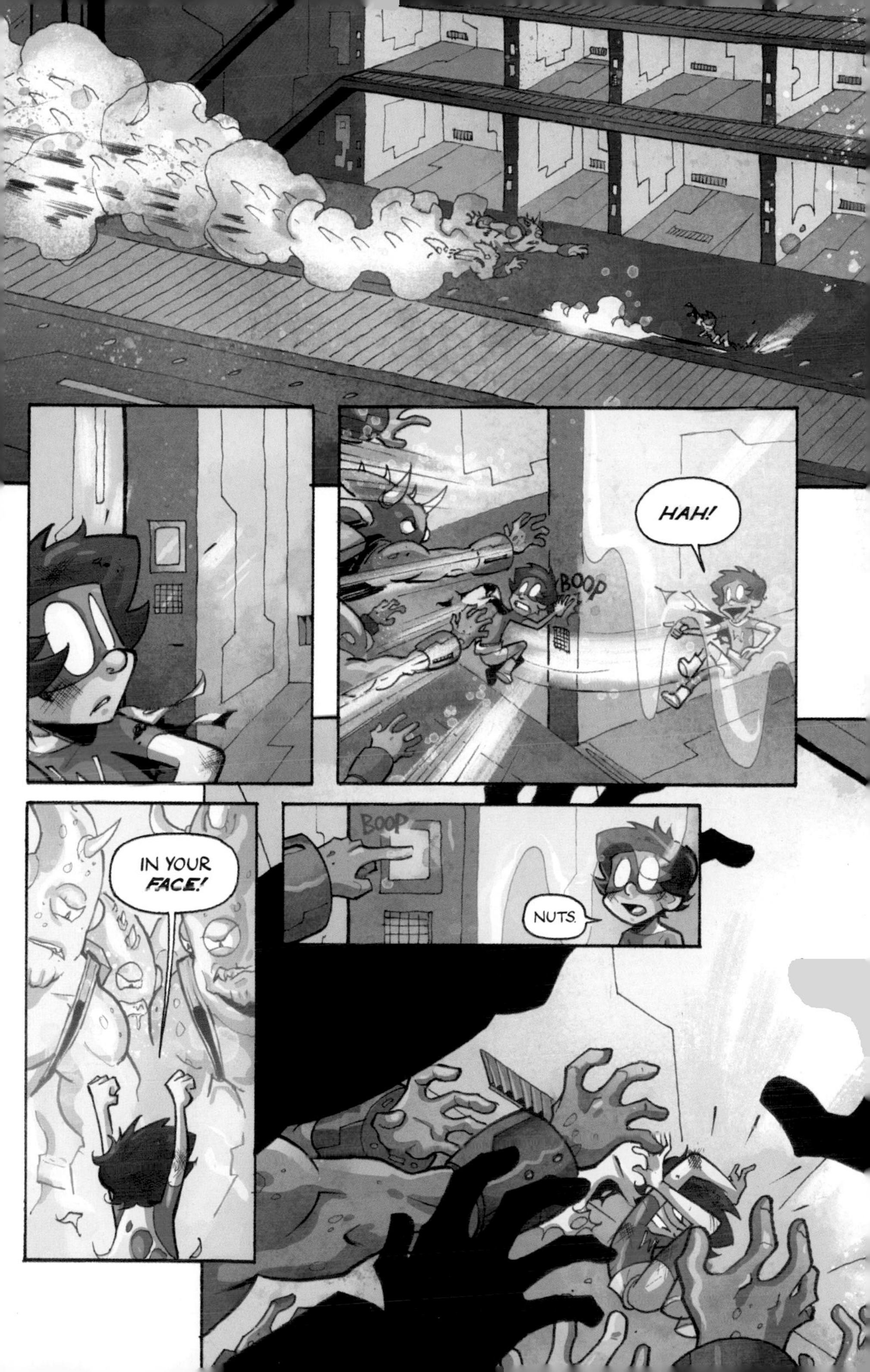
HAH!
BOOP
IN YOUR FACE!
BOOP
NUTS.

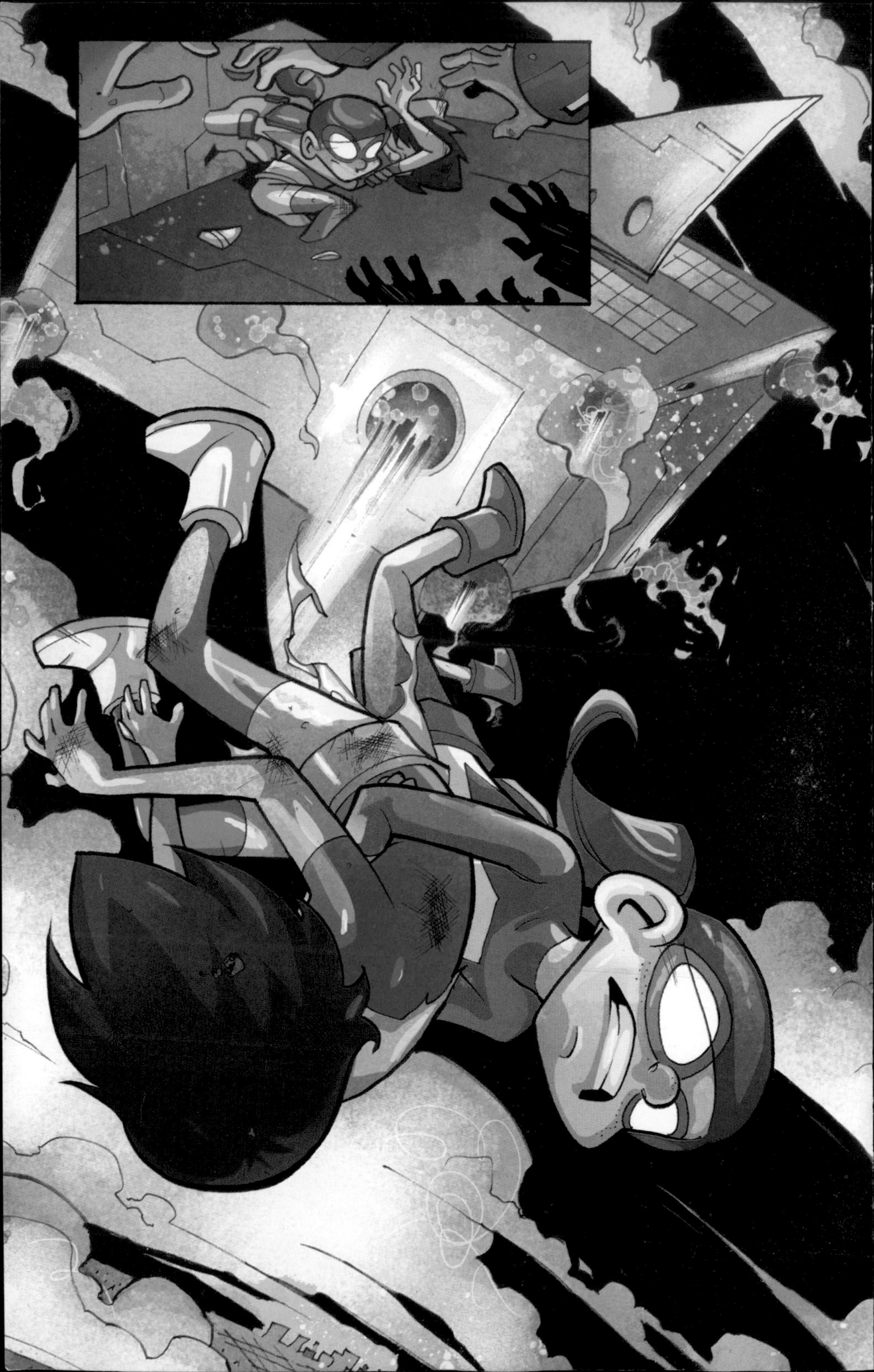

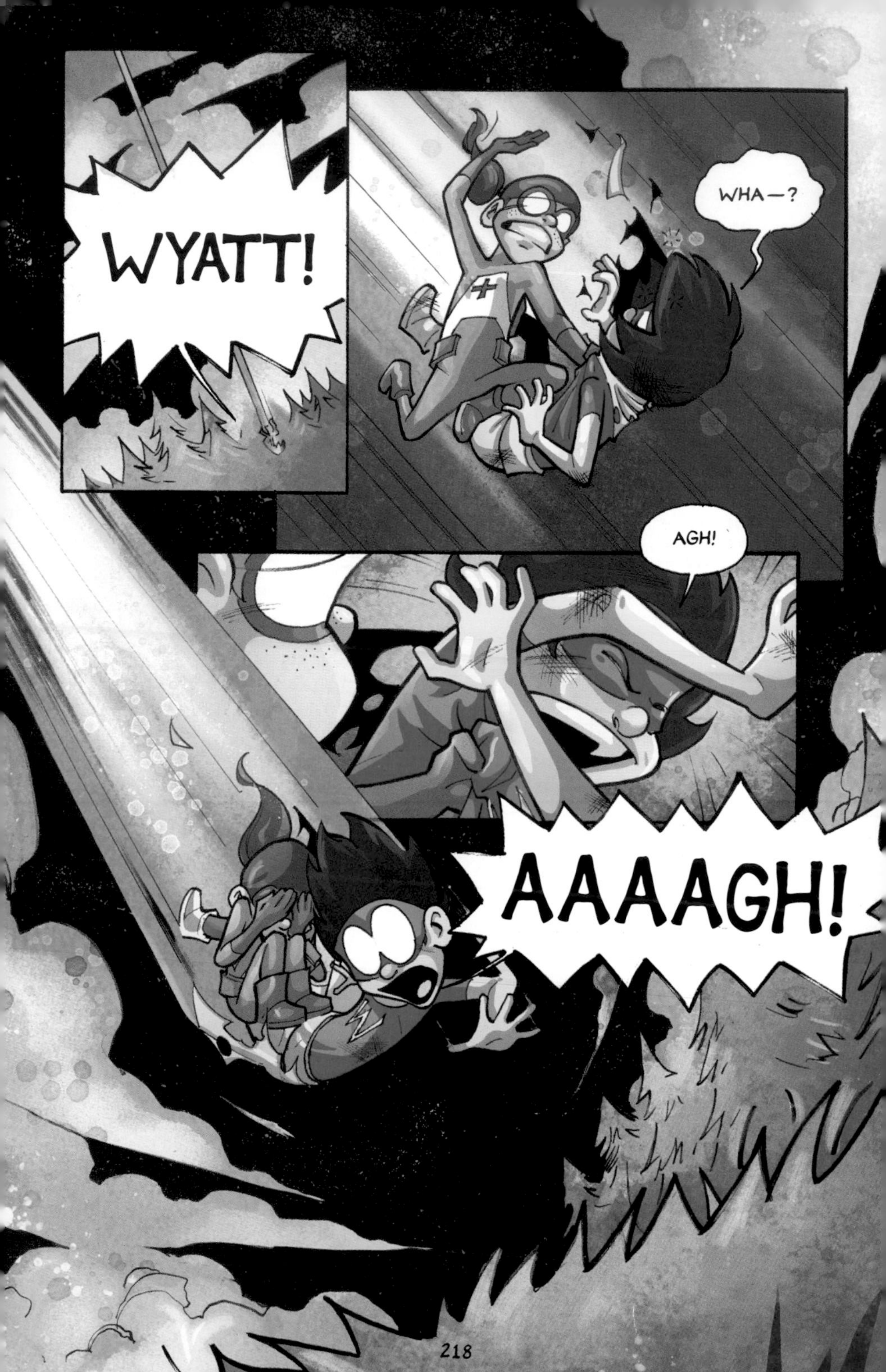
WYATT!
WHA—?
AGH!
AAAAGH!

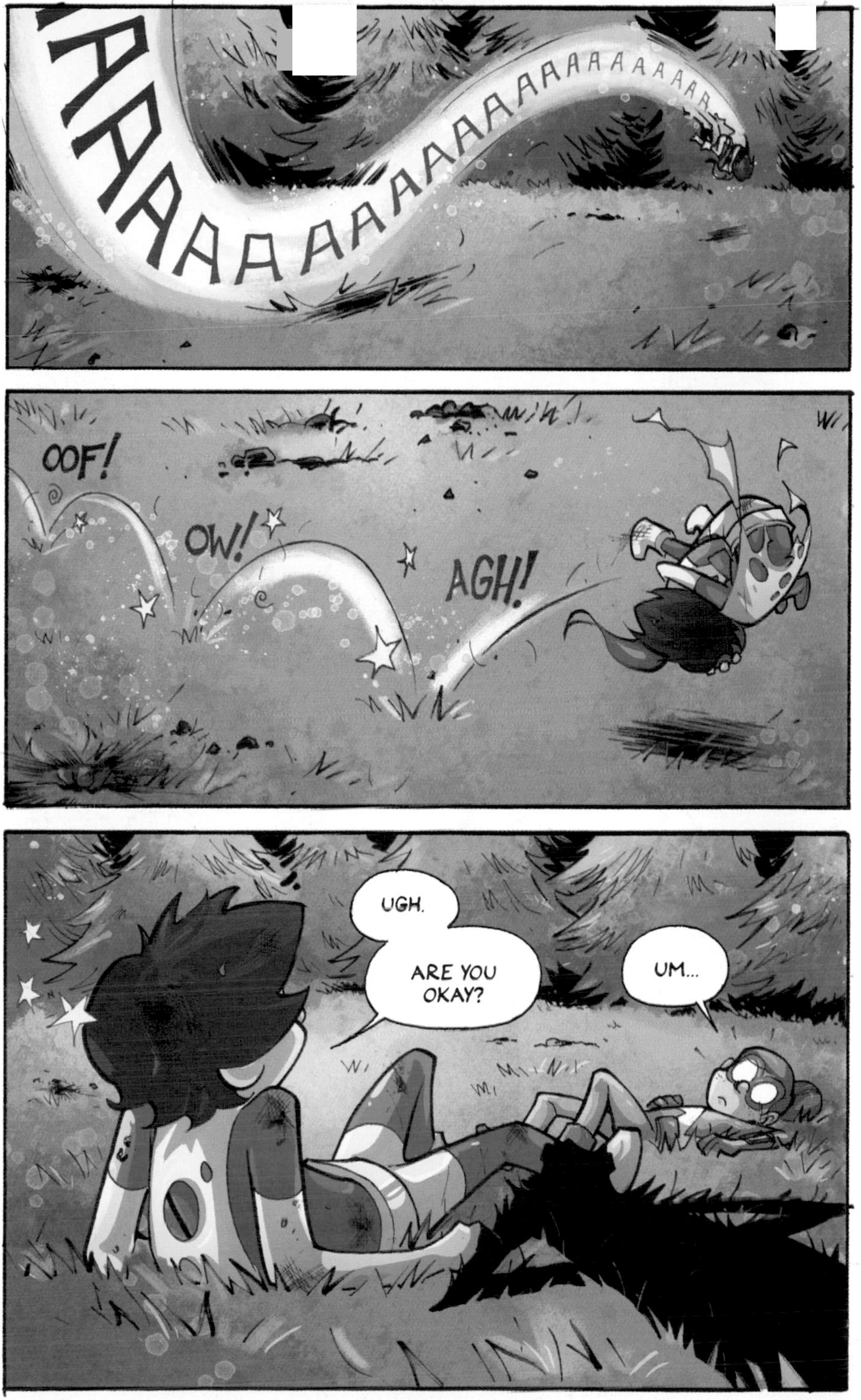
AAAAAAAAAAAAAAAAAAAAAAAAAA
OOF!
OW!
AGH!
UGH.
ARE YOU OKAY?
UM...

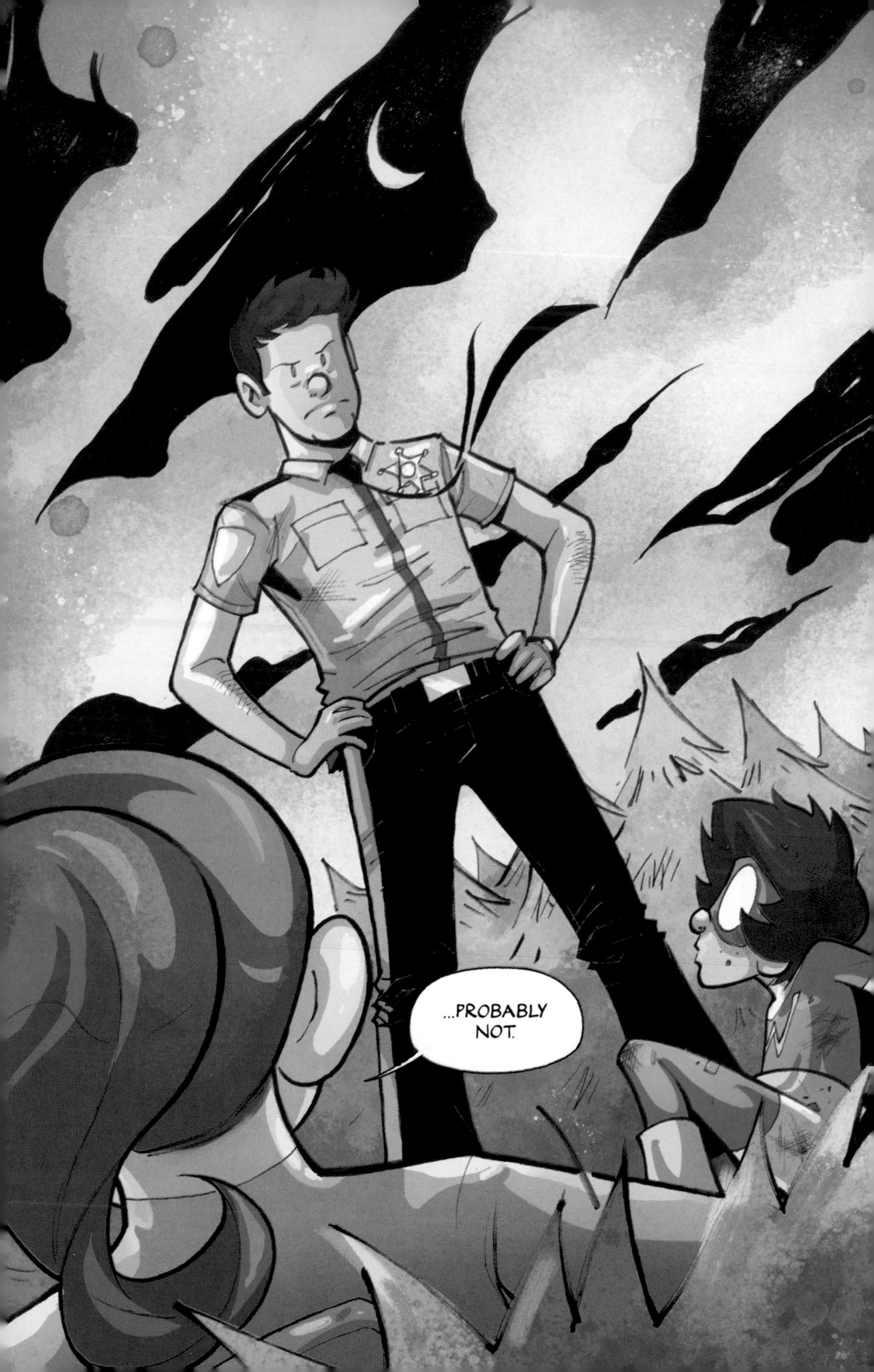
...PROBABLY NOT.

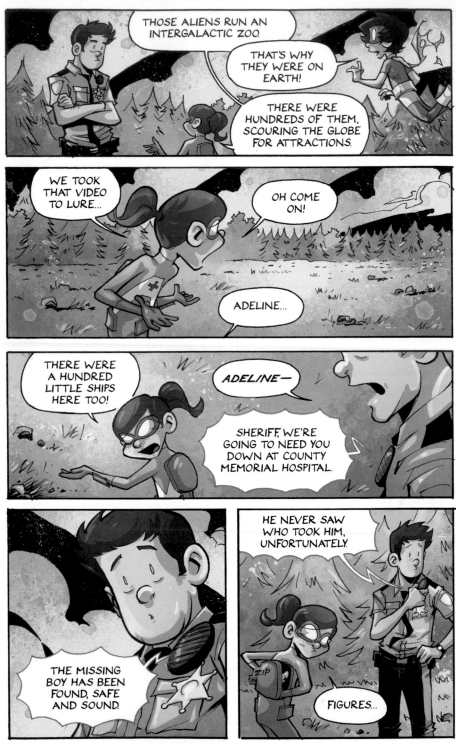

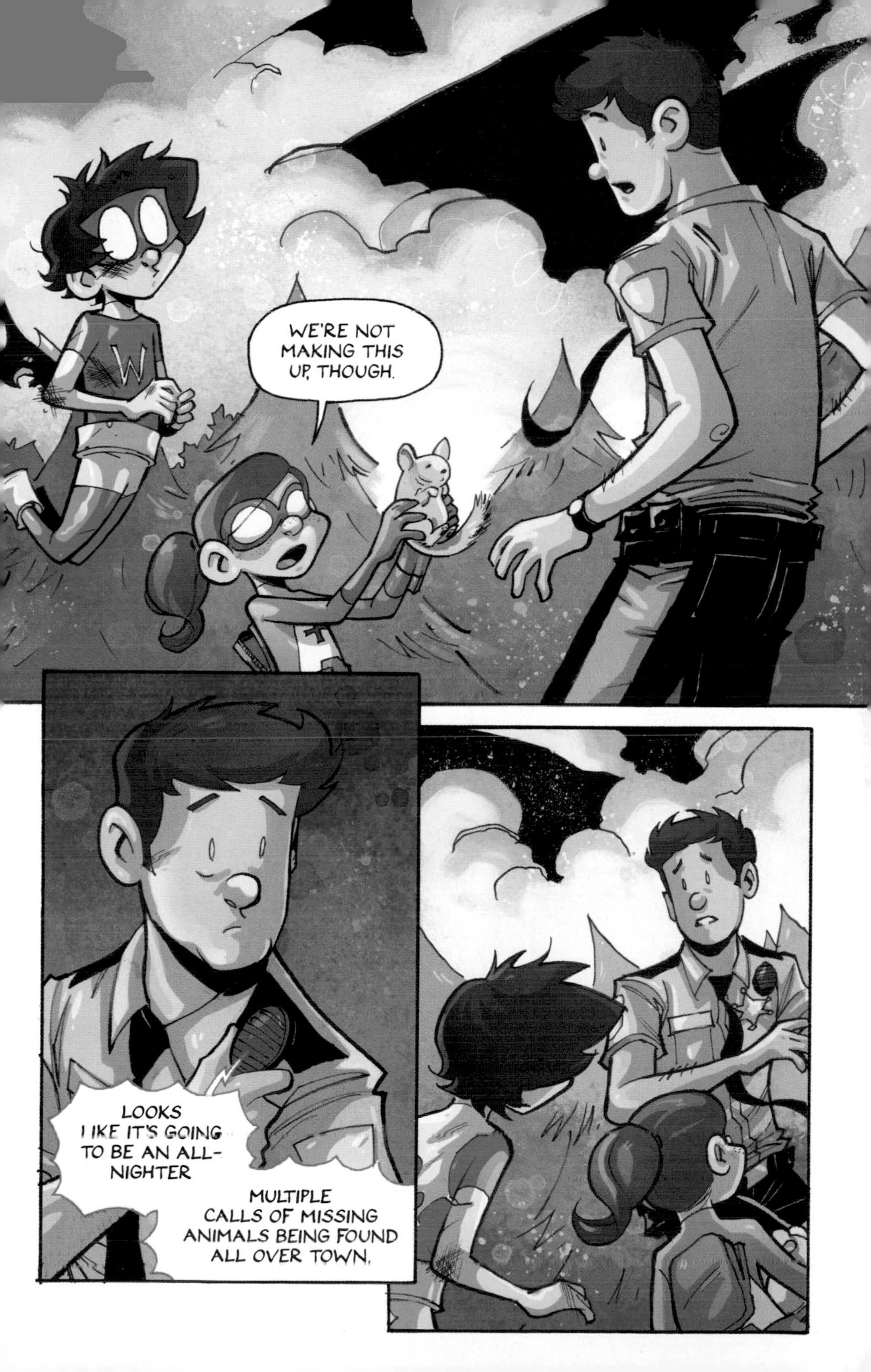
WE'RE NOT MAKING THIS UP, THOUGH.
LOOKS LIKE IT'S GOING TO BE AN ALL-NIGHTER
MULTIPLE CALLS OF MISSING ANIMALS BEING FOUND ALL OVER TOWN.

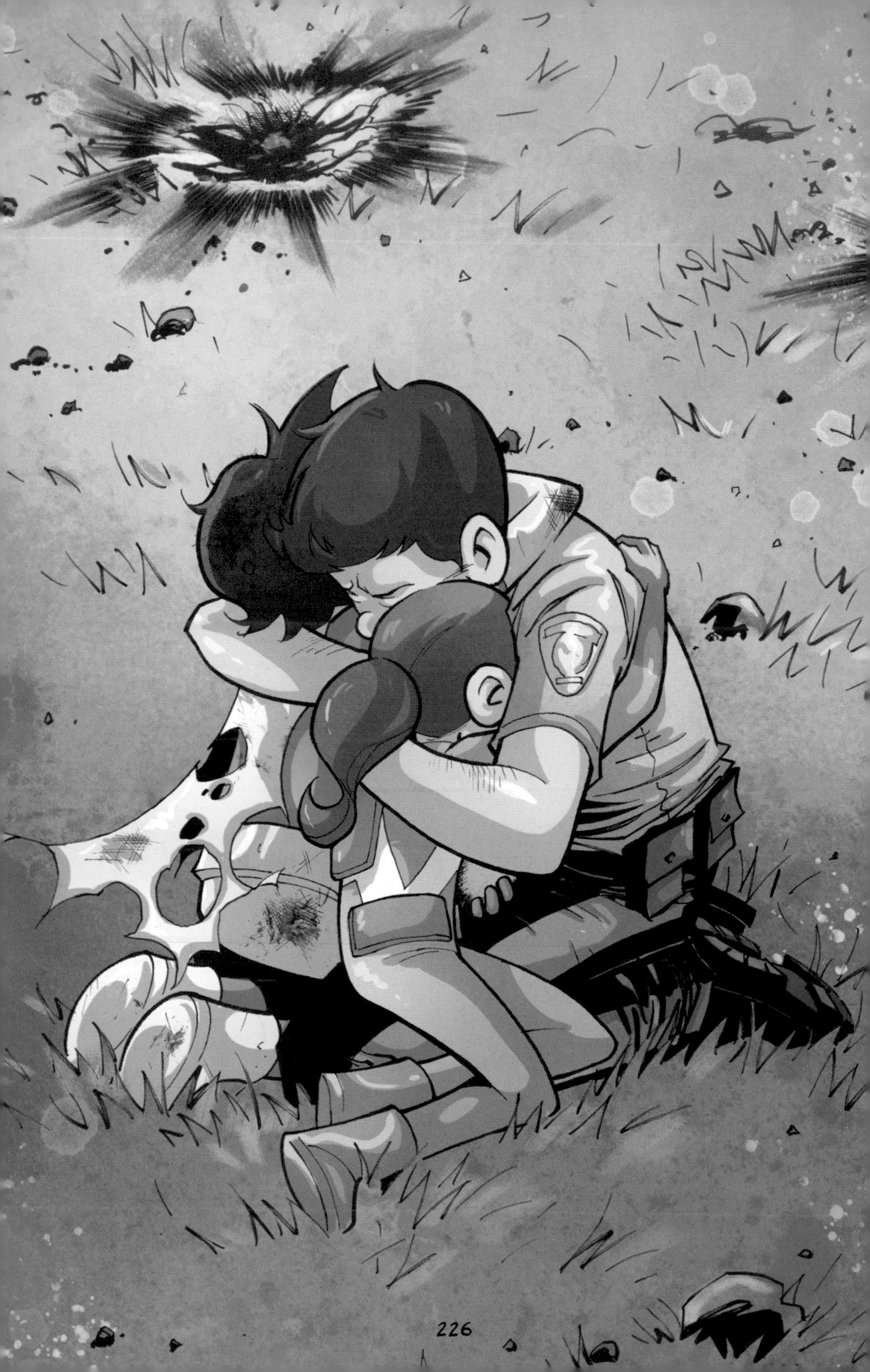

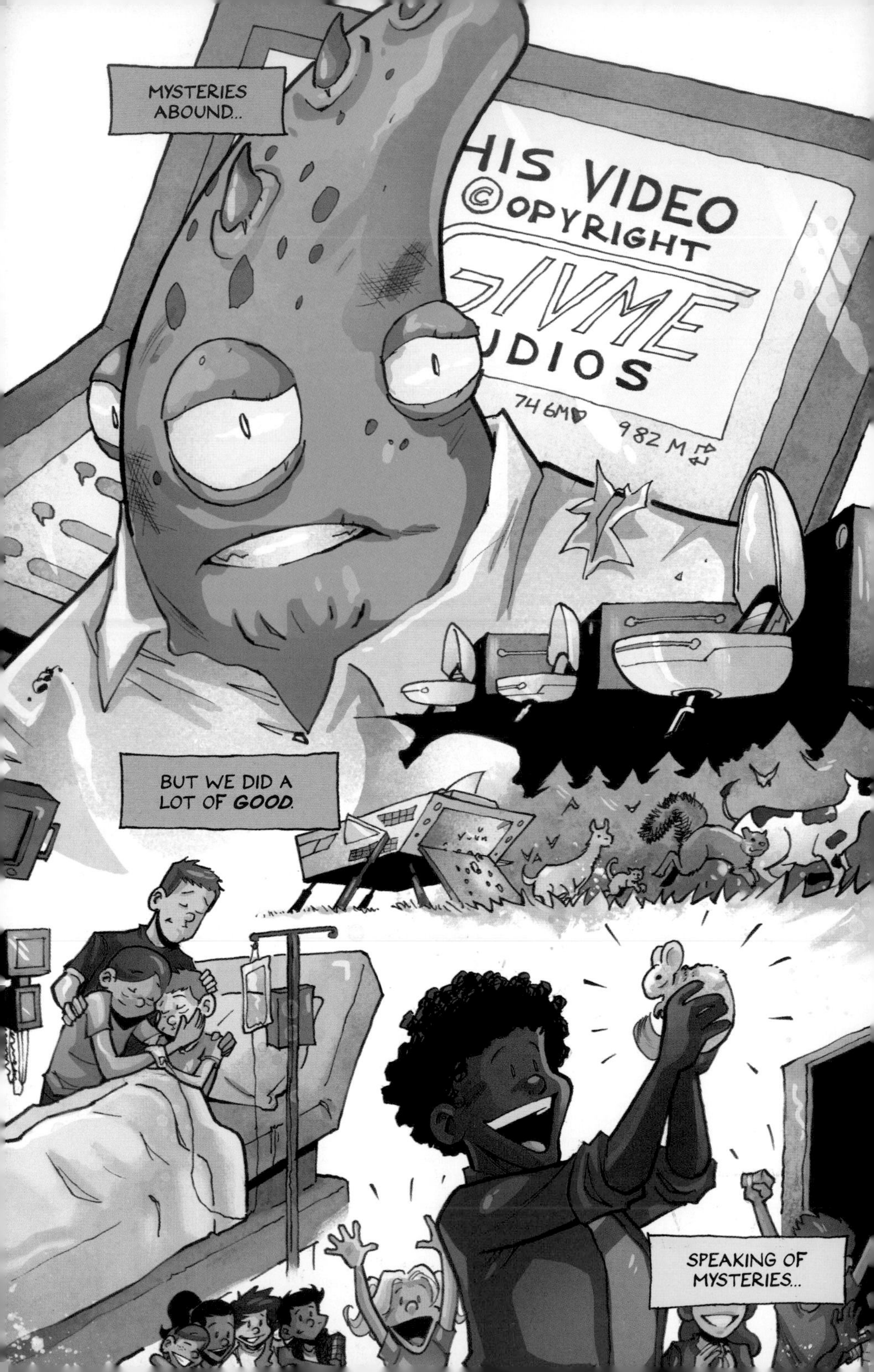
MYSTERIES ABOUND...
HIS VIDEO
©OPYRIGHT
GIVME
UDIOS
746M
982 M
BUT WE DID A LOT OF *GOOD*.
SPEAKING OF MYSTERIES...

231

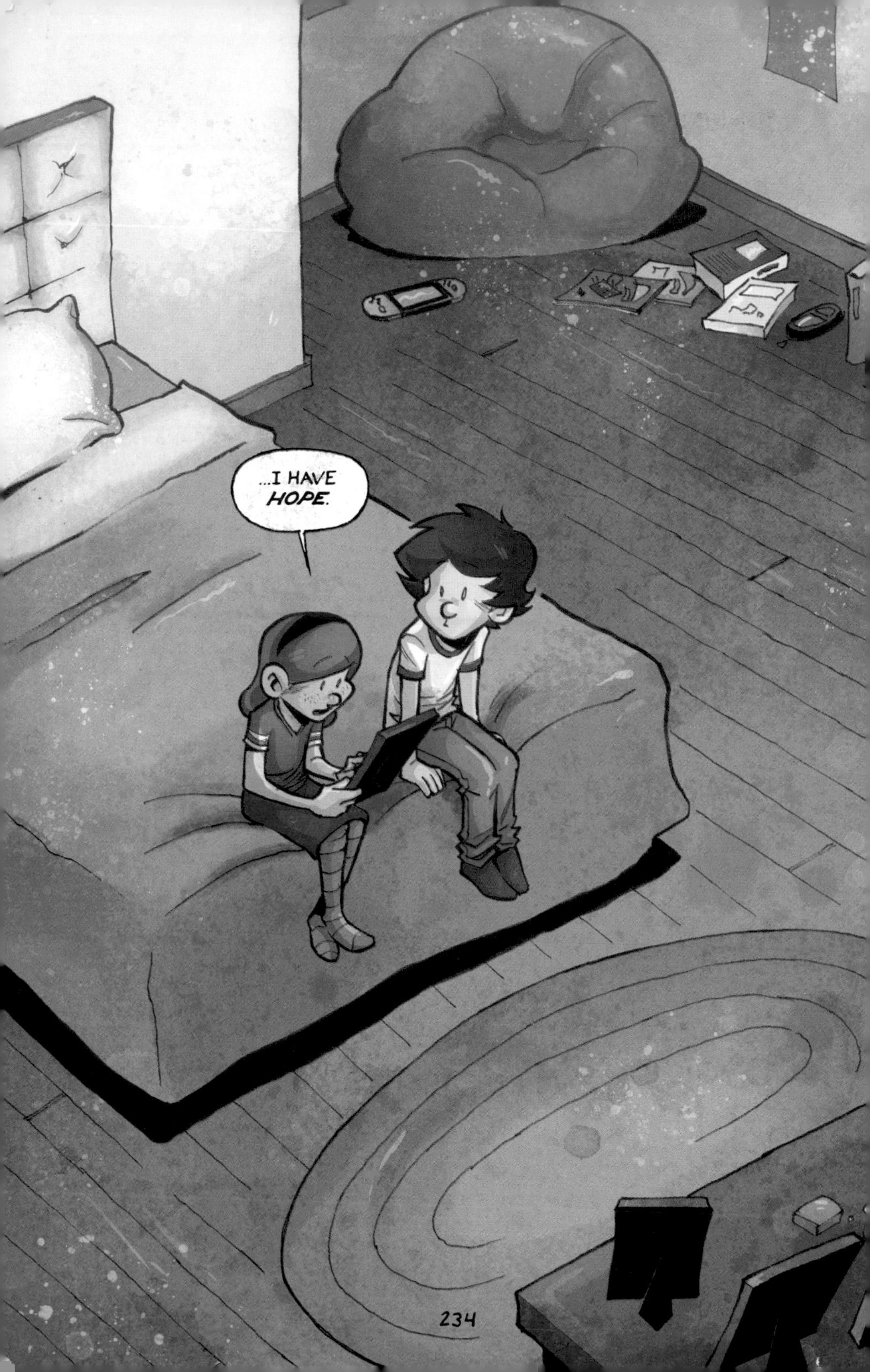
...I HAVE *HOPE*.